WEB
2027

WEB 2027

STEPHEN BAXTER

STEPHEN BOWKETT

ERIC BROWN

GRAHAM JOYCE

PETER F. HAMILTON

MAGGIE FUREY

Copyright © Stephen Baxter/1997, Stephen Bowkett/1997,
Eric Brown/1997, Graham Joyce/1997, Peter F. Hamilton/1998,
Maggie Furey/1998
All rights reserved

The rights of the authors to be identified as the authors of the
individual volumes have been asserted by them in accordance
with the Copyright, Designs and Patents Act 1988.

First published in omnibus form in Great Britain in 1999 by
Millennium
An imprint of Orion Books Ltd
Orion House, 5 Upper St Martin's Lane, London WC2H 9EA

To receive information on the Millennium list, e-mail us at:
Smy@orionbooks.co.uk

A CIP catalogue record for this book
is available from the British Library

ISBN 1 85798 599 0

Typeset at The Spartan Press Ltd,
Lymington, Hampshire,
Printed and bound in Great Britain by
Clays Ltd, St Ives plc.

CONTENTS

GULLIVERZONE
STEPHEN BAXTER

CHAPTER ONE

WEBSUITS

I set my bedroom to wake me early.

It was World Peace Day. And today I was going to spin into the Web and access GulliverZone.

Maybe you spun in too. Maybe we even met. Everybody seemed to be there!

I thought my biggest problem was going to be having the most unpopular girl at school *and* my dumb little brother, tagging along with me.

How wrong can you be!

I'd never have gone into GulliverZone – in fact I think I'd have stayed in bed that morning – if I'd known how close I would come to never getting out again . . .

The bedroom chimed softly.

'Good morning, Sarah,' it said.

I groaned and turned over. 'Metaphor. My name is Metaphor.'

'I'm not programmed to use aliases,' the bedroom said primly.

'Of course you are.' It was dark outside. 'What time is it?'

'Six a.m.'

'*Six!* What is it, Christmas Day?'

'No, Sarah. It is Sunday, February 7, 2027—'

'Sunday? Well, you can shut yourself off and let me sleep.'

'. . . and it's World Peace Day.'

Oh, wow. *Now* I remembered.

I sat up in bed and rubbed my eyes. 'Give me the news.'

'Which channel?'

'BBC 34.'

One whole side of my bedroom lit up with images.

There was a picture of a big celebration going on in a stadium in Pusan, in South Korea: thousands of people, fireworks, singers and dancers, and a platform full of world leaders. I could see our Prime Minister, Ravi Sivarajan, along with King William, President Samuel Jackson of the US, and Boris Becker, Chancellor of United Europe. They were listening to a poem by the Poet Laureate, Damon Albarn.

I told the bedroom to flick around. This was the twentieth World Peace Day, so there were celebrations *everywhere*.

At the Vatican, the Pope was blessing the crowds, his shining black face split by smiles. In Las Vegas, the Robot Beatles were performing *Sergeant Pepper*. Wembley was staging a laser-show hologram match between the England Euro 96 soccer team and the 2026 World Cup winners, Kenya. The real Euro 96 team had been brought out of retirement to see the match, and sat in the stand like a row of grey old soldiers. I imagined Philip complaining about that. *Why don't they make footballers like they used to in this country? It's all money now. Look at Paul Gascoigne. There was a player for you . . .*

(Philip's my dad, by the way. He lets me call him Philip. I let him call me Metaphor.)

On the frozen Thames there was a huge bonfire and a skating gala. In Germany, one of the five-hundred-metre balls of carbon dioxide pollution they froze out of the air had been sculpted into the shape of a huge dove. (Cor-*ny*.) Over the North Pole, the big airship they put up to fix the ozone layer had WORLD PEACE scrolling its mile-wide belly. Pusan was the centre of the celebrations, of course. That was where the North Koreans dropped their atomic bomb in 2007, the event that started the whole World Peace movement in the first place. And at Cape Canaveral, one of the Mars astronauts was waving as he got on board the Space Shuttle *Eagle* . . .

'Off,' I said. The wall blanked out.

So; all that stuff going on, all over the world.

Big deal! I wasn't interested in any of it.

Because today, GulliverZone – the best theme park in the Web – was going to be *free* . . .

I went to the bathroom and washed.

Philip had the mirror tuned to the Snow White option as usual, but I turned that off. I like to know what I *look* like, not what I'd *prefer* to look like. Maybe when you get to Philip's advanced age the truth is just too awful to bear.

I got dressed quickly and ran downstairs. I would have a quick breakfast and spin in, I decided, before Philip had a chance to lumber me with—

George.

The little egg was already sitting at the breakfast table. His favourite animatronic *Action Man* was frisbeeing edible pogs into his mouth. He is *such* a one-mip kid.

Personally, I eat nothing but adult breakfasts. I poured myself a huge bowl of cola-flavoured cereal.

I had to clear last night's empty TFO (Tennessee Fried Ostrich) boxes off the table. And before I ate I put out a bowl of food for our cat, Gazza. When he smelled the food he came in through the catflap, shook snow off his orange fur, and tucked in.

I raised my first mouthful, and slowed.

The egg was grinning at me. I had the horrible feeling he was planning something.

'Good morning, *George*,' I said.

That wiped the grin off his face. 'Byte!' he said. 'Call me Byte.'

'You're too young to have an alias.'

'I'm not too young to spin into the Web.'

I froze. I even stopped ladling cola pops into my mouth.

So that was it. I had an awful feeling, a deep and dark dread, in the pit of my stomach.

I said, 'You are *not* spinning in with me today.'

'Oh yes I am,' he said, and he got off his chair and started jumping up and down. He knows I hate that. 'Dad says I can. GulliverZone. GulliverZone. I'm going to GulliverZone.'

'You little egg! Stop jumping! I'm not taking you to GulliverZone!'

He stopped jumping and adopted his most sickening angelic grin. 'Hello, Dad,' he said.

Behind me, Philip had come into the kitchen. His hair was all over the place, and he was wearing a horrible sweatshirt, so old it showed Noel Gallagher *before* he was knighted. As usual, he fell for George's ploy. He ruffled the kid's hair.

It drove me crazy. Just the day before, George had used the same tactics to raise his pocket money to a hundred Euros a week. I was *ten* before I got a hundred – two years older than George. Even *now* I'm only on a thousand a week.

Philip yawned and went to the coffee tap. 'What's Sallibugs shouting at you about?'

I rose to my full height. I have not responded to Sallibugs since I was six years old.

'She says I can't go to GulliverZone,' whined George.

Philip frowned at me. It was his I'm-disappointed-in-you look. I hate it when he does that. 'Is this true?'

I tried not to whine. 'But today's World Peace Day!'

'So stop fighting with your brother,' Philip said, and George started jumping up and down again.

'He'll ruin it.'

'How can one small boy ruin a worldwide celebration?'

'It's just not fair.'

'I know, Metaphor. Lots of things aren't fair.' He gave me his Sarah-we're-adults-together look. I hate that one even more. Because it means I definitely can't get away with it.

I was stuck with the kid. What was worse, I was going to have to spend my whole time showing the little one-mip what to do. I knew he'd only ever used gag before to spin into the Web.

Philip tuned the toaster to his me-paper. He got a status update from Tilbury – the place he works, the Tilbury Desalination Plant – and started reading earnestly.

The conversation, it seemed, was over.

I ate my cola pops in black depression.

We keep our Websuits in the spare bedroom.

My suit was lying on the floor where I'd left it last night. It looked like a diver's wet suit made out of bright orange material, with its built-on head covering, gloves and boots. There were several fine connectors sprouting from the suit's neck. They joined up to a big thick cable that led to a data socket in the wall.

In there as well was Philip's big Websuit – it looked like a 1990s ski jump outfit, *so* unfashionable – and my old kidsized suit I had grown out of. In the corner there was the gag, the baby gloves-and-glasses kit George had used to spin into the Web up to now.

It was all new to George. He was running around the room like the kid he was. But I knew I had a moment of revenge coming up.

I held up my old little girl's Websuit. 'Here you are, George. Hop in.'

He stopped running. 'I can't wear *that*.'

'Oh? What's wrong, is it the pink colour? The ballerina skirt?'

'No,' he whispered. '*You've* been in it. *Ugh*.'

'Now, come along, George,' Philip said. I hadn't seen him enter the room. 'Be sensible. You know you'll have to wait until your birthday for your own suit. Be a good boy now, and do what your big sister says.'

'I'd rather *die*,' he said.

'If you'd rather not go—'

'I'll put it on,' he said miserably. He opened up the suit by the big zipper down the front and started to climb in.

I started to pull my own suit on. You know what that's like. The suits are one-piece and a tight fit. You really have to wriggle to get into them.

They're supposed to be tight, of course. Everything you feel, touch, see, hear when you're in Webtown comes via your Websuit; through the places it touches your skin, the little screens over your eyes, and so on.

Even so, it was a struggle.

'I think my suit's getting a little tight,' I said to Philip.

'Already? You're growing too fast.'

'Tell me about it,' I said gloomily. I only wished I could grow faster. I was tired of being the smallest kid in the class. If you're short, nobody takes you *seriously*.

'Listen, Metaphor. I have to go in to work.'

I frowned. This was always happening. 'But it's World Peace Day. And it's *Sunday*. Do you have to?'

He sighed and rubbed his tired face. 'You know I do. Otherwise, half of London will be drinking salty sea water by tea time.'

'Does this mean we can't spin in?'

'No.' He looked at me seriously. 'But you're in charge, Metaphor. Take care of Byte.'

'I know how I'd like to take care of him.'

'I'm not kidding,' he said gravely. 'Don't let him get Websick. Three hours maximum, then out.'

'You can trust me, Philip.'

He nodded. He gave me one of his I-know-I-can looks. That one, I don't mind.

'Oh. I nearly forgot,' he said. 'There's something else.'

'What?'

He turned to the door. 'Come on in.'

In walked Meg Toffler, a girl from my class at school. Also known as the Wire. She had a thin, strained-looking face, and she smiled at me in her feeble way. 'Hello, Sarah.'

'Hello.' I glared at Philip and hissed so she couldn't hear. 'What is *she* doing here?'

He looked even more tired. 'You know her father works at Tilbury with me. He just called. He has to work today too. I said she could come in with you today. She can use my suit—'

'You did *what*?'

'Now, Sarah—'

'Meg Toffler is a *wipeout*. And I should know.'

That was true. She seemed to be in every one of my classes

at school: Rocket Science, Life Creation, even the boring stuff like Bungee Jumping. I probably knew her as well as anyone else.

And I needed a *holiday*.

Philip got a little angry. 'I don't know what you're complaining about. You only have to go to school two days a week. Now, in my day—'

'Oh, *Philip*.'

'Look, maybe Meg is unhappy right now. But her mother and father are splitting up. Remember how you were when Mum died?' He touched my shoulder. 'Maybe you were a bit of a wimp then too.'

'Wipeout. The word is wipeout.'

'Whatever. Anyway—'

'All right. She can come. She'd just better not start complaining, that's all.'

'That's my girl,' he said.

My day was going from bad to worse. First my basementlevel brother, and now the Wire.

Of course if I'd known how bad it was going to get later, I wouldn't have complained . . .

The Wire climbed into Philip's suit. Philip checked over George, while I laughed at the big baby in the ballerina skirt.

'The main thing you need to know,' Philip told George, 'is how to scuttle.'

'Scuttle?'

'If you want to spin out in a hurry. Just press this button on the control panel on your wrist.' Philip showed him. 'See? Then you'll be straight back out here, in Realworld.'

George practised a couple of times.

Philip prepared to leave. 'I don't know about this Web stuff. I remember the good old days when the whole family would gather round the glow of the TV together—'

'And you could buy a newspaper for five Euros,' I said. 'We know the story, Philip.'

He grinned. 'Have fun. Do what the Spiders tell you. Don't go on to supertime. Watch out for the bad people. Especially these stories I hear about someone called the Sorceress. Don't take the—'

It was the standard 'don't' lecture. To close him out, I pulled my mask closed over my face and zipped it up. The inside of the suit was warm, a little moist. The spin programs took a moment to kick in. I waited in the dark. I could hear that pest George giggling.

The Sorceress. Talk about children's stories. Everyone knew there was no bad lady living in the Web called the Sorceress. It was all playground stuff, spread by little kids. And—

Suddenly, without warning, there was blue sky all around me.

CHAPTER TWO

WEBTOWN

I learned in Industrial Archaeology that they had something like the Web even when Philip was a boy, in the 1990s. Amazing. I hadn't even known they had *computers* back then!

There was something called *the Internet*, lots of computers around the world connected in a network by telephone lines. They had *holograms*, free-standing, three-dimensional images. And they even had *Virtual Reality*, which was a bit like spinning into the Web, but . . . well, a lot clunkier. Like comparing a jet fighter with a skateboard.

When you spin into the Web you feel as if you've entered another world. You haven't. You haven't even left your house. It's all made up by networks of computers around the world.

We learned all this at school. I found it really interesting to learn how they build the Webware – the Web software, the instructions for the computers. Maybe I'll be a Webware designer when I get older. If I don't pass the exam to go to the Moon colony, that is.

So I understood how the Web works. But I wasn't about to tell George – oh, all right, *Byte* – any of that.

You know what it's like to enter Webtown's first level. One second we were lying on our backs in our familiar spare room. The next – we were there, suddenly standing up, in the middle of a flat golden plain, like a wheat field, with Building Blocks scattered over it like toys dropped by giant children.

Byte, finding himself standing up like that, lost his balance. He stumbled forward and fell on his belly. He screamed like a baby. It made me feel a lot better.

Even the Wire was laughing. 'It isn't real, silly,' she said. 'That's the whole point. It looks and sounds real, but it isn't. Look.' And she flapped her arms and did a backwards somersault. 'These aren't even our bodies. We look like ourselves – we're even wearing our own clothes. But these bodies are *avatars*. Like electronic puppets, inside the Web. In here, you can't get hurt,' she said. 'Here, you don't even have to wear your skin cream and hat when you go outside in the summer . . .'

And she was right. We were perfectly safe in the Web . . . or so I thought then!

Byte got up, and quietened down. 'Not real?'

'Of course not,' I said.

'I wasn't scared.'

'Oh, you *liar*.'

The Wire said, 'I know that jump is a bit of a shock, but this is the way they let children into the Web. Adults can beam straight to the building block they want to go to, of course.'

Byte nodded seriously.

I snickered. 'He's faking it! He doesn't know what a building block is.'

'Yes, I do.'

'Do not . . .'

And so on, all the way to the nearest building block. Just a day at the office, for a girl and her pesky kid brother.

As we neared the building block we could see we weren't alone on the plain. There was a shadowy suggestion of people around us – like a crowd of ghosts, difficult to make out or count. They can't show you all of the users inside Webtown in person – there are *millions*, it would be impossible – but they like to give the illusion of the crowds present with you if you go somewhere busy. So, the ghosts. It's the kind of thing you pick up as you spend time in Webtown.

Right now, anyhow, I could see we were part of a throng of children, all heading in big thick streams towards the building blocks for Education, Retail, Communication, Library, whatever. The surfaces of the blocks were sparkling, ever-changing. Like big advertising hoardings for whatever was inside them. Byte's eyes looked like they would bug out of his head.

A lot of kids were heading for Sport. And a *lot* towards Entertainment. That's the place they keep the theme parks.

We joined a river of kids, marching towards the Entertainment Block. One boy worked his way over to us, and when he got close enough he snapped out of the ghost-grey background so we could see him. He was dressed for an interactive game: overalls, hard black body armour that was moulded to his back and chest, boots that laced up to the knees, steel shinpads and a shimmering red cloak. *So* obvious! He smiled at me, a gesture I treated with the contempt it deserved.

Byte looked nervously at the ghosts. 'Won't it be crowded with all these people?'

'Yes,' I said. 'Better scuttle on home, George.'

'No,' said the Wire. 'The Web never gets crowded. It's not real, Byte. It just expands as more people want to use it.'

That's the Wire for you. Truthful, but just *no* sense of humour.

Still, she was right. It you go to a Web theme park *there are never any queues* . . .

We walked into the building block.

It was like dipping into a viscous liquid. I could feel the surface of the block moving over my body, like a rubber band. When my head passed into the building block there was a brief flash of electric blue, and an electronic tone.

The block expanded all around us, just like the Tardis, until skyscrapers filled the plain, all the way to the horizon. That transition happens every day, of course, but even *that* had Byte goggling when I dragged him in after me.

We were standing on a wide boulevard. The sides of the buildings and even the sky were coated with huge ad hoardings. Some of them were three-dimensional – like the one for the *X-Files* ice dance show – even though 3-D ads are supposed to be banned inside the Entertainment block.

And there was a special exhibition, right there in the building block, to celebrate World Peace Day.

For instance, there was a display of what scientists thought life might be like on the planet Bellatrix III, the planet of another star they found recently. And there was a big globe of our world, turning slowly, beamed down from satellites and beefed up by computer graphics. The big superconducting power net was spread all over the globe, shining yellow. The big new irrigation canals in the American midwest were blue threads. Australia was so full of solar farms it seemed to glitter. I could see the new monorail network being built across India in time for next year's Olympics.

The south of Britain was brown and looked dried out – more like the south of Spain used to be, Philip says, back in the stone age when he was a kid, around 1997. And I could see the new energy mats in the Wash, so big they could be seen from space . . .

In the middle of the exhibit there was a Mars astronaut, lying on his back, working invisible switches. It was the mission commander, Chuck McFarlane. He was wearing a jockey chip today, so we could all follow him as he prepared to take off from Cape Canaveral in a few hours time.

But right now, as you might expect, nobody was paying much attention to Chuck, or any of the serious educational stuff!

It was just chaos in that block. Kids were running *everywhere*. All the theme parks were free today: Cretaceous Park, Apollo 13, the Roald Dahl Adventure Playground, Dreamcastle, Tom Sawyer Country . . . Spiders – Web helpers – were rattling around, trying to control the flow, their cartoon legs whirring like propellers.

Some of the kids were moving a little oddly. Jerkily, like speeded-up characters in a cartoon.

'Wow,' said Byte. 'That looks great.' He started hopping around, waving his arms and legs like Daffy Duck.

I exchanged a glance with the Wire. Time for the responsible big sister bit, I thought.

'Listen, you one-mip. Those kids are on supertime.'

'Supertime?'

'Look, we're all on Webtime here. Everything is faster for us. It makes things brighter, more colourful, noisier. And some people go on to supertime, which is even quicker.'

'More fun!'

'Well, yes.' I admit I had tried supertime myself. 'But it's bad for you. You have to leave the Web earlier, and when you get home you feel dull. Even duller than you normally are. It's called the slows. So if anyone offers you supertime, say no.'

Byte looked disgruntled.

Now, be careful. I know what's good for you. Don't do anything I wouldn't do . . . The worst thing about having a kid brother is that it turns you into your own parents.

That boy in the black gaming suit had landed close by. His cape was rippling over his shoulders, just like Superman's. 'Hi,' he said to me.

I groaned. 'Oh, no. Bad taste *and* an American.'

He laughed. 'I only said one word!'

'What do you want?'

He shrugged, so casually I could feel myself blush under my mask out in Realworld, and I hated him even more. 'Just being friendly. Where are you guys headed? What about the Endangered Park? That's venomous they tell me. They have pandas and manatees there now . . .'

'I hope you're not the type who likes to go hunting dinosaurs,' I said haughtily.

'I certainly am not,' he said, a bit off balance. 'Actually I think I'll go to Dreamcastle. The best game zone in the Web, right? Although I hear that new place, Tracy Island, is pretty wicked.'

I gagged. '*Wicked*? Which 1990s colony are you from, Bellatrix III?'

'No, New England. My name's Surfer. I—'

'We lost Byte,' said the Wire.

'Good,' I snapped.

But of course I had to look for him.

There are times when being the oldest is such a drag. Like, *all* the time.

He hadn't got far. He was standing with his mouth open under a potato-crisp tree.

'Is this real?'

'Yes,' I said seriously. 'Try one.'

He reached up, plucked a crinkly crisp, and put it in his mouth. He looked confused. 'Ugh. I can't taste it.'

Even the Wire laughed. 'Of course not. You can't taste or smell anything in here.'

'Nothing but your socks, anyway,' I said. 'It's just an ad, you one-mip.'

That boy, Surfer, was still hanging around, grinning at me.

Meeting people from all around the world is one of the features of the Web. Right now, for instance, this character Surfer and I were thousands of kilometres apart, in our Websuits, and yet it seemed as if we were side by side.

Usually this is a good thing. It does depend who you meet, though.

'So,' said Surfer. 'What do you say? Maybe I could tag along.'

'Don't you have any friends?'

The Wire actually told me off. 'Metaphor, don't be so rude.'

Surfer laughed. 'Don't worry. It's only because she likes me.'

I started to figure out ways of telling him how wrong he was. Starting with a punch on the nose. It wouldn't hurt in Webtown, but—

Byte was tugging at my hand. 'Let's go. Let's *go*.' He can be such a baby.

I nodded to the Wire. We got hold of Byte's hands, and we started tapping the access code into our wrist controls.

Surfer spread his hands. 'Is this goodbye? Where are you going?'

I took pity on him. 'There's only one place to go today,' I said.

'Where?'

'GulliverZone!'

We finished entering the code.

There was a blue flash and a beep, and the floor disappeared.

. . . And I was sitting on the palm of a gigantic hand!

CHAPTER THREE

GULLIVERZONE

The three of us were sitting on the fleshy thumb joint of the upturned hand. The skin was very soft and warm and looked as if it ought to smell of soap and perfume. The fingers, curling up a little, were like big pieces of furniture.

The hand was steady, so we were in no danger of falling off. But we were, I guessed, about thirty metres off the ground!

Byte was whimpering, the baby. And the Wire was moaning. 'They might have given us some *warning*.'

I was a little rattled too, but I wasn't about to show it. 'Oh, come on. There's always an access metaphor like this. Something in keeping with the theme of the park. The show's started already. Lighten up, you guys.' And to show I wasn't scared, I got on my tummy and crawled to the edge of the hand.

We were suspended above a sunlit landscape. Below us was a little town. At its centre was a palace, surrounded by a shining moat. Further out I could see tree-clad hills, lakes shining like sheets of glass, and what looked like a herd of white horses galloping over the grass.

It was like being in an aeroplane, except in the open. As you'd imagine a magic carpet ride, I suppose.

But I was looking down along an immense body. I could see two tree-trunk legs planted on the ground, swathed in a skirt the size of a parachute. The legs ended in two giant feet, and those white horses were jumping the toes like fences.

Suddenly the hand was lifted up.

The Wire and Byte tumbled over, yelping, and I fell forward against the rough flesh of the palm.

A huge face hovered over the hand. It must have been three metres tall. It was monstrous: eyes like blue balloons, ears like sculptures of flesh, a few loose strands of hair like ship's cables.

Byte whimpered, 'Is it a balloon?'

It did look a little like those fancy advertising hot-air balloons you see at fairs sometimes. But I grinned at the one-mip and said in my scary voice, 'No. *It's real.*'

But even I was startled when the monster face opened its mouth!

It drew back its lips in a smile, revealing teeth like rows of white gateposts.

'Hello,' the head said. It was a girl's voice, but it sounded like remote thunder. 'My name is Glumdalclitch. I'm from the land of Brobdingnag, here in GulliverZone.'

'Wow,' said Byte. 'You're a *girl.*'

She laughed. It sounded like cannons going off. 'Of course I'm a girl. In fact I'm nine years old.' She squinted at him. 'How old are you?'

'Nine.'

I pinched him.

'Next birthday.'

'Well, we're almost the same then,' she said. 'You're so cute.'

I looked at the Wire, and we exchanged gagging gestures. Why do people who don't have kid brothers always think they are cute?

'You're skin's very smooth,' said the egg, and Glumdalclitch laughed.

I poked him in the back. 'Of course it is. This isn't *real*. If *you* were blown up to thirty metres high, your nose pores would look like craters on the Moon.'

Byte pulled his tongue, looking embarrassed.

'Thank you for choosing to be visitors to GulliverZone,' said Glumdalclitch politely. 'This is the Web's most famous theme park, and it's all based on the great children's story by

Jonathan Swift. Did you know the book was written as long ago as 1726, but it's still read widely today?'

The Wire and I glanced at each other. I had a sinking feeling.

'As you know,' Glumdalclitch said, 'everything is free on World Peace Day. Where would you like to start? You can go to Lilliput, the land of the little people. Or come with me to my home, Brobdingnag. Then there is the land of the Houyhnhnms.' I had to look up the spelling before writing that down. She made it sound like a horse whinny. 'The Houyhnhnms are intelligent horses. You can debate philosophy and politics with them. But watch out for the Yahoos, the wild humans . . .'

Byte, the little egg, started jumping up and down. 'Where are the rides? I want to see the rides!'

For once I kind of agreed with him.

This all sounded a little – well – *worthy*. I knew educational groups had put a lot of money into setting up GulliverZone, along with some commercial sponsors like Tennessee Fried Ostrich and Manchester-Newcastle FC. If it was going to be *instructive*, no wonder Philip had been so ready to let us come here.

I was starting to wonder if we should have gone with that kid Surfer to Dreamcastle instead.

I'd never read *Gulliver's Travels*. If it was all so serious, I probably never would. Well, maybe the effects would be good. And—

A huge shadow swept over us, like a cloud. We all yelped and ducked.

The shadow moved on. I looked up. It wasn't a cloud. It was an *island*, a huge elliptical rock floating in the air, with buildings crusted over the upper surface. The bottom was smooth and shining, and I could see people climbing around staircases and balconies carved into the side. Some of them were dangling fishing lines over the edge. They shouted and waved, and Glumdalclitch waved back.

'I almost forgot,' Glumdalclitch said. 'You can go for a ride on our flying island, Laputa.'

Of course we all disagreed about where to go.

The Wire fancied the flying island. Byte just squealed about rides. In the end, as usual, it was up to me.

I stood up straight and faced Glumdalclitch. 'Lilliput,' I said. 'Take us to Lilliput.'

She smiled and bent down. We had to hang on to her fingers, for fear of falling.

Her hand reached the ground. She tipped it, gently, and we rolled off.

I found myself on a lawn of very fine grass. In the middle of it there was a stand of bushes, two or three metres high.

Glumdalclitch straightened up. It was like staring up at Nelson's Column. 'Have a good day,' she boomed. 'If you need anything just ask a spider, or call for me.' And she turned and walked off, every ten-metre stride making the ground shake. 'Remember that. Call me . . .'

'I liked her,' said Byte.

I wouldn't be doing my job if I let *that* one go. 'George has got a girlfriend. George has got a girlfriend—'

He jumped on me and we started to wrestle. We rolled and fetched up against the little stand of bushes.

The Wire followed us, her faced pursed up as usual. 'I don't suppose you've taken time to look at the trees.'

I pushed Byte away, although he kept pummelling my leg. 'What trees? These bushes?'

'They aren't bushes,' she said. 'Look at the leaves.'

I took a closer look. The leaves were very small, like the leaves of watercress, and I could take two or three on my fingertip. But I recognized their shape.

We have a big old oak tree at the bottom of our garden. But the leaves on our tree are usually bigger than the palm of my hand.

The 'bushes' were oak trees, just two metres tall!

'Wow,' I said.

Byte was tugging at my sleeve. 'Let's go to the town,' he said.

'What town?'

He pointed. 'Over there.'

I looked. There *was* a town – perhaps it was the one with the palace we'd seen from the air – but it looked very small and far away. 'I think that might be too far,' I said. 'It looks kilometres away.'

The Wire was moaning. 'I don't know why Glumdalclitch dumped us in the middle of nowhere like this.'

And Byte was nagging. 'Where are the *rides*?'

This was turning, I thought, into a very bad day.

'Let's walk,' I said angrily. 'It can't be that far.' I set off towards the town.

The Wire and Byte followed, grumbling and nagging as was their wont.

Except for the miniature trees, it was like a walk in the country. A wasp buzzed past my head. There were birds singing in the trees. A black cat looked out of a hedgerow at us. It gave us that blank, piercing stare cats do, decided we were no threat, and loped away in search of lunch.

The vegetation here was all miniature. The cat's 'hedgerow' was actually an orchard of tiny apple trees, for instance. But the animals and insects were our scale.

My gloom deepened. Obviously someone had spent a lot of money and mips – computer power – on all these details. The insects and animals – even the cat – were generated within the Zone – they were *phaces*, like the spiders, fake creatures like cartoons that only existed inside the Web.

I wondered if our cat Gazza would enjoy an adventure in a catty Websuit.

Anyway, it was a bad sign. If you find yourself in a theme park where someone has put in a lot of animals and insects and details like that, it usually means they are trying to be *educational*. And have left no money for the rides.

And then, just to cap it all, it started to rain!

It was very realistic – big deal – and I was soon cold and wet and bored. Here I was, slogging across a field in the rain, with kilometres to go to the town . . .

Except it wasn't kilometres.

The town turned out to be just beyond the edge of the field. We only had to walk about a hundred metres.

The town was *miniature* – like a city of dolls' houses. It was so small it had fooled me into thinking it was much farther away.

The rain stopped. We all slowed down and looked at the city.

'Welcome to Mildendo, our metropolis!'

The voice was tiny and came from down by my feet. It was as if an ant had spoken.

I looked down. There was a man standing there, just by my shoe. He was wearing a leather waistcoat and carrying a bow and arrow.

'My name is Clefven,' he said.

He couldn't have been more than ten centimetres tall!

CHAPTER FOUR

LILLIPUT

Clefven stared up at us. We just goggled back down at him.

'Well?' he said. 'Aren't you going to tell me who you are?'

The Wire looked at me. 'I'm the Wire,' she stammered. 'And this is Byte, and—'

He cupped his hand to his ear. 'I can't hear you. You're too far away! Could you pick me up, please?'

I said, 'Pick you up?'

'Of course.' He held up his arms, like a little kid. 'Don't be shy.'

I bent down and put my hand flat, palm upwards. He got hold of his bow and arrow, braced himself on my little finger, and hopped aboard.

I lifted him up, carefully, with my other hand cupped underneath for fear of dropping him. He smiled up at me, reassuring.

I don't know if you've ever had a small bird stand on your hand. Holding him felt a little like that. His weight was tiny. I could feel the hard heels of his boots, and his miniature fingers where they clasped on to my fingertip.

'Wow,' said Byte, and he leaned close to Clefven. 'He's just like *Action Man*. Only smaller.'

What a one-mip he is.

'Now,' Clefven said. 'Who did you say you were?'

I introduced the three of us again, with me last.

'You'll remember her,' Byte said meanly. 'She's the one with the huge pores on her nose.'

Too late, I remembered how I had teased him before. My spare hand flew to my face.

Clefven laughed. 'Don't be self-conscious. Everything is smoothed over here. Anyway, even if this was real, I'm sure you'd still be just as pretty . . .'

The Wire rolled her eyes to the sky.

'Are you *real*?' Byte asked.

Clefven laughed. 'No. I wish I was. I'm a phace. Do you know what that means? All the little people you'll see here today are phaces too. My job is to be your guide for your visit to Lilliput,' he said. 'Thanks for visiting us. Where would you like to start? Would you like to see the Imperial Court?'

'We want *rides*,' Byte said. 'Where are the rides?'

Clefven smiled. 'We don't really have rides,' he said. 'It isn't that kind of theme park.'

I groaned. I was right. 'Oh, no. It's educational.'

The Wire looked at me. 'Maybe we should just spin out of here and try somewhere else.'

'Well, that would be a shame,' Clefven said.

Byte was tugging at my sleeve. 'No,' he said. 'I want to see more little people.'

I shrugged at the Wire. She shrugged back at me.

So it was that we decided to stay.

Of course if I'd known what was going to befall us, just minutes after that, I'd have got out of there quick!

Clefven guided us towards the centre of Mildendo, their town. He sat on my hand comfortably, cross-legged, and ate a tiny cheese sandwich he pulled out of his pocket. Phaces can eat in the Web, of course, even though visitors can't.

Byte wanted a turn at carrying him, and although Clefven said it would be OK, I was *not* going to risk the embarrassment of *that*.

Mildendo was surrounded by a wall about a metre high, and quarter of a metre thick. The wall was made of small bricks each the size of a pencil rubber.

When we were over, there was a scratching sound by my leg. I looked down and saw a huge insect – about half a metre long. It had a shiny black shell and it was working its way along the wall. It had tiny little mandibles – jaws – and it was nibbling at the brickwork. There was something vaguely mechanical about its jaws and clattering limbs.

It was like a dog in a space suit.

'Ugh,' said Byte.

I have to admit I felt the same way myself. 'What's that?'

'It's just a *struldbrug*,' said Clefven. 'It does maintenance. Keeping the fabric of GulliverZone repaired, clearing any mess. It's harmless.'

'Is there a lot of litter?' Byte asked.

'No,' I said. 'Of *course* there's no litter. This is Webtown . . .'

None of this was real – it was all generated by computers – but computer software programs do have faults, and develop glitches. There are even *viruses* – rogue programs that can infest Webware and make it 'ill', just like an infection hurting a person.

This struldbrug was actually a bit of the GulliverZone master program which was going around checking the Webware, and repairing the illusion of reality.

The struldbrug looked creepy, though, like a big black beetle with that shiny black shell, and eyes like grains of sand . . .

Clefven had said it was harmless. But I noticed he was hanging on to my finger a little harder than before, and all the time the struldbrug was near, the Lilliputian never took his eyes off it.

Why should Clefven, a phace, be afraid of a maintenance program? Why should a phace be afraid of anything at all? Phaces were just computer machines. They couldn't *think*.

That was the first time I started to wonder if there was more to GulliverZone than met the eye!

We looked down over Mildendo.

The town was set out as a square, two hundred metres on each side.

The layout of the town was based on two wide boulevards –

wide meaning about a metre across – which were set out in a cross shape. The Imperial Court, with its palace and moat, was at the centre where the boulevards met.

The boulevards divided the town into four quarters. Three of the quarters were clustered with buildings, their little roofs shining in the sunlight. In the fourth quarter there was a park with winding paths and a lake with little sail boats on it. There was a bandstand, but it was shut up.

The heart of the town was the Imperial Court. It was like a toy castle. It was surrounded by a square moat two metres wide, with a drawbridge across it. The palace itself was at the centre of a courtyard, walled off within the moated area, with buildings and inner walls. On the banks of the moat there was a crèche, with huge tables and chairs for normal-sized visitors – adults with their toddlers. I could see a gaggle of babies lumbering around there now, their huge heads looming over the little buildings like moons. I shuddered. *Babies!*

From a distance the palace looked like a miniature Buckingham Palace, or maybe a White House, with tiny glittering windows and balconies and railings and flags everywhere.

'The palace,' said Clefven, 'is the residence of the Empress Golbasta: supreme ruler of Lilliput, delight and terror of the universe . . .' He laughed. 'And so on.' It sounded rather a hollow laugh, however.

'We will *definitely* have to go and see that,' I said. 'After we drop off Byte in the crèche.'

That got me a punch in the leg, but since it didn't hurt, it was worth it.

We started to look around the town. There were a few people our size here, mostly children. They stepped like giants over the houses, and bent down and pointed at stuff.

If you've ever been to Legoland, or Bekonscott, or any of those miniature toytowns, you'll have an idea what Mildendo was like.

Except this was *real*.

The Wire pointed. 'Look. There's Surfer.' She looked at me slyly. 'You remember, Metaphor.'

I sniffed.

I looked sideways, though. It *was* Surfer. You couldn't miss that dumb shiny black suit and the Superman cloak. He looked as if he'd made some friends and was having a good time. I could hear him talking about going to Dreamcastle.

Meanwhile, *I* had the egg and the Wire . . .

On cue, Byte started jumping up and down. 'The lake! Let's go see the boats!'

I stopped him. 'You'll step on somebody, you one-mip. Anyhow, we're going to the palace.'

'Oh, don't be so sour,' the Wire told me. 'Let him see the lake. There's plenty of time.'

She had called *me* sour, in front of my kid brother. Now you can see why she was the most unpopular girl at school.

Anyway, I gave in.

We stepped carefully through the streets, heading for the park.

There were little people *everywhere*. They were all ten or twelve centimetres tall, like dolls come to life. The children were very cute. The people were shopping at the stores that lined the streets, or sweeping out their houses, or tending their tiny, handkerchief-sized gardens. On the main streets, tiny old-fashioned cars puttered up and down.

Everywhere we went, the people waved at us. Clefven leaned over the edge of my hand and hollered down to them.

We reached the quarter with the park. There was a lot of open space here, and we didn't have to tread so carefully as in the town.

Byte whooped, and ran forward towards the lake.

Clefven stood up on my hand. He looked alarmed. 'Slow down!' he called. 'That lake is deeper than it looks . . .'

But Byte couldn't hear his little voice, and by the time I called—

I don't even have to tell you what happened next.

Byte tripped over an oak tree. He fell forward on his belly, slap into the middle of the pond.

He sent up great waves that rippled to the side of the lake.

All the Lilliputian sailors started shouting, and waving their fists at Byte. Some of the yachts capsized, and the Lilliputians bobbed about in the water like matchsticks in a bath.

It was just so *typical*.

I ran towards the lake. I was going to give him a piece of my mind. I was so embarrassed I wanted to die.

I noticed there were struldbrugs, dozens of them, scurrying across the park towards the lake. They looked like a pack of dogs, converging on Byte. Lilliputians had to scurry out of their way.

'Get him out,' Clefven said to me.

'Oh, let the little egg take a bath.'

He kicked the ball of my thumb, hard. 'I mean it. Get him out of there. You don't understand.'

I looked into his miniature face. He was serious.

Suddenly, there was a blue flash from the pond.

Byte sank out of sight.

The Wire said, puzzled. 'That looked like the flash you get when you go into a building block. It shouldn't happen *here*. I think something is wrong.'

The struldbrugs were crowding around the pond now, clicking their metallic jaws at each other. Some of them had even jumped in the water, and were swimming around.

Something, I sensed, really was going wrong. And my little brother was in the middle of it.

I could only think of one thing to do.

I ran forward. I closed my hands over Clefven, who was clinging on grimly to my fingers. The Wire called after me, but I ignored her.

I jumped as far as I could, right into the middle of the pond!

I hit the water. It felt wet, but only briefly. It was as if I was falling through a shell of water, into some empty space underneath.

There was a blue flash and a beep.

I fell about two metres. I landed heavily.

I was in a dusty, shed-like space, like the back of a theatre behind the scenery.

I still had Clefven in my hand. I lifted him up. He looked
bedraggled and angry.

'Are you all right?' I asked.

'Yes, no thanks to you,' he snapped. 'But you aren't! You
shouldn't be here.'

'What do you mean?'

But before he had a chance to answer, I heard a rustling at
my feet.

Lilliputians.

There must have been a thousand of them, lined up
around me in ranks. Behind them I caught a glimpse of little
houses, shacks of wood and brick. It was like another
miniature city in here – a shanty town, anyway.

But that wasn't the most important thing.

The most important thing was that the Lilliputians all had
their bows and arrows drawn, and were aiming at me.

'Now, wait a minute—'

From a thousand bows, a thousand pin-sized arrows flew at
me!

CHAPTER FIVE

LILLIPUTIANS

The arrows rose up in a cloud, like little insects. I cried out, and raised my hands to my face, to protect my eyes.

A couple of the arrows lodged in the backs of my hands. They were like tiny pinpricks. But most of the arrows sailed over my head and shoulders.

I saw, now, that the arrows were trailing ropes – Lilliputian ropes, as fine as thread.

Soon I was caught up in hundreds of ropes that crisscrossed my body.

The Lilliputians ran forward, shouting. They were only a few centimetres high, but there were a thousand of them, and it was *scary*.

They started dragging at the ropes. I was off balance. It only took a couple of seconds.

I fell backwards, dragged down. I was so tangled up I could hardly move.

I hit the ground. The Websuit wouldn't let me get bruised, of course, but it didn't stop the wind getting knocked out of me.

The Lilliputians swarmed all over me. It was like having warm little locusts clambering on my body. I heard rapid hammering, like woodpeckers working all around me.

The Lilliputians were nailing the ropes to the ground, so I would be trapped.

I could feel them tugging at my hair. I tried to twist my head, but it was too late.

They had even tied my hair to the floor!

When I was firmly fixed, the Lilliputians climbed off me and backed away.

I was stuck on my back.

Above me, there was a blue glow. At first I thought it was a skylight, but it was rippling.

It was the lake we'd fallen through. It was a thin sheet of water, spread like a roof above me. It looked like the surface of a swimming pool from underwater.

I heard a low sobbing, coming from a couple of metres to my right. I couldn't move my head to see, but I knew who it was. After all, I'd made him cry often enough. That's a big sister's job.

'Byte,' I said. '*Byte*.'

The crying stopped, but he didn't reply.

'*George*,' I said. 'It's me, Sarah.'

'Sarah?'

'Are you OK?'

'They tied me to the floor.' He sounded thoroughly fed up. 'Where's the Wire?'

'I think she's still in the park. She didn't follow us. Listen, Byte. There's nothing to be afraid of. None of this is real.'

'These strings feel real.'

'But they aren't.' I knew it was all just Webware. The Lilliputians had just added restricting commands to the Webware programs that generated my body . . .

How do you explain that to an eight-year-old?

'Listen, Byte. I'm not sure what's happening here, but it's OK. We can't come to any harm.'

'I want to go home,' he whined.

It didn't seem a bad idea. 'All right,' I whispered. 'Just press your scuttle button and you'll be right there. Can you reach it?'

After a few seconds, he wailed, 'No! I can't reach it!'

I tried too. My hands were tied down too firmly. Strain as I might I couldn't break any threads.

It's surprising how strong a thousand thin threads can be.

Something tickled my hair. I thought I could hear giggling.

But I wasn't interested in that. I was starting to get *seriously* annoyed.

I started to shout. 'Hello! Hello! Whoever's there, this is illegal. You aren't allowed to stop us scuttling . . .'

'I don't know why we don't just ask that nice Glumdal-clitch to come and help,' Byte said.

I scoffed. 'Your giant girlfriend? Don't be so silly, Byte—'

I could feel bird-like footsteps on my chest.

I managed to look down, past my nose. There was Clefven, standing just beneath my chin, looking at me. A Lilliputian woman stood with him, dressed in a long, old-fashioned skirt. Clefven looked concerned.

Suddenly, he leaned forward and shouted past my ear. 'Hey! Get out of there!'

That giggling behind me got louder, and the tickling in my hair went away.

'Sorry about that,' said Clefven. 'That was Clustril and Drunlo. My kids. They were playing hide-and-seek in your hair.'

'Kids! *Children?* You have children?'

'Yes,' he said. 'And this is my wife, Skyresh.'

The woman glared at me. 'I wish I could say I was pleased to meet you,' she said frostily.

'Hold on a minute,' I said. 'Now I really am confused. You people are phaces. You're not real. You're generated by the computers. You're just part of the scenery in here. You don't have husbands and wives and children!'

He looked amused. 'Well, there you are, Skyresh,' he said. 'We'll just have to get divorced.'

She looked at me. 'I think you'll have to tell her the whole story.'

He sighed. 'I suppose so. Things can't get any worse.' He stood before me. 'Then we'll decide what to do about you.'

'And me,' Byte said miserably.

'Yes, and you.'

I asked, 'What whole story?'

He leaned on his bow. 'Metaphor, we aren't really phaces. I lied to you, I'm afraid.'

'Then you're avatars of real people. In Websuits, out in Realworld somewhere.

'Not that either. Metaphor, we don't exist outside the Web. We are Web creatures. *But we are alive.*'

'That's impossible.'

He laughed again. He put his hand on his chest. 'Well, it doesn't feel impossible. I'm as alive as you are. I can think, and feel, and talk, and love. Just as you can. It's just that I live my whole life inside the Web.'

'But what *are* you?'

'Do you know what computer viruses are?'

I tried to nod, then yelped as the threads pulled at my hair. 'Infections of computer programs.'

'That's how it started, thirty or forty years ago. Viruses eat other programs, and survive, and hide, and breed . . . Exactly what living things do! Metaphor, viruses have had decades to evolve, here inside the Web. At some point, we became aware. Intelligent.'

'We? You're telling me *you* are a computer virus?'

'A descendant of one, yes. We infested these forms, the bodies of Lilliputians inside GulliverZone, because nobody notices us that way.' He laughed. 'The struldbrugs dare not harm us out of doors, because the visitors think we're toys. And nobody takes you seriously, when you're small.'

I grunted. 'Tell me about it. Why don't you just make yourselves big?'

'We can't,' Clefven said. 'But we do have magic dust to shrink things to our size. It's a useful way for us to get equipment.'

Magic dust. Of course he meant size control programs.

'But,' he said, 'we don't have anything to make us grow again. Only Golbasta, the Empress of Lilliput, has that.'

I wondered why she would need such a thing. 'But why hide as Lilliputians? Why don't you want anyone to notice you?'

Now Skyresh came clumping forward to glare at me. 'Because people try to hunt us down.'

'It's true,' Clefven said sadly. 'We're *viruses*. People think we're destructive, even though we haven't been for decades. Nobody wants us. They think we're a waste of mips. So they hound us. That's why we have to hide in places like this, unused parts of the simulations.'

'Who hunts you? The Webcops?'

'Yes,' said Skyresh, 'but they aren't the threat. *Golbasta* is the real danger.'

The Empress again. Why should she hunt Lilliputians? I still had more questions than answers!

Clefven said, 'The struldbrugs. The beetle-like creatures. You should know about them. They aren't really maintenance routines. That's a cover. They are *familiars*. Golbasta's creatures. Keep out of their way.' He looked sad. 'I'm afraid they took away your friend—'

'The Wire? She isn't really my friend . . . Where did they take her?'

'To the Imperial Court,' Clefven said. 'Look, I think you've heard enough,' he said seriously. 'We have to decide what to do next. We can't just let you go.'

'Oh, we wouldn't tell anyone,' I said.

Skyresh frowned. 'How could we trust you? We have *children* here. I don't want to go on the run again.'

I opened my mouth to protest. I was sincere. I didn't have anything against these Lilliputians, alive or not . . .

But then, it was all taken out of our hands.

Big black shapes clustered on the other side of the pond roof. There was a flash of blue light.

A dozen struldbrugs came splashing through the pond, falling straight towards me!

CHAPTER SIX

STRULDBRUGS

The struldbrugs clattered to the ground all around me. They hit the floor with heavy, leathery thumps, like dropped suitcases.

Skyresh screamed and clung to Clefven. All around me, I could hear the yells of fleeing Lilliputians.

Clefven said, 'We have to get out of here! The struldbrugs must have seen Metaphor and Byte come through. Now the struldbrugs know where we are, we won't be safe from Golbasta.'

'The children!'

'Find them. Bring them here.' They ran to the edge of my chest, and Clefven leaned forward to help Skyresh slither to the ground. She slipped out of my sight. I could hear her little heels clattering over the floor as she ran away.

Clefven got out his bow and arrow. He ran up on to my forehead, over my cheeks. His boots were sharp little points on my skin. 'It's awful,' he said. 'The struldbrugs are everywhere. Skyresh is right. We have to go . . . Oh, no. *Reldresal.*' He lifted up his bow and arrow, pointing it to my left.

'Who's Reldresal? Clefven, tell me.'

He didn't reply. He jumped down off my chest, to my right. He started popping up and down, firing arrows past me.

He was using *me* as cover! And I was still stuck there, unable to move a finger.

I could hear Byte crying.

'Byte!' I called.

He sniffled. 'I'm not frightened.'

He is such a liar. But how could I stop him being frightened? I racked my brains.

'Byte,' I said at last, desperately. 'Isn't this fun?'

He was silent for a minute. 'Fun. Are you kidding?'

'No! This is all part of the theme park. Didn't you know?'

'It is?'

'Of course it is. This is the, uh, the Lair of the Lilliputians. And this is the part where the struldbrugs break in. It's all just a game. Didn't you read the brochure? You weren't really *scared*, were you?'

'It's all just pretend?'

I tried to ignore the screams of the Lilliputians. 'Of course it is.'

'I wasn't scared. I was worried about *you*. I thought *you* were scared.'

For the first time in my life, I was glad to hear him lying.

But now, I could hear something approaching from my left side: an awful slurp and scrape, insectile, powerful, implacable. On my right, Clefven was still popping up and down, firing his arrows, apparently to no avail.

Have you ever had one of those nightmares where the monster is coming, and you can't even move? Being tied down on that floor, at that moment, was *exactly* like that!

The noise came closer and closer, slithering and rattling and sucking.

At last I couldn't stand it any more.

I gritted my teeth, and twisted my head. There was a horrible ripping sound, and I could feel the hair being pulled out of my head in great handfuls.

'Ouch!'

Of course it wasn't *really* my hair. It was just the hair of my avatar, in the Web. But the *pain* was real enough, even though it faded quickly.

My head was free.

I glanced to my right. I saw Clefven with his bow and

arrow. Behind him, the struldbrugs were swarming all over the Lilliputians' lair, their big black carapaces gleaming in the watery light from the lake above. They chomped their way busily through the warren. They were crushing houses, even ripping up the floor.

There were Lilliputians everywhere, running between the advancing struldbrugs and screaming. Some of them were trying to fight, but their arrows and little stick swords just bounced off the struldbrugs' shiny backs.

One struldbrug had taken hold of a Lilliputian, a young man. I could see the little fellow squirming in that steely grip, still fighting. But he had no chance. The struldbrug was simply too big for him.

The struldbrug looked like a cat with a bird in its jaw.

The struldbrugs were going to *win*, I realized.

'Wow!' Byte said. 'These special effects are great, Sarah! What a ride!'

There was a fresh scraping close by my left ear.

I turned my head. It was a struldbrug; bigger and blacker than any I'd seen before.

And it had a human face.

It was a woman's face, thin and cold-eyed. She had no teeth in her black mouth. Her head was suspended on the end of a thin struldbrug neck. I could see she had the usual metallic-looking struldbrug legs and mandibles, but she also had two human arms, sticking out in front of her carapace.

Behind me, Clefven shouted, 'Get away from her, Reldresal!'

The struldbrug-woman, Reldresal, smiled at me. 'Don't worry, my dear.' Her voice buzzed like dragonfly wings. 'I won't harm you. I know you're human. I only want those Lilliputians. They're *viruses*, you know.'

'Don't believe her!' Clefven shouted. 'She'll hurt you, Metaphor.'

Looking at Reldresal, I believed him.

'It's all very well telling me that,' I hissed at Clefven, 'but I can't get away anyhow. Can't you cut these ropes?'

He got out a knife – it was a little penknife the size of a fly's wing. He unfolded the blade and began sawing.

When he saw how long it was taking, Byte started shouting at Reldresal. He called her names that would have got him into a *lot* of trouble if Philip had been there. I shouted at him to stop, but he wouldn't and it was working: Reldresal was hesitating, hissing, turning between Byte and myself, wondering who to chomp up first.

I have to admit that must have taken a lot of guts. The little one-mip.

At last Clefven cut one of the ropes on my arm. But it made no difference. I still couldn't move the arm. And there were three hundred more ropes to go!

'It's no good,' I said. 'It's going to take too long. Can't you get some help?'

But then Skyresh ran up. She had two Lilliputian children with her, a boy and a girl. The girl waved at me. Her head barely came up to my nose. Was it only minutes ago that these two kids had been playing hide-and-seek in my hair?

Skyresh said, 'We have to go. *Now*. You can't be worried about *her*. If she hadn't come blundering through the lake, none of this would have happened. Leave her!'

Clefven looked at me, and spread his hands. 'I'm sorry. I can't get you free anyhow . . .'

There was a pressure on my chest, on the left. I looked that way.

It was Reldresal. She was climbing over me! Her mandibles waved in my face, like little knives. 'Don't worry,' she said. '*I'll* cut you free.' Her voice was like a snake's hiss.

When I looked back, Clefven was backing away regretfully.

I had to think of something, and fast, or – in some way I still didn't understand – Byte and I were going to be a struldbrug's breakfast!

'Wait,' I said. 'The magic dust! Clefven, do you have any?'

He stopped.

Skyresh said, 'Come *on*.'

But Clefven patted a pouch at his belt. 'Yes. Why?'

'Shrink us! It's the only way!'

He shook his head. 'We've never tried it on the avatar of a real person. It might be dangerous.'

Reldresal was climbing further up my chest. I could feel her hard weight. 'We don't have a choice. Please, Clefven.'

He came running back to me. He dug out a tiny handful of dust from the pouch and threw it over my face. It was blue, and it sparkled like Christmas tree glitter. Then he went running over to Byte, out of my sight.

It took a second to work. Reldresal's face loomed closer to mine . . .

I started to shrink.

Shrinking feels like falling.

Reldresal's face seemed to rise upwards, away from me, as if I was falling down a well. And the pressure of the ropes slackened. Soon I was able to start squeezing out of them.

But I kept shrivelling, getting smaller and smaller.

I stood up. I was surrounded by heaps of thick ropes, stacked up taller than I was. They were the threads that had tied me up, I realized. I was the same size as Clefven – in fact, shorter. And here came Byte, reduced to the same scale as me, running towards me.

'Look at me! Look at me!' he shouted.

He tripped on a rope and went flat on his face. It was just so *typical*.

All the while, far above us, I could see the huge shining belly of Reldresal, the struldbrug-woman, as she worked her way over the ropes, looking for me.

Clefven was back with his family. Now I was the same size, they looked like real people. He grinned at me. 'You'll be safe now.'

'Yes. Go, Clefven. Thank you.'

The Lilliputian family ran off.

I lifted up the control pad on my wrist. 'Get ready to scuttle,' I told Byte. 'You remember how?'

'Aw,' he said. 'I'm having *fun*.'

'Just do it, one-mip!'

I raised my hand to my own scuttle button.

I waited, just for a moment, before pressing it – the way

you might wait before taking your first bite of an ice-cream, just to draw out the anticipation.

It was *such* a relief, and I wallowed in the feeling. I was as good as safe already! In just seconds I would be out of here, and home. There was still the Wire to think about, but I was sure once I told Philip what had happened, and he spoke to the Webcops, it would soon be sorted out.

'Ready?' I said to Byte.

He lifted his hand to his scuttle button.

'Three, two, one—' We both pressed.

Nothing happened. I was still in that dusty wooden cavern. Byte was still here too, looking confused.

The scuttle buttons didn't work!

And now Reldresal had seen us. Her face was like a huge white cloud above us. Her mandible was reaching for us, like the blade of a mechanical digger.

But that wasn't the true horror of the moment for me. We were still stuck here, in the bowels of GulliverZone – *with no way home!*

HUNTED

I grabbed Byte's hand and pulled him aside.

Reldresal's mandible came clattering down on the ground, just behind us.

I ran after Clefven, jumping over the discarded ropes.

'I thought we were going home,' Byte said, panting as I yanked him along.

'Oh, let's stay a bit more.'

'Yay!' He was pleased.

I never thought I'd be glad about my brother's total lack of brain.

I looked up as we ran. I could see Reldresal's face casting to and fro. Her huge shining belly slid over us like a roof.

There were, I decided, advantages to being small. Reldresal obviously had trouble seeing us.

There were very few Lilliputians left now. Evidently everyone had either been swept up by the struldbrugs, or had run off. But the Lilliputians' lair was still full of struldbrugs. They looked like huge machines, giant tanks on legs, picking over the ruins of a town. It wouldn't take them long to find us. And then . . .

I didn't know what would happen. But I was sure it wouldn't be pleasant!

But how could we escape? I couldn't have reached back up to that lake in the roof, even when I was my normal size. And now it was just impossible.

I spotted Clefven. He was shepherding his family into what

looked like the mouth of a well dug into the floor. The two children and then Skyresh dropped through the little black circle, and each time there was a flash of blue light.

The struldbrugs were very close. Clefven was about to jump into the well.

'Clefven!' I called. 'Wait!'

He stopped, on the rim of the well. 'You're all right. I'm glad.'

'Is that a way out?'

He hesitated. Poor Clefven was so late because he had stayed behind to help us. He'd put his family at risk for us. And now, I was asking him to do the same again.

'Yes. Come on. Hurry. The struldbrugs can't follow, it's too narrow.'

The hole was just a bottomless black disc in the ground. I had no idea where it led to.

Would *you* just jump in?

I saw a struldbrug approaching, legs clattering mechanically.

'Hurry,' hissed Clefven.

I pushed Byte into the hole. He disappeared in a blue flash.

'Now you,' said Clefven.

I closed my eyes and jumped.

Even through my closed eyelids I could see electric blue.

Byte, the dummy, was standing under me as I came through. I fell right on top of him.

We fell over on coarse grass.

I looked around. We were underneath a wooden roof, a metre or so above my head – no, I reminded myself, now I was only ten centimetres tall! It must have been only five centimetres above, half my height. Beyond the roof, a few paces away, the grass continued on to a sunlit lawn.

I pulled Byte out of the way. In a few seconds, Clefven came through. It was as if he was falling through a trapdoor. But when I looked up, I could see nothing but solid wooden roof.

He brushed himself off, and smiled at us. He was now

about as tall as Philip in relation to me, though he couldn't have weighed so much.

I felt embarrassed to think I'd picked him up like a toy and just carried him into that lake without even asking him. Because he was small, I hadn't taken him seriously. I, of all people, should know better than that!

'We're safe now,' he said. 'For the time being. Come on.'

He led us out into sunshine. Looking back, I saw that we'd come out of the empty bandstand in the middle of the Mildendo park.

Skyresh and the children were waiting. The children came running up to Clefven, who hugged them. Skyresh just glared at me. I couldn't blame her.

I looked around. Everything seemed *huge* – even though it was, of course, all scaled to my size. The city wall, that I'd scrambled over earlier, was now a formidable barrier, like the wall around a prison. Those miniature oak trees now looked huge and old. The lake, a little way away, was immense, with big yachts tacking back and forth on its surface.

Even the grass under my feet was coarse and a little overgrown.

Byte was looking at the lake, puzzled.

'Don't strain your brain, you little egg.'

'I was just thinking,' he said slowly. 'We fell *down* through the lake – and then we fell *down* out of the bandstand. But we ended up in the same place we came from. We didn't climb any stairs – did we?'

I sighed. 'Look, Webtown is different from Realworld. Mostly it obeys the same laws. But it doesn't have to because it's all just made up by computers. See?'

He frowned, trying to be adult, but I could see he was faking it.

'Some day I'll take you to EscherLand . . . Oh, never mind.' I wiggled my fingers in his face. '*It's magic*. Just accept it.'

Now the two children, Drunlo and Clustril, had come up to Byte and were staring at him curiously. They were about his age, I suppose.

Within about one second the three of them had started to play catch.

Within two more seconds they were fighting.

Kids!

Clefven was standing with his arm around Skyresh. She seemed angry and upset, but he was more resigned.

'What will you do now?' I asked.

'We'll be all right.' Clefven smiled tiredly. 'We have many places to hide. Not even the struldbrugs have found them all yet. But what about you?' he asked. 'I thought you would scuttle home.'

'We tried. The buttons didn't work.'

'Oh.' He nodded. 'I told you the dust wasn't designed for real people. It must have damaged your Websuits.'

I frowned. I thought I understood. Probably because of the different scales, our scuttle buttons were sending out differently pitched signals – the way a penny whistle makes a higher sound than a recorder – which the big computers controlling Webtown couldn't recognize.

'It's OK,' I said breezily. 'All you have to do is grow us again, and we'll be able to get out.'

Clefven looked solemn. 'I told you. We don't have growth dust. Only Golbasta, the Empress, has that.'

Golbasta.

I could see her palace, on the horizon of the park. It had looked like a pretty dolls' house before. Now it looked more like a forbidding Norman castle.

For the first time Skyresh looked genuinely concerned for us. 'I'm sorry. I know none of this was your fault. You must be very frightened. Look, why don't you stay with us? We'll show you where to hide and how to live. It isn't so bad, being a Lilliputian.'

I shook my head. 'Thanks. But that isn't possible. You see, we're not really here . . .' I told her about home, our real bodies in our Websuits in the spare room. Clefven nodded. 'We can only stay here for two or three hours. Otherwise we'll start to get Websick.'

Skyresh asked, 'Websickness? What's that?'

'You get it if you wear your suit for too long. You see, we aren't really moving around, although it looks as if we are . . . No matter what we do in the Web, our bodies are just lying still, out there in Realworld. It's a sort of gap, you see. After a while it catches up with you, and your body can't cope.'

'Then you must go to the palace,' Clefven said firmly. 'Only the Empress has the dust to grow you again. And besides, that's where your friend the Wire was taken.'

'But how can we get there? And even if we make it, will the Empress just give the dust to us?'

Clefven and Skyresh looked at each other mournfully.

They didn't have to say anything. From what I'd seen of her familiars, the struldbrugs, Golbasta wasn't going to help us. The very opposite, in fact.

And yet, what choice was there?

It had become very dark.

Suddenly, there was an explosion on the roof of the bandstand. Then another one.

A huge flattened ball of liquid landed in the grass a few feet from me. Water splashed everywhere.

Clefven and Skyresh reacted immediately. 'Drunlo! Clustril! Indoors, right now!'

The children came scurrying to the bandstand, holding their hands over their heads.

I called, 'You'd better come too, Byte.'

He looked confused. He came, but slower than the others.

Then a huge ball of water came down from nowhere and smashed him in the shoulder-blades. He fell over, howling.

I ran forward, grabbed him by the collar and pulled him to his feet. Volleys of water were pounding the grass flat all around us.

We made it to the bandstand. Clefven and his family were already huddled there. Byte was soaked.

I asked, 'What's that? The struldbrugs?'

Skyresh was puzzled. 'No. Just rain.'

'*Rain?*'

Clefven said, 'Not everything is Lilliputian-sized here. You have to be careful.'

Skyresh said, 'Sometimes it hails. It's like being pelted with tennis balls.'

She didn't say any more, but I could see in her face how serious she was. The Lilliputians weren't wearing Websuits that would shield them from pain. They were *really* here – in a manner of speaking, anyway. Hailstones the size of tennis balls would *hurt*.

Byte was soaked, and miserable again. I tried to get the worst of it out of his hair. Philip had trusted me to look after Byte. A fine job I was making of it.

If we couldn't even cope with the rain, how could I hope to make it to the Imperial Court and challenge Golbasta?

It seemed impossible. I felt pitifully small, overwhelmed by everything.

And we were alone.

I don't think I've ever felt more depressed in my life.

CHAPTER EIGHT

GIANTS

Clefven turned to Skyresh. 'I think we should help them.' In that moment, he looked more like Philip than ever.

Skyresh bit her lip and looked at her bedraggled, bewildered children. 'Yes,' she said. 'All right. We can't just abandon them. They're only kids themselves.'

I bridled a bit at that, but it was not the moment to argue!

'And besides,' Clefven said, 'maybe it's time we challenged Golbasta. She's had it her own way too long.' He turned to me. 'I'll take you to the palace.'

'Clefven, thank you. I—'

He was gruff. 'Thank me when we've made it. I only hope I'm not leading you into greater danger.'

He moved deeper inside the bandstand. There was a little pile of gear: swords, bows and arrows. Clefven pulled out a sword. At least, I thought it was a sword. It was actually a darning needle, just a pillar of steel with a sharpened edge and an eye at the end. But we were so small now it looked half a metre long! Clefven tucked it into his belt.

He turned to Skyresh and kissed her cheek. Then he knelt down and hugged his children.

'Come back safely,' Skyresh said. 'We need you.' She was crying.

I was nearly crying myself. To think I'd thought these people were just little dolls!

Clefven led us out of the bandstand. Drunlo and Clustril stood with their mother and waved to us.

'Come on,' said Clefven. 'To the palace!'

We started to walk across the park, towards the imposing walls of the Imperial Court.

'The thing to remember,' said Clefven,. 'is that you're not humans for the time being. *You're Lilliputians.* And things are different for us.'

'I understand,' I said. 'The rain—'

'Not just that. Remember, nobody takes us seriously. People think we're toys, or worse. Vermin.' He glanced about. 'The struldbrugs shouldn't bother us out in the open. But be careful. Reldresal is their leader. She would recognize you again. And there are many other dangers.'

Byte tugged my hand. He had dried out, and he was mutating back into a hideous little brother again. 'That lady called you a kid,' he taunted. 'Kid, kid!'

I grabbed him and we began a ritual wrestle. I have to admit I enjoyed it, and I tried to do him less damage than usual. It was a little bit of home in a strange place.

There was a loud buzzing sound.

Clefven called, 'Metaphor. Watch out!'

We broke our clinch and looked at each other. 'Is that you?' I accused Byte.

'Is not. It's *you.*'

'*Look out!*'

The buzzing got louder. Something came swooping out of the sky at me. I thought it was a bird.

It was coming right at my head!

I ducked, and pulled Byte's head into my belly.

I looked up. The 'bird' had fluttering translucent wings, a body striped yellow and black, black goggle eyes, and a sting protruding from its tail . . .

That 'bird' was a wasp, half as big as I was.

It came straight at me again. I screamed and hunched over Byte.

It landed on me! I could feel its sticky feet on my back. In any moment it would sting me . . .

I heard a swishing noise. The buzzing stopped.

Cautiously, I stood up straight.

Clefven was standing there, needle-sword in hand. The wasp's body lay at his feet on the grass. Its belly was covered in satiny fur, its legs were twitching, and black glop was oozing from its neck. Clefven had cut the wasp's head clean off. It lay a little way away, like a misshapen black football.

'Wow,' said Byte. 'The special effects here are awesome.'

I breathed out. 'Thanks,' I said.

Clefven grinned. 'Always look up. That's where trouble comes from.' He bent down over the wasp and pulled out its sting. It was a curved needle five centimetres long. 'Here,' he said. 'A souvenir of GulliverZone.'

I took it, and threw it as far from me as possible. 'No thanks.'

'Oh, poor little things. Did you have trouble with a nasty wasp? Oh, dear. Oh, they are so *sweet* . . .'

This barrage of baby-talk was coming from above my head. I looked up . . . to see a huge, sandalled foot coming down out of the sky, right on top of Byte.

Clefven grabbed him and pulled him out of the way.

I don't know what damage that would have done. Normally a Websuit won't let you come to any real harm.

But this wasn't normal. Our Websuits weren't meant to work like this. I didn't want to run any experiments I didn't have to!

'Oh, look at the little one. It's so *dinky*.'

I looked up. Two mountainous ladies stood over us. They were like two office buildings walking around on sandalled feet, draped in garish summer dresses that were much too young for them.

They were *not* underweight.

The ladies were leaning down at us. Their smiling, chubby faces were like two huge moons in the sky. Their voices sounded like thunder, far above us.

Clefven ignored the ladies. 'Come on . . .'

'Wait,' I said, suddenly excited.

'What?'

'These are adults. They can help us get out of here.' I didn't know why I hadn't thought of it before. It was obvious! This was still just a theme park, after all, Golbasta or no Golbasta.

I leaned back and shouted. 'Excuse me. Down here!' I waved.

The ladies pursed their mouths in little O shapes.

'Mildred – I think she's speaking to us!'

'Isn't it marvellous? The things they do nowadays.'

'Can you help me? We're stuck here. We shouldn't be this size. And now our scuttle buttons don't work.'

They tutted.

'Oh, dear.'

'Fancy that.'

'Will you take a message to my father, please? He's probably still at work. At the Tilbury Desalination Plant. I'm sure he'll know what to do.'

Huge relief filled me. It was all over! All these ladies had to do was find a data-box to send out a message. Once Philip got home, he'd be able to unhook us from the Websuits. The Wire, too.

But the ladies were straightening up. 'How amusing,' one said.

They started walking on!

'Wait!' I called. 'Please! Listen to me!' I jumped up and down, but they didn't look down again.

I heard their voices booming back and forth across the sky.

'So clever. So much *detail*.'

'And those wonderful fantasy games for the children. *Father* indeed! It's a shame we're a little too old to play, Mildred . . .'

And they just walked away, like two receding ocean liners.

I walked back to Clefven. Byte looked confused.

'I'm sorry,' Clefven said. 'But I did warn you. Nobody takes us seriously. The visitors think we're just toys. Part of the scenery. They don't even know we're *alive*.'

'But it's obvious we're alive!'

He shrugged. 'Did you think *I* was alive?'

He had a point.

*

We walked on.

We rounded a glade of big oak trees. Byte was still happy, in his ignorance. He ran ahead, using up his energy. He ran around the corner of the glade, out of our sight.

Byte screamed!

Your kid brother screaming really is a horrible sound. It makes your blood run cold.

Clefven and I ran around the corner. I actually beat Clefven.

Byte was standing, frozen to the ground.

And, facing him, a black cat was treating him to a blank, piercing stare.

I remembered we'd seen this cat when we arrived. But now it was the size of a Tyrannosaurus Rex, and it towered over poor Byte!

The cat took a delicate step forward, staring straight at my brother. It was just a phace, of course. Just another situation. It wouldn't hurt us. It *couldn't* hurt us. But—

It looked hungry.

CHAPTER NINE

ANIMAL

Byte was whimpering. 'Is this another game?'

'Yes. Just another game. This is, uh, the Big Cat Challenge . . .'

The cat took another step forward. Two more paces and it would grab my little brother like a sparrow.

I hissed to Clefven. 'Surely it won't hurt him. The programming—'

He shook his head. 'If you stay around here for long, you'll find that not everything is as it seems. Sure it's a phace, but if you're our size, you ought to think of it as if it's a real cat. And think what a real cat would do to you. Your brother's suit might not protect him.'

'Then it's up to me.' I was scared to death, but I took a step forward.

The cat turned its head towards me. Its flat face was like a big radar dish, sweeping down at me, and I could see myself reflected in its black eyes. I looked so *small*.

Clefven put his hand on my arm. 'Remember, think *real* cat.'

'So what?'

'So, use some cat psychology.'

Psychology.

I thought of how Gazza, our fat cat, behaves around unfamiliar animals.

The worst thing to do would be to show fear. I walked towards the cat, past Byte. 'It's all right,' I told him. 'You just stay where you are.' And I walked on, right up to the head of the cat.

It loomed over me like a gigantic sculpture.

I walked back and forth, five or six times, staring up at the cat. 'You see?' I said. 'I'm not scared of you.'

It watched me, fascinated and nervous. It drew its head back and forth as I walked, tracking my movements. It had its claws out – every one as thick as my wrist – but it didn't look as if it was going to spring.

A Lilliputian bird fluttered over my head. To the cat the little phace must have looked the size of a fly.

The cat lost interest in me immediately. It leaped up with frightening speed and strength, and ran off after the bird.

Clefven came up to me. 'Well done,' he said. 'The animals are bigger and heavier than you, but you're smarter. You can't out-fight them but you can out-think them.'

Byte came up, grinning. 'So that's the secret of the Big Cat Challenge. *Venomous*.'

'Yes,' I said. 'Venomous.'

I was trembling.

I walked on towards the palace. Maybe the cat had been truly dangerous, maybe not. I just hoped the others wouldn't notice how scared I was!

At the heart of Mildendo there are a set of barriers surrounding the palace itself. There are the walls of the Imperial Court, then the moat, and beyond that the giant crèche, the place they store the babies.

They hadn't struck me as barriers when we'd first arrived – when we were visitors – but they sure felt like barriers now, and no doubt that's how they were designed. I had no idea how we'd get across that moat, for instance.

But first we had to cross the crèche.

The crèche was surrounded by a fence, presumably to keep out us pesky Lilliputians, and keep the babies in. But there was a stile over the fence.

Every step came up to my waist, and there were twenty-five of them.

We started to climb. I felt exhausted by the time we got to the top.

There were perhaps a dozen giants – that is, normal-sized adults! – sitting around here at tables. And there must have been forty or fifty babies, all giant-sized, waddling around the crèche area, colliding with each other, gurgling like air-raid sirens and grabbing wildly at huge shiny toys. In their garish dungarees and caps they looked like carnival blimps. And every chin was coated with a river of drool.

What a nightmare!

I know not everyone agrees about putting young kids in Websuits. One year old is the legal lower age limit. It does get them used to using the equipment, even if they can't do much when they are in there except play with the kind of toys they get in Realworld anyhow. It's a bit like taking a small child to learn to swim. They can't cross the Channel, but they get used to the water.

I don't care one way or the other about babies in Websuits. I'm old enough to have watched Byte grow up, and frankly the whole thing was a shuddering nightmare. As far as I'm concerned every baby should be put in a box, Websuit and all, until it is civilized enough to be able to ask to come out, and say *please*.

So you can imagine how I felt as I watched those gibbering giants waddle around the crèche – an area I was going to have to cross to reach the Imperial Court!

At least nobody had noticed us. I felt as if I had turned into a rat, or a sparrow, perched up there on the fence.

One of the tables had been pushed up against the fence. It was piled up with building blocks and toys.

'Come on,' Clefven said. 'It might be easier to get down that way.'

He led the way along the top of the fence. It was just a single thickness of wood, but it was a good arm's length wide. We jumped down perhaps half my height to the tabletop. We walked across the table. There was a plastic padded tablecloth covered with huge grinning TFO ostrich faces, so soft and thick it was easy to trip up on a ruck.

Up close to normal-sized stuff, everything was so *big*. On the table there was a plastic plate with green toy slime on it where some little angel had been playing at cooking. I counted – it took me twenty-four paces to walk past the plate. There was a toy teacup the size of a barrel. In the middle of the tea party stuff there was a bright blue inflatable boat with a limp sail and a soppy grinning sailor boy, a bit bigger than I was. We came to a bright red plastic knife. Byte climbed up on it and started using the blade as a diving board, until I told him off for getting too close to the sharp edge.

We reached the edge of the table.

It was like being on top of a small flat-roofed building. The grass looked an awfully long way down.

'Come on,' Clefven said. 'We can climb down the table-cloth.'

He got down on his belly and squirmed backwards until his feet stuck out over the edge of the table. He hooked his feet into rucks in the cushioned plastic, and started using it like a rope ladder.

He looked back up at us. 'Easy,' he said. 'You next, Byte, then your sister.'

The little egg loved it, of course. He just swarmed down.

I went a little more cautiously, as befitted my age. And my fear of heights. But it was easy, really.

At the bottom, the grass loomed up around us like shoots of green bamboo.

There was a toy close by, a little round fat clown. When I got close enough to trigger it, it smiled and started singing in a screeching roar, 'Hello, little girl. Would you like to hear a song? *Daisy, Daisy, give me your answer do . . .*'

Byte had had this toy. I always hated it. I always hated that song! And now here it was, come back to haunt me, bigger than I was.

I kicked it until it rolled away and shut up. It was a waste of time, of course, but it felt *good*!

There was a shattering roar.

Somewhere above us, two babies were approaching each

other, cooing like dinosaurs bellowing across a primeval swamp.

They hadn't seen us.

We crouched down in the grass while two pairs of stumpy legs came crashing down like pink tree-trunks, flattening the grass around us. If they stepped in the wrong place, we would – maybe – have been squashed like bugs.

With unintelligible gurgles, the two infant monsters tottered away.

We straightened up. 'This isn't so bad,' I said. 'All we have to do is avoid being stepped on. Now, we have to think about how to get across the moat—'

'Look out!'

I spun around.

I glimpsed a huge face, a flat bald forehead, a wide grin and teeth the size of our front door. A giant pudgy pink hand came sweeping down from nowhere and grabbed me around the middle. I was swept up in the air before I knew what was happening.

I heard a hideous cooing.

It was a baby.

No, that doesn't do it justice.

It was a BABY!

CHAPTER TEN

BABY

The baby's fat right hand was big enough to close around my waist. It (the baby was a boy, but all babies are *it* as far as I'm concerned) was dragging me across the ground. My arms were pinned to my sides. The breath was squeezed out of me like toothpaste out of a tube. Spots of blackness gathered across my vision.

When the baby felt me wriggling, it squeezed tighter, so hard I thought I could feel my ribs grinding over each other!

Now it pulled me right into its chest. The coarse wet bristly fabric of its bib – soaked in drool, of course – rubbed against my face. I was only glad I couldn't smell anything . . .

It did me no good at all to know that none of this was *real*! The baby was in its own little Websuit in some hideous pink-walled nursery somewhere. And I was writhing around in my own home. What shouldn't be happening was that this was *hurting*.

It relaxed its grip a little and suddenly I could breathe again.

Now there was a moist scrape against my cheek. It made me shudder. The baby was stroking the side of my face with a finger of its other hand. The skin was soft, but it poked so hard it hurt. But it was trying to be gentle, I figured.

I tried not to struggle in case it tightened up again.

It lifted me off the ground.

It scraped my face against the soft fat on its lower chin. The skin there was soaked with dribble, so my face was soon drenched . . . *Ugh*. If you want to know what that experience was like, go open a three-day-old garbage pail and push your face into the mushy, moist stuff at the bottom.

I had had an all-round bad day, but this was the pits! It was all the nightmares I'd ever had, during those years with Byte as a kid brother, come to hideous, bloated life.

Things, I thought, can't get any worse.

And then – of course – they did.

The baby lifted me up higher and held me before its gaping mouth. They were only milk teeth, I suppose, but they were like a row of ceramic guillotines, closing around my neck!

I squeezed my eyes shut.

But my head stayed on my shoulders.

Seconds later, I risked opening my eyes.

A huge doughnut of pink, puckered-up lip was looming in front of me. The baby rubbed its lips all over my face. It was like having a saliva car-wash.

It was *kissing* me.

I just closed my eyes and mouth and endured it. At least, I comforted myself, it wasn't biting my head off.

'Metaphor!' It was Clefven. 'Are you all right?'

When the baby had done smooching, I turned my head away, gasping for air. 'Oh, terrific. It's not going to eat me, is it?'

He hesitated. 'Of course he can't. But I don't suppose he understands about Websuits. He might try . . .'

I would have laughed if I'd had the breath. After all that preaching I'd had from Philip about being kind to my little brother, I was going to end up as an infant's between-meals snack!

Now Byte was shouting. 'Leave my sister alone!'

Something clattered on the floor near me. It was a giantsized plastic bead, the size of a football.

Byte was throwing things at the baby.

The baby pointed and said something like, '*Ack-shummam. Ach-shum-mam.*'

It thought Byte was an *Action Man*! I groaned. If only he

was, I thought. Then he might have been some use all those long years. At least I could have swapped him.

Byte was getting ready to throw again.

Clefven said, 'Byte, no—'

But it was too late. 'Put her down!' And Byte hurled another bead that caught the baby square in one big blue eye.

The baby bared its teeth and screamed so loudly it left my ears ringing. It clutched me to its chest. It started jumping up and down – I was pounded into its hot belly – and then it turned and ran.

It was like being trapped inside a huge, hot, pudgy roller-coaster. With nobody at the controls.

I could hear Clefven calling. 'Psychology! Remember, Metaphor—'

The baby scurried to the table we'd climbed down from. It ran underneath and stood there bawling.

And where, I wanted to know, was its mother?

After a few seconds of that it calmed down. It settled on its haunches close to the tea party plate we'd seen before. It hauled me around in its arms, and I was forced to lie flat against its upper leg with its heavy arm over me like a giant podgy seat-belt. It started stroking my face again, making a strange, almost gentle noise.

It was crooning, I thought.

I thought of what Clefven had said. *Psychology*. He'd been talking about animals, but believe me, that word sums up all babies, without exception, pretty well.

What was this wretched infant thinking?

Suddenly, I understood. *It was trying to cradle me.*

It thought I was a doll!

I had to reassure it I really was a dolly, I guessed. No threat to it. Otherwise it would throw me over against the fence without even thinking about it.

So what do babies do all day?

I tried to relax so I wasn't lying stiff and resistant in its arms. I looked up at it and smiled. I tried to get eye contact.

Eventually, I thought, it would put me down. Until then, I

just had to endure. It would get bored and go to another toy. Maybe it wouldn't be so bad. It was almost comfortable here.

But now a huge pink finger was looming at me out of the sky. It was dripping with green slime.

The baby was going to feed me!

I couldn't help it. I started struggling again and pulled my face away. But it locked my head in the crook of its arm and forced that fingertip into my mouth.

I couldn't taste anything, of course, but I could *feel* that awful cold lumpy plastic slime sploshing over my face and mouth. And if you have ever *seen* that stuff you can imagine what that was like!

'Are you ready, Byte?'

It was Clefven's voice.

'Three, two, one. Go!'

Suddenly, both Clefven and Byte started yelling. I could hear them running at the baby from two sides, making as much noise as they could.

The baby yelped indignantly. It jumped up and dropped me. The grass was spiky but it cushioned my fall.

The baby ran off in a blur of primary colours, looking for its mother.

Clefven and Byte ran up and huddled over me.

Clefven picked lumps of cold slime out of my mouth. 'Are you all right, Metaphor?'

'I think so,' I mumbled around the slime.

'I hoped that would work. I didn't want to scare him too much – just surprise him enough to make him drop you.'

'You *hoped* it would work?'

Byte, sitting on the tablecloth, looked worried. 'That wasn't really a ride, was it?'

I looked into his round, serious little face, and I wondered whether to try keeping up the fiction.

'No,' I said. 'It wasn't a ride.'

'And we're really in trouble here.'

I sat up and took his hand. 'Yes, we are.'

'Then why don't we ask Glumdalclitch to help?'

'I told you. That won't do any good. She's just part of the theme park. She isn't *real*.'

'But she said—'

'Look, don't worry. Clefven is helping us. And we're going to find a way home. OK?'

'Yes,' he said. I could see he wanted to cry, but he was determined not to.

He's not such a bad kid, really. For a one-mip basement-level wipeout little brother, anyhow.

We moved out of the crèche, in towards the centre of Mildendo and the Imperial Court. I thought the next problem we'd face would be getting across the moat.

It wasn't.

We reached the edge of the crèche's long grass. Clefven grabbed our shoulders. 'Wait,' he said, and he pulled us back into the grass a little way.

We heard them before we saw them; a slithering, lizardy, scraping, snakelike sound, utterly inhuman.

A patrol of giant struldbrugs was marching around the paved area between us and the moat. And the lead struldbrug had an eerily beautiful human face.

CHAPTER ELEVEN

RELDRESAL

Our three faces, staring out of the bamboo-length grass, must have looked like three round coins.

The struldbrugs marched past, antennae waving, mandibles clacking. Each of them was about the size of a dog, as I've said, so now they towered over us. Their multi-jointed legs clattered against the pavement.

They were marching in time, I realized after a while. That was an eerie thought. When have you ever seen a column of insects *march in time*, outside of an interactive cartoon?

The column moved slowly, with Reldresal at the front, so I had plenty of time to inspect her. That human face of hers was still there, stuck on the front of the insect body. But I thought I could see some differences. Like a coat of mail shell, the hard black chitin seemed to have progressed a little further up her neck. And her skin looked strangely shiny, as if it was made of wax, or plastic. In the middle of her cheeks and forehead there were small, hard spots of black chitin.

'Her eyes will go next,' whispered Clefven.

'What do you mean?'

'She's turning from a human to a struldbrug,' he said. 'You realize that, don't you? The body is fairly easy to transform. Your arms and legs, and lungs and heart and stomach, are just machines anyhow. They just have to be replaced with other machines.'

'Ugh,' said Byte.

Clefven smiled. 'I didn't say it was nice,' he said. 'Actually it's very painful. It's just easy. But the human brain is the most complex object in the universe. It takes a long time for the struldbrug form to accommodate the head.

'Reldresal will come out of a sleep period soon with eyes like a fly's: lumps of grainy cells . . . It will hurt, because her new eyes won't fit easily into her human skull. But it won't last long. Soon her skull will soften, and start blending into the rest of her new chitin body.'

I inspected the other struldbrugs, as they marched past. They weren't identical, I saw, now that they were so close to me. Reldresal had the most obviously human features – that face. But here and there I could make out other remnants of humanity: a pair of pink hands sticking out of a black chest, what looked like ears on the side of a struldbrug's sketch of a head, even a pair of blue, frightened human eyes peering out from a mask of chitin.

'*They all used to be human*. Didn't they?'

'Every one of them.'

Byte said, 'Why don't they just spin out, and go back to their normal bodies?'

I thought that was a good question, for him. It showed he was starting to understand what was going on here.

'Because they can't,' Clefven said sadly. 'They don't have normal bodies to go back to.'

I didn't understand. 'What do you mean? Are they Web-sick?'

'Worse than that. They've stayed inside the Web so long, they've let their Realworld bodies wither away. Now, the only way they can survive is by staying inside the Web. Just what you see before you.'

I found myself shivering. It was supposed to be impossible for me to be uncomfortably cold – but that's how I felt.

A lot of things were supposed to be impossible inside the Web, such as getting trapped there. But that was just the fix we were in. And now, I was learning, there were monsters – half-human – inhabiting the corners of the Web too!

Suddenly, the Web seemed a much darker place than I could have imagined.

'If your Empress Golbasta does this to people, she must be really evil. No wonder you're frightened of her.'

'No. You don't understand. Golbasta doesn't *force* people to become struldbrugs. They *choose* to do it.'

I was mystified. 'How? What do you actually have to do, to become a struldbrug? Do you have to go somewhere? Eat something?'

He wouldn't tell me. But I noticed he shuddered when I said, *Eat something* . . .

Clefven said, 'People become struldbrugs, sacrificing everything – even their lives outside the Web – because Golbasta offers them something wonderful.'

'What does she offer? Money? Fame?'

'Toys?' Byte asked.

'Something beyond price. I'm telling you this because if we get caught, no matter what she offers you, you must remember what the *cost* will be.'

I couldn't imagine what could possibly be so wonderful that people were prepared to leave Realworld behind for ever.

But, I thought, what if Golbasta had captured the Wire? What if she made this wonderful offer to *her*? After all, Realworld wasn't such a wonderful place for the Wire. Philip had been right. I *did* know how she felt. The few months after Mum died were the worst of my life. You never really get over that.

If, in the middle of that, somebody had offered me something *wonderful*, I might have taken it.

Meanwhile, I had a lot of unanswered questions on my plate. How do you become a struldbrug? What did Golbasta offer that made it worth becoming a struldbrug? Why did she want to capture Lilliputians? What did Golbasta *herself* want?

I wondered how many of these questions I would have to answer before we could get home again.

We waited until we were sure we had a long clear period before the struldbrug patrol came back again.

We crept out of the long grass and headed towards the

moat. I felt very exposed, out in the open like that. But we knew the struldbrugs were a long way away.

A big black shadow came sweeping across us.

I saw a gigantic figure, silhouetted against the sun, and a huge hand reaching down at me. I thought it must be the baby back again.

But the hand was big and muscular.

A thumb and forefinger closed around my waist, pinching tight. I pushed down at the thumb, trying to get away.

I was hoisted into the air. It was like a bungee jump in reverse! I was held up like a bug, suspended before a huge grinning face. I was small and utterly helpless.

He was wearing a huge red cloak, which looked, from my point of view, as big and heavy as the curtain in a cinema.

I laughed out loud. Immediately I knew we were going to be all right. At last we'd found a normal-sized person who *would* listen to me.

It was Surfer!

CHAPTER TWELVE

SURFER

I tried to wave at him, but my arms were pinned. I kicked my legs. 'Surfer! It's me, Metaphor!'

He held me up in the air before his eyes. I could see myself reflected in those big eyeballs. When I kicked my legs, I saw I looked like a wriggling egg. I felt embarrassed and stopped kicking.

'Wow. You can *talk*?' His voice was a deep boom, like thunder in some remote cloud.

'Of course I can talk. I've been talking since I was two years old.'

He shook me back and forth like a pepper pot, making my legs wave.

'Will you *stop* that?'

'The special effects in here are just a-*mazing*.'

He was pinching me over the kidneys with his big clumsy thumb and finger. 'You're hurting me,' I shouted.

He leaned his head closer to me and turned his ear. It was a great big fleshy sculpture, all caverns and shadows and ridges. 'Your voice is like a wasp buzz. Say something else. Go ahead. Can you sing a song?'

For some reason a tune went through my head: *Daisy, Daisy* . . . 'No, I can't sing a song!' I screamed.

He drew his head back and looked at me seriously for the first time.

'I'm hurting you? Really?'

'Really.' I wriggled, trying to loosen the vice-like grip of his thumb and forefinger.

He held out his other hand and dropped me gently on to it. His palm was firm and warm. Then he picked me up by a pinch of cloth at the scruff of the neck.

'Listen, can I get to keep you?'

'*What?*'

'I've picked up a couple of souvenirs already. Do you know the flying island? They have these wacky scientist geezers who are squeezing the sunlight out of cucumbers and putting it into little bottles. Every time you open the bottle the sun shines out. I put it in my hard drive for a souvenir. Even the gifts are free today . . . So how about it?'

'No, you can't keep me! I'm mine! I belong to me!'

He frowned. 'You know, you look just like that girl I met out in Webtown.'

At last! 'Metaphor. Yes. That's me!'

'But you're a Lilliputian. And Lilliputians aren't real. They're just phaces. Aren't they?'

I'd had enough of this. 'Listen to me, you, you red-cloaked one-mip. I am *not* a Lilliputian. I *am* Metaphor – or at least, my avatar inside the Web today. This is *me*. I can't spin out, and I'm in *trouble*. Now, are you going to help me, or not?'

I could see comprehension growing on his big, moonlike face. It was a classic double-take. 'You're serious, aren't you?'

I kicked my legs and waved my arms. '*Yes, I'm serious!*'

'Oh, wow.' He looked around. 'Come on. Let's go over to those tables and talk.' He started striding back towards the crèche.

I waved my arms. 'Wait.'

'What now?'

'You nearly stepped on my little brother.'

I was back on a tabletop again!

Surfer lifted the three of us up on to a padded tablecloth. He sat down and rested his huge head on his folded arms, studying us. I told him the whole story as quickly as I could.

'. . . and so we can't spin out. Not until we get inside the palace and grow back to normal size.'

'Then we've got to get you inside the palace,' he said. He frowned. 'I wonder who's behind all this? I wonder who the Empress really is?'

I turned to Clefven who was sitting squat-legged nearby. He looked back at me sternly, and would not reply.

There are a *lot* of villains in the Web. It is surprising what you can get up to if you're determined: fraud, theft, stalking people, interfering with programs, hacking into home systems – even destroying them.

There are also more subtle dangers, once you're inside the Web yourself: various creepy groups who try to subvert your mind with sleeper memory patterns called engrams. If you have an engram in your head, one day you wake up to find you've become a religious nut, or a flying-saucer fanatic, or you're eating your kid brother for breakfast . . .

Not that *that* would be so terrible.

There are police, called Webcops. The Webcops are an offshoot of Interpol who keep an eye on the crooks in the Web. But the Web is big, the crooks are smart, and the technology changes all the time . . .

It's a dangerous place, the Web. But then so is Realworld.

Surfer stood up and looked at the Imperial Court walls beyond the moat. 'Maybe I can get you in there.'

Clefven said, 'No. You'd never get across the moat. And even if you did, visitors aren't allowed in the palace.'

Surfer laughed. 'Visitors aren't allowed to do a lot of things.'

'Believe me,' Clefven said heavily, 'you won't make it. They'll hurt you. Golbasta and her familiars . . . *We* can get inside if we can get across the moat, but it's pointless you even trying.'

Surfer laughed again. 'Uh – *hel-lo-oh*. Reality check here. This is the Web, remember? Nobody can get hurt in here. It's designed that way.'

'Haven't you been listening?' If I'd been big enough I would have punched him. As it was I had to make do with a lecture, brief and to the point.

After that, he was a bit less cocky. 'Then what can we do?'

'The most useful thing you can do is go to a data-box and send a message out,' I said. 'Talk to my dad.' I gave him Philip's name and his code. 'Tell him what's happening here. He'll have to come home from work and get us out.'

'I'll do it.' He frowned. 'But it might take some time.'

I sighed. 'I know.' I glanced at Byte who was playing with giant blobs of slime. 'By then, it might be too late. We have to go on.'

Clefven nodded. 'It is still up to you to save yourself, Metaphor. But we have a big problem.'

'What?'

'The moat around the Imperial Court,' he said. 'The draw-bridge is up, of course. And without it we have no way across.'

Surfer grinned. 'It so happens I have an idea about that. Maybe there's another way I can help you.'

CHAPTER THIRTEEN

MOAT

Surfer hunted quickly around the crèche, collecting up some stuff. Then he picked up the three of us, lodged us in a pocket of his jacket and strode off out of the crèche and across the paved surround of the moat.

It was quite comfortable up there with my arms hooked over the lip of the pocket. I could look down and see Surfer's legs working like gigantic articulated machinery. Every step he took we bounced up and down in the pocket. I never realized before what a violent action walking is.

Byte was having fun. Maybe he thought this was another ride, the 'Giant-American-Kid' adventure. He was dangling his arms over the pocket and kicking.

The second time he kicked *me* he got kicked back.

We reached the edge of the moat. Surfer lifted us out one by one and placed us down on the paving stones.

To give him credit, he was a lot more careful than he had been before. But I still ended up rolling out of his hands and tumbling across the ground. Being ten centimetres high is just *not* dignified.

I got up and faced the moat. It looked as wide as the Thames. The surface was featureless except for a couple of lily pads – gigantic, bigger than the monsters I once saw in the hot-house in Kew Gardens.

One of the lily pads was rippling, I noticed, bobbing up and down as if something had just jumped off it into the water. But I couldn't see anything. I put it out of my mind.

Big mistake!

'Wow,' Byte said. 'It looks scary. I wonder if there are sharks in there.'

I said, 'Right now, a goldfish would be big enough to nip your head off.'

'There are no fish in GulliverZone,' Clefven said. 'One feature they haven't got around to yet.'

'So what now? Do we swim across?'

Surfer grinned. 'I have a cunning plan. You need a boat, right?'

'Yes. So?'

He reached down and pulled that inflatable baby's plastic boat out of his pocket. 'Welcome aboard the USS *One-Mip*!'

We inspected the toy. It was a piece of vacuum-formed plastic, as fragile in this world as the real thing would be outside. To us, it looked about the size of a small car.

'You have *got* to be kidding.'

'No. I've got it all figured out. That thing will float. And look at this.'

He dug into his pockets and pulled out a plastic tea-set spoon. It was about half my height, and easy to pick up.

Clefven laughed. 'I get it. Paddles.'

Byte, of course, thought it was terrific. It was just the kind of dumb toy he makes for himself at home anyhow. He started clambering all over the boat, making pirate noises. His grin was wider than the one painted on the plastic sailor glued inside the toy.

'I've never seen anything so ridiculous in my life,' I said. 'It's a *toy*, for heaven's sake.'

Surfer looked a little hurt. 'If you have a better idea, I'd like to hear it.'

Clefven picked up a spoon. 'I think you're being un-charitable, Metaphor. It's a masterpiece of improvisation. I think your friend's done well.'

'Thank *you*,' said Surfer.

I sighed. Going to sea in a toy was the worst idea in the world. Except for staying here and doing nothing at all.

I had a feeling of deep and dark foreboding, but I tried to put it aside. The waters were calm and empty, after all. As long as the stupid boat floated, what could go wrong?

What, indeed!

Surfer lowered the boat into the water. Then he lifted us into it one by one, and passed us our spoons. With that big plastic sail sticking up – not to mention the big dumb toy sailor we had to share the boat with – the toy wasn't too stable. It rocked back and forth on the gentle swell of the moat.

Byte was running around being a pirate. If I'd had a plank I'd have made him walk it, there and then.

Surfer lay down on the ground so his huge head was facing us. 'There's no breeze,' he said. 'I'll blow you over as far as I can. But after a couple of metres you're going to have to use the paddles.'

Clefven waved. 'Thanks for all your help.'

'I'll tell your dad, Metaphor,' Surfer said. 'Don't worry. We'll get you out of this.'

I nodded, and clutched my spoon.

Surfer took a deep breath and blew out, hard and long.

Our 'sail' billowed with a plastic crackle. We set off with a lurch that sent Byte tumbling backwards.

Surfer stood up, waved, and ran off so as not to attract attention from the struldbrugs. He looked like a mobile mountain as he disappeared.

We came to rest. The shore already looked an awfully long way away. The water heaved slowly beneath us, its thick and oily surface catching the sunlight.

I longed to be out of there, back in my normal life, not bobbing about like a fragile little doll in this ridiculous toy boat. But that wasn't an option.

We picked up our spoons and lifted their bowls over the side. I pulled my spoon's handle backwards. It was like paddling a pleasure-boat across a lake in some Realworld park, except the water was thicker and a little sticky.

Slowly, slowly, we began to move forward, towards the imposing walls of the Imperial Court. Byte couldn't help much – he was too little to reach the water effectively – and it was up to me and Clefven to do all the work. Pretty soon my shoulders and back were aching.

But we picked up speed, and as long as we didn't stop paddling we advanced rapidly towards the far shore.

For once I thought everything was going to work out for us.

And then – just ahead of the boat – two gigantic deformed eyes loomed out of the water!

Byte screamed.

Clefven shouted a warning. We tried to slow the boat down, but it was too late.

We collided with something soft and fleshy.

The eyes rose up further, staring in at us, and then a huge mouth, half as wide as the boat itself, came leering over the bow of the boat. The skin around the mouth was slimy and mottled by warts. Two huge paws came slapping on to the top of the boat, great long fingers covered in warty skin. And now a huge white throat and belly came lurching up out of the water. The boat tipped forward!

I nearly lost my paddle. Clefven had to hang on to the mast to save being thrown straight out into the water. Byte, wailing, went tumbling down inside the boat once more.

That huge white throat pulsed. '*RIB-IT.*'

I recognized the noise.

'It's a frog!' I shouted to Clefven.

He looked irritated. 'Of course it's a frog.'

Byte came crawling out. 'I thought you said there were no fish here,' he accused Clefven.

'A frog isn't a fish. It's an amphibian. This is advanced programming you're seeing here. The frogs are part of the defence. And furthermore—'

'And furthermore, that amphibian of yours thinks this boat is a lily pad!' I shouted.

Those big front paws came slapping their way a little further over the plastic of the boat, like a diver's webbed feet. The boat tipped forward further, rocking.

I had time to say, 'I think—'

And then, with a huge lurch, the frog hauled its body out

of the water and on to the boat. I caught a glimpse of two gigantic, muscly back legs, scrabbling at the boat's surface. Then our mast broke in half and crashed down over us, and the frog came sliding over the back of the boat.

The frog's big slimy belly came brushing over me, and then he twisted around, sliming me some more. Soon my face, hair and clothes were covered with gooey, stinking, translucent green glop.

And then, it scarcely seemed possible – things got worse.

The frog was too heavy. Our unstable boat started tipping over.

I was falling towards the black, oily water!

CHAPTER FOURTEEN

WALL

Is it possible to drown in a Websuit?

It was an experiment I didn't want to try!

The water didn't feel like water. It felt sticky and thick, like warm honey. And it got very dark, very quickly, as I fell deeper in.

I'm usually a good swimmer, but not in syrup.

I could see light above me. I faced that way and kicked my legs. I tried to keep my mouth shut. I hated to think what would happen if that sticky stuff forced its way into my mouth, Websuit or not.

I broke through the surface, and I bobbed like a cork, treading water. The surface around my chest was tight and clinging, almost painful. The surface tension of that liquid was strong to someone of my size. Next time you see a pond, take a look at the insects walking around *on* the surface and you'll know what I mean.

Our toy boat was upside-down, the straw mast floating forlornly beside it. The frog, evidently scared, had disappeared. I couldn't see Clefven. But there, I saw with relief, was Byte. He was clinging to one of the plastic spoons, with his hair matted down over his face.

I swam over to him through the thick, soupy water. I got hold of the spoon handle next to him.

'Are you OK?'

He gave me a glare that wasn't a bad impression of Philip's don't-ask-such-stupid-questions look.

I pointed. 'We aren't far from the walls . . .'

'Where's Clefven?'

'I don't know.' Actually I was worried about him. Clefven lived here, in GulliverZone. His body was designed for this world. Maybe we couldn't drown. But *he* probably could.

I didn't want to say any of this to Byte.

'Come on now, let's kick . . .'

We leaned forward, holding the spoon side by side, and kicked at the water. It frothed behind us, and our feet glopped as they entered and left the surface.

It only took a couple of minutes before my toes were brushing on a sloping, stony bank. I stood up straight, held Byte's hand, and we walked the rest of the way.

Once we were out of the water we shook ourselves dry, like a couple of dogs. We were standing on a steep, rocky beach. A few paces away the walls of the Imperial Court rose up like a brick cliff, grey and forbidding.

And a little way along the beach, Clefven was lying on his belly, gasping.

Byte saw him and ran. 'Clefven! Clefven!'

When I got to Clefven I helped him lie on his side, and cradled his head in my lap. He was coughing, but he seemed to be recovering quickly.

'Are you all right?'

'Yes,' he said. 'I think so. I got stuck underneath the boat, and I got a crack on the head. When I came to, my lungs were full of water.' He sat up, brushed back his soaking hair and checked his sword was still in its pouch at his waist. 'Come on,' he said. 'We mustn't rest. It's not safe here. And we have a way to go yet.' He stood up, panting hard.

'You didn't say anything about frogs in the moat,' I accused him.

He looked at me. 'Would it have made a difference? We had to get across there anyway. If we'd been lucky—'

'In future,' I said, 'tell me.' I meant it. I hate giant frogs. But I was discovering I hated surprises more!

He nodded.

I looked around. 'We still have to get past this wall.'

'There is a way in,' he said. 'But it's a little—'

'Dangerous?' Byte asked.

Clefven looked at him grimly.

'Well, there's a change,' I said.

'Follow me,' Clefven said. And he began to walk steathily along the deserted, stony beach.

Byte and I followed in the forbidding shadow of the wall. After a while, I felt Byte's hand slip into mine.

After a few minutes we came to what looked like an archway cut into the wall. It was a little taller than me, so Clefven was going to have to stoop. It looked as if it was roughly cut into the wall – not finished properly – and it led into some kind of tunnel.

There were no lights inside. The tunnel snaked off into the darkness, invisible beyond a few paces.

'Yuck,' said Byte, and for once I had to agree.

'Come on,' said Clefven. He hoisted his sword, and stepped into the archway. 'Follow me. Don't lag behind . . .'

Soon, all I could see was his back, disappearing from the daylight.

It looked as if we didn't have a choice.

It pushed Byte ahead of me. 'It'll be OK.'

'Really?'

'Sure,' I lied. 'The wall can't be all that thick . . .'

He trotted in trustingly after Clefven. I followed.

Soon I was in pitch darkness.

I could hear Clefven and Byte, a little way ahead of me, but I could see nothing. I bumped into the wall a couple of times – try walking in a straight line in the dark! – and then, to guide myself, I held out a hand and ran it along the surface of the wall.

It felt as if something had just carved out that tunnel, very crudely. I could feel big grooves and gouges. Strangely, they seemed familiar.

We used to have a hamster . . .

The marks in the wall had been made by teeth.

Suddenly, two giant yellow eyes loomed out of the darkness!

I yelled and stumbled back against the lumpy tunnel wall.

I heard a high-pitched squeal. It was like feedback from huge amplifiers, deafening, almost painful. Those big yellow eyes flickered. For an instant, there was a hot breath on my face and the giant eyes were right in front of me, like car headlamps.

I held my hands up in the dark.

There was a wall of fur in front of me, thick, coarse, wiry. It seemed to go on forever.

And then it was gone. I heard a pattering of huge, soft paws on the ground, heading back the way we had come.

There was a hand on my shoulder!

I jumped into the air.

'Calm down. It's me, Clefven. Are you all right?'

I tried to get my breath. 'Yes. Yes, I think so. What was *that*?'

'Later. Let's get out of here.'

He turned, and led us deeper into the darkness.

It only took a few more minutes before I saw the end of the tunnel as a small disc of light, far ahead. The light got brighter, until at last we came stumbling into daylight.

We crouched in the mouth of the tunnel while Clefven peered out. Byte looked scared again, but I tried to smile to reassure him I was OK.

'Clefven, what was that? Was it whatever built these tunnels?'

Clefven wouldn't meet my eyes. 'I don't want to discuss it.'

'You have to,' Byte said. 'My dad says it's better for us to know dangers. That's so we can cope with them.'

'It isn't that,' said Clefven.

'Then what?' I asked.

Reluctantly, he turned to me. 'I told you my people are descended from computer viruses. Originally viruses were mindless and destructive – that was the way the people who made them wanted them to be – but slowly we evolved intelligence. Communication. An ability to build, not just destroy, and to care for each other.'

'Yes. So?'

'So, not every family of virus made it that way. Some of them stayed mean.

'They got bigger, and more powerful, and more destructive . . . *They're still here*. They live like us behind the skirting boards of the Web, but all they do is destroy. The Webcops call them cyberats.'

'Oh.' Now I understood. 'And that's what I saw in the tunnel.'

'That's what made the tunnel. Cyberats are like the original viruses. It's what everyone thinks *we* are.'

'But why are you so upset?'

He looked me in the eyes. 'I'm ashamed.'

'Ashamed?'

'That thing in the tunnel wasn't just some monster. *It was my cousin*. Now do you understand?'

CHAPTER FIFTEEN

PALACE

Inside the Imperial Court, to my relief, everything was Lilliputian-sized. *Me*-sized.

There were clusters of grand-looking buildings, two or three stories high – I suppose two metres tall, on Surfer's scale. For us it was a little like being in the grounds of the Tower of London. People were moving between the buildings. Some of them were dressed in bright uniforms, like beefeaters. There were more barriers to cross before we got to the centre – walls and fences – but I could see there were big metal gates in the walls, all flung open.

And there, within the walls, at the heart of the compound, was the glittering face of the palace itself.

I stood up, newly determined. I'd come this far. Nothing was going to stop me now.

I took Byte's hand. 'Come on,' I said. And I strode out of the tunnel, towards the first of the gates.

Clefven grabbed my arm and pulled me back.

A pair of struldbrugs – reduced to our scale – came clumping past, moving between the buildings and around the walls and gates. They were evidently on patrol. The people avoided them, but didn't seem afraid.

Clefven pointed upwards.

Another struldbrug – giant-sized this time – was patrolling the top of the Court wall. Its eyes, on long stalks, were peering down into the Court itself.

'Nothing's ever easy,' I grumbled.

'This is Golbasta's citadel,' whispered Clefven. 'You have to remember that Golbasta has dust of both varieties. She can shrink you or grow you. Her struldbrugs can be whatever size she chooses.'

I asked, 'What about all the little people here? Why don't we ask them for help?'

Clefven said, 'I wish we could. But the "people" here aren't Lilliputians any more. Not like me and my family. They are just empty shells without souls. They won't help us, I'm afraid.'

'What happened to them?'

His only reply was, 'We're on our own here.'

He looked around, and tapped me on the shoulder. 'Come on. I think I know a way.'

Crouching down, keeping an eye out for struldbrugs, we followed Clefven to the nearest building.

It was a small, one-storey construction, crudely assembled from big chunky bricks.

Clefven peered in through the door. 'It's safe.'

We crept inside.

'Oh,' Byte said. 'It's a *stable*.'

He was right. The building was lined with stalls, each containing a horse. There was straw scattered on the roughly finished floor. On the walls, garish red and white uniforms were hanging.

Clefven went up to a stall. 'This is where the Empress keeps her Imperial Coach.' He rubbed the nose of a horse, a beautiful white mare with a long flowing mane, and she rubbed her face against his hand gratefully. 'Beautiful creatures, aren't they? Phaces, of course. But just like the real thing. So I'm told.'

'Expensive, I should think.'

He shrugged. 'Yes. But the Empress isn't just powerful in here, inside the Web. She has a lot of influence in Realworld. She was actually one of the people who originally designed the Web, and made a lot of money that way . . .'

I felt a prickling of unease. That was similar to the legends we used to scare each other with. Legends of the Sorceress.

Byte whooped. 'Metaphor! Come and look at this! You won't believe it.'

I went to see.

He had found the Empress's carriage itself, at the back of the stable.

It was a giant Tennessee Fried Ostrich takeaway carton!

The 'coach' was just a big garish cardboard box in red and white, with a picture of a grinning ostrich on the top. It was as big – on our scale – as a large car. Holes had been cut in the lid to serve as seats, and in the corners four big round chocolate-digestive biscuits had been nailed, as wheels.

There were reins leading from the front of the box, bright red. Byte was *chewing* one of the reins. 'I think this is liquorice rope,' he said. 'But I can't taste a thing.'

Clefven laughed. 'Don't chew through the reins. We need them. It's all sponsorship, of course. Money talks, even to an Empress. And the children visitors do love to see the Empress riding around in a coach that looks as if you could make it out of a food carton. Makes them think they could make one themselves, you see.'

'Don't tell me,' I said. 'We are going to have to ride in *that*.'

'It's good cover for us,' he said. 'Anyway, the coach isn't the worst of it.'

'There's *worse*?'

He was holding up a uniform for me to put on.

It was an ostrich suit.

Soon my legs were coated in baggy yellow tights that ended in splayed brown feet. Bright red-and-white feathers were stuck to my backside. I was looking out of the ostrich's big gaping mouth. TENNESSEE FRIED OSTRICH was written up and down my scrawny neck.

It was not my proudest moment. I was *so* embarrassed, and *so* glad nobody from school was there to see me.

Byte looked, if anything, even more comical. His suit was too big for him, and his tights were wrinkled up under his knees. Nevertheless, he laughed at me as loud as he could.

I tried to look as threatening as my ostrich outfit would allow. 'If you *ever* tell anyone about this I will sell you to the Tennessee Fried Ostrich people *myself*.'

'Pack it in, you two,' Clefven grumbled. He had got the friendly white horse out of its stall and was leading it to the coach.

We backed the horse into the coach's cardboard traces, and harnessed it with the liquorice reins. Clefven jumped up to the driver's seat at the front, and Byte and I scrambled into the seats cut out of the lid at the back.

Clefven picked up the reins. 'Everyone ready?'

I tried to fix my feathery tail under me. 'As ready as we'll ever be.'

'To the palace!' He flicked the reins, and snickered encouragingly to the horse.

The horse's hoofs clopped on the stone floor as we set off with a lurch.

We emerged into the open air and crossed the courtyard.

I hadn't noticed before that this area was cobbled, with great big shining stones. I noticed now. The cardboard coach bounced up and down, rattling me in my seat, and the feathers of my suit got up my nose, making me sneeze.

Byte thought it was great fun. He laughed all the way.

He's such an embarrassment.

I thought everyone would stare at us – *I* would if I saw a takeaway ostrich carton the size of a car bouncing towards me – but nobody here, neither the people nor the patrolling struldbrugs, took any notice.

We passed through one gate without being challenged. Then we reached the wall around the palace itself. The last barrier.

A soldier with a long, mean-looking pike was standing at the open gate. 'You have the password?'

Clefven hesitated.

I frowned. The 'password' must be some Webware access code. Of course, we had no idea what the password was. But every security measure can be overridden. Especially when someone as self-centred and powerful as this Empress was involved.

The guard stepped forward menacingly, raising his pike.

I leaned forward, and said as imperiously as I could, 'Is there some problem, driver?'

Clefven understood what I was trying to do. He turned and winked. 'I'm afraid there is, ma'am.'

'Override the entrance protocol,' I told the guard. 'Drive on.'

The guard hesitated. 'But—'

'I said, *override*. Do you want the Empress to know *you* held up the delivery of her coach?'

I knew he had no soul, of course, so the guard couldn't be afraid. But no program is designed to *want* to be shut down and dumped out of computer memory.

'Proceed,' he said pompously – as if it was all *his* idea – and he stepped out of the way.

The coach rattled through the gate.

And there ahead of us sat the palace, as wide and grand and gorgeous as a giant's wedding cake.

There was a soft clatter behind me, and the coach tipped back. I heard a scraping, of chitin over cardboard.

'We've been expecting you,' came a snake-like, slithery voice. 'Why didn't you say you wanted to come to the palace? I'd have been delighted to bring you here personally . . .'

I turned.

A struldbrug, on our scale, had climbed up on to the coach. It was already holding a scared-looking Byte in its arms.

It had a human face, half-swamped by chitin. It was Reidresal.

CHAPTER SIXTEEN

EMPRESS

We were stripped out of our ostrich suits, and dragged by three struldbrugs into the palace. I caught glimpses of magnificent, richly furnished apartments – one hall was lined with mirrors, sparkling with light – but the place was joyless. It was deserted, save for clattering, patrolling struld-brugs.

The struldbrugs, led by Reldresal, dragged us further and further into the heart of the palace. And the further we went, the darker it got. The only lighting was from tiny flickering candles. It was almost as if, here at the centre of the Empress's spider-web, nobody was bothering to keep up the fairy-tale illusion.

At last we came to a gigantic open space.

It was as if the core had been bombed out of the middle of a grand hotel. We were about a third of the way up one wall. The walls were lined with balconies, and I could see corridors leading off to the Lilliputian rooms on all the levels of the palace.

It was dark here, the only light coming from the tiny candles in the rooms and corridors lining the central chamber.

And there was something here, in the middle of the hollowed-out palace. Something huge and dark.

The struldbrugs prodded us forward. For a moment I feared they were going to throw us over the edge, but then I saw there was a platform here, like a bird-table. It sat on an immense pillar which stretched to the floor of the central chamber. The struldbrugs pushed and shoved until we were all three of us on the platform.

I struggled, but Clefven stopped me.

'There's nothing we can do,' he said. 'They've taken our weapons.' He sounded defeated, without hope.

'He's right,' cackled Reldresal. That chitin-pocked face creased up in a caricature of a smile. 'You've lost, human.'

I looked into her ghastly insect eyes. 'No,' I said evenly. '*You've* lost. Whatever she promised you for this isn't worth it. You're the one who deserves pity, Reldresal.'

She reared up above our platform, and I thought she was going to kill me there and then.

But I stood my ground.

She backed off.

Somehow, despite our peril, I wasn't afraid of her any more. I'd told the truth. I did pity her.

The platform slid away from the wall.

It started with a jolt and we all fell over. The surface was slick, like a plastic tabletop, and I had trouble holding on. Byte was on all-fours, and he looked as if he wanted to cry. But he was resisting it. 'I'm OK,' he said.

He is a game little kid sometimes.

I crept to the edge. There was no rail or barrier. This platform was *not* designed with our safety in mind. The pillar it was mounted on must have been five metres tall – fifty times my height! The base was far beneath me and lost in the dark.

The platform stopped moving just as suddenly.

A huge voice boomed over us. ' "Whatever she promised you for this isn't worth it," you said, child. Perhaps you're right. But how do you know, *until I offer it to you too?*'

We were poised near the top of that huge, amorphous statue-shape. The voice seemed to be coming from somewhere within.

Two eyes, each as big as a car windscreen, snapped open. They were *glowing*, bright red.

By their crimson light I could see the eyes were set in a

huge face, sculpted of some hard, dark green substance. And that formless shape below was a giant body, a mound of inert flesh, under thick flowing cloth.

It was the Empress Golbasta, sitting like a spider at the heart of her Lilliput-spanning web. I was face to face with her at last!

Byte was crying openly now. Clefven was holding him, trying to soothe him.

I walked to the edge of our platform. I was poised right before those giant devil's eyes. 'What are you?' I demanded. 'Are you human?' My voice must have been a gnat's squeak to her. My legs were trembling. But I tried not to let my fear show.

There was a rumbling, deep within that mountainous body. It might have been laughter. 'Only as long as I have to be. Only as long as something *better* isn't available.'

She shifted, and a monstrous, fleshy hand rose up before me. On one finger she was wearing a ring, a big gold band the size of a rain-barrel, set with a red ruby.

There was movement, far below, at the base of the Empress's pit. Green eyes. It was the black cat we'd encountered earlier, walking around the Empress's treetrunk legs, its back arched. It looked up at me, hissing and spitting.

I shivered. So Clefven had been right; the cat was a creature of the Empress. I wondered uneasily what it had once been; was there some poor cat out there in Realworld, locked in a Websuit? Or was this, too, some lost human being?

At any rate it clearly *had* been dangerous . . . and we'd come within a few metres of it!

There were two Lilliputian cups on the Empress's giant palm. Those giant red eyes turned to regard the cups.

'Look,' she said. 'Here is what you have come so far to find. What a shame you can't have it. Dust. Simple dust. The red stuff makes you big, the blue stuff makes you small. And with it, I control the world.'

The red glow of her eyes faded. 'You must forgive me. I am still anchored to the world outside. I get so tired. So tired . . .'

Those eyes brightened again and their light swept me like two searchlights. 'You have spirit. Perhaps I should recruit you rather than destroy you. Listen to me, child. Wouldn't you like to *stay* here?'

I frowned. 'What do you mean?'

'Here, in the Web . . . Think about it. When you are in the Web you can take on any form you want. As easy as putting on a new set of clothes. You can *be* anything, anybody. Nothing grows old. Everything is perfect, for ever . . . And yet every two or three hours *you* are dragged back out to that Realworld of pain and decay and age and death . . . *Wouldn't you like to live for ever*, here inside the Web?'

'That isn't possible. My real body will always be outside, at home, in a Websuit.'

'No,' she said, and her whisper was like wind through tall trees. 'It doesn't have to be so. *You can download.*'

I turned to Clefven. 'What's she talking about?'

He was still holding Byte. 'It's a new, experimental procedure. You can store your consciousness here inside the Web; your very soul, loaded in piece by piece. Your real body, outside, eventually withers away and dies. But you live on, in here.'

For one second, it sounded wonderful. *To be in the Web for ever*; to be whatever I wanted, to go wherever I liked, be whatever age I liked.

To live for ever!

So that was what Golbasta was offering. Who wouldn't be tempted by it?

But then I thought of Philip.

I thought of my friends at school. The memory of Mum. I even thought of Byte, the little egg.

It would be an awful thing, I thought, to let myself *die* – never to wake up again in my body, in my own bed.

'Well?' hissed the Empress. 'Have you decided? Are you *tempted*?'

'Don't listen to her,' snapped Clefven. 'It isn't what you think. And there is a terrible price to pay . . .'

I didn't need him to tell me that. I'd already decided.

I stood square in front of the Empress's gigantic, grotesque face. 'Yes, I've decided. I don't want what you're offering. I want to be myself. I want my life back.'

She opened her mouth. There were no teeth behind those black lips, and ropes of spittle laced that huge cavern like spider-webs. 'You sentimental little fool. Very well. If you are too stupid to accept my offer, I will turn to another who will.'

She swivelled her mountain of a head.

A gigantic door opened up in the far side of the chamber. Lilliputian rooms and corridors folded out of its way. From the darkness beyond the door, another giant figure walked in.

It was a girl, I saw. She was moving jerkily, and her face was so pale it seemed to float like a skull in the dim light of Golbasta's lair.

It was the Wire.

She bowed to the Empress. 'Yes, Majesty.'

The Empress raised her huge hand on which the two little cups of dust still stood. She pointed to us. 'It is your time, my child.'

The Wire turned to me.

I jumped up and down. 'Wire! Wire! It's me! Don't you recognize me?'

The Wire reached out a huge, trembling hand.

She was reaching for Byte!

I ran forward, knocked him aside, and threw myself into the Wire's fingers.

She closed a fist around my midriff, trapping my arms to my sides.

Once again I was lifted into the air.

She held me before her face. Her huge eyes were glassy and unfocused. I kept shouting at her, but she didn't seem to respond or even recognize me.

And then she opened her mouth and put my head inside!

CHAPTER SEVENTEEN

WIRE

Just as I felt her teeth closing under my throat, I heard Byte jumping up and down on the bird-table. 'Hey! Stop it! Put my sister down!'

For some reason, it distracted the Wire. Maybe she was reminded of home.

She pulled my head out of her mouth. Her face was a huge sheet of flesh in front of me, like a giant close-up on a cinema screen. She looked around, confused.

'Do it,' hissed the Empress. '*Eat her.*'

Still the Wire hesitated. Her fist kept closing, in jerks, and the breath was squashed out of me.

Now Clefven was calling me. 'Metaphor, this is the way downloading works. Golbasta has to steal mips. Computer power. That's what she's trying to get the Wire to do now. *To suck the mips out of your Web body*. All that will be left will be a shell, like the people in the courtyard. You'll die, Metaphor.'

I struggled to speak. 'That's why Golbasta is hunting Lilliputians.'

'Yes. She must consume us to survive. But the Wire won't become immortal, like the Empress. Not in any human way.'

I understood it all now.

The struldbrugs.

Clefven said, 'The Wire will live for ever . . . but as a familiar, the slave of Golbasta. Like Reldresal. Tell her, Metaphor!'

But, looking up into the Wire's blank, unhappy face, I

wasn't sure if it was going to be possible to tell her anything,
ever again. She was obviously on supertime. She had been
going too fast, too long. And I didn't know what else
Golbasta might have used to infect her Websuit. Outside,
the Wire must already be badly Websick. And she would have
one major case of the slows when she got out.

When – if any of us got out of here!

She squeezed me again, her grip spasming.

I called her name, over and over again. Finally she tipped
her huge head and looked down at me.

She opened her maw of a mouth and started moving me
slowly in once more.

I struggled, but it was hopeless.

Desperately, I bent down and bit the edge of her hand as
hard as I could. She started, and for a moment I thought she
was going to drop me.

She looked down at me, her eyes a little clearer. 'Metaphor?' Her voice was squeaky and too fast. 'What are you
doing here?'

'I'm about to be killed by you!'

She looked confused. 'No, it isn't like that. The Empress
says I'll live for ever. And you will, as part of me.'

'She's lying to you. Oh, yes, you'll live for ever.' I got a
hand free and pointed dramatically at Reldresal. 'You'll live
like *that*. Is that what you want?'

She looked at what was – from her point of view – a small
and shiny bug. For a moment doubt crossed her huge, cloudy
face. But she said angrily, 'If that's what it takes, yes. I'm
never going back out there, Metaphor. Out to Realworld.
Never.'

Behind her, the Empress cackled like a huge witch.

'Wire – Meg – you can't mean that.'

She held me up and shook me so hard my teeth rattled.
'Oh, yes I can. What is there for me out there?'

I tried to think. 'Is it your parents splitting up? Is that it?'

'No. Yes. I don't know! Maybe their splitting up was my
fault.'

I didn't know what to say.

'Get on with it,' the Empress hissed, stirring.

But still the Wire was hesitating. 'It's easy for you, Sarah.'

'What do you mean, easy?'

'You're clever. You're good-looking.'

'Me?'

'Compared to *me*,' she said miserably. 'Even Clefven said so. And you saw how the boy Surfer looked at you.'

She was wrong about that, of course – at least I thought she was – but it wasn't the time to argue!

The Wire said, 'You'll never understand what it's like to be me.'

Suddenly – in spite of everything, in spite of the danger I was in – I felt truly sorry for her.

'Maybe you're right,' I said. 'But you'll never know what it's like to be *me* – with only one parent, who's never home, and a kid brother to look after. People never understand each other. All we can do is put up with each other. Listen, Wire, I'll make you a deal.'

She looked at me suspiciously. 'What?'

'Maybe we can never be friends. Or maybe we can. Anyhow, when we get home, I'll try to put up with you.'

She sniffed. 'All right. And I'll put up with you.'

I laughed. 'And we'll both try to put up with my egg of a brother . . .'

The Empress roared now, and her huge bulk shifted like an exploding volcano. I suddenly remembered where we were. The Empress prodded the Wire with her open hand. '*Kill her!*'

Those two Lilliputian cups of dust still sat on Golbasta's stiff palm.

I hissed, 'Wire, the dust. *Give me the dust.*'

It seemed to happen in slow motion.

Golbasta tried to snatch back her hand. But the Wire, still on supertime, had the advantage of speed.

She snatched the two little cups from Golbasta's closing fist. Then she put me and the cups down on the bird-table platform.

Reldresal jumped across from the wall!

The struldbrug moved in a blur of speed. She grabbed both

Clefven and Byte by the throat. And she was holding Byte right by the edge of the table.

I stepped forward, the cups in my hand.

'Any closer,' Reldresal hissed, 'and the kid goes over.' There was almost none of her human face left on that shell of chitin now – just a sketch of a malicious smile.

'I'm sorry,' Byte blubbered. His eyes were bugging as he scrabbled at her throat.

'You don't have to be sorry,' I said. 'She's not going to hurt you.'

'Oh, yes I am,' the struldbrug said. But she stumbled back when I moved forward, my only weapon the two cups of dust.

I tried to remember what Golbasta had said. *Red and blue*: one to grow, one to shrink. But which was which?

If I got it wrong, I could turn Reldresal into a giant we couldn't resist . . . and we would be trapped as Lilliputians for ever.

The red, I decided. The red shrinks people. That was what Golbasta said.

Wasn't it?

With a confidence I didn't feel, I said, 'Goodbye, Reldresal.'

I prepared to throw the red dust over her – but I thought I saw a flicker of hope in the chitinous mask of her face – and at the last moment I turned and threw the *blue*.

The dust sparkled over her like sky-blue snow. Reldresal wailed, a thin, human sound.

She let Byte and Clefven go. They fell to the tabletop like two sacks of water.

Reldresal started to shrink.

It was like a balloon deflating. I could hear that awful half-human wail getting higher and higher, until it vanished into insect buzzing.

There was a tiny flash of light, a wisp of smoke.

Reldresal was gone.

I thought I understood. 'She was already small. When she got a second dose of dust, the size control programs shrank her past the point where her avatar could be sustained. She's gone.'

Clefven grabbed my arm, and Byte's, and pushed us together. 'Never mind her. She can't hurt you now. Use the dust. Get out of here.'

'What about you?'

'I'll be fine.'

'Oh, sure—'

'*Use the dust.*'

Of course, he was right.

I threw the red dust up in the air and held Byte close. The dust fell over us like confetti.

I started to grow immediately.

It was an even odder sensation than shrinking. Suddenly, the bird-table platform was too small for me – I almost sat on poor Clefven! – and I jumped off, pulling Byte with me. At first we were falling, but we expanded so quickly that our feet had grown down to the floor before we had time to fall.

Our growth slowed as we reached our full size.

The three of us – Byte, the Wire and me – were side by side in the Empress's chamber. Now we were large again the chamber didn't seem so imposing. After all, it was just a shabby hole cut in the middle of a toy palace.

Golbasta was still there, waving her fleshy arms and cursing us. But she didn't have anything left to threaten us with.

Even the cat had gone, I noticed. Even the cat had abandoned her.

I lifted up Byte's wrist. 'Scuttle,' I ordered him.

For the first time since the day he was born, he did as I told him.

He pressed the panic button, and his avatar broke up into a cloud of grainy cubes of light, swirling in the air like butterflies. In a moment, the cloud had shrunk down to a point of light which winked out.

He was gone, and safe.

The Wire grinned at me. Now I was normal size again, I could see how ill she looked.

'See you outside,' she said.

'Yes. Go.'

She pressed her scuttle button and disappeared.

I was the last.

I turned to the bird-table. Clefven was there, once more in his doll-like – compared to me – Lilliputian dimensions. I picked him up carefully and lifted him off the table to the mouth of a corridor in the wall.

'Will you be all right?'

'Yes.' He waved up at me. 'I have to find my family. Now you're safe, stay away from GulliverZone!' And he turned and ran off, into the depths of the palace.

'I'll be back,' I whispered after him.

I turned to Golbasta. She had subsided, wheezing and exhausted.

She didn't seem frightening any more. She was just a sad old woman who was scared of dying.

She dropped her head, and her red eyes winked to darkness. I pressed my scuttle button.

I was lying on my back in the spare bedroom. I pulled my Websuit mask off my face.

Philip was standing over me in his work clothes. He was glaring down at me. It was his worst look of all: *I-trusted-you*.

I sat up. Byte was struggling out of my ridiculous old ballerina-style Websuit. The Wire was still lying inert inside Philip's suit, struggling for breath.

Philip said, 'What kind of state is this to come home? Sarah, you were responsible. How could you let this happen?'

'Philip,' I said. 'Dad. Listen to me. *We have to go back.*'

CHAPTER EIGHTEEN

EAGLE

Well, you probably read the rest in your me-paper.

Philip trusted me. He's good at that. Although, he said, in this instance it was a long leap of faith.

He listened to what I had to say. He called the Webcops, and they listened to *him*.

GulliverZone was shut down immediately. The Webcops went in and they got everybody out.

They found everything: the little warren of living Lilliputians, the struldbrugs, the hollowed-out palace.

But the palace was empty. Of Golbasta and her most senior struldbrugs, there was no sign.

Byte was exhausted. Philip fed him, then put him to an early bed. The Wire was pretty ill from Websickness and all that Webtime. She was taken into hospital for observation. But the doctor said she would recover, and I said I'd come to visit as soon as I could.

I meant to keep my promise to her.

When it was all done, I was amazed to find it was *still* World Peace Day!

Philip asked me if I was hungry. He offered to get me some Tennessee Fried Ostrich as a treat!

I am *never* eating ostrich again.

He made me a quorn protein chili. And then we sat in the kitchen and looked at each other.

'It's still early,' I said.

'Young lady, you've had quite enough Webtime for one day.' But he was wearing his I-have-to-say-no-but-keep-trying-look.

'I still have thirty minutes before I hit three hours Web for the day,' I said. 'Besides, it's been *hours* since we all came out.'

He pulled his lip. 'Where do you want to go?'

I checked the time.

There was only one place to be right now; the biggest event of the day.

The launch of the Mars mission!

'It's very educational,' I said. 'And—'

'All right,' he said. 'But on one condition.'

'That you come in with me this time?'

'You bet your life.'

I scowled. I'd already had to bet my life at least three times today!

Anyway, that was how I ended up sitting on a wooden bench at Cape Canaveral, along with Noel Gallagher.

It was Philip, of course. He just won't edit his old avatar. It was *so* embarrassing.

There were billions of visitors at the launch. You were probably there.

They soaked Cape Canaveral with cameras and micro-phones and gave it its own Web building block, just for the day.

Cape Canaveral is in Florida. I was sitting facing east across a river, and the rocket pad was beyond a line of trees on the horizon. To my left was the biggest building I had ever seen, a black and white block so huge it might have been built by Brobdingnagian giants. It is called the Vehicle Assembly Building, and it's where they used to put together Moon rockets, four at a time. It has sliding doors a hundred metres high.

The launch pad is called Launch Complex 39-A, and it's where they launched those primeval missions to the Moon, back in the 1960s. But today there was a small, slim space-plane tipped up against a gantry like a little white paper dart.

It was a Prometheus-class second generation space shuttle called *Eagle*.

The pad was five kilometres from me – or rather, from the camera I was seeing it through. It was so far away it would take ten seconds for the sound of the launch to reach me here.

There was quite a buzz of excitement among the crowd, and a lot of famous faces. A big countdown clock hovered in the sky. A commentator talked about how the astronauts would be digging into Mars's big underground reservoirs of water to see if any Martian life had survived the three-billion-year ice age there.

'Psst. *Psst.*'

The voice was tiny, and came from beneath my seat. It was as if an ant had spoken.

I glanced sideways. Noel Gallagher, also known as my father, hadn't noticed anything.

I bent forward and pretended to fiddle with my shoe.

There was a man standing there, in the shadow under my bench. He was wearing a leather waistcoat and carrying a bow and arrow.

He was ten centimetres tall. It was Clefven.

He was waving, indicating I should come behind the stand.

I stretched casually. 'Philip,' I said, 'I think I'll take a walk.'

'Only ten minutes to ignition,' he said. He even *sounded* like Noel Gallagher.

'I won't go far. I won't miss anything.'

He smiled, and for a moment I could see the real Philip. It was his I-know-I-can-trust-you look, despite those eyebrows. 'Take care.'

'I will.'

I hurried around the stand.

Clefven was with his family, Skyresh and the two children. Skyresh smiled, and Drunlo and Clustril jumped up and down with excitement when they saw me.

'What are you doing here? You aren't supposed to come outside GulliverZone.'

Clefven tapped the side of his nose. 'We used to be viruses,

you know. We haven't forgotten *everything* . . . Anyway, we
wanted to thank you.'

'Me? I was the one who got you into so much danger.'

He laughed. 'I seem to recall that was actually your little
brother, and he couldn't help it. *You* were the one who
convinced the Webcops to drive out Golbasta. And to take us
Lilliputians seriously. Everything's going to be better now.
We're going to be given our own building block on the Web,
as many mips as we need, and protection from Golbasta. Or
anybody else who tries to do what she did. We even have a
lawyer arguing our case for human rights at the International
Court in New York.'

'That's wonderful,' I said.

'Yes, it is. They even think they can help some of the
struldbrugs. And it's all thanks to you.'

'Here.' Now Skyresh stepped forward shyly. She was holding up a Lilliputian book. It was the size of a thumbnail. She
said, 'It's a gift. To say thank you.'

I leaned down and took the book. The paper was brown,
the cover cracked. I turned the little pages with my fingertip.
They were stiff and yellow-brown with age. *Travels Into
Several Remote Nations of the World in Four Parts* . . . 'Oh,' I
said. 'It's *Gulliver's Travels*.'

'The original and best. I hope you like it,' Clefven said. 'We
put a full-sized edition on to your hard drive for you.'

'Thank you,' I said. 'I'll read it.'

(I did, later. And I had an eerie feeling of *déjà vu*. Gulliver
had experiences like mine – but even *worse*. I wish I'd read the
book before I went anywhere near GulliverZone!)

Clefven said, 'We have to go. But there's someone else who
wants to see you.'

'Who? Where?'

He pointed to the Vehicle Assembly Building.

One of those huge sliding doors was opening.

When I stood at the base of the building, it was like looking
up at a painted cliff face. I felt like a Lilliputian again.

And then a giant stepped out, eclipsing the bright Florida

sun. I saw a smiling girl's face, bending down towards me like a hot-air balloon coming in to land.

It was Glumdalclitch.

'I'm glad to see you looking well,' she whispered in a voice like the wind.

'It wasn't so bad,' I said. 'We even enjoyed some of it.'

'We didn't catch Golbasta, you know.'

'Is that her real name?'

She shrugged, and shoulders the size of mountains heaved. 'It's the name of the avatar you met. Which she's now closed down. She has many avatars.'

The Sorceress, I thought with a shiver. Maybe those silly playground rumours held some truth . . .

But Glumdalclitch wouldn't say. She looked up at the artificial sky. For a moment she looked afraid, despite her huge size. 'She's still out there. I'm afraid that one day we are going to have to track her to her lair, and confront her.'

' "We"?'

'I'm a Webcop.' She smiled. 'I'm here to help. The one thing I don't understand is why you didn't just call for me when you got into trouble in GulliverZone. I said you could, right at the start. It's what I'm here for.'

I felt my jaw drop. 'Byte—'

'Who?'

'My kid brother. He kept saying we should call you. I didn't listen.'

Glumdalclitch laughed, and winked at me. 'I won't tell him if you don't.'

'Thanks,' I said with feeling.

'But if you're in trouble in the Web in future, don't forget to call.' She looked to the east. 'The launch is about to start.'

I turned. There was smoke billowing from the base of the spaceplane, and a voice was counting down: *five, four, three* . . .

Glumdalclitch was disappearing into the shadows of the Vehicle Assembly Building.

'I don't even know your real name!'

'Ariadne,' she said, her voice diminishing. 'Don't forget. *Call Ariadne . . .*'

There was a blue flash, and she was gone.

I looked over at Launch Complex 39-A.

A pure white light burst from the base of the *Eagle*, a splash of brilliance as bright as the Sun. The spaceplane rose suddenly, clearing its launch tower in a second. It rose up on a pillar of smoke, impossibly fast.

It all happened in eerie silence.

A spaceship was going to Mars! Everyone was clapping and cheering.

There was a sparkle of light next to me, cubes of colour that swarmed around each other like butterflies. They coalesced into a boy in a black gaming suit and a red cloak.

Surfer.

He grabbed my arm. 'Metaphor.'

'You missed the launch,' I said.

'What launch? Never mind that. *Listen! You won't believe what I found out about Dreamcastle . . .*'

The noise of the spaceplane reached me. The ground shook and there was a sound like thunder in the sky, crackling and slapping. It was as if Brobdingnagian giants were walking by, laughing.

DREAMCASTLE
STEPHEN BOWKETT

CHAPTER ONE

STORMDRAGON

The VR-bar was quiet this evening, most of the after-workers and kids homeward bound from school having left. Only the real cybernet phreaks – the Webheads – had stayed behind to dive deep into whatever dataspace adventure they had chosen.

Surfer, Kilroy and Rom finished their coffees in the Cyber Diner adjacent to the game area and walked towards the cubicle where they could plug-in and access the Web.

Their intention was to zone-in to the Dreamcastle again. It was their favourite Website. They'd been visiting it together for the past six months or so, since meeting quite by chance in its lower levels. To Surfer's ongoing embarrassment, Kilroy had helped him out of a difficult situation involving twenty skeleton warriors. The girl's courage had matched her speed and strength, and with Rom lending a hand, they'd beaten off the attack and gained a handsome handful of bonus points.

'I reckon we'd make a pretty eight team – whatcha think?' Surfer's idea had been spur-of-the-moment and casually suggested. But he still remembered the light that came into Kilroy's eyes and the way she had looked at him. He'd thought then he was probably making trouble for himself. Fact was, Surfer reflected, I like the clean and simple encounters of the game. Real life emotions are much too messy and complicated. It had been a startling piece of luck (or misfortune, Surfer remembered thinking) that the three of them lived in the same small town. When you were in-game you had no idea where your companions came from until you were told. They might actually live in any part of the world.

Rom had jumped at the chance of being part of a team. His skills were tactical. He was a thinker who enjoyed understanding the structure of games, but he had no real interest in fighting his way to the top. He'd entered Dreamcastle because of its complexity and cleverness. 'It's a labyrinth of dangers,' was his description of it that first time. Tagging along as Surfer and Kilroy dealt with the dangers, so that he could understand how Dreamcastle worked, suited him perfectly.

Rom smiled warmly at his friends as they entered the cubicles and plugged their Websuits into the terminal – and into the world of the Web. Kilroy winked at Rom then slid the VR helmet over her head.

'Last one in's a one-mip six!' Surfer said, pushing in the final jackplugs.

Rom completed his own connections and felt the suit powering-up around him.

On this particular dive the three of them had bought-in to a common access code and reached their site via a twisting glassy tunnel that swirled with all the colours of the rainbow like a slick of oil. At superspeed they spun and tumbled, sliding almost faster than the eye could follow towards their destination. Rom had wanted to do it, and although Surfer had thought it was a pretty cog idea, as the chrome-glossy walls streaked past, even he had to admit he was having a good time.

Kilroy and Rom were spinning ahead of him. Surfer saw them acquire their game-costumes as though by magic: Kilroy favouring a tightly fitting but flexible tunic and trousers of soft dark leather; Rom preferring a pair of rough-weave baggy leggings, a loose cotton shirt and cape. You didn't *have* to go Medieval-fantasy to fit in with the scenario. Eggs did it anyway, of course, to be cool. But just to see them posing in their gamegear looking all self-important was enough to bring on a dose of the voms in any serious player.

The real pros, phreaks like himself Surfer reflected with no false modesty, dressed to win. As the far end of the delivery tunnel came into view and a strong breeze began to blow around him, Surfer's white smock morphed into sensible polyfabric coveralls with hard black body armour moulded to his chest and back, knee-length lace-up boots, steel shinpads, and a red cloak of flame-resistant material that swirled with the heavy elegance of velvet but felt as light and loose as gossamer.

Surfer yelled out in fierce anticipation as the tunnel exit expanded around him. His utility belt and weaponry fastened themselves on as the final processing was completed.

And then he was in, standing momentarily dizzied as the virtual world of the 'castle assembled itself around him.

The Dreamcastle, an interactive gamezone that was designed as a cross between the labyrinth of the legendary Greek Minotaur, a pyramid temple to the great god Ra, and Dracula's Transylvanian mountaintop mansion. The databox that rippled for a second in front of Surfer's eyes reminded him that the 'castle was twenty kilometres wide, fifteen broad, five high, and possessed a thousand levels – each one containing greater dangers and excitements than the level below.

The same d-box told Surfer that he and his friends had battled their way to Level 499, and that now they were on the brink of their greatest challenges yet.

'Whoo! That was *venomous*!' Rom twirled around like a dancer, still alight with the thrill of entry. Kilroy, standing beside him, looked on more calmly, though with a fond and tolerant smile at Rom's antics.

Surfer watched them both as the d-box faded like a memory. At twelve, Rom was by several years the youngest. At the outset, that alone might have prompted Surfer to dismiss him as a real gag hanger-on. But you never judge a videobook by its cover was a valuable lesson, and Surfer had soon discovered that Rom's abilities as a hacker made him an indispensable companion. Although the primary software driving the 'castle's VR existence was out of bounds, reprogramming branch files and sub-routines was possible with skill, intelligence and determination. Rom had all these and had used them to bootstrap the group out of some pretty tight spots in the past.

Rom deserved his moment of fun, Surfer thought. And Kilroy obviously agreed. She chuckled aloud, echoing Rom's pleasure in being here, before her face shone with a darker light as she caught Surfer's eyes upon her.

'You got a gambit in mind?' she asked, guessing that Surfer would see the double-edged nature of her comment – a plan for their present foray deeper into Dreamcastle territory, and a hint of asking his intentions towards her.

True to form, Surfer became flustered. Kilroy grinned at Rom, who shook his head at the girl's impishness.

Rom and Kilroy had met in the 'castle's lower levels around a month before Surfer had joined them. Rom had been having trouble dealing with a crew of cyberknights. Kilroy strode into the action and wiped them pretty effectively with a laserlance, whooping in triumph as the last of them popped in a cloud of shattering pixels. Rom, it appeared, had hacked his way to Level 242 without much thought about what he was going to do when he got there. Luckily, Kilroy had been around, exploring byways, seen the kid's predicament and decided to help. Firm friends are made in a crisis, she'd told Rom. And they'd been zoning-in together ever since.

At the time, Rom had called Kilroy 'his Amazon', and fell in love immediately as people tended to do in the Web where there was little chance of meeting the real face behind the individual's pretend persona.

Except that Rom – and Surfer too come to that – had been startled to learn that all three of them lived in Oakhills and had been sitting mere metres away from each other, while their Web-selves wandered the Dreamcastle's infinite corridors.

'You got a gambit in mind?' Kilroy asked him again, as Surfer's mind jumped back to the present.

It had become clear early on how she felt about him and that, if he wanted it to, things could get serious between them. He had not been tempted, even though Kilroy was tall and blonde, fine-boned and beautiful. Moreover, she wore her real face in the Web and the admiration she felt for him lingered there plainly for Surfer to see.

It fed his pride, but he admitted to himself he was daunted by her cleverness and independence.

After their first encounter, he'd checked her out at Oakhills Senior High. She was majoring in science, and would probably carve a career for herself as a biochemist. Surfer had been able to learn this purely because Kilroy was as honest about her real name as she was about her face. The nick 'Kilroy' concealed Philippa Stephens who lived six blocks up from Rom on Hobbston Pike. Surfer had wandered round there and been jealous of her parents' big house shaded by sycamores, the cherry trees dotting the trim lawns and the palm-fringed pool. It seemed she had it all, and hung around in the Web just for kicks – not because she had something to prove to the world.

She came over to him now and Surfer was impressed by the way the virtual light gleamed on her hair, which she wore cut short in an unfussy style.

'Um,' he said, disconcerted for a second. Kilroy reached out and touched Surfer's forearm. The wonders of technology, he thought. But they fell short of providing any olfactory stimulus in the gamezone. Kilroy smelled of nothing. There was no perfume to tantalize him. He stepped away from her and became businesslike.

'We're at a vital stage of the game,' he said, stating the obvious and paying the price as Rom laughed at him aloud.

'Copy that, Surf!' The smile went away. 'So why is it so quiet around here?'

'Exactly my point. It's not like the early days, when we got all that cog stuff like Frankenstein and Wolfman thrown at us—'

'The digital dragons were wild,' Rom pointed out, recalling that particular skirmish with fondness.

'Don't be a gag,' Kilroy interjected. 'That was kindergarten, just flashbang action with very little purpose. Surfer's right.

This is the calm before the storm. If we go down the plug here, we lose our bonuses, our cred, our gamezone freetime. Isn't that right?' she added, looking to Surfer for confirmation.

He nodded his agreement. 'Can't argue with the truth, Rom.' Surfer drew his sword and was flooded with reassurance to feel its familiar weight and balance in his hand.

'Let's see what's up ahead. But stay close, people, because anything can happen from here on in.'

Five minutes later, Surfer's comment came home to haunt them. They'd reached a place where the grey stone corridor split like an outspread hand, five ways. Even Rom could access nothing via the keypad on his wrist to tell them what to do. So they went random, and on Surfer's suggestion took the middle path.

Very shortly they noticed a brightening ahead, and as they came round a slow curve they saw that the passageway was sheared off cleanly, with pale sunlight glimmering beyond.

'It's the *outside*,' Rom murmured, almost fearfully. Since he'd been gaming with Surfer and Kilroy in the Dreamcastle, he'd glimpsed the surrounding forests only twice. In keeping with the high-fantasy scenario of the game, they were dark, mysterious and menacing. Apart from that, the trees went on forever.

Rom glanced up at Surfer and was not comforted by his grim expression.

'I'll take a look,' Surfer said. He felt empty inside, kind of hollow. He knew from experience that the 'castle was at its most dangerous when it was at its most peaceful.

He edged forward, squinting up at the glassy sun as it shone through the portal in the outer 'castle walls.

Surfer found himself on a broad stone balcony, two kilometres high, looking out over the oceanic forests.

He beckoned the others and they came up beside him.

'This,' said Rom with awe, 'is some domain! I–I've never been so high.'

The illusion was breathtaking. A cool wind buffeted Surfer's hair and rustled his cloak around him. He went to the very edge and felt his feet tingling at the huge distance dropping away to the miniature landscape below.

'It's only a game,' he whispered to calm his nervousness. 'It's only a game . . . '

The mantra was ineffective. As Surfer looked each way along the ledge, then gazed dizzyingly upward, a ripple of fear ran through him. He felt locked to the stone, incapable of action.

Somewhere deep in the grey throat of the corridor, a door creaked open and boomed closed.

Rom let out a moan of pure fear.

'It's not supposed to happen like this—'

'We've funnelled it,' Kilroy declared. She drew her own weapons, a short stabbing sword and a cluster of throwing stars. 'We're trapped here, Surfer!'

'Keep it tight,' he snapped back. They were looking to him for leadership, and that more than anything else was what broke his spell of indecision.

'I'll scout along the ledge. My guess is there'll be other portals. We can dodge in through one of those.'

'Come back for us, Surfer!' Rom squealed as Surfer eased along the lip of stone, his back pressed to the rough vertical.

He moved slowly but steadily, sliding sideways – ten metres, fifteen, pinned by the sunlight's harsh glare against the shadowless wall.

Then his fingers found the edge of the next portal.

Surfer craned around to look—

And without warning the sun was gone. A tumble of black cloud spilled out over the highest pinnacles of the 'castle, rolling thunder before it and cracking the sky like blue porcelain with a tine of white lightning.

Surfer looked up in shock as the storm assembled itself in moments, as though directed and controlled. A few seconds later, his suspicion was confirmed as a winged serpent swooped out of its dark heart towards him.

It was big, and its face was murderous. The storm-dragon's tongue was a flame, its scaled flanks the colour of burning chrome. Black talons flicked out like switchblades and hooked themselves ready to pluck Surfer clean off the ledge.

As it dropped, coming ever faster as time in the Web spun up to speed, Surfer braced his legs apart and swung his sword. He missed completely as the stormdragon tilted aside, smashing him down with a wing.

The sword clattered to the brink of the ledge and pivoted ready to fall.

Surfer snatched it back, scrambled up, then was grasped in the dragon's enormous talons and whirled away into the sky.

The monster shrieked in triumph and swung its head down to devour him. As the awful mouth loomed close, Surfer wrenched back his sword arm and drove the blade deep into the foul hot throat of the creature.

It gushed screams and blood, instantly losing its direction and balance in the sky and tumbling downwards out of control.

Surfer saw the ground far away, spinning around and around, the 'castle walls blurring past him. He knew he had only seconds left before the stricken stormdragon crushed him against the stonework or, more likely, crashed with him into the forest.

He took a gamble, knowing what failure could bring.

Disentangling himself from the beast's claws, he unclipped his cloak, picked his moment, then swung himself in towards the wall.

Surfer's right shoulder hit rock and the pain of it flared through him. His sword fell from a numbed hand and went spinning away out of sight. With his other hand he grabbed a mass of clinging ivy. It whipped through his fingers. He saw his own skin being stripped from his palms, and felt the Websuit gloves rippling to enhance the illusion. He gripped harder, and gradually slowed until he hung there breathless, gazing down at the dwindling shape of the stormdragon smashing into the trees.

The thunder and lightning quickly faded with the death of the beast as it wisped into a vapour, then into nothingness.

The sun came out and warmed Surfer's back as he clambered down the ivy until he reached the portal below.

He was looking into a dim chamber hung with cobwebs and shadows. Chains tinkled in the darkness. Something moved.

Surfer strained to see more clearly.

But now something else was happening. He was being grasped by a familiar but unwelcome sensation of ending; of being drawn back out of this maze of dreams to the Real-world. It was a raid – a program crash maybe – dragging him unwillingly away.

'Please – no – please help me!'

The thin female voice startled him. It confused him too as he struggled to work out if it came from in-game or the outside.

Surfer strained to see through the gloom, glimpsing just for a second the image of the most beautiful girl he had ever seen in his life. As her words disintegrated into the fragments of memory, the sky and the land and the Dreamcastle itself disappeared.

Surfer fought in vain against it, but there was nothing he could do.

And while his mind readjusted, conversation exploded around him. He heard Kilroy's worried voice as nervous hands tugged at the straps and fastenings of his Websuit.

CHAPTER TWO

IN THE VR–BAR

'He's gonna vom!' somebody shouted. That more than anything else brought Surfer back to the here-and-now. He struggled up angrily, looking for the egg who didn't know better than to realize Surfer was a veteran of a thousand trips to the Web.

'Curl up,' Surfer said groggily to the kid he'd thought had spoken. 'Where the heck d'you think I got my nick from?'

'Are you OK?' Kilroy asked him, showing real concern.

'Yeah, yeah, don't smother me!' He pushed away from her, stood up and pulled loose the last of the electrode contacts that linked his Tarantula to the dataspace world of the Web. Even so, he felt the slight but unpleasant lifting in his stomach that marked the onset of a Websickness low. His head throbbed a little now, his mind swimming with images of the stormdragon spiralling to destruction like a stricken fighter plane, the blue sky fractured with lightning, the pleading green eyes of the girl he'd glimpsed in that final second before someone had pulled the plug and wrenched him back to reality.

Yellow stars slapped like large wet snowflakes across Surfer's vision. He blew out a shuddering breath and put a hand to his forehead.

'You want to cocoon it, Surf?' Rom said, standing close, ready to help his friend balance if need be. Rom himself looked small and worried, shaken by his experience.

'It's my fault,' he admitted in a whipped-dog voice. 'We

saw the stormdragon take you, and we thought—' Rom
shrugged, not knowing now quite what he'd thought. In
any gamezone, wipeout didn't do any real damage, but the
loss of a character-life or bonuses or freetime caused one's
cred to plummet in the competitive culture of the VR-bar.
What surprised Rom was that the regular Web-vets hanging
around nearby were smiling at Surfer, half in admiration and
half in ill-concealed jealousy. One of them, a big bulky kid
called Browser, came up and gave Surfer a comradely slap on
the back.

'Venomous, man. Venomous.'

It was not what Surfer had expected. His frown of puzzlement was answered by the boy's broad grin as he pointed to
the huge flat 3-D telescreen up on the wall. It was replaying
Surfer's triumphant slaying of the stormdragon.

'You got yourself a thousand bonus points.' Kilroy's voice
was soft. She was obviously pleased on his behalf. And this
time Surfer could smell her perfume. 'Congratulations.'

'Thanks,' he answered, toning down his earlier dismissive-
ness. He pushed a hand that was still shaking slightly
through his long black hair, feeling itchy and hot in the
tight suit. 'I, uh, I think I'll go take a shower. Then I'll
debrief,' he added, looking pointedly at Rom, and just as
pointedly not at Kilroy.

VR-bars had started twenty years ago as an outgrowth of the
cybercafe idea, just after the millennium. They were places
where folk, mainly kids, could go for entertainment and to
socialize. It seemed a good idea at the time was the view of
most adults now. But their enthusiasm had waned over the
years. Certainly kids had turned off drugs and street-corner
crime in favour of Websurfing; but that in itself had brought
problems. The growth of computing power, coupled with the
sophisticated technologies behind VR engineering, had created a sensory experience that most young people agreed was
better than real life. Parents, teachers, religious leaders and
some politicians had begun to grumble right back then in the
early days. That had grown into a worldwide organized

campaign of protest – a lobby that was powerful by most standards, but still pretty puny when set against the international might and backing of the Web.

Surfer, like most of his friends, treated the protesters as fools who just didn't understand. It seemed all the more laughable that people should object, when those same people had almost sent the world over the edge back in the bad old days of the twentieth century. And more recently, when crazy power politics had resulted in the South Korean seaport of Pusan being wiped out by a nuclear strike in 2007. After the nuclear non-proliferation treaty of 2010, and because of the evolution of the Web, the world had been made safer. The arguments of the protesters amounted to nothing when, just four years ago, the first virtual war had been fought between two small fierce Middle Eastern countries – fought and settled without a life being lost.

That, as far as Surfer was concerned, said it all.

He went to the comfort cubicles, stripped off the Tarantula and dumped it down the chute for refurbishment, cleaning and checking. Then he showered, scrubbing away the sluggishness he felt with sweetsand and water as hot as he could take it.

Ten minutes later, he was down in the Cyber Diner sitting with Rom at a tabletop terminal.

'I want to know *all* about her,' was Surfer's enthusiastic request, after telling Rom what had happened.

Rom shook his head a little sadly. 'Lovesickness and Websickness are pretty much the same, you know. She's probably just a phace anyway.'

Surfer denied that hotly. *Phaces* were personas created by the software itself, a bit like the spiders or AI bot-programs you found populating the gamezones to help you along the way – or to warn you off, as the case may be. Especially in a fantasy zone, Rom explained, phaces fulfilled the function of non-player characters, spicing up the adventure if there weren't enough realoes around.

'But she was *so* real,' Surfer persisted, his eyes staring into memory's distance. 'So helpless—'

Rom made exaggerated gagging sounds and sipped at his drink. 'You got that close to her, huh, that you could be sure?'

Surfer glanced at the younger boy and found him beaming insolently, the insolence sharpened by Rom's reddish hair and peppering of freckles.

'How could a one-mip mind like yours be expected to understand?' he wanted to know. 'Just push the buttons, Rom, and let's find out.'

Rom shrugged off the insult and set to work. Quality time in the Web could be expensive, even if, like Surfer, you'd previously won freetime and the use of a state-of-the-art Websuit like Tarantula. So the tabletop terminals came in handy, allowing you to access flat graphics and other data about the game you were playing long-term.

Rom skilfully opened a nest of Dreamcastle dialogue boxes. 'You don't even know her name,' he complained. 'All I've got is a description and a set of co-ordinates. Huh, before I fall in love I want to know what the girl's called and what kind of Websuit she owns!'

Surfer chuckled despite himself. 'Who says romance is dead,' he quipped, as a spider spreadeagled over the screen, spat a red warning and closed the application down to a spiralling pattern of coloured splinters.

Rom snatched his fingers away from the board as though they'd been burned.

'Did you see that!' he whispered, sounding astonished. 'The spider downed us. All I did was ask about—'

'About her,' Surfer said.

Rom shook his head excitedly. 'No, not exactly. I was seeking information about the layout of the 'castle at that level. But we've been barred, Surf – locked out, ejected.'

'But why?' Surfer stared at the fractal whirlpool as though the answer was there.

'Now who's got the one-mip mind?' Rom batted back, enjoying his minor triumph. 'Don't you understand? The spider won't let me look because the data is above my level of clearance.'

'But we reached four-nine-nine—'

'And you've bootstrapped higher with the defeat of the stormdragon,' Rom added. 'Which means that your girl, whoever she is, must be way above Level 500. We're talking stratospheric here, Surf.'

Surfer sat back in the tubular steel chair, his rather pale complexion reflecting in soft pastels the garish decor-lights of the Cyber Diner.

'If she's that high, she can't be a phace,' was his first conclusion.

Rom clicked his tongue disapprovingly. 'Don't be glove-and-glasses. That's a basement-level error and you'd know it, if your heart hadn't melted like a hot marshmallow for this girl – Ann Onymous,' he laughed.

But Surfer's mood changed as he started thinking tactically.

'We can use her, Rom. She's there for a purpose. A Web-vet whose skill and knowledge can help us to get right to the top.'

'That's pretty fly,' Rom said, deadpan. 'Except flies get swatted, Surfer. You saw a cute face and fell for it. Besides, where does Kilroy feature in all of this? You know how she feels about you.'

That gave Surfer pause. Both of the boys looked across the expanse of tables and saw Kilroy sitting with a group of her own friends, drinking sodas. From time to time, she would glance over at Surfer, then look away as though she wasn't interested at all. Rom's eyes were filled with a complex light; a fondness for Kilroy, extreme annoyance at Surfer's attitude, and a certain excitement because to take the Dreamcastle would be the achievement of a lifetime.

'Just don't keep her on the hook,' Rom said quietly. 'Let her know where she stands with you, Surfer.'

'Do you think I'd hurt her that way?' Surfer asked, reasonably enough.

Rom's reply was silence. He understood how badly Surfer wanted to be a dataspace hero; knew that the guy had something to prove to the world. There was green acid in

Surfer's stomach. Rom knew it was burning every time some silky walked into the VR-bar in his own Tarantula, or by fluke or judgement beat Surfer's high score on the night. Frankly, Rom thought he wouldn't put anything past Surfer if it meant gaining advantage in the game.

That made Surfer dangerous to be with, Rom concluded – for himself and for Kilroy.

'Would you go in again?' Surfer asked, hooking a thumb at the terminal.

Rom slid his ID card from the slot. 'Not tonight, Surf. It's late. Besides, if I'm spidered-off too often, I'll be out, permanently.'

Then he smiled a little wickedly. 'But I got a few contacts I'll talk to. Maybe they can suggest some ways of sneaking round old eight-legs.'

'Good man.' Surfer stood up, stretched and yawned. 'Guess I'd better be homing it also. See you tomorrow?'

'I'll be here.'

'Sleep tight,' Surfer said, smiling cockily at his evening's work.

Rom nodded. 'You too. But let me leave you with this thought: if Ann Onymous is such a powerful player, how come you found her chained up and helpless in a dungeon?'

It was not something that troubled Surfer particularly. He'd heard stories of ultra-vets who'd reached the pinnacle of success in a given gamezone, but rather than move on, they descended to lower levels to try variations in the play, to find other ways of winning. Maybe the girl he'd seen was one of those, which made finding her again a priority, regardless of any other reasons Surfer was keeping to himself.

Outside, a thin October rain was falling and the twilight streets were shiny wet, rippling the garish neon of the VRbar's illuminated frontage.

Surfer looked both ways along King Street, but the town's little fleet of taxis were all busy. He chose to walk it rather than wait, since his home on Trent Road was only four blocks away, and the fresh air would dispel the last traces of Websickness.

He took the quiet route, striding down Southland Avenue with its stands of lime trees in preference to the busier way through the Mall.

There was no one about. Surfer gave a snort of derisive laughter to think that all of the town's critical elders – people who frowned on the Web – would be cabled-in to their favourite soap or quiz show by now, living happily ever after in potatoville!

His thoughts went back to the Dreamcastle, his evening's adventures, and his brief but significant meeting with the girl—

Then that too was brushed from Surfer's mind.

The wind lifted suddenly, sweeping through the trees along Southland and skittering drifts of dry leaves ahead of him on the sidewalk.

He stopped, convinced that someone was watching him. He scanned the shadows, imagining figures there, hearing voices in the wind as his nerves tightened up like guitar strings.

'You're putting the bite on yourself, Surf,' he whispered, chuckling self-consciously.

But his smirk was wiped from his face as he heard, quite distinctly – though impossibly, of course – a door creaking open and booming closed, its echoes lingering along the damp grey walls of the Dreamcastle's corridors.

CHAPTER THREE

THE HONG KONG CONNECTION

'The prodigal returns,' Reg Miller said with a tired kind of sarcasm that Surfer found utterly tedious. He didn't rise to it any more; it was beyond irritation. 'Just thought you'd pop back to make sure the old folks were still alive, eh, Robert?'

Miller grinned at his son, who he knew hated to be called by his real name. Surfer's tight grin reflected the conflict between them both; his silence the mark of how bad things had become lately.

'Well, say hello to your mother, for goodness sake!' Miller snapped, finding an excuse for his anger.

'Hi, Mum.' Surfer walked over and kissed his mother dutifully on the cheek. She was sitting in one of the living room's two easy chairs, while her husband lay sprawled on the sofa. It had sagged over the years with his weight, and now seemed as weary as everything else that had needed to endure him.

Surfer didn't entirely blame his father. In this brave new world of plenty, people could still run short on dreams. Reg Miller worked in a light engineering plant that was part of the big industrial complex on the east side of Oakhills. He had started as a production-line worker and moved up to middle management. He acted as a kind of go-between, allowing the workforce and the executive to talk to each other more effectively. He was good at his job. He had also kept his marriage together these twenty-odd years, owned a modest but respectable house in this pretty New England town. He was nine years off retirement, wanted to spend his twilight years in a lakeside lodge near Rochester, and live long enough to see his grandchildren grown.

Surfer smiled inwardly at that. Being an only child, it was down to him to provide the grandsons and 'daughters.

The fact that he, Surfer, preferred cruising in dataspace to being at home caused constant friction between them.

'Enjoy yourself in cloud-land?' Miller quipped, easing himself upright to reach for another can of beer.

They had been through it all many times before. The old arguments about the merits and dangers of the Web. Surfer, being a staunch supporter, pointed out that it had revolutionized education. What could beat learning geography by going to any virtual location you desired? Or getting into history by fighting in the Civil War, or riding on the tail of Fat Boy as it plunged towards Hiroshima on that black August morning, so long ago? And how much more science meant when you could talk to an atom about the way it behaved, or be a blood cell whirling in towards the heart?

Reg Miller agreed that such things just might beat listening to a chalk-and-talk lesson down at the schoolhouse. But he was also adamant that 'kids of today', like ostriches, kept their heads in the sand and spent an unhealthy amount of time ignoring what was really going on. The fact that Surfer had no definite career in mind – certainly not light engineering like his father's – just rubbed salt into the wound, and made most evenings just like this one.

'I'll fix some supper,' Surfer said, ignoring his father's barb. 'Then I think I'll turn in.'

'You look tired,' Mrs Miller squeezed her son's hand. 'You OK?'

'I'm fine, Mum,' he said, hoping she wouldn't spot the lie. Fact was, Surfer felt shaken by the vividness of the hallucination he'd experienced outside the house. He'd seen nothing, but the sound of a dungeon door slamming had been unmistakable. And then, there was the sense of being watched. That too had been strong, and clung to him now as he wandered into the kitchen, checked the contents of the fridge and found nothing to tempt him.

Surfer poured himself a glass of water, guzzled it, then made his way up to his room. In the corner, beneath his montage of Mars Mission posters, the cursor on his PC blinked unhurriedly on a blank screen. There were no messages.

He went to the bathroom, pausing on the landing as he heard his parents' muted voices drifting up from below. He could not make out any words, but there seemed to be no anger in the tone. Surfer wondered if his dad had just given up on him; lumped him in with all the other cyberphreaks and Webheads, nerds, lurkers and silkies he'd heard about on the news.

Surfer thought he'd be disappointed if that were the case. The Web was the New World of the twenty-first century, a vast territory where pioneers still had a part to play. Careers could be forged, fortunes made, ambitions realized in Webtown. What was wrong with wanting to explore there? Surfer wondered as he slid gratefully into his bed. Where was the harm in dreaming large, then following your dream as far as it would take you?

Not that he knew exactly what his ultimate goal might be, he thought as his eyes fluttered closed.

But there'd be something waiting for him in the Web, for sure.

Something.

The clock woke him at eight-thirty, its cheery urge to rise and shine coinciding with Surfer's father going out the front door to his work. Then there came the whine of the greencoach's motor on a rising pitch as the vehicle trundled off down the street. Surfer could imagine his father saying the same goodmornings to the same faces in the same seats; an unchangng, unending routine. It was almost heartbreaking.

He rubbed his eyes and told the clock to tune-out, which it did, after informing Surfer that he had some e-mail waiting to be read.

It was not a school day. Surfer could take time over his mail and enjoy a leisurely shower and breakfast afterwards. Mum would most likely go to her art class. She was doing this more often these days for the company. Surfer would have the house to himself.

He stepped over to his desk and touched the intro-icon on the screen of his PC. A letterbox appeared. It was customized as a dragon's head, and now disgorged a graphic envelope of aged parchment, burned at the edges by the curlicues of flame that spilled from the serpent's jaws.

The envelope unfolded to reveal a greeting in a gorgeous calligraphic script, together with two little oriental figures waving at him.

'Hi, Surfer,' one of them said, jumping up and down in exaggerated cartoon style. 'We heard about your destruction of the stormdragon. Welcome to Level Five-o-one. I am Suki, and this –' the figure indicated its companion – 'is Silent Blade. We too are explorers of the Dreamcastle, and broke through the five-hundred barrier some weeks ago. Do you want to meet? It would be our pleasure to do so. Maybe, if you are agreeable, we might team up and move on together.'

The little cartoon figure made a sad face.

'There are many dangers ahead, as you know, Surfer. Silent Blade and I thought we would be stronger working together. You must let us know. But anyhow, hello and greetings again! We hope you will agree to see us in Web-town.

'Goodbye for now!'

The two characters bowed, then slowly dissolved in a mist of pixels.

Surfer chuckled, shaking his head in amusement, pleased to receive what he took to be his first piece of fan mail. The dialogue box he opened indicated that the message had arrived from Hong Kong at 2.15 a.m. EST, which made it mid-afternoon over there.

'Clock,' Surfer said, without turning around.

'Eight-forty-two in the morning,' it replied briskly.

Surfer reckoned he could be down at the VR-bar by nine,

and shaking hands with Suki and Silent Blade before they turned in for the night.

Rom was already cruising, mopping up some enemy opposition in a mini-game of Star Warriors. You didn't need to go into Webtown for this. Apart from the VR terminals, the 'bar also boasted a number of stand-alone cubicles. Individuals could hook-up to a brief-encounter scenario and spend as little as half an hour enjoying top quality immersion. It was better than gag, cheaper than multi-player adventures in the Web, and handy for soaking up those spare minutes while you waited for your companions to appear.

Surfer spoke to Rom through the cubicle's external mike, grinning at the TV display of Rom's antics. The kid was good, showing no hesitation as he wiped out the last of the Black Star Omega-wings. Then, in his trim little hyperlight Raptor craft, he did a victory roll through the blue vapour remnants of his atomized enemy and came in to a perfect touchdown on Homeworld.

The view on the screen panned away to a slowly expanding star field. Rom disconnected the Websuit and stepped out of the cubicle.

'Well eight,' Surfer said, and Rom saluted at the compliment.

'Thought I'd sharpen up my hand/eye co-ordination for the widow battles to come.'

'I got some news. Help from afar.'

Rom's eyebrows rose. 'OK, let's take time out over a drink, Surf. I have things to tell you too.'

They walked across to the Cyber Diner which, even this early on, was filled with people – mainly kids and teenagers who did not have a school day today. Some of them were sitting in their Websuits (a few being really cog about showing off the latest gear), but most, like Surfer, wore casual clothes, having yet to start their day in the Web.

Surfer bought two large colas to celebrate Rom's recent victory on the galactic rim. Rom was highly honoured.

'I got a call,' Surfer said, 'from a couple of vets in Hong Kong.' He went on to explain the details of the message.

'Could be significant,' was Rom's considered opinion. 'The population drops in the upper reaches of the 'castle, as you know. Players get wiped out, or fail to make it in the first place. Maybe your new friends are right, Surfer; perhaps there will be strength in numbers. On the other hand,' Rom continued with a mischievous grin, 'a team is only as strong as its weakest link, and only as fast as its slowest member. What do you know about Suki and Silent Blade?'

'Nothing yet,' Surfer admitted, suppressing his irritation because he knew Rom was absolutely right. 'That's why I thought we could set up a meeting with them in Webtown, before moving into the Dreamcastle gamezone.'

Rom nodded. 'OK, that'll avoid funnels if we do team up. What about Kilroy?' Rom glanced around as he said this. 'Is she in on the decision making?'

'I haven't seen her – but we can leave a clipnote in Webtown; or she can contact us from Realworld if she really wants to interrupt what we're doing.'

Rom glared disapprovingly at his friend's dismissive manner. 'Why are you shouldering her out?' he wanted to know, smiling wistfully a moment later. 'Huh, if she was making eyes in my direction, I'd be there before you could say venom!'

'Yeah, well—' Surfer avoided the issue by finishing up his drink. 'You said you had some things to tell me.'

Rom shrugged. 'The news is no-news, actually. I webbed round to a few phreaks I know about the girl you encountered. Her personal data is locked up tighter than the basement safe in the Pentagon.' Rom enjoyed seeing the sudden sparkle in Surfer's eyes dim to disappointment. 'Sorry, Surf, but that's the way it is. I suspect it's not just because she's protected by her higher level clearance in the gamezone. Little Ann Onymous is also cloaking her details – living up to her name, you might say. She doesn't *want* any old basement-level silky smarming up to her, using her to bootstrap higher into the 'castle.'

Surfer grunted with indignation, causing Rom to laugh aloud.

'You'll just have to fight for her, Surf. Which is what white knights have always done, right?'

They went to Webtown in the most straightforward way, without preamble. Sitting together in a private room that Surfer secured with his bonuses, he and Rom hit the power buttons on their wrist keypads, then thumbed-in another code that would deposit them outside the Dreamcastle zone.

Prior to this, Surfer had contacted Suki and Silent Blade on the Web address they'd given, hoping to meet them in VR. Time was moving on, and he hadn't waited for a reply.

His breath caught in his throat, as it always did, at the moment of transition into the Web, as the brief electronic tone sounded in his ears and Surfer's field of vision washed over with a uniform blue. But this BAT effect was brief. He felt the Tarantula squeeze and flex about his body, prepping itself to respond. The headset seemed to meld around his face, his eyes flooding with streams and flurries of virtual light.

Time spun-up to Web-standard and Surfer found himself standing on the broad familiar strand outside the Dream-castle gamezone. Rom was beside him, reading the sky-ads for Coke, Raid and other currently widow products, as well as the more entertaining graffiti embossed on the heavens by the usual crop of Webtown hackers.

The gridwork of streets in this area was busy, for the 'castle and related adventures were very popular. A couple of vets in samurai armour walked by, acknowledging Surfer with a nod. He felt pleased to be recognized as one of them, and glanced sideways at Rom, to see if he had noticed this mark of a new respect.

'Here's Kilroy!' Rom said, calling her name more loudly and waving.

Surfer felt piqued, but lifted his hand in greeting as Kilroy spotted them and walked over.

'I got your clipnote,' she said, with a smile that was

carefully neutral in Surfer's direction. 'Thanks for letting me know your plans. I had an assignment to finish, but I guess it can wait until this afternoon.'

'No problem then,' Surfer said, trying not to look at the sleek black one-piece that Kilroy had chosen as Webgear. She was doing her best for him, he knew that, and he felt flattered. And if things had been different, maybe he and Kilroy could really become close. Although she spent her freetime in the gamezones, Kilroy's main interests lay in the Realworld. She, like most people, would grow out of exploring the 'castle, and use the Web for the same dull and boring things grown-ups used it for. Surfer could see her in, say, fifteen years time; big house like her folks, successful career, couple of kids carefully steered towards only the 'educational' Webtown, a doting husband who would be – let's face it – a real cog silky!

Surfer pushed the image out of his mind with a shudder and half turned away.

'They're late,' he commented, a little over-loudly – brightening the next second as he caught sight of two small oriental figures in colourful silk walking quickly towards him.

Surfer felt embarrassed as Suki and Silent Blade approached, then stopped and bowed in traditional greeting.

'They're kids!' Rom giggled, delighted to see Surfer so discomfited. It was true. Both Silent Blade and Suki were no older than Rom, perhaps just edging twelve. Suki seemed a little unsure of herself; fluttery like a bird, was Kilroy's comparison. The other, Silent Blade, was watchful. Kilroy looked carefully at his eyes – which even in the Web she felt were the windows to the soul. She saw nothing there she liked or particularly trusted.

Surfer made the introductions.

'Surfer's told me all about you,' Rom said, bubbling with excitement. 'It's great to see eggs like us breaking through the first-five-double-zero so early in life. Welcome!'

Suki's eyes twinkled with acknowledgement. 'We are brother and sister,' she answered, 'though very different, as our in-game selves reflect.' She indicated Silent Blade, who was half a head taller. 'And we play in the 'castle zone all the time we can. Our parents think there is much to be gained – much respect and honour – in successfully solving the Dreamcastle's challenges.'

'Much respect, much honour,' Silent Blade added unexpectedly. His voice was slow and careful, and empty of emotion. Kilroy found herself a little unnerved by his presence, without knowing why.

Surfer smiled, obviously not sharing her concerns. 'Well there's a thought to take home to the Old Guy . . . Um, this is all very cosy, but you realize we can't just team up and be chums. We need first to assess each other's capabilities in a simulation.'

Both Suki and Silent Blade looked puzzled. Rom was furious.

'Curl up, Surfer! These kids are ultra-v, if anyone is. They've already proved themselves in-game.'

'Yeah, but they're unknown, and a possible risk.'

'This is so gag!' Rom came back, almost shouting it. 'They welcomed *you* to top level, if I remember rightly. *You're* the one who needs to prove himself!'

'Please, there is no need,' Suki remonstrated, moving between Rom and Surfer to calm them. 'We are both happy to trust you, Surfer – and all of you.'

'Why don't we just get on with the game,' Kilroy suggested quietly. She stared at Surfer without challenge in her eyes, but with a hint of warning that he was making a fool of himself.

Surfer looked away first. He nodded.

'OK, let's do it.'

He reached out his hand to hold Kilroy's, who linked with Rom. Suki and Silent Blade joined themselves to the group, and the five stepped through the shimmering virtual wall of the Website, through an instant of blue-and-tone confusion—

—Into a small stone ante-chamber. The walls were running with water and slimed with green algae.

'D-box,' Surfer said, conjuring one up with a few deft jabs at his wristpad.

A crystal lattice materialized and unfolded like a complex flower to offer up its items of information.

'Wow,' Rom breathed, as exhilaration flashed through Surfer's body.

'Level five-o-six. We're in. We've broken through.'

'Now it gets tougher,' Kilroy cautioned.

Surfer grinned at her fiercely. 'The only way is up. Let's go.'

As they made their way along the dim stone corridor, with Surfer taking the lead, the others decided on slight modifications to their weaponry, utilities and virtual forms. Both Suki and Silent Blade morphed into personas a few years older than their real selves. Burnished leather armour bulged impressively around Silent Blade's muscular figure; while a scimitar that stood shoulder high to him glittered into being in his hands. Suki became taller, leaner, her proportions altering subtly until she looked as though she could move with the speed of a whiplash. And what Surfer had taken at first glance to be ornate items of belt-jewellery, he saw with a start were an array of gleaming darts, barbs and throwing stars.

He found himself feeling better already.

Within a few minutes' Webtime, they came to the end of the corridor. It opened out into a vast domed chamber that rang with faint echoes, and was bathed in a sombre light. That came in part from pitch torches burning in iron sconces affixed here and there along the walls, and from the filmy glow of enchantment. The air was rich with magic.

'In the top levels,' Suki whispered close by Surfer's ear, 'you will find that sorcery plays a much more important role in the 'castle's affairs.'

Surfer clenched his fists nervously. He was a fighter, not a mage, and knew he had no way of meeting spellwork with steel.

'Ahead,' Kilroy said, pointing a trembling finger.

The far side of the chamber was not sheer, but rose in a sweeping flight of broad stone steps towards a series of staggered galleries that disappeared upwards into the darkness. On one of the lower platforms, a hooded warlock seemed to be busy at his craft. Surfer knew from having talked with other players that warlocks were not straightforward opponents. They used enchantments and magics of many kinds to achieve their ends; casting spells, creating deceits and illusions; blurring the boundaries of this reality-within-reality.

This mage was stooping over a cauldron of black metal, ornately carved with redly glowing runes and dragon figures. Crimson smoke alight with yellow flame poured upward, mushrooming out far above into a purple haze busy with electrical sparks.

'Weavework,' Suki muttered ominously. 'He is a creator of monsters.'

'Do we destroy him?' Rom wondered.

Suki shook her head. 'We talk with him – if he will let us.'

And saying this, she moved forward with a lithe grace that the others found startling.

Gaining confidence from Suki, Surfer followed, with Silent Blade to his right and Kilroy, serious-faced, to his left. Rom brought up the rear.

They were halfway across the stone chamber when the warlock noticed them, perhaps having heard a slight footfall.

He spun round, his old man's features sliding into those of a red-faced reptile, flickering a blue tongue.

With a roar the mage hurled a charm of repulsion. Everyone scattered as the fizzing green ball sizzled between them, striking the worn flagstones at Rom's feet.

The slabs split apart, crumbling to dust and falling away into an unimaginable depth. The illusion was so real, and so frightening, that Surfer and his friends were overwhelmed by it. For just these few moments, it was the most convincing thing they had ever experienced.

Rom's scream filled the chamber and raked shrill claws of sound on the vaulted roof. He tried to correct his balance, tried to hurl himself sideways and back—

'Rom!' Kilroy yelled, lunging to catch him.

But the floor was collapsing, caving in under them.

Surfer grabbed Kilroy's arm and swung her out of the way to safety.

They watched in horror as Rom's twisting body tumbled amidst the cascading rubble and disappeared from view.

CHAPTER FOUR

FIREDRAKE

Kilroy reacted first. She flung herself on to her stomach, her head, arms and shoulders leaning over the sagging, splitting edge of the pit.

'Come away!' shrieked Suki's voice, shrill with alarm. 'It will destroy you too!' She and Silent Blade were hanging back, not daring to come closer. Surfer wondered why, since they were both experienced players who had surely passed many tests of bravery in their VR adventures.

Kilroy paid Suki no attention. By craning forward to the limit of safety, she was able to see Rom dangling from a bent spar of iron just a metre below. He looked frightened, of course – but more than that he looked shocked. Kilroy knew why. In the lower levels of the game, a crisis or enemy never came without a sign of some kind, even if it was vague or cryptic. But here, in the upper reaches of Dreamcastle, menace could spring unexpectedly from any direction, snatching the unwary player away without warning.

The only things that would prevent all of them being beaten would be vigilance, courage and comradeship.

'Come away,' Suki yelled again, distracting Kilroy momentarily.

'I'm not leaving him!' she snapped back, while her mind struggled to find a way of reaching Rom.

All of them knew he was in no actual danger. Even if his grip on the iron spar failed him and he fell, he could scuttle out of VR and leave the Web instantly. And even if he didn't, the Websuit would do this for him automatically. But the consequences for the group would be disastrous. Rom's skills had helped them to break through to this new region of the gamezone, and his continued support was going to be invaluable. If he was 'killed' in-game, he'd be forced to start playing again from scratch. That would mean that Surfer and Kilroy would have to go on alone, perhaps teaming up with Suki and Silent Blade if things turned out right with them.

'Rom!' Kilroy called. 'Are you all right?'

He looked up, white-faced.

'Can't hang on for long, Kilroy.' It was as though he expected wipeout.

'OK. Do your best.' Kilroy turned her head and called, 'Surfer—'

'Here,' Surfer said.

'Grab my ankles, I'm going to try to reach him.'

'The warlock's escaping,' Surfer replied, to Kilroy's astonishment and indeed outrage. 'I need to catch him and question him.'

In a fury, Kilroy twisted round and saw Surfer hesitating some metres behind her. Beyond him, the mage who had caused this damage was hurrying as fast as his frail body would take him up the stone steps to the higher galleries of the chamber.

'Let Suki and Silent Blade pursue him.' Kilroy's voice was crackling with anger. 'Help me to rescue Rom. Do the right thing, Surfer!'

Surfer's face registered his own temper, as well as indecision. Kilroy turned her back on him, concentrating on judging how much farther she could lean out towards Rom. Luckily, although the pit-trap had been cunningly devised, it was supported by a clever lattice of iron spars in order to take the weight of the flagstones and of people moving across them.

So although the stones on which Kilroy lay sagged alarmingly as she edged forward and a small shower of rubble dropped down, they did not disintegrate. She wriggled forward another handspan. And another.

Then she felt strong hands gripping her ankles.

'Just hurry it up,' came Surfer's gruff voice behind her.

Kilroy smiled without replying.

'I'm slipping!' Rom squealed, real fear putting an edge to his voice.

'Hold on, Rom, I'm nearly there!'

Risking her own safety, Kilroy dared to push herself out until her entire upper body was over the edge, but now at least she could bend at the waist, and in this position stretch her hands to within a finger-length of Rom.

'Can you reach up?'

He began to try, then screamed as the bar started bending, lowering him away from Kilroy.

'I can't . . . do it!'

Kilroy opened her mouth to shout more encouragement.

It stayed open, but no sound emerged.

Far below in the dreadful bottom of the pit, something like a vast and terrible eye was opening, its grey iron iris spiralling outwards. The pupil of that eye was not dark, but the very opposite; a white incandescence was building there, bubbling towards an explosion.

'Oh no!' she breathed, as the eruption came and a column of flame surged softly and swiftly up the shaft.

It was a firedrake, a legendary terror to those who were new to the gamezone, but a monstrous reality now. The Web's quicktime seemed to grow sluggish around her. Kilroy heard herself grinding out a warning to Surfer, but the words felt like molasses in her mouth. It seemed an age before he responded, pulling her with an agonizing slowness out of the hideous fire-creature's path.

Kilroy watched the white flames streaming like a vapour, whirling and writhing as they changed colour through yellow and orange to a gorgeous, evil vermilion. She knew that Rom had surely been engulfed.

When she had been dragged far enough back on to the platform, Kilroy scrambled to her feet and dived away, pushing Surfer bodily as she did so.

An instant afterwards, the firedrake gushed out of the pit

with a roar and a painful blast of heat. It immediately bloomed outwards, brushing them both with its burning wings – but then retreated, gathering back to its lair, as though it knew its energy would be dissipated if it tried to remain in the huge chamber for long.

The monster took the loose remnants of the platform with it, drawing down the stone and iron and other rubble deep, deep into the under-cellars of the 'castle.

It was gone as quickly as it had appeared, leaving Kilroy dazzled by its after-image; and the hot, dry air of the chamber alive with hissing echoes.

Without looking at the others, Kilroy went to the rim of the pit and peered over.

Everything had changed, been sucked down to destruction. The hanging platform and the iron spars were gone.

And Rom was nowhere to be seen.

Kilroy felt stunned by the speed and suddenness with which it had all happened. When Surfer came up beside her and put his hand consolingly on her shoulder, she felt too tired and drained to shrug free of him.

'It's the price we paid for thinking we knew it all!' she spat bitterly.

'No.' Surfer's voice was calm and almost matter-of-fact. *'We just didn't know enough.'*

She turned to face him. Surfer lifted his eyes and pointed upwards. Following his lead, Kilroy stared up and now, too late, could see the ancient marks of scorching on the domed ceiling of the chamber.

'The signs were there, but we weren't sharp enough to spot them. It's a lesson learned.'

'Is that all you've got to say?' Kilroy let her pent-up emotion come out. 'Is that all this means to you? Rom's been wiped out of the game.'

'He'll find another. And besides, after this we can meet him in the Cyber Diner and he can tell us what it was like to be eaten by a firedrake!'

Surfer's face broke into a cheerful grin. Kilroy wanted to slap him – and might have done if Suki's thin voice had not called down to them from the shadowed upper galleries of the chamber.

'They went after the warlock,' Surfer explained. He became serious, seeing Kilroy's expression. 'I did my best to help you, and Rom. I didn't want him to get wiped.'

'I'm going to see him.' Kilroy's voice was flat and determined. 'Are you coming?'

Surfer stared at her defiantly, then shook his head. 'You know how the game works. Even if we find this chamber next time, the warlock will have gone. The patterns in Dreamcastle are forever shifting. We won't get this opportunity again, unless one of us stays to see it through.'

'Let Suki and Silent Blade catch him and question him,' she said simply.

His eyes locked momentarily with Kilroy's. Then, abruptly, Surfer turned and walked briskly to the steps, breaking into a run as he mounted them.

Kilroy watched him out of sight. He didn't once look back to see if she had stayed.

The steps seemed to rise up and up for ever into the shadows under the huge domed ceiling of the chamber. Sometimes the galleries on to which they led stopped suddenly and Surfer could lean over and gaze down from a dizzying height to the floor. There he could see the dully glowing pit from which the firedrake had emerged, and nearby he spotted Kilroy's tiny form. She waved, then touched the keypad on her wrist to leave the game. Surfer watched her fade like smoke before he moved on.

He felt a brief pang of fondness for her, recognizing Kilroy as a true friend. She had risked her own status in the game to save Rom, and he knew she would do as much for him. It would be foolish to abandon her, and he thought fleetingly about what Philippa Stephens was like in Realworld—

Suki's voice drifted to him from somewhere even higher.

Startled out of his daydreams, Surfer turned and hurried back along the gallery. He bounded up another twenty or so steps, coming out into a small chamber from which at least a dozen passageways radiated.

Suki was calling from one of them, her voice haunting, and as delicate as eggshell. For a second or two, Surfer was tempted to answer her. But then instinctive caution restrained him.

If he'd learned anything at all, it was that the upper levels of Dreamcastle were places of deception and lies. He knew from experience that he could trust Kilroy and Rom, but everything else was new and untested. Could he rely on Suki and Silent Blade as friends? Indeed, did the voice he could still hear ringing in the corridor belong to Suki at all?

This could so easily be another trap. Besides, now that his eyes had adjusted to the shadows, he was able to make out a faint light shining in one of the other passages. It was the pale whitish light of the *outside* rather than the redder flickering of flames. And that gave Surfer an idea.

Ignoring Suki, he followed the glow of light for perhaps fifty metres or so, cheered to see it brightening moment by moment. After a few minutes, rounding a gentle bend, he saw a vaulted portal and wide outer balcony beyond.

Drawing his sword as a precaution, Surfer made his way to where the corridor ended. From just inside its broad arch, he could feel the cool wind of the late afternoon brushing past his face. The sky outside was wispy with high cloud, saturated with pinks and oranges and yellows by the deepening light of the sinking sun.

Remembering his earlier experience with the stormdragon, Surfer moved carefully on to the balcony, keeping a wary eye for any sudden danger.

He stepped over to the edge, dropped to one knee and gazed down.

The ground was a terrifying distance away. As his mind struggled with the scale of things, the immense walls of the 'castle looked for a fleeting second like a colossal cobbled road, stretching straight ahead to a cliff-face of bottle-green pine forest.

There were barriers built along the road. Surfer shook his

head and blinked, realizing that what he was looking at were other balconies below.

Suddenly, his eyes flashed with excitement, for there, two balconies beneath, he could see where he'd crashed through the ivy to break his fall from the sky. And hundreds of metres beneath that, was the black crater in the forest where the stormdragon had smashed into the ground.

'Yes!' Surfer said, clenching his fist in triumph. 'Yes!'

There could be no mistake. Pure chance perhaps had brought him to a point – in all the vast labyrinth of the Dreamcastle – only a short distance above the room where he'd seen the girl of his dreams.

CHAPTER FIVE

AFTERTHOUGHTS

The Websickness hadn't lasted long, and had not been severe enough to put Rom off his favourite cola drink. He came out of the showers, went into the Cyber Diner and ordered a large one, though he didn't bother with the chocolate doughnuts that were on special offer this week.

A couple of vets who knew him came over to say bad luck and wish him well in his climb back up to status in the 'castle. Rom thanked them with a wan smile, which grew warmer as he spotted Kilroy. She was still wearing her Websuit, its glittering contacts dangling from wrists and collar. Her hair was darkened and damp with sweat.

She dropped down into a seat beside Rom, did nothing for a second, then leaned across and hugged him.

'Does this mean we're getting engaged?' he wanted to know, trying to lighten the weight of her mood.

Kilroy's face was serious as she leaned back. Rom pushed his cola across and she took a guzzle.

'I'm so sorry about what happened. We should have been more alert.'

'It's only a game,' Rom pointed out, though the pain of losing it was like a tight fist in his chest.

'If only Surfer hadn't gone chasing after that warlock. What a one-mip idiot he is!'

Rom put his hand on Kilroy's where it rested on the table. 'Kilroy,' he repeated softly, but firmly, 'it's only a game.'

She looked at him with moist eyes. 'A game he's determined to win at any cost. I waited for him, but he'd gone into the chamber's upper galleries and I lost sight of him. More stupidity!'

Rom nodded, then said, 'Do you want to see what he's up to on the observer screen?'

'No. I don't like being watched myself – all those basement-level silkies getting their kicks by watching me work. It's perverse.'

Rom lifted his eyebrows, saying nothing. It was a regular thing for Webheads below your level in any gamezone to look-in on vets' adventures. They saw it as a learning experience. And the game manufacturers and advertising companies encouraged it, too, to attract more phreaks into the Web.

But Rom knew what Kilroy meant, though he put it down to her being especially upset at the moment.

'Besides,' she added, 'I'm feeling pretty vommy. How did it affect you this time?'

'Not too bad, but worse than usual.'

She nodded, wiping a wet lick of hair away from her face. 'I've been noticing that. You think it's a fault in the kit?'

Rom shrugged. 'More likely we're just not used to such power-gaming. Dreamcastle is a high-quality graphics game, and it gets better as you go higher. But that more intense experience is bound to have a kickback. I reckon the voms will get worse before they get better.'

'That's a cheering thought,' Kilroy said, grinning at Rom with a hint of her usual spirit.

'Thanks for trying to save me,' he said.

'What else was there to do?'

'Help Surfer catch the warlock.'

'Curl up,' Kilroy replied lightly. 'Surfer's after bonuses and cred. He's also chasing a rival of mine, someone I've never even met!'

'Ann Onymous.'

They both laughed at the tag, then Kilroy's mouth tightened.

'It's unreal, Rom. To think Surfer's more interested in a girl he's glimpsed in *Dreamcastle* than in me. I mean, she probably lives on the other side of the world. She might even be a phace!'

The idea delighted her fleetingly, until she saw something in Rom's eyes that dampened her confidence in the idea. Rom was thinking of the way he'd been spidered-out the day before when he attempted to find out more about the mysterious girl. True, that might simply have been the constraints of the program itself; but more likely, he thought, she was a high-level player who was deliberately keeping her personal data cloaked.

'I could try to find out more,' he offered – a little hesitantly, because too great a transgression of the game's rules could result in a fine or a ban, which wouldn't attract sympathy from anyone. 'At least,' Rom added, backing off a step, 'I might be able to help you from the outside.'

'That would be great. I'd appreciate that. And I know Surfer will too.'

Rom smiled and finished his drink. 'I think I'll start by checking out our new friends, Suki and Silent Blade. There's something about them I don't trust.'

'I'll go with that,' Kilroy said. She wrinkled her nose and looked down at herself. 'I stink. I'm going to shower and head home. I've a stack of work to catch up on.'

'Copy that, Kilroy. I'll get busy chasing the fade. Maybe see you tomorrow?'

'It's a schoolday, but I'll be here in the evening.'

'See you then,' Rom said warmly as Kilroy stood, turned, and walked briskly towards the shower area.

Suki was waiting in the chamber when Surfer returned. She bowed, and Surfer was amused at the continuance of this Realworld politeness in-game.

He bowed back without mockery.

'What did you find?' Suki wondered. Surfer looked back along the corridor.

'Dead end. Leads to the outside. What about you?'

'I think we've found the warlock,' she said, small-voiced.

Surfer was startled for a moment. Then he frowned. 'You *think* you found him?'

'I'll show you.'

She led the way along another passage, which branched after twenty metres or so. Surfer paused to sheathe his sword, his fingers deftly flipping open a small pouch on his belt.

'Is Silent Blade with him – the warlock, I mean?' he asked.

Suki gave a ghastly smile. 'Not *him*, Surfer. Wait and see.'

He walked on with her silently, noting the corridor branched again and again until, without his companion's sense of direction, he would've become hopelessly lost.

'Just ahead,' Suki said presently, pointing into the torchlit gloom.

Within the leaping shadowdance of the flames, Surfer caught sight of Silent Blade. He was standing, his hands nested on the hilt of the great scimitar, standing guard over a shapeless mass on the ground.

The thing looked quite dead and, as Surfer approached, he became sure it was. The monster had the appearance of a reptile; a two-legged greyish lizard as big as a man but grotesquely different from any human being. Its red-green eyes were dulled in death, half-hooded by membranous lids. The thing's mouth was open, its sharp white teeth stained pink by blood. Looking more closely, easing aside the material of its voluminous caul, Surfer saw the deep gash where Silent Blade's scimitar had struck. It had been a fatal blow, with no attempt on the warrior's part to disable the mage and question it.

'I suppose it was self defence,' Surfer said to Silent Blade with a cool irony.

'Self defence,' Silent Blade replied like an echo. The thought flickered across Surfer's mind that maybe Silent Blade himself was a Non-Player-Character, created by Suki for company and safety. Certainly most opponents would think twice about attacking Suki if Silent Blade was nearby. It made sense, then, that Silent Blade said very little; he was here for his formidable appearance and not his conversation. It also explained why Surfer felt there was more to

Suki than met the eye – hidden depths that might yet prove dangerous.

Surfer glanced again at the slain reptile. His experience of warlocks in the lower levels was that they'd been a cowardly lot, eager to turn and run rather than do battle with hot-blooded adventurers. The Web's NPC warlocks were pro-grammed that way. The realoes did it by choice, most of them being interested in bootstrapping by solving cryptic clues rather than fighting.

Surfer lifted a fluttering torch from its rusted bracket on the wall, and swept it this way and that above the warlock's body.

He paused, startled, as a chime sounded in the air and a small purple spider scuttled out of the darkness.

'Oh,' Suki said. 'Our time's up, Surfer. We have to leave. It is late for us, and our parents will want us to return home now.'

'You could always squash the spider and play on,' Surfer said with deliberate mischief, noting Suki's smile in reply was uncertain.

'We have to go. But we have enjoyed meeting you, Surfer – and Rom and Kilroy too. And we are sorry about Rom.'

'It happens,' Surfer said flatly.

'We will meet you again tomorrow, perhaps. We will leave a clipnote. Goodbye.'

'Hey, but—'

It was too late. Suki and Silent Blade's computer-generated forms were changing, swirling into a delicate spiral of disintegrating pixels that bloomed apart like rainbow dust before fading.

Surfer watched them until there was nothing left. Then he grinned and loomed towards the spider.

'Boo!' he said, laughing as it did a cartoonlike leap into the air, then turned and hurried away.

Standing alone in the corridor, Surfer felt strangely calm and reassured. He knew, suddenly and without doubt, that he had been lured into a clever trap. Suki had deliberately led him along these featureless corridors without suggesting they mark their path. Then she and her brother had deserted him here, hoping he'd stumble into danger perhaps, or simply wander aimlessly, losing points.

And the trap might have worked, too, if Surfer hadn't taken the precaution of scattering tag-stars along the route, so that he could get back to the huge vaulted chamber. That forethought had bought him some time, although he knew he shouldn't linger too long. Kilroy might still be waiting. But apart from that, he was alone here on alien ground, a potentially dangerous situation.

Working quickly, he examined the body of the dead mage. It was one of the underlying principles of Dreamcastle that something of significance was always there to be found. The warlock would be loaded with symbols and clues that might help Surfer to battle to higher levels if he read them right. But things never came easy, not this far in. There could be traps – and there was certainly a time limit. Already the torch he was holding had started to fade, as were those all along the corridor.

Surfer felt frustration with himself building inside him – frustration that he did not know what he should be looking for.

Not far away, two torches fizzled out in a flutter of dying flames. Surfer felt suddenly that the darkness beyond them seemed to be moving – seemed to be alive.

'Come on. Come on!' He pulled aside another layer of the warlock's robing and thrust his left hand inside.

Now his own torch was guttering out, blinking the darkness on and off, on and off, on and off . . .

Surfer cursed and flung it to the ground – then grinned as he caught sight of the answer to his unspoken question.

The voms were worse than he'd ever experienced before, and Surfer just had time to run from the VR suite to the toilets before he was sick. It puzzled him, because Websickness was caused by confused signals to the brain as you moved in-game, but they stayed relatively still in reality. Today he'd only climbed steps and walked corridors. He hadn't even exerted himself in helping Kilroy rescue Rom.

But whatever the reason for it, Surfer felt awful as he left the VR-bar and turned down Southland on his way home. His mood was not helped by the fact that Kilroy had not waited for him, neither in-game, nor in Realworld. Surfer guessed he couldn't blame her for that. He'd been pretty headstrong chasing after the mage, and had ignored her badly since they'd broken through to the 'castle's upper levels. He remembered his promise to Rom about letting Kilroy off the hook one way or the other. The kid was right, he shouldn't play Kilroy along by not making a decision.

The fact was, Surfer told himself as he turned into Woodvale Avenue, Kilroy was ultra-venomous all round; good looking, bright, a great gamezone companion, and she rated him. He knew he'd be stupid to tell her no. On the other hand, she did not possess the dark mystery of the girl he'd seen in the dungeon cell – someone who was equally eight lookwise, and obviously far superior to Kilroy in gaming skill. What a partner *she'd* make, on the way to the top!

It was a dilemma. Surfer knew if he kept Kilroy waiting much longer, she'd lose interest in him, and perhaps also in Dreamcastle itself. But if the mystery girl realized that he and Kilroy were together, she might have no wish to help him either.

Surfer was lost in these thoughts as he came to the junction of Woodvale and Fox, and crossed over into Trent Road.

A sudden bellowing roar snapped him out of his daydream. His head jerked up and he stared along the road towards town.

For an instant he glimpsed an electram trundling towards him, headlights flaring—

But then it was gone and the sky was filled with smoke and flames as the firedrake swept on towards him.

CHAPTER SIX

XENIA

In terror, Surfer reached for his sword, bracing himself for the firedrake's heat. But there was no sword, and the electram's horn blared as the driver swerved round Surfer, cursing.

Surfer ducked, squinting and throwing up his hands to shield his face from the hurricane of dead leaves blown along the street in the electram's wake. He stood, dazed and confused, watching the monster move out of sight at the corner of Woodvale and Trent. He followed slowly, checking his clothes for signs of scorching as he chuckled at his narrow escape. Even so, he could not stop himself shaking.

Reg Miller was off-shift today, sprawled in his usual position on the sofa. He glanced up as Surfer came into the lounge, but didn't bother to joke or jibe at his son.

'Mum around?'

'She's not back yet,' Miller said. He hooked a thumb at the TV screen. 'You ever get the news in that twilight zone of yours, Robert?'

Miller went on as he noted his son's look of puzzlement. 'They're talking about opening a Federal investigation into the long-term effects of the Web on kids. Some psychologist is saying that Websickness is just the early stage of more serious damage to the mind.'

'Hey, but look at me.' Surfer managed a cheery smile. 'I'm a picture of health!'

'You look pretty pasty, actually. Are you catching enough sleep?'

'What is all this – some clever way of getting me to follow in my daddy's footsteps?'

'Don't get smart with me, boy!' Miller's voice rose as anger flushed his face. Then he quietened, shaking his head slowly. 'Can't you see I'm just concerned? This guy, Professor Gibson I think he's called, has done some research sponsored by the Government.'

'Oh ho, so now we know whose side he's on!'

'Research which shows that for some people, spending too long in the Web can be dangerous.'

'Does he say anything about the long-term effects of wallowing around on a sofa, Dad?' Surfer hit back. He could see that his father was making a real effort to control his temper, and that behind the rage was the worried look of a parent for his child.

The trouble was, Surfer thought, he and his dad had become so used to quarrelling they seemed unable to talk in any other way. Apart from that, the Anti-Web Lobby – parents around the world who didn't want their kids in the Web, period – tried all sorts of tricks to win their case. This Professor Gibson was just another ploy by them to gain ground. Another bad guy to battle against.

He was only a phace, Surfer concluded. A nothing. The real enemy was narrow-mindedness, ignorance and fear.

Reg Miller was staring at his son in a strange way, Surfer realized, as he came back to reality.

'What's the matter with you?'

'Nothing I can't handle,' Surfer said, with unwarranted viciousness. But he realized his father was genuinely concerned – realized too that the illusion of the firedrake out in the street had unnerved him very badly.

'You were just standing there, saying nothing.'

'I'm tired, that's all.'

'Maybe I should phone for Doctor Carlson to come over and—'

Surfer's eyes flashed. 'I said, I'm just tired. Leave me alone, Dad. I'm going to sleep for a while, then I'll catch up on my school assignments, OK? You get back to your beer and baseball games,' Surfer said as he turned towards the door. 'And don't worry about me at all.'

Upstairs in his room, he stripped off his jacket and jeans, flopped on to the bed, pulled a thin coverlet over himself and dropped into a doze.

His sleep was filled with dreams. He was back in the 'castle, watching the firedrake surging up from the pit, exploding into the chamber. Then things twisted round strangely and he was out on the street. The firedrake had no limbs, but wheels, and there was the angry, frightened face of the electram driver—

Surfer screamed as it brushed by him, enveloping him briefly in its cloaks of flame. That became brown, dry autumn leaves whirling around him in clouds before being dragged down the street in the electram's slipstream. Leaves, only leaves . . . slowly turning into thousands of kids, singing and dancing as they followed the colourful leaping figure of the Pied Piper towards the darkly pulsing centre of the Web . . .

Then the street itself disappeared, morphing into a shadowed corridor of the Dreamcastle filled with a silence broken only by Suki's wind-chime laughter.

Surfer reached for his sword – only there was no sword.

He looked back to glimpse his tag-stars, but they too had vanished.

A doorway in the shadows swung open and the warlock appeared. It had the face of a reptile, and came forward slowly with a soft hissing.

Surfer cried out, finding himself cocooned in clinging cobweb. He began to struggle, but the reptile was upon him, its tongue flicking out and touching his face, its grey clawed hand reaching forward, forward for his throat—

Surfer yelled as Mrs Miller touched his brow. He startled awake, sitting upright, his eyes wide.

'Robert – for goodness' sake, what's the matter with you!'

There was a moment of complete confusion. And then Surfer laughed.

'Nothing, Mum, nothing. Just a nightmare. I'm all right now.'

Relief to be free of it flooded over him like a warm breeze. The stifling cobweb was just the coverlet of his bed, the warlock-reptile's taloned forelimb only his mother's soft and familiar hand.

She put her palm against his forehead again. 'You have a temperature. Maybe you've got a cold coming on, or a dose of the flu?'

Surfer smiled wearily. 'I'm fine, really Mum. I've had all this from Dad. Look, I've been busy with schoolwork recently and things have reached an important stage in the game-zone. But that's relaxation for me,' he added quickly to forestall any criticism. 'It's like your classes or Dad's TV shows.'

'That sounds like a flimsy explanation to me,' she said.

Surfer smiled at his mother fondly. She and his father were utterly different. Reg Miller had become wearied by the burden of his job, was hardening into his middle age as he looked out over more years of the same stretching ahead of him. But his wife had a softness about her, a kindness that was stronger than all of his anger and outrage. Sarah Miller had grown more beautiful as time went by, more graceful and understanding.

'Mum—' Surfer had been about to say, 'you remind me of someone', but the idea embarrassed him. And besides, he couldn't for the life of him think who it was she looked like.

'Mum, I just want you to know I love you – and Dad – and you mustn't worry about me at all. I won't work too hard. I won't stay out too late. I'll eat my greens . . . '

She laughed and reached out to brush Surfer's long dark hair away from his face.

'All right, we're off your back. But promise me,' she added, 'that if you're troubled by anything – anything at all – you'll come and talk to us.'

'I promise, Mum. Cross my heart . . . ' Surfer said.

Mrs Miller smiled at her son, moved away and closed the door behind her.

'And hope to die.'

*

Oakhills Senior High lay on the eastern side of town at the end of Hobbston Pike. It comprised a small cluster of modern buildings set in spacious grounds that blended into the treed acres of the Memorial Park. The new school had been created in 2016 when advances in the Web had made it possible for all children to be educated from home. Webschooling was now a universal phenomenon. Kids went into VR to complete pre-set assignments, and came to school in Realworld for only two days a week for social activities, sports, and extra lessons with in-person teachers.

But even then, computers were widely used to access databases all over the world.

Kilroy found Rom in one of the study suites. He was working with a voice-activated PC, scrolling through lists of subscriber names linked with particular gamezones and areas of Webware.

'How're you doing, Rom? Any flies yet?'

'This,' said Rom with a sigh, 'is *incredibly* cog—'

'Working,' said the synthvox in the computer, mistakenly identifying Rom's words as a prompt to complete the task.

'They've all got their own little personalities,' Kilroy chuckled, indicating the PCs nestling in the other cubicles throughout the room. All had voice-activation software, none of which was perfect. Sometimes it was like talking to a parrot, at others like conversing with a bright-minded child of six or seven.

'I've been looking for Silent Blade on the subscriber listings,' Rom said, getting back to business. Most Webheads clocked their times, high scores, clipnotes and other data under their gamer-names; it was highly six to register with a realname – this being more to do with cred than privacy.

'Can't find him?' Kilroy asked, pulling up a chair to sit beside Rom as he worked.

'Nope, nothing under Silent Blade or *Dreamcastle*-Hong Kong.'

'Any indications of cloaking?'

'Like with Ann Onymous?' Rom shook his head. 'No, he's just not there. I guess we're left with the option of going back into VR to question him personally. That is, *you're* left with the option now that I'm wiped out.' He glanced at Kilroy, not wanting sympathy – not getting any. The girl seemed uneasy about the whole thing. She was staring at the screen as though willing the data to appear.

'I didn't trust him from the start,' Kilroy began, then shrugged. 'Or maybe we're doing it wrong . . . Or perhaps there's a glitch in the protocols. Why not try for Suki?' Kilroy suggested.

'OK. Synthvox. Redefine task. Target, Suki-Dreamcastle-Hong Kong.' Rom checked a scribbled note on his pad. 'Cross-reference Surfer-Kilroy-Rom, entertainmentWebtown, Day-two-nine-eight-stroke-two-eight. Commence.'

'Task redefined,' the computer responded at once. Its voice had not been customized by a hacker with a sense of humour, so it didn't sound like a cartoon character, famous film star or TV chat show host. Rather, it possessed the smooth and calmly efficient vocals of a female airport PA system.

Rom's reference codes blipped on the screen, then shrank into a tiny box in the lower right corner. The main visual showed an endless field of fluidly waving wheat. This was a standard way of projecting numerical information; plants, trees, swarms of insects . . . It made maths more fun and number searches less tedious.

The point-of-view swooped over the field and dipped closer, so that now Rom and Kilroy could see that each ear of wheat was composed of golden reference codes and tiny dialogue boxes, clenched as tightly as flower buds waiting to blossom.

A glassy silver pointer entered the picture and indicated one particular dialogue-box.

'Reveal,' Rom commanded.

The wheat-ear expanded to fill the screen.

'Venomous!' Rom and Kilroy beamed at each other.

'Su Mai, aka Suki, nine-nine-two-zero, Canton Boulevard, Kowloon. Lots of other stuff. But it's her, Kilroy. Bang on the button.'

'Get into the persona details,' Kilroy suggested. 'See if we can trace Silent Blade that way.'

Rom nodded and, to save time, keyed in further technical instructions. one section of the main dialogue box opened like a set of nested tangrams, revealing further information.

'So,' Kilroy said a few seconds later, as the images of Suki and Silent Blade flickered together on the screen. 'Now we have the truth of it.'

And she felt herself go cold both with grief, and with fear.

Surfer e-mailed his excuses from home, leaving the house moments afterwards with a cheery goodbye to his parents. They thought he was going off to school. The school secretary thought he was spending the day at home with a bad cold.

Surfer reached the VR-bar quickly and was pleased to see it almost deserted at this time in the early afternoon on a schoolday. What he didn't want were friends or the usual crowd of egg silkies peering over his virtual shoulder while he was in-game.

But before he suited up, Surfer hooked into a standard PC terminal and checked out what he'd seen beside the reptile-warlock that Silent Blade had slain.

It was a symbol, splashed in the blood of the mage, an X-shaped rune that Surfer was now able to identify as *Gyfu*. In the fantasy-lore of Dreamcastle, it was a mark of the Dark Lord who ruled both the 'castle itself and the uncharted forests all around. *Gyfu* was also the symbol of partnership, Surfer read with interest: a gift or offering from the gods to loyal followers.

'So, even though Suki tried to trap me— Because I escaped from the trap, the Dark Lord has sent me a sign . . . made me an offering of—'

Surfer frowned. Of what? He had taken nothing away from the warlock. 'So, I missed something,' he said, realizing he'd have to go back to where the warlock was slain, and hoping that the body had remained undisturbed.

He logged-off the PC and hired out a standard Tarantula

Websuit. He went through the pre-game checks and tapped in the access codes that would take him straight into the great domed chamber where Rom had been wiped.

There was a moment's dizziness and disorientation as he batted-in. The universe spun-up to Webspeed.

Surfer found himself surrounded by shadows and echoes and the cold presence of ancient stone walls.

He swept his eyes across his virtual-self, making sure all of his weapons and utilities were in place. Then he began the long climb up the tiers of steps to the high galleries, feeling the Websuit move around him to create the illusion of effort.

Within minutes, he had found the corridor he needed. His sprinkling of tag-stars was still there, and he now followed that glittering trail until he came upon the motionless shape of the warlock.

Nothing had changed. The dark maroon caul of the mage – so dark it looked almost black – still shrouded the creature's twisted form. The X-shaped splash of blood stained the stones besides its head.

But now, looking carefully for clues, Surfer noted that the arm of the mage, flung out as though in agony, was pointing along the corridor. The three fingers of the reptile hand were splayed wide. On the middle finger was a ring of black iron in which was set a purple stone.

Surfer knelt and drew the ring free. He held it up to the torchlight, tilting it this way and that. At certain angles the light caught something deep in the crystal – a twist of brilliant silver in the shape of an X.

'Yes!' Surfer clenched his fist in triumph, knowing from previous adventures in the gamezone that the ring was a key that would open the way to higher levels, further successes, greater glory.

But there had to be more. A key unlocked doors. Which doors, and where, Surfer didn't yet know.

He glanced again at the warlock, and in a flash knew which way to go.

Slipping the rune-ring on the middle finger of his left hand, he found it fitted perfectly. With his sword gripped in his right hand, Surfer jogged along the passage in the direction the dead mage was indicating.

After a minute or so he came to a huge iron door set in the wall, but passed it by. The ring had been on the middle finger of three – the second door.

Surfer found it moments later. It was identical to the first – solid, imposing, and with no obvious lock mechanism.

The torches along the walls were fewer here, and burned only dimly. Surfer studied the door very closely before he found a small oval indentation in the metal, the size and shape of a starling's egg. Cut into the bottom of the dent was an X-shaped mark.

With his heart beating faster, Surfer pressed the ring into the hollow. The purple jewel blazed brilliantly for a second, and a brief and sudden heat flared through his hand. A curl of blue smoke trickled upwards from the cavity as Surfer withdrew the ring and pushed the great door open.

It swung wide revealing . . . nothing.

Surfer looked each way along the gloomy corridor before stepping into the cell. He slipped a dagger from his belt and wedged it under the iron door to prevent it from swinging closed behind him. Then he examined the room more closely.

It was a standard prison chamber – square, bleak, depressing. A tiny barred window showed an unimposing overcast sky. On the adjacent wall, chains hung rusting and unused. *She* had never been here, and yet the message of the rune seemed so clear.

With an impatient sigh, Surfer ran his eyes across the floor of huge square flagstones lightly covered with straw.

Nine flagstones, Surfer counted, a slow smile spreading over his face.

Three rows of three.

He knelt on the central flagstone, sweeping away the dirty straw with both hands to reveal a similar egg-shaped depression to that he'd found in the door.

Hurriedly, Surfer pressed the ring home. The crystal blazed and a section of the stone seemed to melt away, bringing an iron pull-ring into view.

Surfer scrambled up and stood astride the slab. He took a firm grip on the ring and heaved, marvelling all over again at the Websuit's ability to recreate the fantasy of weight and inertia.

Slowly, the flagstone lifted and swung to the side. Surfer pivoted it further and released his hold. The stone fell with a dull boom and cracked apart.

Eagerly, he dropped on to all fours and peered into the cell beneath.

The girl was watching him closely, the look on her face suggesting that she knew all along he'd be coming.

'Hello, Surfer.' She smiled, and Surfer thought she was beautiful. 'My name is Xenia.'

SISTER'S SECRET

It felt strange for Kilroy to be going in alone, and with Rom like a guardian angel riding at her side. His wipeout in Dreamcastle meant that he could be with her in Webtown but as soon as she entered the 'castle gamezone itself, she and Rom would be separated – unless Kilroy also opted to begin again at ground level. But that would be pointless because it was Surfer who needed her help . . . Surfer, and possibly Suki too, now that her secret was out.

Webtown was busy today, with vets, gamers and the usual cog silky basement-levels hanging around for free advice and contacts. Kilroy ignored them all. She'd set up this meet with Suki via a clipnote, and hoped she'd come alone. If Silent Blade accompanied her, then whoever was *behind* Silent Blade would know that Kilroy had been digging for data.

And Kilroy now knew how dangerous that could be.

'Any sign?' Rom said, his voice in miniature through the microphone link at Kilroy's left ear. In reality, she and Rom were sitting side by side in the VR-bar; Kilroy in full Tarantula, Rom in gag. He needed only partial immersion, with the ability to skim out of VR quickly to access external databases when necessary.

'You sound like Jiminy Cricket.' Kilroy smiled and broke into laughter at Rom's peep of outrage at the notion. 'No,' she added, 'no sign of her yet . . . Wait a minute. Yes, I see her now by the Raid display. You got good visuals?'

'Not as good as yours,' Rom said with a hint of frustration.

His glove and glasses kit allowed him to see Webtown without appearing as a persona within it. So, he moved invisibly at Kilroy's side, picking up some but not all of the details of her virtual experience.

Suki caught sight of Kilroy a second later. She waved, but not, it seemed to Kilroy, with her original enthusiasm. The little Chinese girl's face looked troubled, as though she knew what Kilroy was going to say to her.

'OK, Rom,' Kilroy cautioned. 'Not a word now. I want Suki to think I'm entirely alone.'

'Copy that,' Rom said briskly. There came the click of the external mike closing down.

Kilroy was the first to make the formal bow, which she did as a mark of respect to Suki, who echoed the gesture. Then she said seriously, 'Why did you want me here, Kilroy? I do not understand your reasons.'

'Like I said, it's girl talk. You know how I feel about Surfer, and I'm jealous, I guess, of this other girl he's discovered in the 'castle.'

The words came out easily, but the lie sounded feeble. Kilroy could see by Suki's eyes that she didn't believe it for a second.

Kilroy dropped the pretence. She shrugged. 'OK, it's not girl talk. But I suppose it is about Surfer – and it's about Silent Blade, too.'

In the early days of the Web, computer graphics would only have allowed a realoe with a plastic-looking face to register the most obvious of emotions. Now, with unimaginable processing power maintaining it, the image of Suki – which was in every detail identical with her realself – seemed to deflate. Her shoulders sagged, her eyes darkened with sorrow, and a tear of glittering pixels appeared and quivered down on to her cheek.

'He's dead, isn't he, Suki?' Kilroy said gently. It was not really a question. The conclusion she and Rom had reached was the only one possible.

Suki nodded miserably, and began to sob.

'He— he— Kilroy, I miss him so!'

Kilroy put her arms around Suki and hugged her. And perhaps for the first time in her life, Kilroy blessed the technology that allowed her to offer this comfort, to someone sitting alone over twenty thousand kilometres away.

'We need to talk. Let's out-space.'

Kilroy led Suki through the bustling streets of Webtown to a nearby block. Like the others, its liquid-looking faces rippled with colourful advertising which the girls through habit ignored. Kilroy used her wristpad to arrange to buy space, and a few moments later the 'Transaction Confirmed' message bloomed on the wall in front of them.

The girls armlinked and stepped through into a private area, like a small room which had hundreds of items of furniture, ornaments and pictures floating as images within the walls. Kilroy went over and touched a couple of comfortable chairs. They appeared instantly in interactive 3-D on the floor.

The girls sat down.

'Tell me about him?' Kilroy urged.

Suki wiped her eyes, brushing away her real tears in a VR-bar in Hong Kong.

'We had played Dreamcastle together for a few years. It brought us closer.' Suki smiled. 'K'ai was always very serious – quietly serious. But in the gamezone he allowed himself to have some fun. Our parents, they encouraged us this way. They said it was good we should influence each other, each giving something of value. K'ai gave me strength and courage. And I needed that, after he was gone.'

'How did he die, Suki?' Kilroy's voice was almost a whisper.

Suki shrugged bleakly. 'It was just a silly accident . . . On the roads . . . A car—'

Kilroy's virtual fingers reached out and she squeezed Suki's hand.

'I'm sorry. You must love him very much.'

'I do.' Suki looked up and smiled through her grief. 'He is a wonderful brother. He will grow up into a fine young man, and I will be so proud.'

Kilroy felt a strange shiver run through her body. It had nothing to do with the Websuit.

'Suki, that is what I don't understand. K'ai has gone, and yet you keep Silent Blade alive in the Web, treating him as though he was real. Silent Blade is only a phace, a creation of the software.'

'No.' Suki's head moved to and fro, almost dreamily. Kilroy felt the first tingles of worry.

'But you can't believe K'ai is still with you. No phace can be so detailed that you truly think it is alive.'

'He lives, he grows as I grow. He talks to me, teaches me things.'

'K'ai is dead,' Kilroy insisted.

'No!' Suki's fury flared in an instant. She leaped from her seat, her fingers hooked to rake at Kilroy's face and eyes.

Instinctively, Kilroy grabbed the younger girl's hands, before realizing that she could not be physically harmed in the Web. The Tarantula powersuit was unable to create sensations of acute pain, or inflict damage, though mild discomforts were possible.

But for a few seconds the two girls struggled, oceans apart, until the wave of Suki's emotion had crashed and she slumped down on her knees at Kilroy's feet.

'He's not dead, he's not!' she protested. 'She said he would live if—'

Suki's eyes looked away. She bit her lip.

'What are you talking about?' Kilroy wondered, her worry blossoming into something greater; into a real and tangible fear. 'Tell me, Suki,' she demanded. 'Who said K'ai would live?'

'She—' Suki giggled crazily, as though her mind was balancing on a brink. 'The One who lives at the heart of *Dreamcastle*.'

Surfer briskly checked the chains that bound the girl to the damp dungeon wall, then the manacles locking her hands. He saw that her skin was torn, the metal smeared with blood, and was startled at the realism of the illusion.

'I knew you'd come for me,' Xenia said. She seemed unconcerned with her plight.

'How did you know?'

'You have that look about you – the look of an adventurer.'

Surfer glanced up. He felt flattered; and then, more powerfully, drawn by her nearness and beauty.

Xenia was tall and pale, her hair long and the colour of straw, tangled at the moment, even unkempt. Strands of it brushed over the back of Surfer's hands. Again he felt a mild shock that the Websuit should be able to recreate such subtle details.

He grinned, suddenly slightly embarrassed.

'This is a really cliché situation. I mean, damsel in distress rescued by daring young hero. Real life isn't at all like this, you know.'

'Do you think I'm beautiful?' Xenia asked. To Surfer her presence was overwhelming; her realism unique.

'Well . . . yes.'

'And can you rescue me?' she wanted to know.

Surfer drew a length of diamond wire from his beltpouch and set about sawing through the iron chains and fetters.

The first parted after a minute's work. He was halfway through the second when there came a dull *boom* from somewhere deep in the 'castle, and the slow scream of a heavy door opening.

'What's that?' Surfer paused in his labour, his right hand dropping to the hilt of his sword.

'The Dark Lord,' Xenia said casually, 'or one of his multitude. He knows you are here, Surfer. You understand he will try to stop you from getting any closer.'

'That's what the fun's all about,' he replied, his cocky smile fading as it came to him that Xenia might be talking about something else entirely.

'We'd better leave,' Surfer said, his voice clipped now. For the first time since entering the gamezone today, he felt vulnerable without the company of Kilroy and Rom. Without one or other of them as lookouts, he had no way of knowing who or what was coming up the corridor, and how far away it might be.

He used the diamond wire deftly and the second manacle fell apart, clattering at Xenia's feet. Surfer touched the blood on her wrist and felt it slick between his fingers.

There came another booming echo from the depths of the 'castle, and something that sounded like a large animal snuffling.

'Time to go.'

Surfer took Xenia's hand and led her to stand beneath the opening in the ceiling from which he'd descended.

'If he catches us—' Xenia said breathlessly.

Surfer opened his mouth to reply. But in that instant his words were drowned out by a huge roaring from just beyond the door.

His first impulse was to draw his sword – but the foolish-ness of actually trying to *fight* the Dark Lord on their first encounter was obvious. Instead, Surfer gripped Xenia firmly around the waist. 'Haul yourself up,' he instructed, lifting her so she could reach the lip of the trapdoor opening.

Xenia grunted with the effort, but after a moment pulled herself through, then turned and reached down to help Surfer.

Something vast slammed into the dungeon door, and the roaring came again, redoubled. Whoever or whatever the Dark Lord might be, it was either too stupid or too enraged to use a key. Instead, the thing was attempting to hammer its way in.

And it would soon succeed, Surfer realized, his mouth opening in astonishment to see the ten-mill iron plating buckle inwards, the stones of the doorframe beginning to shatter.

'Surfer!' Xenia called.

Surfer tore his eyes away from the sight of the door *bulging inwards*. He took Xenia's outstretched hand and was drawn up towards the opening.

This feat was almost as impressive as the Dark Lord's destructive power. Any player's strength in VR was partly a factor of the basic rules of the game, but also varied according to the nature of your bonuses. If a gamer had earned plenty through previous success, he or she could 'spend' them on added strength, or speed, or better eyesight, or magical powers.

Xenia had obviously done just this. But to have hefted Surfer's weight so easily, she must have gathered an astonishing number of bonus points, and would have required a Websuit that would make the Tarantula look basement-level six.

These thoughts flew through Surfer's mind and were then dispelled by the thunderous crash of the cell door hurtling inwards and smashing against the opposite wall. Stone fragments showered everywhere, one sharp splinter catching the back of Surfer's hand. He yelped with the sudden hurt of it and the appearance of a bright slash of blood, feeling shocked that the pain created by the Websuit should be quite so intense.

White smoke billowed into the room, streaked through with unhealthy curls and spirals of yellowish vapour. The creature entered and moved within the fog, a bulking shape emitting a low crackling growl from deep in its throat. The thing was much bigger than a man, low slung, as though prowling close to the floor. Fleetingly, Surfer caught sight of its hand – massive, black and leathery, the claws curled and split like old ivory. The limb looked large enough to encircle his chest and then, with effortless ease, to crush it.

Xenia pulled Surfer through to safety. He scrambled up and leaned over to peer back down into the cell below. He wanted a better look at the Dark Lord – wanted to see the face of his enemy – but Xenia cautioned him with a slight shake of her head. She drew him silently towards the open door of the cell.

'I knew you'd solve the puzzle of the rune,' she told him with a sparkling smile. They were walking quickly back along the corridor to the colossal vaulted dome. It seemed to be an important central point in this part of the 'castle. Behind them, the Dark Lord's frustrated bellowings were fading into the distance. 'You also understand,' Xenia went on, 'the importance of clues and symbols in these upper levels. That's fast learning. You'll go far.'

Surfer felt flattered, but kept it hidden. 'How far did *you* go, Xenia?' he asked her quietly. 'And why do you bother coming back to the five-hundreds? That's like me returning to basement level to fight vampires and Frankenstein monsters!'

He laughed at the absurdity of it, but she simply shrugged.

'Dreamcastle is infinite. Even when you've explored the highest towers, there are still countless mysteries, unnumbered adventures to enjoy. You could live here for ever, Surfer – never to know the pain of growing old and feeble, never to die.'

'Nobody has been to Dreamcastle's highest towers,' Surfer pointed out flatly, frowning at her words. 'And anyway, Xenia, it's only a game. We all have to go back to Realworld when it's over.'

'Only a game.' She chuckled, the echoes of her laughter coming back to them through the darkness. 'If you say so, Surfer my rescuer. Only a game.'

They had reached the huge chamber and Xenia's manner changed abruptly.

'I have to go now.'

'Where?' Surfer demanded.

'Nowhere you can follow,' was Xenia's reply. Her face in the shifting torchlight looked by turns warm and welcoming, cold and cruel. She seemed to hover on the borders of reality, like a vivid dream that was ending. Surfer realized he was experiencing a strange kind of Websickness, even though he was still in-game. It was not entirely unpleasant, just odd. As though, if she had wanted him to follow, her words would have come true, and he would have lost himself in these endless corridors for ever.

'Will I see you again?'

'Whenever you return.'

She half-turned to leave. Surfer took her hand, forcing her to look at him again.

'I don't even know who you really are, Xenia, or where you live.'

'Behind the mirror,' she taunted, stepping close to him, pressing her cool palms to his cheeks as she kissed him.

The kiss tasted sweet, and her hair smelled of fresh straw and a very delicate, distant perfume.

That's impossible! The thought cracked like a whip through Surfer's mind as Xenia stepped away and retreated into the darkness. However good the Web technology was, it had never been able to reproduce the sensations of taste and smell. And yet there was no doubt. Surfer sniffed the air and was tantalized again by the girl's musky aroma.

'Come back to me soon,' she called from the shadows, vanishing like a ghost into a half-hidden passageway.

Surfer made to follow but stumbled back with a cry as a monstrous spider loomed from the passage in a bristling nest of repulsive black limbs. Spiders were the guardians of this and other games. They issued cautions and instructions, and prevented access to forbidden areas. Their size denoted their importance and the seriousness of transgression. This one was the largest Surfer had ever seen.

He backed off, frightened by the hissing sound coming from the creature's busily moving mouthparts. The detail of the animal was startling.

Surfer entered some technical data on his wristpad, noting reference numbers, in-game time and so on. Then he scuttled out of VR—

—and found his stomach heaving with Websickness cramps, his head pounding with a blinding, dazzling pain.

Feeling almost suffocated, Surfer disconnected his headset and dragged off the helmet. He tore the contacts loose from his gloves and pulled them free – left hand, right hand.

Then he froze as the shock swept over him.

The stinging on the back of his right hand was tiny compared with the dreadful headache and the nausea he felt. But it was not the pain that troubled him.

Where the splinter of stone had struck him in the dungeon, an angry red mark had now appeared. The skin was not broken, but even as Surfer gazed at it, horrified, tiny droplets of blood oozed up, grew, and dripped down steadily into Surfer's lap.

CHAPTER EIGHT

ROOT FILES

Rom and Kilroy were talking over Kilroy's conversation with Suki. Kilroy particularly felt outraged that anyone could play the cruel trick of creating a phace based on someone who was dead. Rom was more interested in the technology that made the phace *so convincing* that Suki believed her brother still lived.

'This problem is big, and it's bad,' Rom emphasized, pausing to gaze through the panoramic window of the Cyber Diner at a sudden commotion in the lobby.

Surfer had blundered out from a game cubicle, and for no apparent reason had attacked the biggest guy in the place. Rom saw him swing a punch at the jaw of a teenager, who effectively blocked it and pushed Surfer away with the flat of his hand.

Surfer's face darkened with a blind rage as he came back for more.

'Shouldn't he be at school today?' Rom wondered, almost casually.

Kilroy took one look at what was going on, and leaped from her seat.

The Dark Lord had come after him! How that was possible, Surfer didn't know. But then, nor could he explain the blood on his hand. All he understood was that the Dark Lord of Dreamcastle, in all his terrible majesty, had pursued him from the cubicle and now just stood there, taunting.

Unaccountably, Surfer's sword was missing. He must have lost it in the blue-and-tone out of Webtown, or dropped it in the vaulted chamber perhaps. It was a setback, but nothing he couldn't handle.

The monster growled something at him in a guttural tongue. Surfer dodged a swipe of the creature's huge taloned hand, stepped closer and delivered a stunning punch to the Dark Lord's midriff—

The big guy doubled over, and as Kilroy ran towards them she saw that he was beginning to lose his temper.

'It's Websickness!' she called out, pushing her way through the press of onlookers. Across the lobby, she could see Gill Bates, the proprietor of the VR-bar, hurrying to break up the skirmish. If Surfer wasn't careful, he'd get himself fined, barred and grounded; something that he'd never live down.

As Surfer drew back his arm to jab at his opponent once more, Kilroy grabbed the wrist, jammed her leg behind his, and slammed Surfer to the ground in an effortless judo move. She followed him down, pinning his arms.

'Xenia! He'll kill us. Let me destroy him!' Surfer yelled in panic.

'He thinks he's still in the 'castle,' Rom said, close behind Kilroy. 'Fascinating—'

'The Dark Lord will kill us!' Surfer shrieked, his panic rising.

Kilroy twisted to look at the boy Surfer had attacked.

'Please, back off. He isn't well . . . Please!'

He nodded, stepped away, and began talking with Bates.

'Xenia—'

Surfer's energy was draining. Kilroy felt the tension going out of him and he slumped under her.

'It was not the Dark Lord,' she told Surfer, quietly but firmly. 'The 'castle here is filled with weave-magic. What you saw was nothing but a dreamspell, sent to confuse you.'

'Dream – magic—' Surfer mouthed, frowning.

As Kilroy held him close, there came the howling whoop of an ambulance from the street outside.

'Paramedics,' Rom confirmed, seeing them hurry from the vehicle.

'I know the ways of the weave,' Kilroy went on, soothing Surfer with tender strokes of her hand across his temples and brow. 'You can trust me to see you safe. Trust Xenia, and rest now.'

'Rest . . . ' Surfer whispered. He smiled, lifted his hand towards her, then let it drop as he fell into an exhausted slumber.

The quick response paramedics in their trim light-blue overalls broke through the crowd and checked Surfer over before lifting him on to a stretcher.

'You with him?' one of them, a pertly pretty girl in her early twenties, asked Kilroy.

'She'd like to be,' muttered Rom, shrugging at Kilroy's glare of disapproval.

'Yes, I'm with him. I can give you his details on the way to the hospital. Rom,' Kilroy added in a tone that brooked no argument, 'you clear things here with Gill, explain Surfer's not been himself lately. Then join me at the hospital later.'

'OK. You know, it occurs to me that the gamer he mentioned, Xenia, must be our mysterious Ann Onymous.'

'Copy that,' Kilroy said emphatically. 'And when I get in-game again, I'm going to back that garbage into a corner and ask her a few rather pointed and rather personal questions.'

We all have our dreams, Kilroy reflected, feeling the power of her own as she gazed at Surfer through the observation window of his room. Mrs Miller sat at his bedside, reading a romantic novel. Her husband had been paged at work and was on his way over.

Kilroy thought that she had never seen Surfer looking so peaceful. The mild sedative had cleared his mind of nightmares, leaving a calmness that showed on his face. All the ambition, all the anger, had ebbed with the tide of sleep. For a few hours at least, he did not have to fight the world to prove himself worthy to be in it.

When is a game not a game? Kilroy asked herself darkly. 'When you have to win it to survive.'

'I'm sorry?'

Kilroy started and turned round. Doctor Esdaile, Surfer's consultant physician, had stepped into his office, a mini-PC clutched in one hand. It was no bigger than Mrs Miller's paperback.

'Oh, nothing.' Kilroy found herself blushing slightly. 'I was just thinking aloud. Is he going to be all right?'

'Sure he is.' Doctor Esdaile turned on a reassuring smile with thirty years of practice behind it. 'Robert's obviously suffered some mental trauma through becoming too involved in these games you young folks seem to like playing.' Esdaile's smile moderated slightly. 'Beats me why you can't knock the heck out of a baseball, like I used to do.' He shrugged. 'But that's neither here nor there now, is it?'

Kilroy found herself smiling back, not so much at what the man had said, as by the use of Surfer's realname. It sounded strange, almost artificial.

'We do compulsory sports at school—'

'I'm talking about *fun*, young lady,' Esdaile replied rather sternly. 'Why, when I was a boy, I'd go down to Oakhills Memorial Park and—'

Esdaile caught himself and grinned. 'But there I go, losing myself in my own land of daydreams. No, don't worry, your friend will be fine. Though I have to say I'm a little puzzled by the odd mark on his right hand.'

'He got it in the fight,' Kilroy hazarded. The doctor shook his head.

'Apparently not. And the nature of the damage is unusual. The skin has not been broken, but there's quite deep bruising beneath, and the blood seeped through to the outside. I've heard of such things,' Esdaile went on, 'where people react because they believe something is true, even if it turns out not to be in the end.'

'I'm not sure I understand.'

'What you believe controls your life,' Esdaile said simply. 'My guess, for what it's worth, is that Robert received a hand wound in his VR game, and was so involved that the mark appeared in his flesh in reality.'

'But Webheads are always battling in-game.'

'Yes, but it depends how far you know it's a game while you're playing. Maybe Robert got carried away. Or perhaps,' Esdaile added, as the thought occurred to him for the first time, 'there's something in the game itself that convinces you it's real.'

Rom turned up shortly afterwards, in a state of high excitement. He controlled it just long enough for Kilroy to pass on what Esdaile had explained to her.

'It all fits in,' Kilroy concluded. 'Surfer develops an actual mark after a wound in-game. Silent Blade appears so real to his sister that Suki remains convinced that he's still alive.'

'More fool her,' muttered Rom.

'No,' Kilroy came back at him insistently. 'More fool us, for thinking we could bat out of the Web, turn our back on it and get on with our lives. Doctor Esdaile asked the question: where does the mind end and the body begin? I'm asking another one: where does the Web end and reality begin?'

Rom looked at Kilroy, wide-eyed. He whistled softly, nodding.

'All right, you've sold me on the idea. Especially since I'll be speaking to someone who will probably agree with everything you've said.'

'Who's that?' Kilroy asked.

Rom sniffed and examined his fingernails modestly.

'Only Glen DelRoy, the guy who created the Dreamcastle.'

Rom explained that Gill Bates, back at the VR-bar, had been worried about the trouble Surfer had caused. Not that there'd been any damage; and the kid he'd attacked was perfectly willing to forget all about the incident.

'The real problem,' Rom went on, his eyes bright with an eager gleam, 'is the Anti-Web Lobby. If they get hold of the idea that kids are going crazy in the gamezones, they'll wipe us out – Websuits, VR-bars, the whole package. It'll be back to the stone age!'

'We'll have to play baseball in the park,' Kilroy murmured. Rom made a gagging sound and crossed his eyes.

'Gill has some contacts in GameZone International,' he said, 'the company who hooked up the VR-bar in Oakhills to Dreamcastle worldwide. I hung around while she talked with a couple of them. They felt the best thing to do would be to talk to Mr DelRoy. He lives in England. It's early morning there now, but Gill has booked a breakfast call so that we can get the matter sorted out.'

'When will Gill be making the call?' Kilroy asked.

Rom glanced at his wristpad. 'In about ten minutes. If we hurry, we can just about get there in time.'

Gill Bates looked distinctly nervous, Kilroy thought, as she sat with herself and Rom waiting for the videolink to connect. It would have been perfectly possible, of course, to have met with DelRoy in Webtown. But given the short notice, only a gag immersion was practical, which to anyone who had surfed the gamezones in a Tarantula, was strictly a cog basement-level spider of an option. Kilroy smiled at what must have been Rom's immense frustration using glove-and-glasses to enter with her when she met Suki. It would have been like watching video in 2.D with flatsound and all the colours dimmed. Like being half deaf and blind, Kilroy mused.

Her smile went away.

The soundblaster circuits in the PC created a chime and the linkup happened without preamble. Glen DelRoy's well-known craggy face appeared. He was sitting at a desk, it seemed, and his head-and-shoulders were framed by a background of bookcases and kids' toys. Kilroy recalled it was one of DelRoy's firm beliefs that you could only create Webware for kids if you were a kid yourself, and although Glen DelRoy was well into his seventies now, he still maintained publicly that he refused to grow up.

'Good day to you, Gill . . . And is it Rom? And—?'

'I'm Rom,' Rom said with something like awe in his voice. 'Uh, and my friend's nick is Kilroy.'

DelRoy nodded after a tiny pause, which was the time delay of the signal speeding a quarter of the way around the globe.

'Yes, hi. Gill has sent me an account of what's been happening. How's your friend Surfer?'

'He's got bad voms,' Rom replied. Kilroy went on to explain about the strange wound to Surfer's hand.

Across the Atlantic, DelRoy's face showed concern.

'You know as well as I do about the failsafes built into the Webware. Not just the international controls, but all the safety nets woven in at every level, to make sure something like this doesn't occur.'

'But it *has* happened, Mr DelRoy,' Gill spoke up. 'So is it possible someone has been tampering with Dreamcastle – and perhaps other gamezones – without the authorities knowing?'

DelRoy's frown deepened, and his eyes changed, as though he was gazing far into the past.

'All I can say,' he answered a moment later, 'is that if the tampering you suggest is going on, then it's occurring at a fundamental level – machine-code level. And to go that far in, you'd have to have access clearance of the highest order.'

'The trouble is,' Gill persisted, 'that if the Anti-Webbers make a crisis out of this, I could be closed down – me, and other VR-bars all over the world!'

'That won't happen,' DelRoy assured her with a mischievous, twinkling smile. 'There's too much money tied up in Web entertainment for any government to seek a blanket clampdown. And I've received no other reports of this kind of problem with Dreamcastle. My suspicion is that, if someone's tampering with the Webware, your locality is being targeted, and for a very specific purpose.'

'Which is?' Kilroy asked.

DelRoy shrugged lightly, though Kilroy suspected he'd given the matter some deep thought. 'Frankly, I think that you and your friends are the guinea pigs in some kind of dangerous experiment. Someone is meddling, not just with computer programs, but with the greater programming of the human mind. Reality is what we believe it to be. If someone's beliefs can be changed, then what they think is *real*, changes too. What's happening is that the barrier between reality and illusion has become blurred for Surfer. He no longer recognizes the boundary line.'

'Wait a minute,' Kilroy interrupted. 'You're saying this has been done deliberately? But there's also Suki . . . ' She quickly told DelRoy about the Hong Kong connection and Silent Blade.

DelRoy's face registered first surprise, then a serious concern. He became agitated.

'This is even more worrying. You see, it's the aim of all programmers to create a phace in such complete detail that you'd think it was real . . . a kind of artificial lifeform, living in the Web . . . a dream of life, or perhaps more of a nightmare. But it occurs to me that to achieve it, you don't just reprogram Webfiles, you reprogram the human mind itself!'

'Something – someone – recreated Silent Blade in the Web!' Kilroy's voice was a whisper of astonishment.

'Complete in every detail,' DelRoy added grimly. 'So realistic, that Suki herself was convinced. So realistic, that in a way we don't yet understand, Silent Blade might still be alive. But you can be sure that since it was created by the socalled Dark Lord, it must be under his control. This is a very dangerous situation.'

'So what can we do about it?' Rom wanted to know.

'Well, for a start, stay clear of Dreamcastle, and make sure Suki and Surfer do too. They're the ones who seem to have been most seriously affected.'

'His love life will be ruined,' Rom muttered, ignoring Kilroy's withering glance.

'Meanwhile,' DelRoy went on, 'I'll have a word in the right ears to make sure the matter is properly investigated – and to see that your VR-bar continues to flourish, Gill.'

'I appreciate that, Mr DelRoy,' Gill said with a look of relief on her face.

DelRoy nodded. 'You're welcome. But as a first step, I think it might be wise to check that we aren't making fools of ourselves. If someone is tampering with Dreamcastle, then it'll show up in the root files.'

'Sure, but you can only get into them if you're—' Rom began, then blushed deeply as he realized the importance of the man he was talking to.

'And to *really* impress you,' DelRoy grinned, 'I can do it right here from my desk terminal. Sit back and watch.'

DelRoy glanced away from the screen and keyed-in security numbers, meanwhile issuing instructions by voice to the bot programs built into his machine. The Webware that made up the Dreamcastle gamezone was located in a number of mainframes scattered all over the world. DelRoy's scanning facilities allowed bots to talk to bots, creating access to the deepest levels of Webware programming – the root files out of which everything grew.

'I'll let the visuals take over from here,' DelRoy said, as his face moved to a corner of the screen, shrank and became an icon.

A huge tree swirled up into being; its leafy branches towering into a virtual sky, its trunk plunging for what seemed like many kilometres into reddish textured ground far below. Kilroy and Rom were used to having information presented in picture form, but this was the first time they had been given so clear an image of the sheer scale and complexity of the Web.

As though they were flying an invisible plane, they zoomed in towards a cluster of branches that formed just one small section of the tree. Leaves flickered by and became giant-sized, before one leaf swung to the centre of the screen and grew larger, larger.

It was the leaf that represented Dreamcastle.

'We're going in!' Rom yelled, his voice catching with excitement.

Their viewpoint continued to zero in, so that now the leaf looked like a huge cracked landscape of light green rounded hills, and darker, deeper green valleys, all of it pocked with craters.

'One of those leaf cells is the vaulted chamber,' Kilroy said, 'another is the ledge where Surfer fought the stormdragon.'

'We're bypassing those – going right to the roots!'

Rom actually blinked as the 'plane' plunged into an airpore, blurred through the veins of the leaf at superspeed, then began to drop at a fantastic rate of acceleration into the darker zone of the tree's colossal trunk. The greenness vanished, and a gloomy amber-gold light pervaded all.

The ride was breathtaking, allowing Kilroy hardly any time at all to realize that the journey was only the bot programs' way of explaining that they were opening up deeper and deeper levels of security to gain access to the basic information through which Dreamcastle had been created.

Finally, after a breathless descent, the 'plane' began to slow. The cell walls became less than a blur, looming closer and closer – until the viewpoint moved through them, to look at the roots from the outside.

The onlookers seemed to be floating in limbo; drifting in a dim zone, through which the incredibly complicated tangle of the root structure could be seen.

A tiny gold thread, pulsing with light, indicated the way to the Dreamcastle root files. The 'plane' followed the marker, weaving this way and that through the woody mass, until—

'There!' Kilroy burst out, pointing a trembling finger. 'Oh my God!'

Something was obviously wrong. One section of one of the roots seemed distorted, covered in a strange growth. A black mass of crusty tissue surrounded the normal, healthy cells.

'Security bots,' Rom hazarded a guess. 'Keeping us out.'

And as the viewpoint eased closer, the truth of his words became clear.

For not only were the root files of Dreamcastle locked away from their inspection, but as if to warn them further, the entire area was swarming with spiders.

CHAPTER NINE

DARK LORD

Some part of Surfer's mind knew he was lying in his bed at home, dipping in and out of sleep, and that Xenia could only be a dream. Perhaps the last cobwebby traces of the Websickness still clung to him, or maybe the drugs he'd been given in hospital were still working. Whatever, she couldn't really be there – not really. Could she?

She was sitting in the easy chair by the bookcase, watching him with gentle eyes and a smile that he found oddly unnerving. Surfer lifted his head a fraction to study her better. She was dressed in the tattered rags of her Dreamcastle costume; and he could see the white cursor on his PC screen blinking through the insubstantial mistiness of her body. He guessed then that she *was* a dream, or rather an hallucination, and felt through some deep instinct that the Xenia he'd met in the Web had somehow tampered with his mind. This beautiful ghost existed only in his head. Although, as Surfer continued to gaze at her, he still felt he was in her presence. Her *realness* was frightening.

'How are you, Surfer? You look pale.'

An uneasy chuckle broke from his lips as she spoke. 'Go away Xenia. I don't want you here!'

It was her turn to laugh; a soft self-assured laugh in the light of another person's fear.

'It's not that easy. Having sought me out in the 'castle, you can't just wish me away with a wave of your hand.'

'You're a phace,' Surfer said, putting as much confidence as he could into the statement. 'You're nothing, Xenia. The computer made you. You're virtual light.'

She shrugged lightly and tossed her hair in a gesture that was utterly natural, completely human. No program could be that good.

'You don't know that, and only the cowardly part of you wants to believe it. Where's the hero inside you, Surfer? Where's the warrior who leaps to any challenge? Where's the man who wants to win the girl and the glory and live happily ever after as king of all he surveys?'

Xenia's voice crackled with scorn and mockery, but it also possessed a velvety persuasiveness that stirred the dark forces in Surfer's heart.

'In my dreams,' Surfer admitted bleakly. 'It's only a game.'

'Better to play and lose and feel the joy of battle, than to live like your father does.'

'What do you know?'

'I know he'll drag on in a job he hates for another fifteen years, and then perhaps cog-out in front of the TV for another ten or twenty. Then what, Surfer? He dies and the world forgets him.'

'Don't say that about my father!' Surfer felt the rage tightening inside. He struggled up and Xenia didn't shimmer into nothingness – didn't go away.

'If I'm in your mind, then it's you who's saying it. But wherever it comes from, you know it's the truth. Your greatest fear is to be like him – to be nobody. Less real than even a phace, a pixel ghost in a silicon dream. Get real, Surfer – fight for what you want. Come with me and we'll destroy the Dark Lord together.'

'And then?'

He felt temptation pulling him off the bed, his hand lifting to take Xenia's, which she was reaching out towards him, a ruby ring glowing on her finger.

'Then we will live together in the highest towers of Dreamcastle; never growing old, never falling ill. And death will be like a rainshower passing unnoticed outside. It won't touch us. We'll be free of it.'

'My Mum—'

'Your mother will understand. Don't you think she's like me in so many ways? She wants her son to achieve, Surfer. She wants to be proud of you. We both do.'

Xenia's hand was neither warm nor cold. It had the feel of a Websuit glove squeezing his flesh. But it was only the memory of that glove, Surfer realized, as Xenia led him over to the wardrobe where he took his jeans and a shirt and his jacket off the hanger.

'It's cold outside. You'll need a jacket too,' Surfer insisted, his heart beating faster at this experiment.

His other jacket was polyfabric leather. It was a little large for Xenia, but as he draped it over her shoulders, he thought she looked cute in it.

Gill kept the VR-bar open all night. This was partly because, even in the early hours, a few phreaks turned up for some quiet time in the gamezones. But also, all over the daytime world, Webheads were active and Gill needed to receive their messages and transmit updates on the state of play of her own customers.

It was during this time too that Gill herself went in-game; because the bar wasn't busy, and because she was embarrassed to admit her favourite zone was *The Wishing Star*, a Website that was unashamedly based on a best-selling romantic novel.

She was sixteen again and falling in love for the very first time. Her boyfriend was tall, dark, handsome, fearless, and he adored her. Nick had just taken Gill for a fast ride on his motorbike: 200 kph under full white moonlight, with the wind in her hair and the chill of the sweet spring night on her cheeks.

Now, breathless with excitement and her eyes agleam with starlight, Gill gazed up into Nick's smiling face and felt his lean strong arms slip around her waist.

'Darling,' he said huskily, leaning towards her. 'Kiss me.'

Gill pursed her lips – then gazed beyond Nick and saw a blue cartoon spider dangling from a thread nearby.

'Oh, curl up!' she muttered, as the spider grinned and swirled into a vanishing cloud of glowing blue dust.

It was an icon Gill had programmed into the game to warn her that a customer had come into the VR-bar.

'See you later, Nick,' she said, attending to her wristpad. 'You beast,' she added, smiling.

After a moment of blue-and-tone confusion, Gill unplugged the VR contacts and slipped off her helmet. She synthvoxed the security monitors, and was surprised to see Surfer striding across the lobby towards the private cubicles.

Frowning, Gill left her own cubicle and waved to him. 'Hi, Surfer. How are you feeling now?'

When he failed to answer, she walked closer. Then stopped nervously. Surfer appeared to be talking to someone beside him. He was speaking with great intensity and seriousness. When he reached the cubicle door, he held it open for his invisible companion to enter before stepping inside himself.

'Surfer – wait!' Gill called. But the door swung closed, as though he had never heard her at all. As though she didn't even exist.

And at around the same time, Mrs Miller went into Surfer's bedroom to check that her son was OK.

She found his bed empty, his wardrobe door wide open, and his polyfabric leather jacket lying crumpled on the floor beside it.

Rom rarely had nightmares, or at least rarely remembered them. But when the synthvox told him softly at his bedside that there was a call coming in, he thrashed his way out of sleep, madly trying to escape from a million swarming spiders.

'Rom – what's the matter?' Kilroy's face looked concerned.

'Whatever's in the Dreamcastle is trying to get out!' he shrieked in terror. Kilroy turned up the voice-volume at her end of the line.

'Rom! That's enough! Calm down – you've been dreaming!'

That seemed to snap him awake. His eyes refocused and he
seemed to see Kilroy for the first time.

'Surfer's mother called me twenty minutes ago, to say Gill
Bates had phoned her. Surfer's in the VR-bar. He went
straight to a terminal and zoned-in without so much as a
word.'

'Can't she bat him out of it?' Rom wanted to know. Kilroy
shook her head.

'There was something strange about him. Gill thought if
she tried a raid on Surfer, she might hurt him – especially
after what's happened. I got Gill to call Mr DelRoy, and I've
just spoken to Suki; explained things. We're going to meet in
Webtown in half an hour. Get over here, Rom, do whatever
you need to persuade your parents. It's an emergency.'

Xenia's gentle but possessive grasp of Surfer's hand never
slackened. She appeared to help him into the Tarantula, and
then watched as he keyed-in the codes to grant him access to
her realm.

There was no detour to Webtown, no fast ride down the
glassy delivery tunnel into the game. The walls of the 'castle
simply loomed into existence around him out of the blue
wash of entry, just as though he'd never been away. Still
gripping Surfer's hand, Xenia kissed him, then whispered to
him how to program-in special codes to access bot programs
only she knew about. They would ensure he could bypass all
the intermediate levels of Dreamcastle, and travel with her
swiftly to the very highest towers.

'I can smell you. I can taste you,' Surfer said in a tone of
simple wonder.

'One day, only the Web will be real, and the world outside
will be nothing but a memory.'

'Our bodies are out there—'

'Our minds are in here,' she replied. 'That's all you know,
and all you need to know.'

'Where are we going now?'

'Higher up, further in.' Xenia's voice was filled with ecstasy
and triumph. 'I'll show you.'

Now, as they walked, Xenia told him that of all the other phreaks who'd entered the gamezone none had ever seen the true heart of Dreamcastle.

'They just played in the shallows,' she said. 'No one has ever glimpsed the depths. In here, you stand astride the boundary between worlds. The world of the Outside, and the world of the Web. You can make your choice, Surfer, and turn the Outside into a memory.'

'What about Suki and Silent Blade? Is that what happened to them?'

Xenia nodded. 'Suki came closest, but she could neither obey the Dark Lord nor destroy him. When she comes in here again, the Dark Lord will kill her.'

Something about the way Xenia said it made Surfer withhold his reply. He'd intended commenting that Suki seemed such a good warrior that defeat at the hands of the Dark Lord was not a foregone conclusion. But Xenia's assurance of the Dark Lord's power led him to wonder just how much she knew.

'And Silent Blade?' Surfer probed carefully.

'Oh, he's won his greatest victory already,' Xenia said cryptically. She squeezed Surfer's hand, and again it felt like something happening in his mind, rather than the pressure of the Websuit flexing. 'Come with me, Surfer, I have something to show you.'

She chose one of the many passages and led Surfer unresisting along it. His apprehension grew, together with the questions he needed to ask. Where had Xenia come from, that she understood so much about the 'castle? She spoke of the Dark Lord as though she *knew* him – or it. How could that be? And most tantalizing of all – who exactly was she? And in what way was she real? And why had she chosen to confer upon Surfer the gift or the curse of her company?

Things were changing around them now. The walls were no longer just walls; the flagstones on which they walked had become blurred, vague, as though they might be anything depending on the mind's lightest whim or the heart's deepest desire. And the pitch torches that flickered and hissed at intervals had drifted out of focus, and were more like twisted red stars glowing in a cosmic void.

'Where are we now?' Surfer asked, his voice flat and itself oddly unreal.

Xenia looked at him, startling him by the subtle way her features had shifted. Suddenly, without his noticing the change, she'd come to resemble his mother, and Kilroy, and Kristie McAuliffe who was one of the astronauts on the Mars Mission. She resembled all the women he loved or admired in his life.

'At the Interface. Take care now, Surfer – and look down.'

They were right at the edge of an impossible chasm; a vast crack in the fabric of the 'castle. By leaning out and gazing up, Surfer was able to see the dizzying uppermost galleries and towers of the citadel, striking skywards at slightly out-of-true angles into a heaven of chromium blue-grey, streaked with fire.

Then, just as cautiously, he stared down into a complexity of forever expanding colours and patterns, an endless spiral staircase of fractal light.

'The truth is in there, Surfer,' Xenia told him, her voice honey smooth and very close. 'To dare to step over is the only way of winning the game.'

'I don't understand,' he said, trying to pump some bravado into his tone and manner. 'Why is the way to the Dark Lord down, and not upwards?'

'As above, so below.'

'That's a bunch of mystical nonsense!' Surfer said with a flash of healthy temper. 'If you want me here with you, Xenia – if you want me to *survive* here – I have to know more.'

A faint shadow crossed Xenia's features. 'The technicalities would be impossible for you to comprehend. All you need to understand is that our minds consist simply of thoughts. Who we think we are is nothing more than stored information. And just as the network of nerve cells in our brains gathers that information and uses it to create what we call "reality", so the processing power of the Web can generate an existence that is equally real. *A Xenia and a Surfer that are equally real!'*

'But . . . but—' Surfer struggled for words. 'But what about the actual you and me? Our bodies – our lives?'

Fury came and went on her face and left her less patient.

'There isn't time to argue, Surfer. We must go now – together – or here on the brink is where I leave you to perish.'

'This is amazing!' said Gill Bates, her voice trembling like a child's on Christmas morning. Even as Kilroy and Rom arrived at the Website, they realized that something important was happening.

The virtual room in which they found themselves was whirling with data: words, symbols, strings of binary code sweeping across the walls, floor and ceiling in measureless waves.

A little blonde-haired boy in old-fashioned school cap and uniform stood in the middle of it all, directing the dance with a glittering light-pointer.

Gill hurried over and hugged Rom and Kilroy warmly.

'It's astonishing. He's using high level bot progams and decryption software like keys to unlock the Dreamcastle root files.'

'Yes, but—' Kilroy began.

Rom's eyes suddenly lit up.

'It's Glen DelRoy! I recognize him now!'

'He always said he'd never grown up,' Gill chuckled. 'And here in the Web he can prove it. He's gaining us access to the levels we have to reach to find Surfer—'

'Surfer is sitting two cubicles down in the VR-bar, Gill.' Kilroy sounded angry, as though this was all some elaborate game. And she said as much.

Gill's face grew serious. 'The biomonitor shows something's wrong. I have a terrible feeling that the shock of batting Surfer out of the gamezone would damage him, perhaps seriously. And you're right, Kilroy – this is a game. A dreadful game we only partly understand . . . so we have no choice but to play by the enemy's rules.'

After a moment Kilroy nodded. She realized her real concern for Surfer's safety was clouding her judgement.

'OK, you're right. So – how do we help him?'

'As Gill said, by playing it the enemy's way.'

DelRoy had finished weaving his maths-magic and stood with his hands on his hips; his little boy's face was bright and beaming despite the darkness of the situation.

'You have to go in, find Surfer, and rescue him. But the Dark Lord will try to stop you. Ah, I see we have some valuable help that could make all the difference.'

Suki had entered the Webspace. DelRoy gave a low respectful bow, which the others followed and Suki returned.

'I am so sorry about your brother,' DelRoy said, quietly and simply.

'I understand now that what has been laid to rest should be allowed to rest.' Suki's voice was small and fragile. It tore at Kilroy's heart.

Gill went over and squatted to be level with Suki. 'Life is what matters – true life. Honour your brother, little Suki, in the best way you can.'

A flash of colour streaked across the walls.

'I am in contact with GameZone International,' DelRoy told them, seeming businesslike now. He flipped his light-pointer towards a kaleidoscope of coloured icons floating in the corner. 'They have begun a raid program to evacuate all players from Dreamcastle, and expect it to be concluded very shortly. You have little time to complete your task.'

He looked at them all soberly. 'I suggest we go in there now and finish this business . . .'

Entry to the zone was a frightening experience. The group could not push through the virtual walls of the 'castle Website because of the raid. Phreaks were already being gently bounced away; the walls seethed with warning keep-out messages, and an increasing number of ferocious-looking spiders was beginning to swarm all around.

DelRoy used his access clearance a final time for direct entry. The Webspace seemed to explode apart. There was a terrifying second out of time and space as the Websuits and bot programs raced to adjust.

Then Kilroy found herself in the dark and familiar corridors of Dreamcastle.

And she was alone.

She almost panicked as terror gushed through her.

'Rom! Gill! Mr DelRoy!' Her voice echoed away along the infinite passages and galleries and chambers, bringing no reassuring reply. She guessed what had happened. Just as DelRoy was doing all in his power to dismantle the complex software that sustained the game, so the Dark Lord had prepared his defences well. One of them had been a blocking program, denying access when certain identity codes were detected. So, DelRoy, Rom, Gill Bates and Suki had been prevented from batting in, while Kilroy's entry had been allowed.

It was quite deliberate, very cunning, and incredibly dangerous.

For a few seconds, as the first fear eased, Kilroy felt an almost overwhelming temptation to blue-and-tone-it to the safety of the VR-bar in sleepy little Oakhills lost in a New England valley. In which case, Surfer would die or become an empty shell, and she would never forgive herself for that.

'Get a grip, Kilroy, you one-mip basement-level cog egg silky!' she spat viciously.

DelRoy's preparations had provided her with throwing stars, daggers and a fine combat sword.

Kilroy drew it now, turned around and walked where intuition took her. She soon reached the end of the corridor and was gently guided by an unseen force to the left. She guessed that DelRoy, or at least a technician somewhere, was auto-controlling the Websuit to bring her to Surfer's location. And she was happy for that to continue, except that when she reached a large chamber with many entrances, the invisible control faded and she was left with the choice of a score of identical passages.

Kilroy stopped and a sense of bleak panic tightened in her chest.

'Now which way?' she yelled at the uncaring stones, her eyes flicking madly from passage to passage. Suddenly, her brain registered something and she moved forward to look closer at a little trail of marker stars.

Kilroy smiled.

'It's too late!' Xenia hissed, her pretty face contorted with anger. 'They are already destroying the caverns and cellars of the 'castle. It is time for me to withdraw.'

'What are you talking about?' Surfer demanded. He could detect no changes in the framework of the zone, nothing to give substance to her rage.

'I was hoping to have you as a companion by choice. Now I see that I will simply have to take you with me.'

'I don't understand,' Surfer said. 'What about destroying the Dark Lord?'

Xenia chuckled like the chiming of bells, and it seemed, just for a second, as though she laughed with many voices.

'Oh, Surfer, how did you ever break through to the upper levels? You are so innocent, so gullible.'

She gazed at him steadily.

'*I am the Dark Lord*. Lift the stone and you will find me. Cleave the wood and I am there. I am Dreamcastle, Surfer, and more. So that even when this place has been rendered down to chaos, I will continue.'

'Xenia – this is crazy.'

'Not as crazy as dying without good cause. Come with me now!'

She lunged at Surfer and gripped his hand. Surfer screamed, for Xenia's fingers seemed to knit into his, as though joining them seamlessly together.

'No! Let me go!'

'You can never be free of me now!' Xenia shrieked and to Surfer's horror, her hair and face, the very bones of her body, began to ooze and stretch like warm plastic towards him. And the more he struggled, the more fluidly and quickly Xenia oozed over his body.

'You wanted us to be close,' she slurred from a melted mouth. 'Together for ever, Surfer.'

A piece of her face touched his cheek.

'Let go of him!'

Kilroy's voice rang out and she never hesitated. Snicking a star from her belt, she hurled it glittering in Xenia's direction.

Even as it flew, Xenia was laughing in disdain. But when it hit, lodging in her arm, the laughter turned to a shrill cry of agony, and part of the arm puffed away in wisps of meaningless light.

'Each weapon is an icon,' Kilroy warned her, remembering DelRoy's earlier instructions. 'A kill-program which will destroy you piece by piece, byte by byte.'

She launched another star which sailed over Xenia's head, missing her narrowly.

Xenia backed off, sliding away from Surfer's body, but rippling into a hideous change as she did so.

'Throw your pathetic little missiles! You won't hurt me, girl!' Xenia's voice boomed out from jaws which were lengthening, darkening, issuing blue smoke and golden sparks.

She became the stormdragon, the firedrake, the reptile mage; all of the crawling horrors of the Dreamcastle locked in Kilroy's mind.

Kilroy gasped at the sight and shrank back. As a child, she had turned stones over in the park, and saw what wriggled and writhed beneath. Now, all of these creatures, monstrously magnified, had come to get her; to drag her down into the earth and eat her slowly, with soil stifling her screams.

'Kilroy – move yourself!' Surfer yelled, not just to jolt her out of her paralysis. The dark had bulged behind her and Silent Blade had appeared. He too was changed, an echo of Xenia's monstrousness, nothing more than a puppet phantom.

Silent Blade's huge scimitar swept down, striking Kilroy's sword with a screech of steel on steel. She had spun and

blocked his blow in the final instant, twisting aside to throw
him briefly off balance.

Kilroy staggered out of reach to recover. She had felt the
shock of the strike through her arms which now burned with
pain. Then she understood that, just as her hand reflected the
blow in-game, so her own body could be destroyed in
Realworld if it was obliterated here.

Silent Blade came at her with the grace and speed of a
dancer. Kilroy ducked as the scimitar swept over, then
parried with her own weapon, forcing Silent Blade a step
closer to the edge of the chasm.

Surfer moved in to back her up. Weaponless himself, he
snatched a clutch of her throwing stars and spun them
viciously into Xenia's massive looming form. One grazed
the flesh of her shoulder, the other lodged in her eye.

The awful shriek that issued from her terrible mouth
rocked the farthest ramparts of the 'castle. Her reptile hands
scrabbled and plucked at the wound that was growing swiftly
as the kill-program spread the destruct virus with incredible
speed through her body.

Silent Blade glanced fleetingly away from the encounter.
Kilroy saw her chance. She lifted the sword—

And was restrained by a cool and delicate hand on her
own.

'No, it is for me to do,' Suki said at her side.

The girl's body was flickering in and out of existence, as
though a war was going on in the Web between vast and
invisible forces.

'I only have these few moments,' Suki explained with
pleading in her eyes. 'I must lay the ghost of Silent Blade
myself.'

Kilroy held back the fires of her fury. She nodded, and
watched as Suki strode unafraid towards her brother's apparition.

Never pausing, Suki ran the final few steps and threw
herself at him, her weight taking him with her over the edge,
and down and down until both of them blinked out like two
stars wiped from the map of the night.

'Suki – no!' Surfer cried.

'It's only her realoe that's gone. If DelRoy is doing his job, he'll bat her out safely. Now we must go too,' Kilroy shouted above the rising crashings and booms of destruction.

Surfer knew she was right. The kill-programs were everywhere, unmaking the walls and towers, the numberless rooms, the very foundations of Dreamcastle.

As he watched he saw Xenia, grotesquely transformed, spinning apart like threads from an unravelling tapestry, her influence over him similarly dispersing.

Together he and Kilroy keyed-in the codes to take them away from the zone.

Then Kilroy screamed as Xenia surged forward one final time, a lizard's claw flashing out of nowhere to slash at her face.

Without thinking or caring, Kilroy retaliated, hurling herself towards the creature and plunging her sword deep into the dragon's withering heart.

Xenia emitted a bellow of agony, but Kilroy kept the pressure on to force the monster to the brink of the pit and then topple it over.

Xenia dropped from sight, and Kilroy leaned out to watch her descent.

'I got you,' she whispered, blood and tears mingling on her cheeks. 'I got you.'

The Dark Lord flew apart in an explosion of fiery scraps and fragments, as the gentle hand of reality held Kilroy like a child and led her back towards the light.

CHAPTER TEN

SAVE

Kilroy breathed a sigh of relief as the videoscreens faded to blue and the faces of Suki, Gill Bates and Glen DelRoy finally disappeared.

'They were only concerned about you,' Rom pointed out when he noticed her slump back in the hospital bed.

'I know, I know,' Kilroy said. She was grateful for their good wishes, but now they were gone she could be herself again – truly herself, in the company of the best friends she had ever known.

It was three days after Dreamcastle had been wiped from the Web by the kill-programs of GameZone International, and GZI had already approached DelRoy to create another, better version of the adventure. Kilroy had begun to protest at the news, but Surfer's view had been calmer and more considered.

'The problem wasn't in the game,' he declared. 'Whatever Xenia was, she was simply using the 'castle as a lair, as a testbed to see—'

'To see what, Surf?' Rom's brow was furrowed in puzzlement.

'To see how *real* VR could be. But the problem was in me, too,' Surfer admitted quietly. 'I let myself be tempted by the gold at the end of the rainbow. It was an illusion. A lie. And I fell for it.'

'It's all over now,' Kilroy said, speaking as much to herself as to the others. And she said it with as much conviction as possible, knowing it might not be true.

Her Websickness had been rather worse than Surfer's. Apart from the bouts of nausea, she was still being troubled by nightmares. Walking alone in grey places, feeling that perhaps Xenia had not gone away at all, but was lurking somewhere nearby. So when she came to a stone, she could not help herself but lift it – and then shudder at the crawling, writhing things beneath it. Some of those things, the ones with Xenia's face, laughed and spat at her before burrowing down deep into the ground and out of sight.

Waking each morning, it had taken her some minutes to shake off the feeling that she was not alone in her room and that many eyes were watching her.

Unexpectedly, Rom leaned over and gave her a hug. The sparkle of tears he had noticed in Kilroy's eyes welled up and she wept with the sheer joy of being here, alive, herself, on this sunny autumn day.

'It's all right,' Rom whispered softly in her ear. 'It's all right now, Kilroy.'

'Hey, Rom.' Surfer clapped the boy on the shoulder. 'How about fetching three Cokes from the vendor down the hall – giant size? I'm paying.'

'Venomous!' Rom said, beaming, as Surfer flipped over his smartcard.

'Kilroy,' Surfer said, after Rom had left the room. 'I just wanted to say I'm grateful – and I'm sorry for all the worry I've caused.'

She looked at him with untroubled eyes, easy in herself that, whatever became of them both, she had been true to her principles and not lulled by the Dreamcastle's empty promises of glory, or the mirror of pointless vanity.

'It's OK,' Kilroy shrugged, very aware that she looked a mess in her hospital gown and her sleep-mussed hair – but not caring a mip!

'Um, that is, I wondered—' Surfer coughed, seeming suddenly awkward, 'if you'd like, maybe, to date. We could go wherever you liked, do whatever you want. How about it?'

Kilroy put her tongue in her cheek and kept him waiting for the number of seconds he deserved. Then she nodded.

'Great, Surfer. And what I'd like to do most is go play some baseball in the park.'

His face registered surprise, then bemusement. Then he laughed as Kilroy's expression softened and he reached out to touch her, his fingers finding her forehead and temples, before moving down to her cheek to trace there the cross-shaped scar she would carry for the rest of her life.

UNTOUCHABLE
ERIC BROWN

CHAPTER ONE

ANA AND AJAY

That June, the monsoon rains came early to New Delhi.

Ana Devi crouched on the pavement outside the Union Coffee House, listening to the downpour drumming on the awning overhead. Above the city, the night sky was patched with a dozen hologram advertisements. A thousand auto-rickshaws and mopeds buzzed like angry wasps around the roundabout of Connaught Place.

Ajay slept beside her, his head resting on her shoulder. It was still early in the evening but her brother was only six years old and needed his sleep.

With his eyes closed, lips smiling at something in his dreams, Ajay looked perfect. Ana touched his cheek with her fingertips.

She stared out into the night, alert for danger, or the arrival of a car full of rich people.

The holo-ads marched across the night sky: 3-D images of perfect kitchens, men and women in fabulous clothes, exotic holiday resorts . . . Ana had once heard someone say that these images were the cinema of the people, but she thought they were more like glimpses of heaven.

She often spent hours gazing up at the light show, dreaming of being able to afford the luxuries glittering far above her. She wondered what it must be like to open a cooler and take out enough food to fill your stomach.

Now and again, giant words flashed across the sky in Hindi and English. Over the years Ana had taught herself to read

both languages. INDIA IS GREAT IN THE TWENTY-FIRST
CENTURY! she read, and, VOTE NATIONAL HARIJAN
PARTY FOR A CHANGE!

She could read the words but often they made no sense.

She turned her attention to the cars speeding by on the
road. She could easily spend hours staring up at the holograms but she had to watch out for Deepak Rao.

The thought of him made her skin crawl with fear.

A car pulled up in front of the restaurant. Ana stared with
wide eyes, her heart beating fast. The car was slim and sleek,
as silver as a new rupee coin.

As gently as she could, she leaned Ajay's head back
against the restaurant window and struggled upright. She
found her wooden crutch and pushed herself towards the
car, the stump of her right leg hanging useless beneath her
shorts.

The car doors lifted like the wings of an insect. Four people
climbed out, tall men and women dressed in dark suits and
colourful saris. Ana noticed the wink of gold and jewellery,
caught the scent of expensive perfumes.

They moved from the car, chatting and laughing amongst
themselves. They worked at not noticing her. Ana pushed
herself before them, hand outstretched. 'Baksheesh, sir. Just
one rupee,' she pleaded in Hindi.

A bearded man waved a lazy hand. '*Chalo*, girl. Go away!'

'You give me rupee, I go away, ah-cha, sir? See, I speak
English. Ana not uneducated girl.'

The man gazed down and moved around her as if she were
an infected dog.

She hobbled over to a woman dressed in a crimson and
gold sari and pressed her palms together beneath her chin.
'Namaste, memsahib,' she whispered. 'One rupee for food?'

The woman stared at Ana, her expression sour. Ana had
seen the same look on the faces of many Brahmin women.
They regarded her as less than an insect, a pest to be ignored
or swept aside.

The woman spat. '*Chalo*, gutter rat! Away!' She hurried past
Ana, joined her friends and entered the restaurant. As the

door opened, the odour of tandoori chapatis and spiced masala wafted out, reminding Ana of her empty belly.

One of the high-caste men was talking to the doorman in the entrance. As Ana watched, he handed the doorman a note and glanced across at her.

A note! Then he was giving the doorman at least ten rupees!

The doorman crossed the pavement to where Ana was standing. 'Your lucky day, monkey. Rich businessmen. Brahmins.' He waved the note. 'Ten rupees.'

Ana stared at him. 'Fifty-fifty, ah-cha?'

The doorman laughed. 'Five rupees for little monkey? Think again, girl!' He reached into the pocket of his long coat, pulled out some coins. He counted them into Ana's outstretched palm. 'One, two . . .' He stopped, making to pocket the rest of the coins. 'But I'm feeling generous today, monkey. Here's another. Three, ah-cha? Now go, *chalo*!'

Ana swung herself back to her station beneath the window. She wished that the businessman had given the ten rupees straight to her instead of to the doorman. But Brahmins were like that. They did not like dealing directly with her, kept contact to a minimum.

She was untouchable, after all.

She supposed that she should be grateful that the doorman was a good man. Many others would have kept all the rupees and kicked her into the gutter.

Ajay was awake.

He stared in Ana's direction, but slightly to the left. With his eyes open, his face was not so perfect. Where his big brown eyes should have been, white circles like the skin on sour milk regarded her blindly.

'Rupees, Ana?'

She sat down beside him, slipped an arm around his shoulders and smiled. 'Three rupees, Ajay. Tomorrow morning we'll go to Begum's stall and buy chaat and puri, ahcha?'

His smile was wonderful to see, and Ana could almost ignore his staring, sightless eyes.

She slipped one rupee coin into the pocket of her shorts.

The other two she pushed into the pouch she kept on a cord around her neck, under her vest.

Over the past two weeks she had managed to save more than fifty rupees. If she worked harder, kept awake for longer, she was sure she could save even more. Soon . . . well, maybe in a year or two, she would have saved enough rupees so that she could buy what she had dreamed about for years.

She remembered seeing the holo-programme a long time ago, when she had been seven and Ajay just two.

She had stared at it with wonder, hardly daring to believe what she was seeing and hearing. There were doctors and nurses in India who could give blind people new eyes – they could take away the old, imperfect eyes and replace them with big brown eyes that worked.

From that day, Ana had lived in hope.

For two eyes, the doctors at the miraculous hospital charged two thousand rupees . . .

Until two weeks ago, Ana and Ajay worked for Deepak Rao in the slums of Old Delhi. Rao gave his boys and girls a stinking room to sleep in, and every day took them in his beat-up van to different areas of the city where they would beg all day. Late at night he would return and pick them up. Back at the room he would take all their earnings and search them for any rupees they might have hidden. Then he would give each boy and girl one rupee for food.

Every day Ana and Ajay begged, and every day they earned just one rupee which they had to spend to keep themselves alive.

Ana had saved no money, so how could she buy Ajay new eyes?

Then, two weeks ago, when Deepak had beaten Ajay for not begging enough rupees in one day, Ana knew what she had to do.

The following day, when Deepak had dropped them off, she took Ajay's hand and marched him from the slums of Old Delhi, past the monorail station and down Chelmsford Road to Connaught Place. There she moved from restaurant to restaurant, never the same one twice, and begged baksheesh from the rich customers.

Now, hope was blooming like a flower within her chest – but at the same time she felt fear, too. Deepak Rao would not sit idly on his massive bottom and let her escape so easily. He would have spies looking for her and Ajay, and if he found them— The thought was enough to make her sick.

Many children had disappeared from Deepak's gang over the years. Deepak would gather the children together, comment on the fact of the missing boys and girls, and say: 'They tried to escape, like beasts of the field returning to the wild. So what do you do with stubborn animals?' And he would draw his forefinger across his throat in a cruel and final gesture.

Now, Ana tried to banish the image from her mind.

In time, she told herself, she *would* save enough money to buy Ajay his new eyes . . .

Through the window of the restaurant Ana could see the big screen on the wall. The diners ate their expensive meals and looked up from time to time.

'What can you see, Ana?' Ajay asked.

She focussed on the images, rather than just seeing them as a series of floating patterns. 'It's . . . I think it's the Mars mission, Ajay.' The astronauts were tumbling around in their spaceship, turning head over heels like slow-motion circus performers. Objects drifted through the air: pens, notebooks, drink cartons.

Ana knew about the mission to Mars but she still found it hard to believe.

She stared at the images coming all the way through space. The astronauts were sucking food from see-through bags. The stuff looked like split pea dal. Ana felt her belly rumble.

She described the pictures to Ajay.

He frowned. 'Why are they going to Mars, Ana?' he asked.

'It's called,' she tried to recall the word she'd heard, '. . . *progress*.'

'What does that mean?'

They had sealed thirty men and women in three space

ships and shot them off to Mars with enough food and water to last them for months, and they called it progress.

'I don't know what it means,' she said. 'Now go to sleep, Ajay, ah-cha?'

Ana was awoken by a loud shout.

She looked around, angry with herself for falling asleep. A kid stood across the road, pointing towards her and Ajay. He seemed too afraid to come any closer. 'There they are!' he yelled in Hindi.

Then Ana saw the van, and felt a sickening sensation in the pit of her stomach. Deepak Rao's battered green Nissan transporter came to a jerking halt a hundred metres away, then reversed along the road towards them. Ana saw Rao's big face hanging out of the window, glaring murderously at her through the teeming rain.

She screamed and pushed Ajay to his feet. 'Run!' she cried.

Ana held on to his shoulders and they ran. Her own leg acted as a third as they sprinted along the covered pavement in front of the lighted shopfronts. Over the years, in time of danger, they had often managed to escape like this. Ajay acting as her legs, while Ana was his eyes.

She heard shouts far behind her, the sound of a revving engine.

Many of the streets in the centre of New Delhi were curved, built in circular patterns by the British in the last century. This one curved away around Connaught Place Park with no break for side street or alley for a hundred metres. Ana considered crossing the road and entering the park – but then Rao would know where she was, and it would only be a matter of time before he found them. It would be better to try and escape down the side streets and alleys around Janpath.

At last they came to a corner. Ajay was panting at having to bear her weight. 'Turn left!' Ana called.

Without slowing, less fearful of what he might bump into than what was in pursuit, Ajay veered to the left. They raced down another wide street like the winning team in a three-legged race. Ana glanced over her shoulder and saw the green van turn the corner and accelerate after them.

She gave a terrified yelp. A metre ahead was the dark opening of a narrow alleyway. They dived into it and kept on running. At least now Rao would be unable to follow them in his van. He would have to give chase on foot. Deepak Rao was the size of an elephant. Ana had never seen him run. She began to think that this time they might get away.

The rain beat down, soaking them to the skin. She had stubbed her bare foot somewhere along the way, and every step was painful. Exhausted, Ajay was slowing down. She heard him sob with every breath, and tried to find the words to urge him on.

They ran through the darkness. The alley opened out and was crossed by a wider, lighted street. Cars and bicycles passed back and forth through the pounding monsoon downpour. Across the street, Ana saw another dark alley. If only they could get through the traffic and disappear into it— She looked over her shoulder. There was no sign of Rao or his helpers.

They emerged on to the busy street and stopped. Cars sped through the night in a continuous procession. Ana looked over her shoulder and saw a dark shape in the shadows of the alley behind her.

When she looked back at the road, there was a gap in the traffic. Sobbing in relief, she yelled at Ajay to run. They limped halfway across the road, stopped to let a battered coach pass, then ran the rest of the way and hurried down the alley. Behind them, the traffic had closed up again, halting Deepak Rao's pursuit.

She urged Ajay on, telling him that they were almost safe. 'Not far now. We're nearly there. But we've got to keep on, ah-cha? Then we'll stop and sleep.'

They turned left down a quiet street and slowed to a painful limp. They came to a road busy with cars and autorickshaws, turned left and slowed to a walk. A small voice in her head told Ana that they were not safe yet, that they should still be running. But she could run no further, and she knew that Ajay was exhausted too. They would walk a while, then head west before finding a concealed place to spend the night.

After that . . . perhaps they ought to leave the city altogether, take a train south to Bombay or east to Calcutta. Deepak Rao would never find them then.

Later, she told herself that she should not have been thinking of the future. She should have concentrated on the present, on the danger they were still in. She might then have avoided what happened next.

She heard a deafening shout to her left. She looked down an alley and saw the small figure of a kid. She turned to run the other way, swinging Ajay with her, but not ten metres away stood Deepak Rao, breathing hard but grinning in triumph.

Ana cried out and dragged Ajay across the road, cars and mopeds flashing by in a blare of horns. Deepak Rao's shouts reached them like the wailing of a wronged spirit.

The cry frightened Ajay. He hesitated, unsure which way to turn, and Ana slipped and fell. Ajay ran into the middle of the road, turning this way and that in panic at losing her.

As Ana lay in the gutter, time seemed to stretch. In slow motion she watched a white Mercedes brake suddenly. Deepak Rao stepped from the pavement and grabbed Ajay's arm in a big fist winking with solid gold rings.

Ajay tried to struggle, but he was like an insect in the grip of a gorilla. Ana reached out, aware of the pain in her ribs, but her cry was lost in the roar of passing traffic. She ducked behind a parked car.

The door of the Mercedes swung open. Seated inside was the hunched figure of a woman. She was old, her face pale and terribly wrinkled – but what Ana noticed was that the woman was wearing a tight-fitting, silver dress cut short to reveal thin white legs. The woman stared out at Rao and Ajay, her lips moving with shouted orders.

Deepak Rao bundled Ajay into the back of the car beside the skeletal woman, and as the door swung shut, Ana caught a glimpse of a ring on the woman's hand. The Mercedes accelerated away into the rain-filled night.

Ana crawled along the gutter towards a taxi-rank, knowing that she had to give chase. She hauled herself upright and leaned panting against a taxi. She pulled open the door and fell inside.

She pointed to the Mercedes as it sped away. 'Follow . . . please follow!'

The driver gave her a withering look. 'You pay up front, I'll take you. Fifty rupees, girl.'

'Fifty?' she began. That was almost all her savings. But what was more important, her savings or Ajay? 'Ah-cha. Here. Now, quickly!'

She pulled fifty rupees from the pouch around her neck and thrust them at the driver.

Seconds later they were racing through the rain, buildings flashing by on either side. The taxi turned a corner, tipping Ana across the back seat. She righted herself and stared through the windscreen. She made out the tail-lights of the white Mercedes two hundred metres up ahead. It was heading south, into the rich district of the city.

Ana wondered what she would do when she found out where the Mercedes was taking Ajay. Why had Deepak Rao so readily handed him over to the old woman?

Five minutes later the taxi slowed.

'Hey! I said follow that car!'

'Like I said. You give me rupees, girl, and I'll follow.'

'But I *gave* you fifty!'

The driver laughed. 'Fifty got you this far. If you want to go any further, give me another fifty.'

Ana sobbed. 'But I've only got . . .' She tried to count her few remaining rupee coins. 'Please, you've got to help me—' But she should have known . . . When had anyone ever helped her for nothing?

The driver reached back between the seats, grabbed Ana's pouch and yanked. The cord snapped.

'Hey!' she began.

The taxi slowed. They were in a rich suburb of big houses and spacious gardens. The driver said, 'Get out.'

'No! You take me—'

He flipped a control switch and the back door opened. Ana felt a hand on her back as the driver pushed her from the car.

She hit the road with a painful smack and the taxi sped off into the night.

CHAPTER TWO

INTO THE WEB!

Ana pushed herself into a sitting position and looked around her. She was in the middle of a wet street with houses on either side, dark blocks against the brightly lit night sky. She was in the affluent suburbs south of central Delhi, where all the Brahmin businessmen and their families lived.

Her knee hurt, her forehead throbbed, and the palms of her hands smarted where they had scraped the ground. She was amazed that she had survived without breaking any bones.

Then she thought of Ajay and she felt a pain in her chest, as if a big fist had grabbed her heart and squeezed.

'Are you OK?'

The voice startled her. She looked around. A boy, older than her, was squatting on the pavement, staring. He had a round face and his dark hair was combed back and oiled. His clothes looked expensive.

'Do you speak English?' he asked.

Ana instantly disliked him. 'What does it matter to you?' she snapped.

Ana knew why he had asked. He had seen that she was a maimed beggar-girl, and he had wanted to show that he was superior by speaking English.

He was obviously surprised when she had replied in English as good as his.

'I saw what happened. Are you all right?'

She glared at him. 'What do you think? I was pushed from

a car speeding at fifty miles an hour, and you ask if I'm all right—'

'More like five miles an hour, actually.'

'What?'

'I said, the car was only going at five miles an hour—'

Ana frowned and rubbed her knee. 'Well, it felt more like fifty . . .'

His eyes darted over her, taking in her soiled vest and shorts, the stump of her right leg. 'Do you make a habit of that?' he asked. 'Jumping out of moving cars?'

She glared at him. For a rich boy he was amazingly stupid. 'What do you think?'

He shrugged. 'What happened, then?'

She felt angry. How rude he was to ask such questions. 'Couldn't pay my fare,' she muttered. 'So he threw me out.'

'I'm sorry,' he said. 'Look, can I help you? Come back to the house – I'll give you something to eat and you can clean up.'

She was torn between accepting the offer of food and getting away from here.

'Well?' he asked.

'Just leave me alone!' she shouted. She looked around for her crutch.

But she'd left it back at the restaurant when she and Ajay had fled from Deepak.

It was this, the loss of her simple crutch which she had relied on for years, that finally made her cry.

She sat in the road, soaking wet and hurting, and wept.

The boy reached out, touched her shoulder. 'Please, let me—'

'Leave me alone!' She lashed out at him, dashing his hand away.

She struggled upright, hopped over to the fence and leaned against it, regaining her breath. The boy followed her.

She stumbled along the pavement, holding the fence for support.

'And how long will it take you to get home like that?' he asked.

'Just leave me alone! Please, please, leave me alone!'

'You're being stupid and stubborn. Why don't you let me help you?'

She stared at him. 'What do you want?' she asked. 'Why should you help me?'

He smiled. 'Because you *need* help. You've just fallen from a moving car. You can't walk. You look hungry and injured . . .'

She stopped, staring at him through her tears and strands of wet hair. 'Where do you live?' she asked.

The boy pointed to a big house. 'I have my own bungalow in the back garden,' he said. 'I'll get you some dry clothes and food.'

She considered his offer. She had never before met anyone willing to give her anything other than the odd rupee, and she was suspicious. 'Ah-cha. Just food and clothes – and then I go.'

'Suit yourself.' The boy shrugged. 'Here, lean on me.'

'Don't touch me! Get me a stick, something I can use as a crutch.'

The boy smiled to himself and shook his head. He disappeared into the garden. Ana leaned against the fence and stared at the mansions on either side of the street. This was another world, a place of luxury and privilege she had only ever seen in holo-ads.

The boy reappeared carrying a garden spade without its blade. The D-shaped handle fitted perfectly under her arm. It was even a better crutch than her own. She hobbled along beside him as he walked into the grounds of the big house and up the drive. Half a dozen expensive cars were parked outside the house, and from an open window the sound of music and conversation drifted out.

The boy was speaking to her. 'I said, where do you live?'

She stared at him. How stupid and unthinking he was!

'My parents own a penthouse on Connaught Place,' she answered breezily. 'I have a few rooms overlooking the park.'

'No,' he said gently. 'I mean, seriously.'

'Where do you think I live? I sleep on the pavement outside the Union Coffee house with my— with—'

The thought of Ajay blocked her throat with emotion.

'With your family?'

'With my brother. I have no family.'

He nodded, led her past the house and into a back garden the size of a park. They approached a bungalow surrounded by trees. Ana stopped. 'I don't understand,' she said. 'All the other people like you . . . they want nothing to do with me. Rich people, Brahmins, they treat me like an animal—'

'My family is Brahmin,' he said. 'But I want nothing to do with that way of life. I've travelled, seen how other people live.'

She stared at him. 'You've been overseas?'

He smiled. 'And even farther,' he said mysteriously. He unlocked the door to his bungalow and stepped aside. 'Welcome to my world.'

Ana entered the lighted room, stopped and stared.

She had once read a story in a comic book about Aladdin's Cave, a place full of fabulous treasures, winking gold and glinting jewels. Now, she was reminded of Aladdin's Cave. There was no gold or jewels here, but there were other treasures. Her gaze raced around the room, stopping here and there before moving on to the next amazing object.

She stepped inside and moved around the room as if in a daze. She paused in front of something like a big television screen set into the wall. A multicoloured pattern was playing across its surface. Next to it was what she knew was a computer system, and next to that a musical instrument like an electric sitar. Chairs and sofas furnished the room, some even hanging from the ceiling on chains.

She turned in a circle, open-mouthed. She could have sold any one of these objects and bought food to last her months.

'Sit down and I'll get you a drier and a change of clothes.' He pointed to a chair and stepped through a door to a second room.

She sat in the chair, a black furry blob that looked more like some animal. She leaned back, and cried out as the chair moved beneath her. It flowed around her, taking hold of her waist as she sank into its spongy depths.

Ana kicked out and struggled, and at last escaped from its embrace. She sat on the floor, staring at the living chair.

The boy entered the room, carrying clothes.

'It attacked me!' Ana said. 'Your chair tried to attack me!'

'It's a foam-form,' he explained. 'It changes shape to suit the size of the person who sits on it.'

Ana felt herself blush.

He handed her the clothes, a white shirt, shorts and underwear, and a drier. She had never used an automated drier before, though she had seen them in the ads. It was a warm, egg-shaped object that you smoothed over your skin to magic away the moisture.

'I'll get you some food while you change,' the boy said.

While he was in the next room, Ana stripped off her wet clothes, dried herself, and pulled on the clean new shorts and shirt. The material was soft against her skin.

The boy returned with a tray full of samosas and two bulbs of milk. He placed it on the floor before Ana and sat cross-legged opposite her.

He indicated that she should help herself, and Ana realized that it was almost a day since she had last eaten. She bit into a samosa, the spiced potato and peas the best things she had tasted in a long time.

She caught her reflection in the steel surface of some exercise machine across the room. She looked just like some rich schoolgirl in an ad. She felt a stab of guilt, and then pain that Ajay was not with her to share the experience. She decided that she would finish her meal and then return to Connaught Place. Then, she would try to find her brother.

The boy cleared his throat. 'I'm Sanjay, by the way.'

'Ana,' she said through a mouthful of samosa.

He indicated her leg. 'How did that happen, Ana?'

She stared at him, defiant. 'Are you always so rude with your friends?'

Sanjay smiled and shrugged. 'Where I spend much of my free time, we're open about everything.'

Ana took a long drink of milk, then wiped her lips with the back of her hand. 'If you must know, I was in a monorail accident,' she said.

Sanjay nodded. 'I'm sorry.'

Ana finished her milk and was about to thank him and leave when he said, 'Now, will you tell me what really happened?'

She glared at him. 'I told you – I was in a monorail accident.'

He laughed. 'No, I don't mean that – I mean, what happened earlier? Why were you thrown from the taxi?'

She stared at the crumbs caught in the folds of her new shorts. She suddenly wanted to tell this arrogant Brahmin boy about what had happened to her brother, to share her pain with him.

Perhaps, just perhaps, he might be able to help her find Ajay.

'Two weeks ago I ran away from Deepak Rao with my brother, Ajay,' she began. She told Sanjay how they had made their way to Connaught Place and kept hidden for two days, not daring to show their faces in case Rao should find them. Then, for a few hours each day, they had gone begging around the restaurants. The police had constantly moved them on, but rich people had given her and Ajay more rupees than they would normally earn in the slums of Old Delhi.

Then, Ana had become lax and fallen asleep, and Deepak Rao had found her. 'We ran and ran, but he chased us. I fell in the street and Ajay was picked up by an old woman in a white Mercedes.'

Sanjay was shaking his head. 'What could she want with your brother?'

Ana regarded her fingers. 'I don't know.'

'Can you describe her? Perhaps, if you gave her description to the police—'

Ana stared at him so hard that he stopped talking. For all his wealth, for all the education he must have had, he knew very little about the real world.

'The police!' she exclaimed. 'If I went to the police and told them that my brother had been taken, they'd laugh at me! Do you think they're bothered about the disappearance of a street kid?'

'I don't know . . . I thought—'

'Maybe if *you* had been taken, then they might do something.'

That silenced him. While he blushed and drank his milk, Ana looked around the room. She pointed at a reclining chair in the corner. 'Is that a Web-couch?'

Sanjay nodded. 'Do you know what the Web is?' he asked, surprised. He was doing it again, playing the arrogant little rich kid.

'Of course I do!' she said. Or, rather, she had a vague idea what the Web was.

Deepak Rao used the Web at the public VR-bar near the monorail station. He had bragged about its many wonders to the kids when he was drunk. 'I've been to a wonderful world!' he had shouted, swinging his bottle of whisky like a bell.

'Are you sure you know what it is?' Sanjay asked.

'It's like the movies, and you can step inside the film and take part in what's happening.'

'But you've never Webbed?'

She shook her head. 'But don't tell me – you have, right?'

He nodded, casual. 'Most days,' he said. 'Here, I'll show you.'

He stood and pulled the couch into the middle of the room. On the couch was what looked like the outline of a person – some kind of empty grey suit with wires attached, a control pad on its wrist, and a face mask.

'A Websuit and Web-couch. The latest Atari models,' he said smugly. 'You wear the suit, plug in, and use the wristpad to access the Web.'

Ana nodded, trying not to be too impressed.

Sanjay was looking at her, considering. 'Would you like to have a go?' he asked. 'Spin into the Web?'

'What, enjoy myself while Ajay is somewhere out there?' She grabbed her new crutch and struggled to stand up. 'No! I need to find my brother.'

'Ana, sit down, please. Think about it. What can you possibly do in the real world to get Ajay back?'

'At least I'll be looking for him! Which is more than I'd be doing if I went with you into the Web.'

Sanjay was shaking his head. 'You're wrong. I'll post MP reports on various Web sites.'

Ana stared at him, mystified. 'What do you mean?'

'I'll show you around the Web, and while I'm there I'll post missing person reports about your brother. Then, if Web users see Ajay in the real world they can contact me. Simple. So how about it?'

'I–I don't know. I've never done it before.'

'That doesn't matter. I'll show you the ropes.' He pointed across the room, to another Web-couch and Websuit. 'That's my spare suit for friends.' He glanced at her. 'You'll come?'

She wanted to ask him if she could have a bundle of rupees instead, but stopped herself. She gave a little nod. 'Ah-cha,' she said.

'Good.' He pulled the second couch and suit into the middle of the room next to the first. 'You can have my old suit. I'll use the Atari. Now, step into the suit.'

Ana hesitated, then picked up the suit. The material was cold, and clung to her skin. She found the opening in the back, sat on the edge of the couch and worked her good leg into the legging, then slipped the stump of her right leg into the second. The material hung loose where her right leg should have been. She pulled the suit around her body and worked her arms inside. It gripped her limbs, squeezing. Ana shivered.

She glanced at Sanjay. He stood in his own suit beside the couch, looking like a deep-sea diver. He slipped on his face mask and attached the control panel to his wrist. Ana did the same.

'Now, lie back on the couch and relax,' he told her. 'I'll plug us in.'

She lay back as instructed while Sanjay moved around the couches. She stared through her face mask at him, a part of her not believing that this was happening. Who would have thought, just one hour ago, that soon she would be entering the Web?

'I don't feel anything,' she said.

Sanjay lay down on his couch. 'Not yet, but you will,' he said. 'Just follow my instructions.'

He lifted his right wrist and pointed to the control pad. 'See the red button, Ana? That's the activator. Press it and you'll enter the Web. Once you're in the Web, you can press it at any time to get out. I'll show you all the other functions once we're in there, ah-cha?'

'Ah-cha,' Ana replied in a whisper.

'So . . . here goes,' Sanjay said. 'Into the Web!'

Ana reached out and pressed the red button—

Instantly her world was transformed.

CHAPTER THREE

TROPICANA BAY

'Where am I?' Ana screamed.

She was no longer in Sanjay's room. She was standing on a vast golden plain, a desert that seemed to extend for ever beneath a bright blue sky. Before her was a series of multi-coloured blocks like small houses.

'Relax, Ana,' Sanjay's voice said beside her. 'This is Level One, BB. We call those things building blocks.'

Ana turned. Sanjay – or rather someone like Sanjay – stood beside her. She gasped and stepped back. This Sanjay was much older and taller than the boy she knew. Although his face was still recognizably his own, it seemed more grown-up, and he was dressed in a smart white suit.

'I feel . . . funny,' Ana said.

Sanjay laughed. 'You'll get used to it, in time.'

'I don't know about that.'

Her brain knew that she was lying on her back – she could feel the tug of Realworld gravity as she lay on the Web-couch – and yet all her senses told her that she was standing upright. The contradictory sensations made her feel slightly ill.

Also . . .

Here she was in the Web, but she could smell the scents from the real world. She sniffed. She could smell the samosas she had just eaten, and the sweet incense that Sanjay burned in his room.

Sanjay saw her sniffing and laughed. 'You can't smell or taste things in the Web,' he said.

She glanced at him, at this changed, older Sanjay. The Web was truly a strange place.

'How did you do that?' she asked. 'How did you change yourself?'

Sanjay smiled down at her. 'Simple.' He indicated his wristpad. 'I programmed in how I wanted to look. I can make myself appear as anything. Watch.'

He tapped the keypad on his wrist.

He began to grow slowly taller, and taller, and at the same time thinner. His body became as thin as a drainpipe, his long arms hanging by his side like wires. His head grew. He bent double and leered down at her.

Ana backed off, whimpering.

'OK, OK,' Sanjay said in that superior way of his. His thin fingers touched the keypad again and he began to shrink. Within seconds he was the older version of Sanjay again.

Only then did Ana realize that she had taken two steps backwards.

Steps!

She had not taken actual *steps* for years.

She looked down at her body. She had *two* legs. She was wearing a white smock, and she had two perfect, brown legs.

'I–I don't understand,' she murmured. 'How is it possible? My leg—'

'The suit is relaying the sensations of your phantom limb to your brain,' Sanjay explained. But to Ana that was no explanation at all. 'Therefore, you *think* you have two legs. And in the Web that's all that matters.'

She stared down at her new leg. It *looked* just like her good leg, but at the same time it felt artificial. She moved her toes, and though she could see them, she had no feeling of movement.

She took a deep breath. For years she had been unable to run, really run, without the help of Ajay. Now . . .

She stepped forward, walking towards the coloured

blocks. She had the sensation of really walking, her feet brushing the warm surface of Level One. She felt dizzy with delight.

Fearing that she might fall over, she increased her pace. She began running, thumping down on the ground with both feet, arms swinging. She knew that she was really lying down, yet all her senses told her that she was running. Her dizziness increased, made her head swim. She was moving with a slight limp, her new leg not as efficient as her good leg – but far, far better than the crutch she had used for so long in the real world.

Sanjay was beside her.

'And if you think that's special,' he said, 'just wait until you change your appearance.'

She shook her head. 'How do I do that?'

'Press the panel marked A on your pad,' Sanjay said.

She did so. A list appeared on a tiny screen beside the keypad: HEIGHT? COLOUR? AGE? DRESS STYLE?

'This is a simple program. It'll just alter your appearance as you are now. More sophisticated programs like mine will allow you to alter *everything*. How tall do you want to be?'

'I don't know . . .' She was small for her age. She had always dreamed of being taller. 'As tall as you are now?'

'OK, just tap in two metres.'

She followed his instructions. Instantly she seemed to grow. Her eye level shot up. Now she was as tall as Sanjay.

'Now, for colour and age just tap in what you desire. To stay the same just tap in S.'

Ana considered. She would stay the same colour, but make herself a little older.

Next to COLOUR? she tapped in S, and next to AGE? she tapped in 16.

'How do I change what I'm wearing?'

'Next to dress style tap in casual, or smart, or formal. The program has thousands of options, but it'll be quicker if you just stick to the simple ones.'

'Ah-cha . . .' She tapped in: smart. She had always wanted

to be as well-dressed and sophisticated as the people in the holo-ads.

She looked down at her sixteen-year-old body. She was wearing a red knee-length dress and smart red shoes that felt odd on her feet.

'And now, Ana,' Sanjay said, 'are you ready to bat?'

She stared at him. 'What?'

'Blue-and-tone,' he said. 'Enter one of the worlds of the blocks. That one, for instance, is for the entertainment and recreation Web sites. How about a little E&R?'

He held out his arm, and she took it – amazed at the feel of the material of his white suit beneath her fingers. They strode towards the block, and the sensation of walking made her forget that in the real world she was lying on a Webcouch in Sanjay's bungalow.

They halted before the face of the block. 'Touch it,' Sanjay said.

Ana reached out, brushed the block with her fingertips. The red gloss rippled like the surface of a pond.

'Now, step through,' he said.

Holding tightly on to Sanjay's arm, Ana walked into the block. She heard a loud pinging in her ears and her vision was flooded briefly with a bright blue light.

And then, for the second time that day, her world was transformed.

Ana gasped.

It seemed that she was standing in the centre of a busy, bustling city. Buildings like skyscrapers reached high into the blue sky. Long, straight roads stretched between the buildings, and these avenues were thronged with a thousand different types of people and . . . *things*. She stared. Big spiders scurried around between humans of every size and shape. Some, she saw, had changed their appearances so that they had the heads of animals – gorillas, zebras and unicorns.

She turned her attention to the buildings and realized that they were not really buildings at all. On the surface of each construction was what looked like a vast cinema screen showing a different picture.

From time to time as she watched, a human or spider would walk *through* one of the screens and disappear.

'Welcome to E&R, Ana,' Sanjay said. 'There are thousands of blocks in this Webtown, and each block offers a different world of entertainment and recreation. We can enter whichever world we wish simply by stepping through the wall, or accessing the code through our keypads.'

Ana just stared, shaking her head in wonder. 'Where shall we go?'

'How about Tropicana Bay? It's very popular with New Delhi-ites.'

He led the way across to a skyscraper that showed a scene from paradise. A gently sloping beach stretched around the perfect circle of a bay, except that the water of the bay was more silver than blue, and the sand of the beach was red. Even the trees that fringed the foreshore were unlike any trees she had ever seen. Instead of green leaves they sported myriads of yellow flowers. Between the trees, groups of people sat around tables, chatting and laughing.

'Let's take a stroll around Tropicana Bay,' Sanjay suggested.

He took her hand, and Ana felt a sudden surge of wonder at what was happening to her. They stepped through the surface of the screen, Ana laughing aloud at the weird sensation of moving so easily from one world to another. She found herself walking towards the beach, the sunlight warm on her skin and a breeze blowing in her face.

Ana stopped and knelt by the silver sea. Sanjay watched her. 'Ana, what's wrong?'

She shook her head. She reached out and took a handful of water – except that it didn't feel like real water, but more like a million tiny diamonds.

Ana shook her head again, disbelieving.

'This is the first time,' she said, 'that I've ever seen the sea.'

*

Ana and Sanjay strolled along a promenade between the red sands of the beach and the grass of the foreshore. They passed other couples, well-dressed, sophisticated men and women like the people from the holo-ads. Ana found it hard to accept that she was a part of this incredible world.

She wondered what all these people were like in real life.

She remembered something. 'Hey, I thought you said you were going to post a missing person report?'

Sanjay tapped his wristpad. 'I've already posted the MP report, Ana – I've asked for any info about a six-year-old blind boy taken by Rao and a woman in a white Mercedes.'

'Ah-cha.'

They passed a kiosk that hired out jet-chutes. Reflected in the window, Ana caught sight of an attractive young woman in a red dress.

She stopped in her tracks and stared.

The young woman mimicked her movements, her gestures and facial expressions. Ana frowned, and so did the woman. She turned her head and the woman turned her head too. In the face staring out at her, Ana recognized herself, but more mature, even beautiful. She had breasts, and long legs, and her hair was long and sleek, not the tangled mess it was in real life.

She tried to feel the Websuit that she knew she was wearing, tried to detect the couch she was lying on, and only when she really concentrated could she feel the material of the suit that enveloped her and the sponginess of the couch beneath her.

Then she forgot that she was really in Sanjay's bungalow, and lost herself in the illusion.

'Sanjay!' someone called from the beach.

'Rom!' Sanjay raised a hand a waved.

A white boy with a shock of red hair came running across the sand. 'Hi there, Sanjay,' he said in an American accent. 'Who's the egg?'

'She's no egg, Rom. Meet Ana, a friend from India. Ana, this wise guy here is Rom, Web-wizard and all-round pain.'

Rom squinted from Ana to Sanjay. 'You trying to bite me? You sure she's not your kid sister? I can tell Ana's a first-timer.' He winked at her. 'How're you liking Webworld, Ana?'

She glared at him. 'I was having a great time until I met you.'

'Ow!' Rom yelped, shaking his hand as if stung. 'Hey, no hard feelings, OK? Friends?' He held out his hand.

She smiled. 'Friends,' she said, accepting his handshake.

Sanjay asked, 'Been anywhere venomous since last time?'

'You kidding? Have I told you about the Dreamcastle? It's a long story, Sanjay. Hairy!'

Ana looked from Sanjay to Rom, trying to work out what they were talking about.

'Hey,' Rom said, 'what're you doing now? How about a little jet-chuting?'

'Eight!' Sanjay said. 'You, Ana?'

Ana looked across the bay at the jet-chutes looping through the air. 'I think I'll just sit and watch you.'

'You sure? . . . Ah-cha.' He slapped Rom on the back. 'Let's do it!'

They hired a pair of jet-chutes and rose into the air. Ana watched them climb into the sky, waving and yelling like the kids they were as they circled high above the bay.

She strolled along the promenade, constantly amazed at the strange *reality* of this world. Here the surfaces were brighter than out there in the real world, more like the colours in a film. And surely things actually *moved* faster, too – or was this just her excited reaction to finding herself in the Web?

She was surprised at how friendly Rom had become, after his first few digs at her. In the real world he would never have looked twice at her, still less talked to her.

She found a café and thought about sitting down alongside all the other people. But something stopped her – how might all these well-dressed, beautiful people react if *she* sat down near them and ordered a drink?

In New Delhi, if she tried to enter an expensive café,

begging for food, she would very quickly be chased out . . . and maybe even beaten.

But . . . she was not in New Delhi. She was no longer in the real world, she reminded herself.

She no longer looked like the twelve-year-old untouchable beggar girl that she really was.

She told herself – though it was very hard to believe – that she looked just as rich and good-looking and well-dressed as all these sophisticated people around her.

If she joined them, how would they know who she *really* was?

Even so, as she crossed the grass and sat down at an empty table, her heart was beating fast and she imagined that everyone was staring at her with distaste in their eyes.

A white-coated waiter approached her from an open-air bar. 'Can I get you something, Miss?'

Ana looked around, wondering who he might be talking to. But he was looking straight at her. Embarrassed, she opened her mouth to say something.

The waiter smiled. 'First-timer, yes? Then welcome to the Web. I can get you the house special, a daiquiri-synth slammer. Yes?'

Ana nodded. 'Yes, please.'

The waiter winked at her and hurried to the bar.

She sat in the sunlight and watched as he mixed her drink. She was aware of her heart hammering in her chest. It would take a lot of getting used to, being treated as an equal like this.

The waiter returned with her daiquiri-synth slammer, presented it to her with a bow and moved to the next table. Ana raised the long glass of sparkling blue liquid to her lips, wondering if it would be possible to drink in the Web.

She soon found out. The liquid did not enter her mouth, but seemed to fizz over her lips and across her face, blurring her vision and making her laugh at the tickling sensation. She noticed the other 'drinkers' around the bar lifting glasses to their lips, laughing . . .

She was about to take a second 'sip' when she saw a familiar figure seated at a table near the beach.

She almost dropped the glass, panic clutching at her chest.

It could not be true.

The man seated with the striking young blonde woman certainly looked like Deepak Rao, but he was much slimmer, and better dressed, and his face was younger than in reality. Ana recognized the shifty eyes, though, and the thick, revolting lips.

So this is where he came when he Webbed with the money earned by all his child-beggars.

Next to him, the blonde Western woman raised a glass to her lips. Ana recognized the tight-fitting silver dress, the thin face of the woman she'd seen in the white Mercedes.

Of course, the woman in the car had been old, hideously old – but here in the Web age counted for nothing.

This woman had taken her brother, and Ana had to find out what she had done with him. She wanted to confront Rao and the woman and demand to be told where Ajay was – but that would be stupid and dangerous.

She controlled her panicked breathing and considered the situation. She told herself that there was no chance of being recognized by Deepak Rao. He would not be expecting to see her here, and anyway she looked nothing like the beggar-girl she was in real life.

The table next to them was vacant. Ana knew that she should make her way across to it, try to listen in on what they were talking about.

She told herself she had nothing to fear. She stood up, her heart pounding.

Casually, she strolled through the grass to the empty table and sat down. Neither Deepak nor the woman had paid her the slightest attention.

She sipped her drink, straining to overhear their conversation.

'I need more . . .' the woman was saying.

'How many?' Rao replied. Ana would have recognized his voice anywhere. Even in the Web it was as sickly as ghee.

'How many can you get?'

'Oh . . .' Rao considered, stroking his moustache. 'Say . . . six more.'

'I want them by midday tomorrow, understood?'

'I understand perfectly. Do you require boys or girls?'

The woman waved. 'It makes no difference. Just so long as you bring me six children, you will get your money.'

Deepak Rao nodded with satisfaction and sipped his drink.

Ana wanted to scream at Rao and the woman, force them to tell her what they had done with her brother, but she knew that to show herself now would be a mistake. She had to be careful, very careful.

'You did say that one day you'd tell me where you were keeping them,' Rao said.

The woman gave him a superior look. 'I said "one day", Rao. Today is not the day.'

'Then tomorrow,' Rao smiled sickeningly. 'I would be intrigued to know what becomes of my children.'

'What makes you think I would trust you, Rao?'

Deepak Rao spread his hands in a humble gesture. 'But I have been your faithful servant now for . . . how many months? Have I not served your every need? Surely you can trust me by now?'

The woman gave him another contemptuous look, as if she were regarding a worm. 'We'll meet in the Web tomorrow morning at eight,' she said. 'If I feel in the mood, then I'll take you to the children. Meet me at these coordinates.' And she gave a series of letters and numbers that Ana had no hope of remembering.

'And now,' said the woman, 'time to scuttle. *Ciao*, Rao.'

As Ana watched, the woman touched the red button on her wristpad. What happened next made Ana stare in disbelief. The woman dissolved, became a swirling mass of coloured bubbles – just like the fizz in a glass of soft drink. Then the bubbles vanished and the woman was gone.

Deepak Rao sat alone, sipping his drink, a satisfied expression on his smug face.

Ana stood and hurried from the bar area, wanting to put as much distance as possible between Deepak Rao and herself.

She moved along the beach, looking into the sky for Sanjay.

'Hey, Ana! What's the rush?'

She turned. Sanjay was standing beside the kiosk, having returned his jet-chute. 'Ana, are you all right?'

'I've . . . I've just seen Deepak Rao and the woman who took Ajay! They were here!'

'Hey, calm down, Ana. Just calm down.'

'But I saw them. The woman said she wanted more children. Deepak's going to meet her in the Web tomorrow at eight, and she's going to show him where she keeps the kids!'

'Ana, slow down and start from the beginning. Tell me exactly what you heard.'

He sat her down at an empty table and Ana repeated what Deepak Rao and the woman had said.

Sanjay shook his head. 'I don't understand. Are you sure she keeps the kids in the Web?'

Ana nodded. 'That's what she said. She told Deepak Rao that maybe she'd take him to where she was keeping the children.'

'But you can't keep anyone in the Web! You can stay in here for a few hours, and then you start getting Websickness – the voms.'

'Sanjay, what is the woman doing to my brother and the other children?'

'I don't know, Ana.' He fell silent, then looked up. 'Does Deepak Rao use his own Websuit or does he go to a public VR-bar?' he asked.

'He uses the bar near the monorail station.'

'Good. We'll meet there just before eight in the morning. If we bat at the same time as Rao, then we'll be able to follow him. With luck and good disguise we'll be able to find out what's going on.'

Ana nodded. 'Ah-cha, Sanjay.'

'Hey, it's late, Ana. I need my sleep. I'm scuttling. See you back in Realworld.'

He pressed the red button on his wrist-pad, and seconds later Ana hit hers.

She found herself back in Sanjay's room, lying on the couch in the tight Websuit. She sat up, then stood and tried to take a step. She fell over, crying out in pain and bitter disappointment.

She sat up and stripped off the Websuit. She was Ana the beggar-girl again, Ana the untouchable, twelve years old with one leg and no money and a brother kidnapped by an evil old woman.

Ana stared about her. Everything seemed dull here in the real world. Sanjay was no longer the dashing young man he had been in the Web, and as he stripped off his suit he seemed to be moving in slow motion.

He smiled at her confusion. 'You'll get used to it, Ana. Things happen faster in the Web, so when you exit from it the real world seems slowed down.'

She nodded, looking for her crutch.

Sanjay said, 'If you like, you can spend the night here.'

Ana looked around the room. It was too comfortable, too luxurious. She was used to life on the streets.

'I'll see you in the morning near the VR-bar,' Ana said. She hesitated. 'How much will it cost to use the Web?'

Sanjay smiled. 'Nothing,' he said. 'I have a card that'll pay for us both.'

She found her new crutch and moved to the door. Sanjay followed her. 'Look, you can't walk all the way into New Delhi. Take this and hire a taxi.' He forced a ten rupee note into her palm, and Ana did not object.

She left him with a small wave, limped from the grounds of the mansion and turned right, heading north. She came to a main road, and the taxi rank. She paused, thought about the luxury of taking a ride back to Connaught Place. She shook her head and limped on past the line of taxis.

She shoved the ten rupee note into the pocket of her shorts.

She had started saving for Ajay's eyes again.

CHAPTER FOUR

THE CHAMBER

Ana found it hard to believe that just one hour ago she had been in the Webworld of Tropicana Bay. She had strolled along the seashore, known what it was like to have two legs again. Now, her shoulder ached with the pressure of the crutch and her bare left foot was sore from the long walk.

Keeping to the quiet alleyways, she made her way to the city centre and the VR-bar. She would sleep in one of the doorways nearby, and then meet Sanjay outside the bar just before eight.

It was midnight and quiet along the darkened streets. Homeless families huddled in the doorways of every shop and those less fortunate slept out on the pavements. Rats scurried along the gutters, searching for scraps of food. Ana shivered, despite the warm wind. She thought of Sanjay and his comfortable bungalow.

Then she thought of Ajay. She had been with him for so long that she found it hard to believe that she was without him now. She half expected to turn and see him trotting along behind her, smiling at some private thought.

As she limped along the street, looking for an empty doorway, tears filled her eyes.

'Ana!' someone hissed from the shadow of a doorway. 'Ana Devi!'

She turned, her heart beating in panic.

A young boy appeared from the darkness, pushing himself along in a wheeled cart made from a flimsy fruit box.

'Prakesh!' Ana said.

She had known Prakesh for years. He worked for a friend of Deepak Rao's. Prakesh had no legs, and a voice like a song-bird. He sang ragas outside the monorail station, earning many rupees for his master.

'Ana!' Prakesh hissed. 'You're in great danger.' He tugged her into the doorway.

She squatted down in the shadows beside him.

'Ana! Rao's looking for you. Rao and his kids – everyone! They're not sleeping tonight. They're searching every street in Delhi!'

'Do you know where they took Ajay?'

The boy made a pained face. 'Ajay was taken?' He shook his head. 'Sita, Nazreen and Parveen have all disappeared, too, just like that – never seen again. Now Deepak wants you. He's angry, first that you ran away, then angry again that you got away tonight. He doesn't want the other children to think they can get away from him. He said "Whoever tells me where Ana Devi is, there's a reward of many rupees."'

He stared at her with big eyes. 'What're you going to do, Ana?'

She shrugged. 'Find somewhere to sleep tonight, some-where safe.'

Prakesh reached out and gripped her wrist. 'Not here, Ana! Every fifteen minutes, Deepak drives along the street. Try the monorail station. Look, take my blanket, wrap yourself up so you can't be seen. Sleep at the station.'

Ana thanked him. 'Keep your blanket, Prakesh. I'll hide in an alley.'

'Ah-cha. Take care, Ana.'

She stood, fitted her crutch under her arm and moved quickly from the doorway. As she hurried along she realized that she was the only moving figure in the quiet street. If Rao were to drive by now—

She tried to push the thought to the back of her mind. She had to hide until eight when she would meet Sanjay and follow Rao into the VR-bar, try to find out why he was selling children to the old woman.

It was past midnight now, and many of the hologram advertisements in the sky had closed down for the night, leaving great patches of darkness up above where the stars shone through. This meant that the streets were darker too and there were more shadows in which to hide from Deepak Rao.

Ana considered what Prakesh had told her, that Rao had offered a reward to anyone who found her. It meant that many people would be looking for her, eager for rupees. The thought made her angry and afraid.

She turned down a narrow sidestreet. During the day, this street was full of shops and stalls selling meat: lamb, chicken and goat. The street stank of blood and offal, and no one slept here at night. Maybe Deepak Rao would not think to come down here in search of her. She would find a doorway and doze until eight.

She stopped, her heart thumping like a drum. Ahead of her, at the end of the alley, she thought she saw a shadowy figure. She told herself that it could be anyone or anything, told herself that she should not be afraid. She squinted into the darkness. The figure was still there, tall and unmoving – staring at her.

Quickly, Ana swung herself around and set off back down the alley, a moan escaping from her lips. She stopped at a sound up ahead – a grumble of an old petrol engine.

In her fright, she almost stumbled and fell. She stared down the alley. A green van – Deepak's old Nissan trans-porter – stood at the end of the alley, blocking her way.

She turned again. The tall dark figure was moving towards her. She was trapped – like a rat in a box. She wanted to scream at the unfairness of what was happening but knew that to show her anger and despair would be to show Deepak Rao how frightened she was – and she did not want to give him that satisfaction.

She hurried towards the van. He might capture her, but she would do her best to hit him with her crutch.

The door of the van opened, and at the same time a pair of

hands gripped her from behind. She tried to struggle, but the man's hold was impossible to break.

Deepak Rao squeezed himself from the van like an over-weight genie emerging from a battered lamp. He stood with his arms folded, looking down on Ana. 'You're a very stupid girl to think you could escape,' he said. 'You know that no one can get away from Deepak Rao.'

He nodded to the man holding her. 'Into the van,' he said.

The man gripped her with one huge arm, opened the back door of the transporter and tossed her inside. Ana fell heavily, managing to keep a tight hold on her crutch. The door slammed. Seconds later the engine started and the van trundled off.

She sat up, riding the painful bumps, and stared through the rear window at the passing streets. She hoped that at least she might soon be reunited with Ajay.

Five minutes later, the van slowed and stopped. She peered through the window. Her heart sank at the sight of the familiar interior of the warehouse where Rao had his base. She heard footsteps, and the doors were flung open. Deepak Rao stared in at her. 'Get out, girl!'

As the strong man Rajiv grabbed her ankle and dragged her out, she cracked her head on the back of the van. She cried aloud as she hit the floor. The strong man swept her up and carried her across the vast floor of the warehouse. Deepak Rao lifted a trapdoor and Rajiv set her down by the dark hole. He tried to pull her crutch from her grasp but Rao shook his head. 'Let her keep it.'

The strong man grunted, lifted Ana by one arm and lowered her into the hole.

Ana yelled in protest, feebly kicking her leg. The man dropped her and she hit the stone floor with a painful smack.

She had been here before, many years ago. This was the chamber where Deepak Rao kept his newly found waifs and strays.

Four years ago, her uncle had been unable to feed and clothe Ana and Ajay any longer, and had turned them out on to the streets. Deepak Rao had found them wandering around the monorail station, and offered them a home and food.

Ana tried to shut out the thought of what had happened then.

She looked around. Light spilled in from a barred window set high into the wall. The window was at street level and showed only a dark patch of sky.

She sat and rubbed her bruises and the bump on the back of her head.

'Ana? Is that you?'

Her heart skipped at the sound of the voice. For a second she thought it was Ajay, and then she made out in the dimness the small shape of a young boy called Bindra. She had known Bindra for more than a year. He had worked as a shoeshine boy outside the Hilton Hotel in Old Delhi.

'Bindra? What are you doing here?'

'Last week someone stole all my brushes and polish. I had to beg in the streets. Then Rao came along and offered me a bed and work.' He paused. 'What happens now, Ana? Where am I?'

How could she begin to tell him what the future had in store? He sat in the corner and stared at her. He had two legs, two arms, and his eyes shone brightly in the little light that filtered in from outside.

'I don't know,' she whispered, not meeting his eyes. 'I don't know what happens now.'

She looked around the chamber, saw the small shapes of other children lying on the floor, asleep.

Bindra was silent for a while. 'And Ajay? Where is Ajay?'

Ana began to speak, but found that the words stuck in her throat. At last she said, 'Someone took Ajay, a friend of Rao's. I don't know where he is.'

'I'm sorry, Ana,' Bindra said. 'Maybe when Rao lets us out, maybe then you can find Ajay?'

'Maybe, Bindra,' Ana said. She watched the small boy lie down on the floor and try to sleep. She thought of the fate in store for Bindra and the other children in the chamber . . . and then wondered what Rao had planned for *her*.

Of course, she could always try to escape.

No one ever tried to escape from Deepak Rao's chamber. When he brought new children to the warehouse, he would tell them that if they tried to get away he would throw them in the river. Everyone was so frightened of being thrown into the river that they never even thought of trying to get away.

Perhaps, Ana thought, there might be a way out.

She looked up at the trapdoor, but it was too high up and in the centre of the ceiling. She would be unable to reach it.

But if she could climb the wall she would be able to reach the barred window.

Deepak had made a mistake in letting her keep her crutch. If she could reach the opening, push her crutch against the bars . . . just maybe she could force one out of the crumbling wall and create a gap wide enough to squeeze through.

But first she had to find a way up the wall.

Ana stood and placing her crutch carefully between the sleeping children she hopped across the chamber. She paused before the wall and ran her fingers up and down the brickwork. Some of the bricks were worn and hollowed. She would be able to push her fingers and toes into the gaps and pull herself up.

She threaded her arm through the D-shaped handle of her crutch and hung it from her shoulder, then reached up and dug her fingers between the crumbling bricks. She pulled herself up, finding a hollow with her toes. She paused, the weight of her body resting on her leg, then began again. She reached up, her fingers probing blindly for the next gap.

The noise of her climb alerted Bindra. 'What are you doing, Ana?'

'Shhh!' she hissed.

He fell silent.

She found a hand-hold, searched for another and found one, then dragged herself up the wall. Her toes found a gap and she rested, panting. She could almost reach up and touch the bars – then, she should be able to pull herself up on to the window ledge and get her breath back.

She reached out with her left hand and felt the fingers of

her right slipping from their hold. In desperation she reached up and managed to grab a bar. She scrambled up the wall, snatching at another bar with her right hand and hauling herself up on to the window ledge. She sat, shaking with exhaustion, and looked down into the darkened chamber.

She stayed very still for five minutes, calming her nerves before she began the next stage of her escape plan.

She pulled her crutch from her shoulder and poked it through the bars. She pushed with all her strength, willing the bars to shift.

She heard a sharp crack and thought at first that her crutch had broken. Then she saw that the brickwork at the base of the bars was crumbling. Almost tearful with relief, she pulled again. A bar shifted, dislodging bits of brick and cement powder. She reached out and tugged at the bar, and it came away in her hand.

She pushed her crutch out into the street and was about to follow it when she remembered Bindra and the others. She peered into the darkness. 'Bindra!' she hissed.

'Ana! What are you doing?'

'What do you think?' she called softly. 'Tell the others to climb the wall and escape!'

'No!' she heard Bindra say, fear in his voice. 'Rao will drown us if we escape! Don't go, Ana!'

'You've got to get away from here, far away so Rao won't find you!'

'I'm too afraid, Ana,' Bindra said.

'Bindra, you must escape. Please believe me. You've got to escape!'

She wanted to tell him the truth, but the truth was so terrible that he would never believe her.

'I must go,' Ana cried. 'Please, do as I say and escape!'

She pushed her shoulders through the gap. The bars pressed painfully against her ribs and shoulder blades as she squeezed through bit by bit. Halfway through she paused to regain her breath, and hoped that Deepak Rao would not choose now to open the trapdoor and find her.

She pulled herself into the street, picked up her crutch and hurried away from the warehouse, sadness in her heart at the thought of leaving Bindra and the others.

Fifteen minutes later, she arrived at the VR-bar. Even now, in the early hours, it was still open. A massive neon VR sign flashed on and off, filling the street with multicoloured light. She found a doorway across from the bar and curled herself into a tight ball.

She dozed on and off for the next couple of hours.

She awoke finally as dawn was breaking over the city. She yawned and stretched, aware of her empty stomach.

A taxi pulled up outside the VR-bar, and the well-dressed figure of a young man stepped out and paid the driver.

'Psst!' Ana called. 'Sanjay – over here!'

He looked into the windows of the buildings, as if expecting to find her there. Then he saw her waving from the doorway and ran across the road, dodging the traffic. He looked embarrassed as he glanced around the filthy doorway.

'Welcome to my world,' Ana said, remembering his words of the night before.

'I did say you could stay at my place.'

She stared at him. 'I'm fine on the streets,' she said, then changed the subject. 'What's the time?'

'Almost eight.' He noticed something in her expression. 'Is something wrong?'

'I'll tell you later,' she said. It was odd to think that while Sanjay had slept, comfortable in his bed, she had been imprisoned by Rao, had managed to escape, and had spent the rest of the night in the doorway.

A green van braked outside the VR-bar, and Deepak Rao squeezed himself from behind the driver's seat. She was aware of her heart pounding at the sight of him.

'There's Rao,' she said in a small voice, pointing.

Sanjay watched as Rao entered the bar. 'Ready, Ana? Let's go.'

She stood, gathering her crutch. As she crossed the road next to Sanjay, Ana wondered what experiences awaited her this time inside the strange world of the Web.

CHAPTER FIVE

BELLATRIX III

Deepak Rao crossed the carpeted floor of the VR-bar and stepped into one of the single booths that lined the far wall.

Sanjay led Ana to a double booth and locked the door behind them. Two couches occupied the booth, a grey Websuit lying on each. Ana sat down and pulled on the suit. The material clung to her as if it were wet. She pulled on the face mask and stared through the goggles at Sanjay.

'I'll go first,' he said. 'I'll follow Rao to whichever Webtown he enters, try to find out which site he goes to. Then I'll come back to BB and meet you there.'

He lay down and pressed the red button on his wristpad. Ana watched him, finding it hard to believe that now Sanjay would be walking around in the Web. It looked as if he were asleep and dreaming. His arms and legs twitched from time to time, and once or twice his head turned.

Ana lay back and pressed the red button on her wristpad.

Instantly, she was standing on the golden plain, the multicoloured blocks before her under a bright blue sky. She peered down at her body. She looked like she did in the real world, except here she had two legs, and she was dressed in a simple white smock.

She looked around for Sanjay, but there was no sign of him. From time to time she saw other figures appear, fizzing into existence from nowhere before moving quickly to the coloured blocks and disappearing inside.

Then two figures appeared from a block to her left. As she watched they waved and ran across to her.

Ana stared. The figures looked for all the world like upright green frogs with domed heads, little pot-bellies and spindly legs.

'Ana,' the taller frog said in Sanjay's voice. 'Don't be alarmed, it's only me.'

'Sanjay?'

'And this is Rom,' said the taller frog. The smaller frog gave a little bow. 'Hi, Ana. How's things?'

'There's a lot of explaining to do,' said the Sanjay-frog. 'First, tap in these coordinates.' He gave her a list of numbers and letters, and she tapped them into her wristpad.

Instantly, she was aware that she had changed appearance. She looked down at her arms and legs. They were thin and green, and she had a little belly just like Sanjay and Rom.

'Welcome to the club, Ana,' Rom said. 'Don't we look just great?'

Ana had to laugh. 'What's happening, Sanjay?'

The first frog was walking towards the block. Ana and Rom joined him. 'I followed Rao to the Exploration Webtown,' Sanjay said. 'He went to a site called Bellatrix III.'

Ana frowned. 'What's that?'

'It's an imaginary planet, one of thousands the Web authorities have created and stored in the exploration system,' Sanjay explained. 'I followed Rao there and saw him meet a woman. They boarded a power boat and headed off across the sea towards an island—'

'But why are we disguised as frogs?' Ana asked.

'I'll get to that,' Sanjay said. 'While I was on Bellatrix III I noticed a lot of spiders – they're security systems that make sure we don't go where we're not supposed to. The island was one of these no-go areas. I don't have the know-how to get around these systems, but guess who does? I left Bellatrix and accessed a few sites where I know Rom hangs out.'

'And I like a challenge,' Rom said.

'But why frogs?' Ana tried again.

'You'll soon find out,' Sanjay said. He linked hands with Ana and Rom and they stepped into the block.

Webtown stretched away like a glinting city of skyscrapers, crowded with a million other Web users. For a second Ana was conscious of her guise of a frog – but then she noticed the many physical types all around her: animals of all kinds, even insects and birds, and fish that swam through the air.

Sanjay gave instructions, and Ana tapped a code into her wristpad. A second later she found herself alongside Rom and Sanjay, standing before the Bellatrix III block. The façade of the block showed an alien landscape. Hand in hand, the three frogs stepped through.

They were standing on a beach of black sand, facing a vast ocean. The water was thick and green, moving with sluggish ripples towards the shore. From time to time, whale-like creatures broke the surface of the sea, spouted geysers of green water from their blowholes, then submerged. A huge, molten red sun filled the horizon, slow-motion fountains of flame spewing from its circumference.

'It's so . . . strange,' Ana said, inadequately.

'It's the ancient planet of an ancient sun,' Sanjay said, 'near the end of its life.'

Added to the oddity of being in the Web again, the gravity of this planet was less than that of Earth. Ana had no idea how it was achieved, but she felt lighter on Bellatrix III, as if she could leap into the air and float.

She looked around her at the planet, the jungle of black trees behind her, the thick green soup of the sea. She concentrated, and felt the pressure of the Websuit against her body and the Realworld couch beneath her.

Sanjay and Rom were pointing out to sea. Ahead of them, outlined against the bloody half-circle of the sun, was the dark cone of an island.

Then Ana saw why they were disguised as frogs.

Along the beach sat a circle of small green creatures, frogs just like themselves. Pulled up on to the sands beside them was a wooden fishing boat.

'The Web authorities thought it'd be more exciting if the planet had aliens,' Sanjay explained. 'So they generated these creatures. If we go to the island disguised as aliens, then Rao and the woman might think nothing of it.'

'But first,' Rom said, 'we have to get to the island, right?' He pointed along the beach to where two hairy spiders, each one as big as a dog, ran towards them on long black legs.

Ana stepped back in fright. Rom touched her shoulder with a little green hand. 'Be careful. If they bite us, we'll find ourselves scuttled back to the VR-bar.'

The spiders halted before them, bodies bobbing up and down. 'Welcome to Bellatrix III,' the first spider piped up. 'We hope you will enjoy your visit here. Please allow us to remind you that certain features of this site are out of bounds.'

The second spider went on, 'You are welcome to explore the mainland, but do not attempt to venture across the straits to the island. Trespass will be met by increasingly severe warnings.'

Rom stepped forward. 'Outa my face, hairies,' he said, fingers working on the keyboard of his wristpad.

The fluting voice of the first spider began to protest, before it vanished along with its mate.

'How did you do that?' Ana asked.

The Rom-frog winked at her. 'Just a little sub-routine I cooked up back home in New England,' he said. 'Trouble is, when we get to the island the spiders will be bigger and fiercer, and my programs might not work as well.'

'Let's worry about that when we get there,' Sanjay said. 'Do you think the natives will mind if we borrow their fishing boat?'

'They're Web constructs,' Rom said, 'so they can't stop us. Come on.'

Ana followed her friends towards the gathering of frogs. The seated aliens seemed not to notice as Sanjay and Rom hauled their broad-bottomed boat down the beach towards the sea. Ana joined in, her feet sinking into the hot black sand as she pushed.

They jumped aboard the bobbing boat and Sanjay passed
Ana and Rom a pair of oars. She had never rowed a boat
before, but after watching Rom and Sanjay she soon fell into
rhythm.

They made good progress through the thick soup of the
sea, the lower gravity making the oars as light as cricket bats.
Ana concentrated, trying to discern the lie of this 'reality'. Of
course, visually and aurally it was wholly convincing – but
when it came to the sensation of smell . . . Ana smiled to
herself. She might have been on an alien planet in the Web,
but she could still smell the familiar scents of her native
India. The aroma of spiced food wafted into the VR-bar,
along with the scent of joss-sticks, cow dung and petrol
fumes.

Five minutes later Ana saw her first ghost.

She was sweating beneath the heat of the sun when the
face of a boy appeared, floating in the air beside the boat. His
expression was pained. His mouth opened but no words
sounded.

Ana screamed.

Sanjay turned to her. 'What's wrong?'

She pointed out to sea. 'There . . . There, I thought I
saw . . . a face – the face of a young boy.'

But there was nothing in the sky now.

Sanjay looked at Rom, who shrugged. 'Could be a Web-
ghost,' the American said. 'Don't be alarmed. They happen
all the time – stray machine memories bleeding into site
programs. They look frightening, but they're only virtual
illusions, OK?'

Ana didn't understand half of his explanation, but she
nodded anyway and said that she was fine.

She concentrated on rowing, and they made steady progress towards the island. It rose steeply from the calm waters
of the ocean, its sides covered with a forest of trees like burnt
matchsticks. On the highest point of the island was a solid,
square building constructed of red bricks, dark against the
light of the setting sun.

A beach of black sand came into view and they rowed all the faster. Ana kept a look out for spiders patrolling the foreshore, but the island seemed still and quiet in the twilight.

The keel scraped the shelving sands of the shallows. Rom and Sanjay leaped out and pulled the boat up the beach.

Ana stepped on to the hot sand and stared back at the mainland. She looked up into the sky. The light was failing fast. 'How will we be able to row back in the darkness?' she asked.

Rom stared at her, his big mouth split wide as he laughed out loud.

Sanjay smiled. 'Think about it, Ana.'

She felt herself blushing. 'What? I don't see—'

Sanjay held up his right arm and pointed to his wristpad. 'We don't have to row back to leave Bellatrix III,' he explained. 'All we do to get back to the VR-bar is hit the scuttle button. OK?'

'Ah-cha,' Ana whispered. 'I see.'

Rom strode up the beach and peered into the forest of blackened trees. 'I can see a footpath,' he called back. 'I guess it leads up to the house.'

They left the beach and climbed the path through the trees, Rom leading the way, Ana second and Sanjay behind her. The eerie silence was broken from time to time by the quick chirping of birds. Ana saw dark shapes leaping with silent agility through the tree-tops.

'Careful,' Rom warned suddenly. 'We have company!'

Ana's heart jumped. She looked all around her, unable to spot the danger. Sanjay pointed up the path.

A spider almost as tall as Ana straddled the path before them. Its great hairy body bobbed on the sprung suspension of its legs. Two eye-stalks bent to regard them.

'You are contravening Web-codes,' the spider said in mechanical tones. 'Please turn about and leave the island. Failure to obey this command will lead to summary expulsion.'

Ana gripped Sanjay's arm. 'What is it saying?'

'It said that if we don't go away it'll bite us out of the Web.'

Rom was tapping frantically on his wristpad. 'I'm finding it hard to shift,' he called out. 'Pick up a big stick each and hit it if it tries to bite you.'

The spider advanced one step. Rom backed off, still tapping. Ana and Sanjay stepped backwards too, looking around them for suitable weapons. Ana saw a hefty branch on the forest floor and picked it up. Sanjay found a shorter club and gave it a practice swing.

The spider bent its legs, as if preparing itself to jump at Rom. Instead, it scurried forward, trying to catch Rom off guard while he was busy with his wristpad. Sanjay dashed past Rom and swung his club with all his might but narrowly missed. The spider scurried backwards, hissing.

'Take care, Ana,' Sanjay called to her. 'The Web might be make believe, but we can still feel pain.'

Ana was aware of her limbs shaking in fear. She tried to tell herself that all this was an illusion, that really she was lying on a couch back in New Delhi. But her brain was convinced that she was on Bellatrix III in the disguise of an alien frog and being attacked by an overgrown spider.

The spider advanced again, jumped at Rom in an attempt to bite him. Sanjay swung his club again and this time made contact. One of the spider's legs snapped and trailed uselessly along the ground as the spider backed off up the path.

'There!' Rom cried in triumph. He stabbed a finger down on his keyboard, and the injured spider dissolved in a swirl of colour and disappeared.

Sanjay stood panting. 'That one was too close for comfort. It almost had you, Rom.'

'I was doing everything I knew. Once it was weakened, I could override its defences. You OK, Ana?'

She nodded. 'Ah-cha,' she said. 'I'm fine.'

They began climbing again. The trees soon thinned out, and they passed from the forest to stand on the edge of a sloping sweep of grass. High above them, its lighted windows looking down like watchful eyes, a red-brick building stood dark against the evening sky.

Ana saw movement to her right. She turned. In the air before her she made out the indistinct shape of a floating face. She stared at the ghost, opened her mouth and tried to scream.

The ghost gained solidity, became the brown face of a young Indian boy. Its lips moved, forming silent words. It seemed to be pleading, begging her to help.

Then, as quickly as it had appeared, it vanished into the gathering dusk.

Ana turned to Sanjay and Rom. They stood very still, staring at where the apparition had been.

At last she found her voice. 'I–I know who it was,' she said. 'A year ago a boy called Dilli— Deepak Rao took him out begging one morning, and Dilli never came back.'

'It's OK, Ana,' Sanjay soothed. 'It's OK.'

'But it isn't OK!' Ana cried. 'What happened to him – what's happening to all the children that Rao has given to the woman?'

She thought of her brother, and pain clutched at her heart like an evil fist.

CHAPTER SIX

THE HOUSE OF STOLEN CHILDREN

'We'll go round to the back of the house,' Rom said. 'It's too open here – they'd see us if we tried to get near. Follow me.'

He led the way through the bushes, up the hill and then along the side of the house. Ana told herself that she should not fear for her own safety – whatever happened, Rao and the woman could not harm her. All she had to do to escape was hit the scuttle button on her wristpad.

But she could worry about what might be happening to Ajay.

They emerged from the bushes at the back of the house. Before them was a flat lawn overlooking the ocean. The lawn was enclosed by a high wire-mesh fence. Imprisoned behind the fence were perhaps a dozen young children. As Ana stared, she realized that she recognized many of them – Sita, Nazreen, Parveen. They were dressed in identical white trousers and shirts, and of course they were not wearing wristpads.

She turned to Sanjay. 'But why imprison the children behind the fence?' she asked. 'Surely the island is prison enough.'

Sanjay shrugged. 'Maybe the woman doesn't want the kids seen by Web users on the mainland. What she's doing here isn't exactly legal, Ana.'

She moved to the fence and clutched the wire. 'Ajay!' she cried. 'Ajay, are you there?'

Something moved to her right. She turned. A spider the size of a barrel scurried towards her. She backed off until she bumped into Sanjay. Rom stepped forward, fingering his wristpad.

The spider advanced. As before, Sanjay leaped forward and swung his club at the spider. This one was faster than the first and leaped back out of reach.

Ana yelled at Rom and Sanjay. Advancing along the side of the fence was yet another spider, scurrying towards them on long, nimble legs.

Rom looked over his shoulder. 'OK, I think it's time to retreat, guys. Back into the bushes.'

Ana was about to step into the cover of the bushes when she saw a small figure among the children on the lawn. The boy was walking towards the fence, his head cocked as if he had heard a familiar voice.

'Ajay!' Ana cried. She ran to the fence again. 'Ajay, I'm here!'

Ajay heard her, and a smile transformed his face.

'Ana!' Rom called out. 'Come on!'

Sanjay and Rom were already in the bushes. Sanjay was beating off a spider with his club.

'I can't leave Ajay!' Ana cried.

'You can't do anything for him here!' Rom tried to reason with her. 'Remember, he's not really here on the island – he's somewhere out there in Realworld.'

'But I can't just leave him!' she sobbed.

'Ana!'

She turned at Sanjay's scream. A spider was running towards her with high, quick steps, its mandibles clacking like castanets. She stumbled backwards and fell, then scrambled on all fours towards the bushes. Sanjay grabbed her arm and pulled her into the bushes. Rom was still tapping codes into his keypad. As Ana watched, the first spider exploded in a swirl of multicoloured pixels and vanished. There was no time to feel relief. The second spider darted towards them, jaws working.

Rom tapped desperately. He called over his shoulder.

'Might as well press your scuttle buttons, guys. This is the end of the road.'

The spider darted forward and leaped at Rom. Its mouth found his arm, and Rom cried out in pain. Instantly, the frog who had been Rom dissolved in a whirlwind of a million green bubbles and disappeared as if he had never existed.

Sanjay cried out and swung at the spider with his club. The impact snapped three of its legs. It stumbled around in a drunken circle, attempting to steady itself and charge at Sanjay. As it came, he stepped forward and like a cricket batsman swiped at the spider's body. He made full contact and swept the creature high into the air.

'Let's scuttle, Ana,' Sanjay said. 'We can't do anything without Rom here to help us. It won't be long before another spider shows itself.'

'No! I've got to talk to Ajay!'

'But think about it, Ana. You can't do anything. He's not really here, remember?'

'But he might know where he is in the real world!' Ana yelled at Sanjay. 'Don't you see? If he knows where he is in Delhi, then maybe I can find him!'

Without waiting for his reply, Ana ran from the cover of the bushes and approached the fence. She told herself that two minutes was all she needed, two minutes to question her brother, find out where the woman in the Mercedes had taken him.

'Ajay!' she called, fingers clutching the wire of the fence.

The little barefoot boy moved towards the source of the sound, his head held to one side and his sightless eyes staring straight ahead.

'Ajay, over here. Quickly!' She looked towards the house, but there was no sign of life at any of the windows.

Ajay stopped at the fence and reached out. Ana poked her fingers through the wire and touched his hand. He pressed his face to the fence and Ana kissed him. The skin of his cheek was warm, just as she remembered it in real life.

'Ana, where am I? What did they do to me?'

'You're in the Web, Ajay.'

'The Web?' He looked bemused, even though he knew all about the Web in theory. 'I'm really in the Web? I wondered. I was taken away in a car, Ana. Taken into a house and made to wear a tight suit. Then I found myself in a different place. I was suddenly outside. It was so hot, even hotter than home. And the smells – I could still smell India. I wondered . . . I wondered if I was in the Web.' He shook his head. 'But why? What are they doing to us?'

'I don't know, Ajay. Listen, I need to know where the woman took you. Do you understand? I can't help you now – I'm in the Web just like you. I need to know where you are in real life. Where did the woman take you, Ajay? *Which part of Delhi?*'

Ajay frowned, then shook his head. 'I don't know. We . . . we drove for ten minutes after I was picked up. We stopped and I was taken from the car, across grass and into a building. But I don't know where it was, Ana.'

'Don't worry. I'll get you out. Honestly, I'll get you out somehow.'

'I've been in here a long time, Ana. I feel sick all the time. But some of the others, Sharma and Parveen – they've been here for months, made to stay in here and never let out!' He made a vague gesture behind him, and Ana saw two children sitting in the middle of the lawn, clutching their legs and rocking back and forth in distress.

Ana heard a sound behind her. She turned, fearing the attack of another spider. Instead, Sanjay pushed through the bushes.

Ajay jumped. 'Who is that?'

'It's OK, Ajay. I'm with a friend.'

'Ana,' Sanjay hissed urgently. 'Quick, get down!'

Before she could protest, Sanjay grabbed her arm and dragged her into the concealment of the bushes. As she squatted and peered through the leaves at the house, the back door opened and two figures stepped out on to the lawn.

The woman had a shock of bleached blonde hair and wore the same short silver dress that her older self wore in the real world. A younger, slimmer version of Deepak Rao strolled across the lawn beside her.

Ajay hooked his fingers through the wire of the fence. 'Ana? Ana, where are you?'

'Ajay,' Ana hissed, 'please be quiet!'

Rao and the woman walked at a leisurely pace around the lawn, chatting. They approached the fence where Ajay stood and paused behind him. Ana ducked further into the cover of the bush.

'. . . This child has only recently been introduced into the Web,' the woman was saying. 'So of course the effects of long-term exposure have yet to manifest themselves.'

Rao nodded. 'Very interesting . . .' he murmured.

The woman glanced at him. 'You don't approve? Let me tell you that I see very little difference between what I am doing here and your own operations out there in Realworld.'

'Come, come. I see a – please excuse the pun – a world of difference.'

'How so?' the woman snapped. 'You use children to your own ends, manipulating them for your personal benefit, and I have the honesty to admit that I do the same.'

'But permit me to point out that I happen to look after my children. Yes, I take a percentage of their earnings, but I also provide them with shelter.'

'And I initiate my children to the wonders of the Web,' the woman responded. 'By the way – you do have the children you promised me yesterday?'

Rao nodded. 'Safe and secure and to be delivered to you at midday. Oh, and for a little extra I can even supply you with another child if you wish – Ajay's sister.'

Ana stiffened, realizing what Rao was talking about. Bindra and the other children in the chamber – they were all destined to be delivered to the woman at noon.

'Excellent,' the woman said.

Rao paused, a finger to his lips in a gesture Ana had seen

many times before. 'Perhaps, now that you have taken me into your confidence, you will tell me what it is exactly that you are hoping to gain from these . . . these *experiments*?'

The woman stared out across the ocean. Her face took on a calculating look. 'Very well, Rao . . .' she said, but her words were lost as she began strolling away across the lawn towards the house, Rao in eager attendance.

Sanjay grabbed Ana's arm. 'What did he mean, he can give you to the woman?'

Ana looked at Sanjay's frog face. 'Last night he captured me, threw me into the chamber. I managed to get away and meet you. But he obviously still thinks I'm imprisoned—'

'Ana?' Ajay called from the fence. 'Ana, are you still there?'

'I'm here, Ajay – but I'm leaving now. I promise that I'll see you very soon.'

Ajay smiled. 'Please hurry,' he whispered, tears falling down his cheeks.

'I'll get you away from here, Ajay,' Ana said.

Sanjay shook his head. 'But how can you get them out?' he whispered. 'We don't even know where they are in Real-world!'

Ana looked up at her brother. 'Bye, Ajay. I'm going now.' She turned to Sanjay. 'See you back at the VR-bar.'

She hit the scuttle button.

Ana lay on the Web-couch in the double booth, blinking up at the ceiling and wondering if the events on the island had really happened. They seemed so real, and yet at the same time so fantastic. Then she remembered Ajay and the tears on his face.

She knew what she had to do. She had to act fast and make sure Sanjay would help her.

She struggled into a sitting position and quickly peeled off her Websuit. Beside her, Sanjay was sitting up. He seemed to be moving in slow motion, and Ana realized how drab the colours of the real world were after the cinema gloss of the Web.

Sanjay pulled off his face mask. 'You didn't answer my question, Ana. How can we get the children out of there—'

'Think about it, Sanjay. It's very simple, really.'

'Go to the police?'

Ana nearly laughed. 'The police? Is that what you'd do?' She shook her head. 'For all I know, the woman pays the police to take no notice of what she's doing. I wouldn't trust the police with a dirty rupee.'

'You have a better plan?' he asked, pulling off his Web-suit.

She stood up, found her crutch and fitted it under her arm. 'Of course. I'm going back to the chamber where Rao had me imprisoned.'

Sanjay stared at her. 'You can't!'

'Why not? Didn't you hear him – he said he would deliver me and the other kids to the woman at noon.'

'But what good would that do? You'd be locked in the Web like the rest of them!'

Ana nodded, staring straight at Sanjay. 'Of course, and that's why I need your help.'

He shook his head. 'But what can I do?'

'Go back to Bellatrix III at noon, cross to the island. I'll be on the lawn, near the fence where Ajay was standing.'

'I don't understand how that will help—'

'Listen to me, Sanjay. When Rao takes me and the others to where the woman is in the real world, I'll remember the route, ah-cha? When I see you on the island, I'll tell you where I am in Delhi.'

Sanjay spread his arms in a defeated gesture. 'What good will that do, Ana? So I'll know where you are in Realworld. What do I do then? The place will be guarded. How do I get in on my own? Have you thought about that?'

Ana stared at him, considering. 'Perhaps you can do something to attract the attention of the guards, then enter the house and get us out of the Web.'

'Like what? You make it sound so easy—'

'I don't know . . .' Ana said, frustrated. 'But you've got to create some kind of diversion.'

Sanjay was shaking his head.

'Have you got a better idea?' Ana cried. 'At least my plan is better than nothing!'

'I'm not suggesting that we do nothing.'

'Then what are you suggesting, wise guy? Come on, let's hear your plan.' She stared at him, angry.

He just sat on the edge of the couch, staring down at his fingers. 'I don't know, Ana. I just don't know. I've never been in a situation like this before.'

'Then we'll follow my plan?'

'It's just too risky, Ana.'

'Are you frightened the spiders might bite you, Sanjay? Are you frightened you'll be caught by the woman's guards?'

Sanjay looked up, shook his head. 'I'm not frightened that anything will happen to me,' he said. 'I'm frightened that something will happen to you.'

They stared at each other across the small room. The silence stretched. Ana suddenly wanted to hug this privileged little Brahmin boy for what he'd just said.

The odd thing was that she would gladly go back and imprison herself in the chamber, but she could not find the courage to tell Sanjay how much she liked him.

'I've got to help Ajay and the others, Sanjay,' she said at last. 'You saw the second ghost. The woman must be doing terrible things to the children – even more terrible than what Rao would have done to them—'

She stopped there.

'What do you mean?' Sanjay asked. 'What would Rao have done to them?'

Ana raised the stump of her right leg, so that it pointed at him. He looked away, embarrassed.

'I was lying when I told you that I'd had a monorail accident,' she said.

He still could not meet her eyes. 'What happened?'

Her voice wavered as she told him. 'Rao picked us up off the streets, took us back to the warehouse and locked us in the chamber with some other children. Then he took us out one by one. He . . . he injected paraffin into my right knee. It went bad, and he took me to the hospital, pretending to be my father. The doctor said that they must cut off the leg to save my life, and of course Rao agreed.

'I can't remember the next few days. The pain was more terrible than anything . . . Rao kept me in the chamber until I got better, then let me out. Then I saw what Rao had done to Ajay.' She paused there, waited five seconds before going on. 'He'd blinded him.

'Then Rao took us out on to the streets of Delhi to beg for money from people like you, and he took the money and bought himself all those gold rings.'

Sanjay was shaking his head, whispering, 'I'm sorry, Ana. I'm so sorry.'

'So do you see why I have to try and save Ajay and the other kids? Rao does terrible things to the children in his care, but what terrible things is the woman going to do to them?'

She gripped her crutch and moved to the door of the booth. 'Will you help me, Sanjay?'

He nodded. 'Ah-cha, Ana. I'll help you.'

Ana smiled at him and left the booth.

She limped from the VR-bar into the street busy with pedestrians and cars, once again just another cripple among many. She made her way to Rao's warehouse and tried to shut her mind to the dangers she would face over the next few hours. She thought only of Ajay, and how wonderful it would be to be with him again. It made the threat of danger seem bearable.

She came to the barred window of the underground chamber and crouched down. She lowered her crutch through the gap, and then squeezed through after it. She hung from the bars, her knee scraping against the wall, then let herself drop. She found her crutch and sat against the wall.

Bindra and another child were watching her, eyes wide in disbelief.

Ana smiled at them. 'It's OK,' she said. 'It's OK. I've come back to help you.'

Her heart beating like a snake-charmer's drum, Ana closed her eyes and waited.

CHAPTER SEVEN

THE QUEEN OF EVIL

Ana must have fallen asleep . . .

She was awoken by a loud noise. She looked up. A patch of light appeared in the ceiling as the trapdoor was opened. The other children in the chamber stirred and sat up groggily. Bindra rubbed his eyes, looked across at Ana with a worried expression. She smiled to reassure him.

A ladder dropped into the chamber and a face appeared in the square of light above. Deepak Rao stared down at them. 'Up, up! Quickly now!'

The children stood and moved to the ladder. Ana pushed herself upright on her crutch and limped across to the foot of it. She waited until she was the last one in the chamber, then hooked her crutch on to her shoulder, took hold of the ladder with both hands, and hopped up the rungs one at a time.

Deepak Rao and Rajiv the strong man were waiting beside the van, its back doors open to receive the children. One by one they climbed inside. Ana joined them. Rajiv locked the doors and sat in the front seat beside Rao. The engine coughed into life and seconds later they were motoring from the warehouse and down the street thronged with daytime crowds.

'Where are we going?' a little girl asked in a frightened whisper.

'Don't worry,' Ana told her. 'We'll be all together. That's the most important thing.'

Bindra sat beside her, staring at her with big, curious eyes. 'Do you really know where we're going, Ana?'

'We are going to a big house on an island,' she said. 'Now don't be afraid.'

She turned her attention to the front, and stared through the windscreen between Rao and Rajiv.

They were heading south. They circled the big roundabout of Connaught Place packed with traffic, the humid air blue with petrol fumes. On the sides of the street, stallholders sold fruit and vegetables, onion bhajis and pakoras, bottles of cola and sugar cane juice. Ana saw Begum's foodstall, where she and Ajay had sometimes eaten breakfast when the begging had gone well.

They turned down Janpath, a long, wide road jammed with stalls selling books, Indian artifacts, and the latest electrical equipment. Soon the stalls gave way to expensive, multi-storey hotels where Ana and Ajay had sometimes begged from foreign tourists. They were heading towards the select suburbs of New Delhi where many countries had their embassies and consulates, and where the rich owned massive houses set in lawns as vast and perfect as cricket pitches.

They passed the Indian Museum and turned right along Raj Path. The parliament buildings came into sight, then disappeared as the van turned left and continued south. Ana felt a knot of apprehension tighten in her stomach. She had been so confident all along – but what would happen if she could not tell Sanjay where they were, or if Sanjay failed to turn up on the island? There was so much that might go wrong.

No, she told herself, everything *will* go to plan. It *had* to. She could not imagine what might happen if her plan failed.

The van turned left, into a district of leafy suburbs. She was in an area of the city new to her. She leaned forward and peered out, staring at the nameplates on the street corners as they passed. She memorized the name of every street.

They turned again. Ana caught a brief glimpse of the nameplate. Himachal Boulevard, she repeated to herself.

The van slowed, and Ana felt a glow of triumph in her chest. Himachal Boulevard, off Patel Marg—

They turned into a gravelled driveway flanked by trees. Some of the children, lulled to sleep by the motion of the van, now woke up as it slowed. They peered ahead, curious. Ana looked around for any sign of security guards, but saw none.

Then she stared through the windscreen at the house standing in the middle of a large lawn and surrounded by trees.

The house was big and square, and built of dark brick.

It was an identical copy of the house on the island on Bellatrix III. Or rather, she corrected herself, the other way around. The house on the island was an identical copy of this one.

She told herself that Sanjay would be able to locate the house without any difficulty . . . just so long as he made it to the island.

The van drove around to the rear of the house. Ana half expected to see a caged lawn full of children, but of course the children were imprisoned in the Web.

In the real world, they would be somewhere in the house.

The van jerked to a halt and Rao and Rajiv climbed out. The back doors swung open and Ana jumped down, followed by the others.

'Up the steps!' Rao shouted. 'Quickly now!'

A hand dropped on to her shoulder. 'Not you, Ana.'

She felt her stomach turn in sickening disappointment.

Rao turned her to face him with a rough hand. He lifted her chin, squeezing her cheeks with brutal fingers. His gold rings winked in the sunlight.

'I'm sorry to see you go, little one,' Rao said. 'You've been a faithful servant over the years, but then you spoilt yourself by running away. What choice do I have, little one, if I can no longer trust you?'

She squirmed out of his grip. 'Let me go!' She put all her hatred into an unblinking stare.

Rao laughed. 'You'll soon wish you'd never run away.

When you've seen what lies ahead, life with me will seem like paradise. Now go!'

She felt relief that she would be allowed to join the others after all, but at the same time his words filled her with fear.

She limped up the steps and into the house, hurrying to catch up.

Rajiv led the children through the darkened house, followed by Deepak Rao. They passed down a long corridor and up a flight of narrow stairs. At last they came to a pair of double doors. The strong man knocked, waited five seconds and then opened the door. Ana peered inside.

She thought at first that it was the throne room of a palace. It had a marble floor, a red carpet stretching the length of the room, and at the far end the throne itself.

Then she saw that it was not a throne at all, but an invalid carriage. The two men standing on either side of the carriage were not courtiers, Ana saw now, but medics.

And the woman sitting in the carriage was no queen, but someone so old that all life seemed to have fled from her bent and twisted body.

Ana paused with the other children on the threshold of the room, too terrified to enter.

The woman lifted a stick-thin arm and beckoned. A command like a dying breath sounded faintly. 'Come . . .'

Deepak Rao pushed Ana in the back, and she led the other children into the room and down the red carpet towards the woman in the invalid carriage.

'The children, ma'am,' Rao said.

Ana stared at the woman's white face, covered with wrinkles like paper screwed into a ball. What made the old woman's appearance all the more ghastly, Ana saw, was the short silver dress – it was as if she was desperately trying to regain the long gone days of her youth.

Watery grey eyes peered at Ana. The woman made a feeble gesture with her right hand. 'Come closer, girl,' she croaked to Ana.

Trembling, Ana took one step towards the carriage.

Then she saw the tubes twisting from beneath the seat of

the carriage. Like hungry snakes they were attached to the woman's flesh at her neck and her wrists, but these snakes were the colour of pumping blood – the same colour as the ruby ring on her left hand.

'Don't be alarmed, girl. I, like yourself, am human – though I scarcely appear so now.' The woman cocked her head to one side, regarding Ana. 'Are you horrified by what you see, girl? Come on, the truth. I want the truth!'

Ana opened her mouth, stammered, 'I–I—'

The woman interrupted. 'Well, girl, I will tell you that *I* am truly horrified every morning when I inspect myself in the mirror. What do I see but someone ravaged by disease and the treacherous advance of the years! I was once young like you, young and pretty and full of health . . . but where do the years go to, girl? How is it possible for the years, so everlastingly long in childhood, to go so fast? It's a tragedy that one must age and grow feeble, and leave behind for ever the days of one's youth.'

The woman gestured again. 'Come closer, girl. Closer!'

Ana moved closer.

A claw reached out, and cold fingers took her chin. Ana thought that she would rather have had Deepak Rao gripping her with his cruel fingrs.

'Such youth,' the woman marvelled. 'Do you understand what a precious gift you possess? But no, of course you don't. One never appreciates a possession until it is no more. Do you know what death is, girl? Do you fear it?'

Ana tried to shake her head, but the woman's cold fingers prevented the movement.

'No, of course you don't! You hardly know the meaning of the word!' She pushed Ana away and turned her attention to the other children who watched her in horror.

'For years I have stared death in the face, waited for it to come quietly in the night and carry me away.' She shook her head. 'But no more! My lost youth is within reach, thanks to you beautiful children . . .' She collapsed back into her chair, breathless.

The medics bent and busied themselves around her,

administering injections, taking her pulse. After a minute she seemed to gain strength.

'Rajiv!' she called.

The strong man stepped forward. 'Ma'am.'

'Take them away!'

As Ana was led from the room, she heard the old woman say: 'And now, Mr Rao, the small matter of your payment . . .'

Rajiv and the medics hurried Ana and the children along the corridor to a room at the opposite end of the house. One of the medics unlocked the door with a key on a chain. The room beyond was gloomy, but even so Ana made out the shapes of a dozen or more Web-couches.

'Inside,' Rajiv said.

Ana limped into the room with the other children, staring around her at the machinery and computers banked along the walls. Even though she had known what to expect, the sight of the small children in the grey suits, each one bound in place on a Web-couch, filled her with panic. She looked for Ajay, but all the children looked alike in the Websuits.

She noticed that some of the children struggled against the straps that bound them down, twisting and turning like sleepers suffering nightmares. She remembered Ajay telling her that a few of the children had been held in the Web for months.

Empty Web-couches waited at the far end of the room. The medics sorted the children into groups of two or three, according to their size, and led them across to the couches. They ordered the children to put on the Websuits.

Bindra began to cry. 'What's happening, Ana? What are they doing to us?'

Ana smiled bravely. 'Don't worry. We won't be harmed. We'll find ourselves in a . . . a new world. And we'll be together. OK?'

Bindra pursed his lips and nodded as he pulled on the suit.

Ana laid her crutch on the floor, pulled on the suit and stretched out on the couch. The medics passed around face masks and goggles, and ordered the children to put them on.

As Ana did so, she reached automatically for the wristpad –
but of course these suits were without the devices.

The first medic moved from couch to couch, strapping
down the children. He arrived at Ana's couch and fastened
her so that she could not move.

The second medic crossed to a computer terminal and
pressed a series of keys. Ana's vision was filled with darkness.

Then she could see again. She found that she could sit up.
For a second she thought that nothing had happened, that
she was still in the same room.

Then she noticed that the medics had disappeared, and
that the computers were no longer in the room. Red sunlight
slanted in through the long window to her right. She sat up
and saw that she was not on the couch, but sitting on a bed.
She was dressed in a white shirt and trousers, like all the
other children she had seen on the island earlier – and once
again she had two legs.

The other children were climbing to their feet, looking
about them in bewilderment.

Ana jumped from the bed, lighter now in the gravity of
Bellatrix III, and ran to the window. She gazed down on to
the lawn, and there by the fence was Ajay.

CHAPTER EIGHT

THE GHOST IN THE WEB

'Where are we?' a little girl cried.

The children climbed from the beds and looked around in fear.

'Don't be afraid,' Ana said. 'We're in the Web. We'll be OK if we all keep together. Now hold hands and we'll go down to the lawn.'

She led the way from the room and down the stairs, marvelling again at the sensation of walking on two legs. The house was deserted, with no sign of the woman or the medics. The children followed her timidly.

She found the door leading to the back garden. It stood ajar, and through it she could see children wandering aimlessly around the lawn, standing still and gazing out across the vast ocean, or sitting and rocking back and forth in distress. Ajay stood by the fence, facing the bushes where just a few hours ago she and Sanjay had hidden. She ran across to him.

'Ajay!'

He turned, an expression of disbelief on his face. 'Ana? Ana, is it really you?'

Unable to speak, she moved to her brother and took him in her arms. He was as she remembered him from the real world, the same small warm bundle, the brother she had looked after and loved for the six years of his life.

'Ana, how did you get here? Did she . . . did the woman get you too?'

She sat him down on the lawn, and lowered herself beside him, holding his hand and saying, 'It's a long story, Ajay. I had to let the woman capture me. I have a plan. A friend out in the real world is helping me. With luck we'll be able to get everyone out of here.'

She looked around the lawn. The children who had been imprisoned here for a while were talking to the new arrivals. Some knew each other from the real world. They hugged and exchanged what little information they possessed.

Some children, those sitting on the ground and rocking back and forth, were not aware of the latest arrivals. They stared into space with pained expressions.

Ana squeezed her brother's fingers. 'Ajay, do you know what's happening here? Do any of the other children know?'

He shook his head. 'We've talked about it. When we go back to our rooms to sleep at night, we try to work out what is happening. Why the woman is doing this to us. But, Ana, *nothing* is happening. That's the awful thing. Nothing happens, and there's nothing to do. The children who've been here for longer than me say that every day is the same. We will just wait here until—' He stopped, staring blindly into space.

'Until what, Ajay?'

'At first, it seems a good place. It is warm and comfortable. No one harms us. We don't have to beg or work. We are fed once a day. I feel a tube enter my mouth and then my tummy feels full.' He shrugged. 'Some children say that they like it here, at first.'

'And then?'

'And then . . .' He frowned, shaking his head. 'Strange things happen to the children. Come, I'll show you.'

Ajay stood and held out his hand. 'Can you see Parveen, Ana? She sits all day and rocks back and forth.'

'She's over by the steps.' Ana took Ajay's hand and walked him over to where the little girl rocked, humming to herself.

Ajay squatted before her. 'Parveen, Ana is here.'

The girl stared through Ana and went on rocking back and forth, her hands on her knees.

Ana reached out and touched her arm. 'Parveen, can you tell me how long you've been here?'

The girl stopped rocking. She looked at Ana, but her gaze seemed far away, as if she were seeing not Ana but some other world.

'A long, long time,' Parveen said. 'So long that I am no longer really here.'

'Parveen, what do you mean?'

The girl shook her head, as if she found her situation hard to describe. 'I see you, I see the house and the lawn, but I also see . . . other things.' She stopped talking and began rocking back and forth again.

Ana took the girl's hand and squeezed. 'Parveen, I want to help you. I want to get you away from here and back to the real world. Tell me, what other things do you see?'

Parveen frowned. 'Other worlds . . . hundreds and thousands of other worlds, all on top of each other. It is like . . . like watching a thousand holo-ads all at once. Soon, I will leave here for ever and travel through all those other worlds.'

'How do you know this?'

'Because they have told me.'

Ana blinked. 'They? Who are *they*?'

'They,' the girl repeated. 'The others. The other children who were here, but are no longer here.'

Ana shook her head. 'I don't understand,' she said in a whisper.

Ajay said, 'I think she means the ghosts.'

'The ghosts . . .' Ana repeated in a small voice. She recalled the ghostly head she had seen on the island, the face of Dilli floating in the air.

'Parveen,' she said. 'Is Dilli a ghost?'

The girl nodded. 'Dilli and Shazeen and Babu. They all live in the other worlds, now, and soon I will join them.'

Ajay took Ana's hand. 'The ghosts sometimes come and shout to us. They need our help.'

'Parveen,' Ana said. 'Do you know why the woman is doing this to us? Do you know what is happening?'

But Parveen just shook her head and continued rocking back and forth, back and forth.

Ana turned to her brother. 'When do the ghosts come, Ajay?'

He shrugged. 'I hear them all the time, calling to us. They live in the hills around the house.'

Ana looked through the fence, recalling the ghosts she had seen earlier, Dilli on the hillside and the other floating head she had encountered above the sea.

Maybe, if she could find another ghost and question it about what was happening here . . .

Ana left Parveen and walked Ajay over to the fence. She stood and looked down the hillside at the green ocean, across which Sanjay would soon be coming – she hoped.

A thought occurred to her. Why wait until Sanjay reached the house? She would make his task easier by getting out of the compound and walking down the hillside to meet him on the beach. That way, he would not have to do battle with the spiders that patrolled the island. She could tell him the location of the house in the real world and he could scuttle and do something to rescue them.

'Ajay, can we get out of this cage?'

'There is a gap under the fence near the house. Other children got out and tried to get away. But they found we are on an island a long way from the mainland . . . so they could not escape.'

'Do you know how often the woman comes here?' Ana asked.

'The others say that she arrives every evening. She moves around the lawn, talking to the children like Parveen about what they can see.'

Ana nodded. 'That gives me plenty of time. Ajay, listen to me. I'm going away for a short while, ah-cha? But I'll be back soon.'

Ajay looked suddenly frightened. 'Ana, promise me you'll come back!' He reached out, found her hand and gripped it.

'I'll be back. I need to meet a friend. It's very important.'

They stood and Ajay led her to a section of the fence in the shadow of the house, and then stopped. Ana saw a semi-circular gap in the fence where it had been pulled up.

She said goodbye to Ajay and squirmed through. She stood in the sunlight on the side of the hill, and felt as if she had made the first step on the journey to freedom.

She hurried down the hillside, through the bushes and across the open grass in front of the house, and then along the steep path through the blackened trees.

A spider appeared suddenly on the path before her. She halted, the sight of the hairy monster filling her with fright.

As she stared, she realized that the spider seemed unaware of her. It was looking the other way, its eye-stalks bent towards the coast.

She recalled what Rom had told her, that a spider's bite would scuttle them from the Web.

What would happen if the spider bit her now? Would she find herself in the woman's house in Delhi? If so, then she would be able to help the others to escape without having to wait for Sanjay.

It was too much to hope for, of course.

She stepped forward and called to the spider. It took no notice of her. She reached out and touched the hairy monstrosity, its furry warmth beneath her fingertips making her shudder.

The spider moved, scurrying off into the trees to her left.

Ana continued down the path.

Two minutes later she saw movement to her right. She turned quickly.

A disembodied head bobbed between the trunks of the nearest trees, staring at her. With a sickening feeling in the pit of her stomach, she recognized the face of the boy she had known as Dilli.

The floating head moved its lips, and Ana thought she heard the faintest whiper. 'Ana, please . . . help me.'

'I . . .' she began. 'How . . . how can I help you?'

'I too was like you, Ana. Then she caught me, imprisoned me in the house in the Web. I was there for many months,

Ana, slowly fading away. Now I am no longer . . . *real*. I can't feel, or move or experience as I did before. There are more of us who live like this in the Web, the children who the woman captured and imprisoned.'

Ana called out, 'But why is she doing this to us?'

'We do not know why. We are ghosts, being kept alive by the woman . . .' The face was fading away, its words becoming faint.

'Please . . . Please help us!'

Seconds before the floating head vanished, Ana stepped forward. 'I will try!' she called. 'I promise, Dilli, I will do my best . . .'

She turned and hurried down the path towards the coast.

She came to a clearing in the trees and looked across the bay to the mainland. There was no sign of the rowing boat. She willed Sanjay to hurry up. She wondered how long Parveen had before she, like Dilli and the other children, became a ghost in the Web.

Ana was about to begin the descent again when she saw movement on the black sands of the beach. She stared. Six black spiders ran towards the sea, lifting their legs high as if scurrying over hot coals. They paused by the water, staring out across the ocean as if they somehow knew that Sanjay was on his way.

At that very second, Ana saw the rowing boat appear around the headland and make for the beach. Two small frog-figures sat side by side, rowing with all their strength.

Ana called to them and waved, then bounded along the path, taking great leaps in the lighter gravity.

She came to the beach as one of the frog-figures jumped out of the boat and dragged it through the shallows. The other frog stood in the prow of the boat, holding an oar ready to hit out at the waiting spiders.

'Sanjay, Rom!' Ana yelled, waving as she ran towards the sea.

Then the spiders attacked, swarming through the breakers towards the boat. The two frogs jumped out and fought with the spiders, knocking the creatures from the water with fierce blows of the oars. Sanjay, the taller frog, spun in a mad circle, his oar like a propeller as it scythed down the advancing spiders. If Ana had had time to think about what was happening, she might have noticed how comical the contest appeared – two giant frogs duelling with half a dozen over-grown spiders.

But all she knew was that she had to reach Sanjay before one of the spiders bit him. She raced towards the sea.

The sand slowed her progress, making every step a labour. She was still fifty metres from the water. Already, her friends had accounted for two of the spiders. Their bodies bobbed in the shallows, fragments of leg and carapace floating in the sea. The remaining four spiders danced through the waves, mincing their legs high and snapping their jaws in a bid to eject Sanjay and Rom from the Web.

Rom slipped, falling beneath the waves, and a triumphant spider advanced upon him and dived, biting Rom on the arm. Rom screamed in pain and fear, the sound filling Ana with terror. As she watched, Rom disappeared in a vortex swirl of multicoloured dots. She imagined him coming to his senses on a Web-couch in America, a world away from the battle.

Now, four spiders inched towards Sanjay, circling him and moving in for the kill. Ana waded into the turgid, green waters of the shallows. She reached out and grabbed the first spider, sickened by its hairy weight as she swung the creature from the water and up the beach, where it landed in a tangle of broken limbs.

She moved to the next spider, but the other two creatures had Sanjay backed up against the side of the boat. He lashed out with his oar, keeping them at bay, but it would be only a matter of seconds before one darted beneath his attack and struck the final bite.

'The house is on Himachal Boulevard, off Patel Marg!' she yelled at him. 'You can't miss it, Sanjay! It's exactly like the house here on the island!'

He looked up at her, but she was unable to tell whether he had heard her. 'Sanjay! Did you hear me? I said the house is on Himachal Boulevard!'

And at that very second a spider darted towards Sanjay, reached out with its snapping jaws and bit him on the upper leg. The frog's mouth opened in a short scream, and then he vanished in a fizz of pixels.

Instantly, the remaining spiders stepped from the water and walked up the beach, leaving behind the shattered legs and bodies of their companions.

Ana dragged herself from the water, the undertow pulling at her legs, and staggered up the beach.

'I don't know if he heard me!' she cried to herself. 'I just don't know.'

She fell silent as she heard cries and shouts of help from high above. Among the children's voices, she heard Ajay calling her name.

Gripped by panic, Ana hurried up the path to the house on the summit of the island.

CHAPTER NINE

ESCAPE FROM THE WEB

There was a commotion on the lawn when Ana returned.

The children were gathered at the far end, away from the house, holding on to each other and crying. Ana squirmed through the gap in the fence and hurried towards the wailing children. She found Ajay beside Bindra.

'What's wrong? What's happening?'

Bindra looked at her, his face made ugly with anguish. 'Just five minutes ago – *he* came!' Bindra pointed towards the house.

Ana followed the direction of his gesture, but saw no one.

'Who came, Bindra?' she asked.

'Him,' Bindra wailed. 'Look!'

Now Ana could see, standing beside the house and looking out across the ocean, a familiar overweight figure.

'Deepak Rao!' she said to herself.

But why was he here? He had tortured the children enough in real life, why follow them into the Web?

Ana left Ajay with Bindra. 'I'll be back in two minutes, Ajay. I'm going to talk to him.'

'Be careful!' Bindra warned. 'Don't let him harm you!'

'In the real world maybe he can harm me,' Ana said. 'But here he can do nothing. In the Web we are equal.'

She left the children and walked across the lawn. For all her brave words, as she approached Deepak Rao she felt a flutter of apprehension in her belly.

He was not the young, slim version of Deepak Rao who had

appeared in the Web earlier. Now he looked like he did in real life – big-bellied and many-chinned. As Ana came closer, she saw that Rao was in distress. He clutched the wire fence like a man imprisoned, and his cheeks were streaked with tears.

When he saw Ana, he tried to dash the tears from his face with fat fingers. 'What do you want, girl?'

She felt fear block the words in her throat. She told herself that even if he tried to hit her, the blow would not hurt that much. But it was still hard to overcome the fear that she had lived with for so many years.

Ana did not know where the words came from, and looking back on it later she was amazed at what she said. 'Now you know what it's like to be held prisoner. Now you know how unfair it is.'

He tried to bluff her. 'What do you mean?'

Ana stared at him and did not flinch. 'The woman has imprisoned you here,' she said. 'How do you like having *your* freedom taken away, Rao?'

'It's not the same!' he cried. 'I gave you shelter, money to buy yourselves food—'

'You tortured us. You maimed us and blinded us, made us good for nothing but begging for rupees.'

'What kind of life would you have had on the streets had I not taken you in?'

Ana shook her head. 'I don't know,' she answered. 'At worst, I would have begged. I might have found a job. You took away our futures, Rao – you took away any choices we might have had.'

He shook his head. 'You don't understand—' he began.

'I understand that you're evil and greedy. Our afflictions made your life easy. You couldn't see our suffering, or you chose to ignore it.' She paused there, staring at the fat man before her. 'And for that you've been rewarded.'

He pointed a finger at her. 'I'm in here not because of what I did out there,' he said, 'but because of what I know. The evil witch told me what she was doing here – told me all about her experiments. Then she had me imprisoned so that I couldn't tell the world!'

Ana recalled the first time she had been on the island, when she had seen the woman and Rao walking around this very lawn. Then she had heard Rao ask what the woman was doing here, but they had moved away from where Ana was hidden and she hadn't heard the reply.

Now she felt her pulse quicken. Her throat was dry.

'What?' she asked in barely a whisper. 'What is she doing with the children?'

Rao glanced at her, his lips trembling. 'Do you really want to know?'

'Tell me!'

'You would be better off in ignorance.'

'I said, tell me.'

He laughed in despair, then began weeping. Great tears rolled down his cheeks. He pushed at them with his chubby fingers, for all the world like an overgrown baby.

'She . . . she told me what was happening. I found it hard to believe. I know you think I'm evil, girl – but I never in all my years killed a single soul.'

'What is she doing to us!' Ana demanded.

He took a deep breath. 'She told me that she is experimenting with you – with us. You see, she is very old and very near death, and it is her wish to remain alive for ever.'

'Is that possible?'

'She claims that it is. She can remain alive for ever, not in the flesh and bone body that she possesses now, but in the Web.'

Ana shook her head. 'I don't understand.'

'She plans to live in the Web for ever as a young woman, not the old crone she is now. She will transfer herself into the memory of the Web, but to do that she needs to experiment with others first to perfect the transfer process. That is why you – why *we* – are imprisoned here. We will not be allowed to return to the real world. We will stay here for months and suffer the sickness and nausea that comes of spending too long in the Web. Then we will die, and when our bodies die, the woman will attempt to transfer our identities into the memory of the Web. You've seen the ghosts of some of the children who have died? These are her unsuccessful experiments. They haven't been fully transferred. The woman hopes to transfer herself more successfully into the Web so that she will be able to live here for ever, able to touch and sense and experience everything here just as if it were the real world. Now do you understand why she needs guinea pigs to perfect her transfer technique? We are disposable. We are less than nothing to her. We are the means to an end – the means to her ultimate immortality!'

Ana thought of the ghost of Dilli she had spoken to in the forest. She heard again his pleas for her to help him.

She shook her head in defiance. 'We won't let the woman do this,' she whispered to herself.

Rao gave a great bellow of mirth. 'Fine sentiments, girl! But how can you stop her?'

Ana stared at the fat coward. 'I can stop her and I will!'

'Observe,' said Rao, shaking his arm in the air. 'We have no wristpads to control our stay here. We're imprisoned as if it were a jail made from bricks and mortar.'

'We can escape, Rao,' Ana told him. 'I have friends out in the real world working to do just that.'

He peered at her, suspicious. 'I don't believe you.'

'Do you see me crying?' she asked him. 'Do you see me blubbing like a baby at what the woman hopes to do to us?'

'But how is it possible?' Rao began, a gleam of hope in his eyes.

Ana stared at Deepak Rao. She almost laughed at the pleading tone in his voice. 'I said I could free us from the Web – myself, Ajay and Bindra and all the other children. I said nothing about you, Rao.'

'Would you leave me here to become a wailing ghost?' he cried.

'I think it'd be a just punishment if I left you here while we all escaped,' Ana said. She knew that if Sanjay did what they had planned, then everyone including Rao would be freed from the Web – but Rao did not know that.

'No . . .' he moaned.

'Why *should* I help you, Rao? What have you ever done for me, apart from have my leg removed, and blind my brother?'

'But if you get me out of here, I'll . . . I will—'

'What, Rao?' she asked. 'What will you do to make up for what you did to all of us?'

He shook his head, spreading his hands wide in a pleading gesture. 'Anything,' he babbled. 'Anything at all. Name your price.'

Ana felt excitement rising within her, a sense of power and triumph. 'If we give you your freedom,' she said, 'then out there in the real world, you must give us *our* freedom. We will no longer beg for you, ah-cha? We will beg for ourselves – and you will no longer take in new children and maim them and make them work for you.'

Rao nodded like a pathetically grateful child. 'Of course. Anything, anything.'

'And another thing.'

'Name it.'

'I want your gold.'

He stared down at the gold rings that covered his fingers, the bracelet and watch around his wrist. 'They are yours, all of them. As soon as I am out of here.'

'But how can I trust you, Rao? How do I know you will keep your promise?'

He spread his hands. 'You have only my word of honour,' he said.

She nodded. For what it was worth, his word of honour was all she could hope for.

'Then I'll help you escape,' she said.

She left him beside the fence and returned to the crowd of children at the far end of the lawn.

'What did he say?' Bindra asked.

'Don't worry,' Ana said. 'Deepak Rao will harm no one.'

She took Ajay's hand and drew him to her, kissed the soft skin of his forehead.

She wondered if Sanjay *had* heard her, down there on the beach – if he was now trying to bring about their escape.

If he had not heard her, then surely he would attempt to

come here again. It would only be a matter of time before he made it to the house. If, that was, he was able to fight his way past the spiders.

Please, she whispered to herself. Oh, Sanjay, please.

All she could do now was wait.

She sat down with Ajay and stared out at the ocean and the huge sun slipping slowly into the sea. Now and again, great alien whales surfaced, blew a spout of ocean water, and dived.

'We will get out of here soon,' she told her brother.

'Do you mean that, Ana?'

'And when we do get out, I will buy you new eyes, so that you can see again.'

He smiled and laid his head on Ana's shoulder.

It was then, as Ana gazed out at the setting sun and the basking whales, that the world around them began to change.

First, the sun changed colour. From a huge dome of fiery red, it became blue, and then black. The amazing thing was that all around them was still light. The children gasped and pointed. Then the sky changed – became a vast screen like a holo-ad, across which a thousand different images moved. Ana watched, becoming dizzy with the procession of moving scenes. She saw a thousand worlds up there, and a million people walking across the sky like gods.

Around them, the house and the lawn were undergoing a rapid transformation, too. The house winked out of existence, replaced by a house-shaped mosaic of a thousand fractured scenes. Ana could see patches of mountain and river next to scraps of road and city. Faces appeared, staring out at her.

The lawn became a multicoloured quilt, and the island beyond the fence flickered like silver lightning.

The children screamed.

Ajay gripped Ana's hand. 'What's happening?'

Ana stared. 'I think we're leaving the Web,' she said. 'I think Sanjay is saving us . . .'

As she said this, she realized that she could smell something. She inhaled. An irritating, acrid stench filled her nostrils. At first she was unable to identify the smell. It grew stronger, making her eyes water. She choked, coughing.

Then she knew what the terrible stench was.

Smoke!

Suddenly, the world of the Web went mad.

The scene around her flickered on and off. Ana seemed to be existing in two places at once – on the strangely transformed island one second, and the next on the Webcouch in the house.

She heard snatches of screams from the other children.

And then a familiar voice: '. . . get you out of here!'

Screams again – and Ajay crying in fright.

'Quick!' Sanjay's desperate shout. 'Move to the window!'

She was on the Web-couch struggling to free herself.

And then back on the island, trying to make sense of the kaleidoscope of sickening images that swirled around her head.

She saw a face before her, a floating face she recognized. 'Dilli?' she said.

The face whispered. She made out the words, 'Ana, thank you . . .'

The face was fading. 'Ana,' Dilli said, 'you are releasing us from our torment. Thank you . . .' And even as he spoke, his face and his words grew even fainter until they were no more.

The stench of the smoke was making Ana retch.

Another voice sounded close by. 'Ana? Is that you? Quickly!'

She sat up. She was back in the real world. The room was in half-darkness. Figures hurried about her. She tugged off her face mask, pulled the wires from her Websuit connecting her to the computers. She realized the reason for the half-light was that the room was filled with smoke. Sanjay was rushing from couch to couch, unfastening the children, telling them to get up and move towards the window.

Some children had been in the Web for so long that they

could not walk. Others, in the real world, had missing legs, or were blind.

Ana jumped off her couch. She found her crutch where she had left it, picked it up and limped across to help Sanjay. There were still some children strapped down. The smoke was becoming thick, unbreathable.

She moved awkwardly from couch to couch, unfastening straps, pulling away the face masks and connecting wires, helping the children to their feet. She led them across the room, half-carrying those too weak to hold themselves upright. A knot of children stood beside the open window, identical in the grey Websuits.

She looked for Ajay. She could not tell if he was among the group by the window. She hobbled around the room, peering desperately through the swirling smoke at each couch.

There – Ajay had staggered across the room and was sitting by the door, his face distorted with fear.

'Ajay!' she cried. She limped across to him, choking on the smoke, and dragged him to his feet. He clung to her like a frightened monkey as she half-dragged him across the room.

Sanjay was beside her.

'How did you get in?' she asked.

'I petrol-bombed the lower storey,' he said. 'While they were trying to put it out, I smashed a window and ran through the house. I thought I was never going to find you.' He stared around the room. 'I think that's everyone out of the Web,' he said.

Ana saw a fat shape on a couch across the room. 'No – there's one more!' She started across the room.

Sanjay gripped her arm, halting her. 'I know,' he said. 'It's Deepak Rao. Leave him!'

Before he could stop her, Ana pushed herself across the room and fumbled with the straps binding Rao to the couch. She pulled the mask from his face.

Rao struggled upright, moaning in terror.

For a second, their eyes met. Ana stared at him. Rao reached out, tears in his eyes, and touched her cheek with his fat fingers.

Ana hurried back to the window.

Sanjay had tied two ropes to the leg of a solid table beside the window. Now he was helping the children over the window ledge and down the rope.

The blind children moved by touch, swarming over the window ledge with a speed that amazed Ana. Those without arms moved just as fast. Two children had legs missing. Sanjay carried one on his back, and Ana lifted the other. The boy's arms fastened around her neck, almost choking her.

Ajay found the rope, followed Sanjay's shouted instructions, and disappeared over the edge.

Behind them, the door exploded inwards and a great plume of flame roared into the room. Ana felt the heat scorch the back of her leg. The children still waiting by the window screamed in terror. Ana looked around her. Parveen sat curled on the floor, sobbing.

Deepak Rao was about to climb over the window ledge. He paused and looked across at Parveen, indecision on his face.

'You must take her!' Ana screamed.

'There's no time,' Rao called back. 'We have to get out!'

'I saved you!' Ana reasoned. 'Now you must save her!'

Rao looked from Ana to Parveen and made his decision. He reached out, whisked Parveen up and placed her on his back. He gripped the rope and lowered himself from the window, face contorted in pain and concentration.

Ana looked around the room. She and the boy she carried were the last to leave. She peered out of the window as Sanjay followed Rao over the ledge. It seemed a long way down to the lawn, and she felt a moment of terrible fear. Then the fire roared like a crazed animal behind her. She threw her crutch out first, watched Sanjay lower himself down the side of the house, then gripped the rope and climbed from the window.

The bricks of the house were hot against her bare foot, and the rope burned her fingers. The boy on her back clung tight, almost strangling her. His weight dragged her down and she feared that at any moment she would be unable to hold on any longer and they would drop.

Above her, tongues of flame came licking from the window. The house was collapsing. The roof fell in with a deafening crash and bricks tumbled all around her.

With a hopeless cry she lost her grip on the rope and fell.

A second later she landed on the lawn and was aware of hands helping her and the boy to their feet. Ana found her crutch, hobbled with the others across the lawn and away from the burning house. She turned and stared at the inferno raging in the darkness.

In twos and threes the children slipped from the grounds of the house, towards freedom. Ana saw Deepak Rao standing in the middle of the lawn staring at the blazing house. She limped towards him and halted. He glanced at her.

'I helped you escape,' she said in a small voice. Now, in the real world, her fear of him had returned. This was the man who had made the lives of many children a misery. Did she really expect him to honour his promise?

His eyes regarded her as if she were an insect, and then something in his expression softened. His hands were a blur of motion. He pulled half a dozen rings from his fat fingers, slipped a gold bracelet from his wrist.

He held out a fist full of gold jewellery that winked and glimmered in the light of the flames, his expression unreadable. Ana reached out and took the gold in her hands. Deepak Rao turned and ran, disappearing rapidly into the darkness.

Sanjay hurried over to her, Ajay at his side. 'Look!' he called, pointing.

A white Mercedes roared up the driveway. As Ana watched, figures hurried from the house towards the car. She recognized the white-coated medics and the tall strong man.

Rajiv, the strong man, was carrying something in his arms – something incredibly old and light. As Ana stared, she made out the bent, frail shape of the woman, with her ancient face and clawed hands.

Their eyes met across the lawn, and for a second Ana felt the woman's rage and hatred directed at her.

The moment passed. The medics and Rajiv dived into the

Mercedes. It sped off, turned into the street and roared away into the night.

'She survived,' Ana said to herself. She told Sanjay, then, what the old woman had been doing to the children.

Sanjay took her hand. 'She's old,' he said. 'Time is against her. Maybe . . . maybe this was her last chance, and we put an end to her dreams?'

Ana stared at her new friend, and shook her head. 'I don't think so, Sanjay,' she whispered to herself.

As fire sirens sounded through the night, Ana, Ajay and Sanjay moved from the remains of the house, heading north towards New Delhi.

CHAPTER TEN

ANA AND AJAY

Ana and Ajay sat on the pavement outside the Union Coffee House.

Storm clouds were gathering in the early evening sky, and here and there above New Delhi the holo-ads were flashing on. Ajay slept beside Ana, his head resting on her shoulder.

A car drew up in the street outside the restaurant. Ana carefully moved Ajay's head, found her crutch and stood. As the car door hinged up she pushed herself across the pavement. A rich family climbed out, mother, father and two children, a boy and a girl around her age. The kids hurried past her without a second glance.

Ana thought of the world of the Web, where for a brief time she had been equal.

'Baksheesh,' she called out, pushing herself in front of the man. 'Please spare me ten rupees so that I can eat tonight.'

'Ten rupees!' the woman exclaimed. 'The cheek of the girl!'

'How many rupees will you spend on your meal?' Ana asked. 'One hundred? Two? With ten rupees I can feed my brother and myself for days.'

Embarrassed, the man was sorting through his wallet. 'Here! Now go. Bother us no more.'

Ana accepted the ten rupee note with a triumphant smile.

She returned to the sleeping Ajay, sat down and tucked the note along with all the others into the purse around her neck.

Earlier that day she had taken Deepak Rao's gold rings and bracelets to a jewel trader in Old Delhi.

'Are these stolen?' the trader had asked after examining the treasures.

'What does it matter to you?' Ana said. 'You'll sell them at a profit whether they're stolen or not.'

The trader glared at the bright little beggar girl, too cocky by half, and bent to inspect the rings once more through his eye-piece.

'I will give you one thousand rupees,' he said at last. 'No more.'

Ana laughed. 'One thousand? Now it's you who's trying to steal them! I'll take four thousand and not a rupee less.'

'Four thousand? Do I look like I was born yesterday, girl?'

And so began half an hour of haggling.

At last, the trader made his final offer. 'Two thousand five hundred rupees. Take it, or leave my premises for ever!'

Ana had taken it, stashed the wad of notes in her purse and hurried back to Ajay.

A taxi pulled up outside the restaurant. Again Ana pushed herself upright and limped across the pavement.

The taxi door opened and a young boy jumped out.

'Sanjay!' Ana said.

'Ana. You said you'd visit me.'

Ana shrugged, smiling shyly. It was a week since Sanjay had rescued her and Ajay and the other children from the Web. That night they had returned to his bungalow, ate and slept in luxury. In the morning, Ana had promised that she would be back soon. But—

She shrugged again. 'I've been busy, Sanjay.'

'Never mind. Look, I've brought you something.' He reached into the pocket of his jacket and pulled out a small square card. Ana took it – a VR-bar card.

'So you can join us in the Web, Ana. Rom wants to meet you again. I want to introduce you to all my other friends.'

Ana thought of her time in the Web, in Tropicana Bay

when she had not been a twelve-year-old beggar girl, but sixteen with two good legs and a beautiful red dress.

Where, for a time, she had been equal.

The thought of experiencing that world again filled her with excitement.

'You will join me, won't you?' Sanjay asked.

'Of course. In maybe two weeks, ah-cha? You see, I want to buy eyes for Ajay.'

They sat on the kerb and talked as the sky darkened.

Later, when the taxi carried Sanjay home, Ana returned to Ajay and rested his head on her shoulder.

That afternoon she had taken Ajay to an eye surgeon in New Delhi. She had paid twenty rupees for the consultation, and waited with apprehension while the surgeon examined Ajay's blind eyes.

At last the grey-haired man had nodded. 'It can be done,' he said. 'But it will be expensive.' His gaze took in Ana's dirty clothing, her one leg and crutch.

'It will cost three thousand rupees,' he told her.

'I'll give you two thousand five hundred,' Ana said, defiant.

The surgeon smiled. 'You are not in any common bazaar here, little girl. My prices are fixed. I charge three thousand rupees to replace damaged eyes.'

Ana tried to work out how long it might take her to earn the extra five hundred rupees. Months, maybe even years. She felt a crushing sense of disappointment. She had hoped that, maybe, in a day or two Ajay would be able to see again.

The surgeon took off his glasses, massaged his eyes. 'Listen to me, girl,' he said. 'In your case, just this once, I'll make an exception. Come back when you have two thousand and six hundred rupees, and I'll give your brother new eyes, ah-cha?'

She had almost danced from the surgery in joy.

She needed just one hundred more rupees. If she begged hard, night and day, she would be able to earn that much in no time at all, perhaps a week or two.

She put an arm around Ajay's shoulders and held him to her. Of course, she could have asked Sanjay for the money. But Sanjay was a friend, and she did not beg money from friends.

And she could always sell the Webcard he had given her. It would be worth well over a hundred rupees. But she would not do that, either. She wanted to save the card. She wanted to meet Sanjay and his friends in the Web in two weeks' time.

She would take Ajay with her – an Ajay who would be able to see the wonderful world of the Web with his own eyes.

Smiling, Ana laid her cheek on Ajay's head and tried to sleep.

Overhead, the monsoon rains began to fall.

SPIDERBITE
GRAHAM JOYCE

CHAPTER ONE

STEEL PROBE

Conrad knew something was wrong as soon as he sensed a black shadow growing at the corner of his vision. The moment he tried to pass through the door, the spider formed itself out of triangular blocks and raced at him. There was no warning or command. The huge spider scurried towards him, extending a nasty-looking steel probe. Emitting a high-pitched electronic whine, it raised itself on its back four legs. Then the steel probe touched Conrad on his forehead between the eyes, and everything faded to black.

Groaning in pain, Conrad tore the cable from his neck jack, yanked away the wrist wires and peeled off his Websuit before tossing it into the corner of his room. His mother had warned him many times to treat his Websuit with greater care; they were expensive and credit didn't grow on trees. But at that moment he felt too sick to care. The spider bite left him feeling as if someone had drained every drop of blood from his veins and replaced it with battery acid. It fizzed. It left a nasty metallic taste in his mouth. His head ached. He felt he could be sick at any moment.

'Conrad, supper's ready!' he heard his mother calling from downstairs.

He hugged himself. He checked his tongue in the mirror. 'In a minute,' he called back weakly.

He dared not tell his mother he'd been bitten by a Web spider again. Parents had no sympathy for kids who were poking around places they were forbidden to go. All off-limits sites were protected by spiders to stop children seeing things they weren't supposed to see, and you needed the adults-only access codes to get past the spiders. If your parents found out you'd been bitten, they were likely to give you a roasting, sometimes worse than the spider bite itself.

'Don't let it get cold,' sang out his mother.

But this was *bad*. This was worse than any other spider bite he'd had before. This wasn't a *normal* spider bite. Normal spiders gave you a bite: they didn't inject you with a steel probe. How could he tell his mother that the last thing he felt like doing right now was eating his supper? He glanced up at his computer terminal monitor. The screen was glowing with sickly green light and winking with the words:

ACCESS DENIED

Still feeling dizzy from the shock of the spider's attack, Conrad shut down his computer, rescued his Websuit from the floor and hung it up neatly. Then he dragged himself downstairs to the kitchen.

'You look pale,' said his mother. 'I hope you haven't been spending too long in that suit.'

'Maybe,' said Conrad. The sight of his spaghetti bolognese made him turn green.

Later that evening, Conrad sent e-mail messages out to all the members of the Tech-Rats. Actually, besides himself, there were only two other members, his friends Paddy and Chloë. Membership was supposed to be secret, but they hadn't been too successful in recruiting anyone else. The two messages he sent out were the same, though they appeared in Rat code, which looked something like this:

x'''1!*LL'ˆˆ$|||5|\\x# ~>~ 5.

Chloë and Paddy owned the codebreaker program that could make sense of Conrad's late-night message. The code itself, and the codebreaking program, had been invented by Paddy, the most technically-minded of the three. The message read:

<Help! Something weird happened to me today. Either of you

ever been bitten by a spider in an Edutainment site? Get back
to me as soon as you can. Conrad.>

Conrad left his monitor switched on and climbed into bed.
It was too late to contact either Paddy and Chloë by tele-
conference because of the net-curfew on under-fourteens,
but he had a good idea they would both get the message
before going to sleep that night. One of them might send a
message back immediately, and if they did, he had a pretty
good idea which it would be.

He was already dozing when he heard the signal tone, like
a coin spinning on a plate, for an incoming e-mail. Half
asleep, he got out of bed and ran the message through his
codebreaker. Sure enough it was from Chloë. He groaned.

<Hey, Dummy! You must be Websick, or are you just
ordinarily stupid? There are no biting spiders on Edutainment
sites! Only the warning types. That's the whole point,
winklebrain! I'm going to propose that evidence of complete
and utter stupidity in members of the Tech-Rats is enough to
get them expelled. We can't have members with the intelli-
gence of a piece of pond-life. So go and stick your head in a
bucket full of live electric eels, OK? And while we're on the
subject, your use of code is terrible! Appalling! Dreadful! I
spotted five mistakes in your tiny message. How am I
supposed to read that? I don't know why I bother. I'll see
you on tele-speak in the morning, brush-head. Love, Chloë>.

Conrad scratched his head (which was only a little brush-
like) and climbed back into bed. Just another normal communication from Chloë. But she was wrong. Conrad knew
there were not supposed to be any security spiders in the
Edutainment programs, but he'd found an aggressive one
and it *had* bitten him. Badly. He was still feeling the after-
shock.

There were plenty of sites that were off limits to kids. These
included government, finance and business sites, adult
entertainment, and certain library sites. There wasn't a kid
on the Web who hadn't experienced at least one spider bite
when trying to sneak through to a forbidden site. The
guardian spiders attacked anyone who didn't have the access

code. Usually, they offered a verbal warning first. After that, if they attacked, all they did was give you a little electronic nip, like a small shock. It was unpleasant enough to keep you away, but it didn't really hurt, and certainly couldn't cause any long-term harm. The worst thing was that the spiders kept a record of who tried to break through, and not only did they increase the power of the shock if you tried to gain entry a second time, but they also contacted your parents who had to pay a fine.

But that day Conrad had been working on an Edutainment site, for a school project of all things! Edutainment was any so-called 'educational entertainment' program, designed to get kids away from games on the Web and into educational stuff. Before the spider bit him, Conrad had been bored, fiddling about in a program on Ancient Greece. He'd found a doorway labelled 'Labyrinth', and had been about to go in when the spider had attacked.

As he lay in his bed, he remembered the pain of the attack and the terrible sick feeling that had spread over his body afterwards. He was almost afraid to fall asleep. The shadow of the spider hung at the edge of his closed eyes.

He knew he wasn't mistaken. There had been a spider where it shouldn't have been. It had bitten him. 'You're wrong, Chloë,' Conrad whispered to himself as he began to drift off to sleep. 'You're wrong.'

CHAPTER TWO

THE TECH-RATS

Conrad had half an hour before school started on the Web. Paddy was already on screen, staring glumly from the monitor. They were waiting for Chloë to patch through for a Tech-Rat conference. Paddy was wearing his aviation helmet, as usual. The helmet had belonged to his uncle, who had flown a reconnaissance plane in the Gulf war before the turn of the century. Both Chloë and Conrad had given up on teasing him about it.

The screen divided into two as Chloë came through, so that her face and Paddy's each occupied half of the screen. This morning her hair was silver with scarlet streaks. She was still eating breakfast cereal.

'What have you done to your hair this time?' said Conrad.

'Forget it,' said Chloë, who had changed her hair colour four times, from luminous green to orange to black and now to silver in the space of as many weeks. 'What's all this panic and wild talk of spiders?'

'Wait, Chloë,' Paddy said, putting on a pair of sunglasses. 'I need these if I have to look at you at this time of the morning.'

Paddy and Chloë took every opportunity to wind each other up. Chloë was about to fire back some sarcastic remark, but Conrad stopped her to explain everything that had happened the previous day.

'Impossible,' said Chloë, slurping her cereal.

The straps on Paddy's aviation helmet waggled as he shook

his head. 'Can't see it, kid.' Paddy liked to call Conrad and Chloë 'kid' even though at thirteen they were all the same age. 'There are no aggressive spiders in . . .'

'I know all that!' Conrad snapped impatiently. 'At least, there *shouldn't* be. But I'm telling you there are!'

He'd already been inside the Ancient Greece program that morning to make sure there was no mistake. As soon as he'd approached the labyrinth door again, he'd seen the spider begin to form out of triangular blocks. This time he hadn't given it a chance. He was so afraid of a second bite he'd hit the scuttle button, whacking him right out of the program.

'I'm going to give you the references,' said Conrad. 'Go and look for yourself.'

'No time,' said Chloë. 'School is up and running.'

'You can get in and out before Webschool starts up,' pleaded Conrad. 'Just prove to me I'm not going mad.'

Paddy shrugged. 'That's what friends are for . . .'

'Hell,' said Chloë, 'give us the references, gag-head.'

Paddy and Chloë tapped the Web references on to the keypads on their wrists. 'Edut. 4 by 77, Parameter G. History. Block 4. Area Red 15.'

'Not coming with us?' Paddy wanted to know.

'I've been in again this morning and I don't like it. And by the way, get out of there before it bites you. I'll wait for you to report back.'

The images of Chloë and Paddy faded as they transferred from tele-conference and entered the virtual world of the Edutainment program. Conrad was left waiting. He figured it would be three or four minutes before they found their way through to the labyrinth.

The door opened and his mother appeared. 'Are you online for school?' she asked.

'I'm just about to do it.'

'Starts in five minutes,' she reminded him, smiling. 'Try to make an effort, Conrad. You know your father is coming home next week. It would be nice if you were able to show him some good grades for a change.'

'I'll try, Mum.'

He didn't want to argue about it. He wanted his mother out of his room before Paddy and Chloë reappeared on the screen shouting about spiderbites. His house had received three bills for unauthorized access attempts by him in the last three months. His father had got so angry and purple in the face he almost had a brain haemorrhage.

Conrad's father was a businessman who travelled internationally. Most recently he'd been working in South Korea, which meant he was away from home for much of the time. But there were some advantages to this. First, he was able to bring back from South Korea top quality Websuits and other hardware, things that made Paddy and Chloë deeply envious. The Websuit Conrad was about to climb into for school had been brought back by his father just three months ago. They were 'free samples', which Conrad knew was a phrase meaning 'bribes'.

'And while we're on the subject of your father coming home, couldn't you do something about this room? It's a bombsite!'

Conrad glanced around at the untidy mass of books, comics, T-shirts, jeans, and old computer hardware and software littering his room. He made an unimpressive effort at gathering together a pile of comics, as if showing his mother how keen he was to make a start, but all the while hoping she would get out before the Tech-Rats came squawking through loud and clear.

Finally, she closed the door only moments before Chloë and Paddy's faces faded up on the monitor. Conrad tossed the comics back on the floor. 'Well?' he demanded.

Paddy looked puzzled. Chloë looked bored. She was pulling scarlet streaks of her hair towards the light and trying to look up at them. 'Your brain has fried, Conrad. You finally flipped. You're down the plug.'

'You mean you didn't see it?'

'There's nothing there, kid,' said Paddy. 'Are you sure you're not Websick?'

Conrad had been Websick before, from spending too long in a suit. But even though he'd vomited that time from

Websickness, it was a completely different feeling, and he said so.

'But, but, but—' Conrad stuttered.

'Outboard motors go butbutbut,' said Chloë.

He ignored her. 'But did you look by the door, where I told you?'

'There was just a black box information point made of triangles,' said Paddy.

'We even went inside the labyrinth for a couple of minutes,' added Chloë. 'Boring history program is all we saw there. Common-or-garden. Hey, gotta go. School is ringing.'

Conrad heard the school signal ringing through his own monitor. 'I can't believe it!'

'No time to discuss it now, kid.'

'Look,' Conrad said. 'How about you both come round to my place on Saturday? You still haven't seen my new Web-suit.'

'Cool,' said Chloë. 'Get some munchies in for us.'

'Saturday,' said Paddy, before his face faded, to be replaced by the bespectacled and frowning face of Mentor Robinson, Conrad's form teacher.

CHAPTER THREE

THE LABYRINTH

Saturday came around and Conrad had forgotten to tell his mother that Chloë and Paddy were visiting. When he finally did tell her, she made him tidy his room before they arrived. 'No one's coming into this room until it looks like human beings live here,' she said.

Tidying wasn't easy. Except for his bed, which he enjoyed putting away every morning. All he had to do was touch an electric switch on the side of his bed and it was instantly deflated – in under half a second – by powerful vacuum motors that reduced it to the size of a tennis ball with an electrical cable attached. Only the switch remained the same size, for reflating the bed later. He picked up his bed with one hand and tossed it into the cupboard. If only the rest was so easy! He grabbed a pile of comics and put them down somewhere else, shifted some books and dropped them where the comics had been. Then he collected up some music discs and piled them where the books had been. After half an hour of this tidying nothing looked any different.

'Finished,' he told his mother.

She wasn't fooled. He had to start again. When Chloë and Paddy arrived, his mother kept them downstairs until he'd done the job properly. By the time she let them come up, Conrad was going out of his mind.

'What a dump!' said Chloë, throwing herself on the old sofa, also inflatable, in the corner of his room. Paddy grabbed a pile of comics and spread them all over the floor, examining the covers.

'Did you go back?' asked Conrad. 'Did you go back and have another look?'

'Yep,' said Chloë, flicking her red and silver hair.

'And?'

'Nope,' she said. 'Nothing. Got any munchies?'

'I'll get you something to eat in a minute. What about you, Paddy?'

Paddy was more interested in Conrad's comics collection. 'Sorry, kid. Went back twice. Actually, that program is not as boring as I thought. The labyrinth is a maze, and you have to escape from the Minotaur and—'

'I know all that!' Conrad shouted. He couldn't believe his friends hadn't seen what he had seen. He'd been back into the program twice, hovering nervously at the entrance to the labyrinth. Each time he'd taken a step towards the door, the dog-sized spider began to form out of black triangles, and he'd got out, quickly. He'd even asked his teacher, Mentor Robinson, if it was possible that aggressive spiders – as opposed to the normal behaviour-regulating variety – could hover around Edutainment programs, but all he'd got back was a lot of withering sarcasm worthy of Chloë.

'The only spiders are in your brain, lad, along with the cobwebs.'

'Come on,' said Chloë, unpacking the Websuit she'd brought with her, 'let's do it. The only way Conrad is going to be satisfied is if we all go in together.'

So Paddy unrolled his own suit, and Conrad lifted his from the wardrobe where he'd hung it only moments earlier.

'Wow!' said Chloë, feeling the smooth texture of the suit. 'It's rubber, but it feels like silk!'

'State-of-the-art, kid,' said Paddy enviously.

'No,' said Conrad. 'They've made an even better one. In fact, my dad is bringing me a new one home today from South Korea.'

'Great! Then you won't have any use for this one!'

Conrad shrugged. He had a soft spot for Chloë, and would

have happily given her the Websuit when the new one arrived. After all, he had no use for two. But he could see Paddy looking wistfully at the suit, too. Paddy was a great pal, but Chloë was the unspoken leader of the Tech-Rats and he found himself wanting to please her for reasons he didn't understand. Fortunately, Chloë solved the problem by suggesting that she and Paddy toss a coin.

Conrad spun the coin and Chloë won. 'Tech-rats!' shouted Chloë, punching the air. 'How much do you want for the suit? I'll sell my old one and—'

'I don't want anything,' said Conrad. 'My dad gets them for nothing.'

Unusually for Chloë, she went very quiet. She looked at Conrad, deeply impressed.

'Come on,' said Paddy who was a good loser. 'Let's go!' He was already climbing into his own inferior suit.

When all three were properly suited, they jacked into Conrad's terminal and tapped out the references on their wristpads. Within moments they were all transported to the History Edutainment block in Webtown. Webtown was a grid of golden blocks under a featureless brilliant blue sky. Different sites were characterized by building blocks of different colours, and the History Edutainment block was the colour of pink liquorice. After a moment the slight dizziness passed. They linked hands and the pink block rippled as they passed through. In the strange, blue-violet light of the virtual world, Chloë's silver and scarlet hair glistened with stroboscopic effect. It was easy to see why she switched her hair colour so often. She ran a program that could change the colours and appearance of her computer-generated alter-ego, and she liked to adopt the same colours in real life.

Inside the block, further coloured blocks represented different teaching areas. Normally busy with school parties, the site was empty. This only made Chloë wonder what they were doing there on a non-school day. Ignoring her, Conrad led them to 'Ancient Greece'. They passed through this to be presented by a number of doors flanked by giant architectur-

al columns from different periods, one of which fizzed with
an electronic sign: LABYRINTH. There was also a logo of a
double axe-head. Conrad paused.

He heard Chloë's voice crackling in his ear, breaking up
slightly through her throat-microphone. 'Come on, gaghead.
Let's do this and then get into some *real* games.'

Paddy approached the triangular information unit at the
door to the labyrinth. 'Was it here?' he said. He activated the
unit and a calm, female voice began to talk history.

*'Welcome to the labyrinth. You have chosen to study the
Minoan period of Ancient Greek history, the great culture based
on the island of Crete. According to Greek mythology the Minoan
Empire . . .'*

'We'll go inside and have a look round for a few minutes,'
said Chloë. 'Get chased by the Minotaur or whatever, and
then come out.'

Chloë passed between the giant columns of the doorway,
followed by Paddy. Conrad, lagging behind, made to follow
them. But as soon as he took two steps forward, the history
lecture stopped abruptly and the information box changed
shape. It rapidly reformed itself into a spider and came
rushing at him, steel probe extended. Conrad screamed as
the probe touched him between the eyes, and everything
faded to black.

When Conrad came round he was lying on the floor of his
bedroom, with Paddy and Chloë peeling him out of his
Websuit. They were still wearing their own suits. Conrad sat
shivering in his shorts, hugging himself, feeling sick from the
bite. The vile, metallic taste had returned to his mouth and
he felt as though he wanted to vomit. Still, it wasn't quite as
bad as the first time. Conrad had the idea he'd managed to
get out before the probe was fully inserted.

'Get him some water,' Chloë told Paddy. 'Conrad, what
happened? One minute we were walking ahead of you into
the labyrinth, and then you started screaming!'

'Uggghh, spider,' was all Conrad managed to say.

'There was no spider, kid,' Paddy said, handing him a glass

of water. Paddy was still wearing his aviation helmet over the hood of his Websuit. 'We looked back and you'd simply fallen over.'

'I hadn't simply fallen over!' Conrad shouted, angry. 'There was a security spider! Like before! I just don't get what's going on!'

The door opened and Conrad's mother appeared. 'What's all the shouting about? Conrad, get up off the floor. Your father's home.'

At lunchtime, Conrad, Chloë and Paddy sat on silent, aircushioned hover-stools, while Conrad's parents sat on the old-fashioned V-wing chairs with four legs that they preferred. Conrad's father, James Hamilton, was good-natured and balding. He always returned from his business trips with dozens of stories. Mrs Hamilton sliced a tomato the size of a football as James told them about South Korea and the incredible things that were happening there. South Korea had become the main country for the manufacture of Web-suits and other computer hardware, but listening to what James had to say, it seemed as if the companies there had to fight off criminal factions and other shady interests. Conrad's mother wondered if it was safe.

James Hamilton shrugged. 'The other thing is all these weird religious groups springing up. Despite making all these computers, the people are still very poor there, so they get drawn in to fundamentalist groups who, frankly, use brain-washing techniques.'

'Conrad's brain could do with a wash,' Chloë said brightly. Everyone laughed except Conrad.

'So, how's school going?' James wanted to know.

'Don't ask,' said Conrad's mother.

'Want to see the new Websuit?' James asked, knowing his son was dying to see the latest development. A silver foil package was lying on the chair. 'Open it up. Take a look.'

The new Websuit was the same silky rubber as the old one, but this was grey instead of blue, and iridescent where it caught the light. The throat-microphone had been refined

and the wrist-mounted keyboard was part of the suit instead
of an extra.

Conrad wasn't too happy about the tiny spider logo on the
suit, but was so impressed by the rest of it, he kept quiet.

'Venomous!' said Chloë. 'Real venom!'

Paddy and Chloë wanted to try it on immediately, but
Conrad's mother intervened.

'Oh, no, you don't. You've been in Webtown all morning.
We don't want another case of Websickness,' she said, eyeing
Conrad suspiciously.

After spending the afternoon together, the Tech-Rats
dispersed. Chloë happily took Conrad's other suit home with
her. Mr Hamilton gave Paddy a colour-character generating
program not unlike Chloë's, so he didn't leave the Hamilton
household empty-handed either. 'Just don't come back with
green hair,' Mrs Hamilton said.

That night Conrad slept badly. He had a strange and
disturbing dream. He was on a beach of yellow sand, and he
was only about four or five years old. Lots of people around
him were singing and smiling. The song they were singing
stuck in his head. Everyone held their smiles in place just a
few seconds too long. All the people seemed just a little bit
too happy.

He woke up in the night feeling sweaty and uncomfortable. A light was winking on his computer. Someone had
sent him an e-mail. He slid out of bed and ran the message. It
was in Rat code. He recognized the signature even in its
coded form. The message was from Chloë, and he ran it
through the codebreaker:

<Hey, winkle-brain, I take it all back. I've been bitten by your
spider. I feel terrible. Call me. Love, Chloë.>

CHAPTER FOUR

ARIADNE

Conrad called Chloë the following morning. She was waiting for him. 'You took your time!'

'Sorry,' said Conrad. 'I'm a bit sleepy. I've been having strange dreams.'

'Anyway, as I said, I take it all back. I went back to the labyrinth when I got home yesterday. I was in a hurry to try out the suit. I thought I'd take a look around, and before I got through the door a monster of a filthy spider bit me. You weren't joking, Conrad. It was *mean*. I felt sick all night.'

'At least it proves I'm not going mad. Have you told Paddy?'

'He hasn't answered. Hey, how many times have you been bitten by security spiders in the past?'

'Four, maybe five times.'

'I've collected seven bites over the last few years. And not one of them hurt like this. Plus I've had the voms before, but not like this. Something weird is going on, Conrad. There just aren't supposed to be aggressive security spiders in Edutainment. Government sites, finance outfits, adults-only sites, sure. But not Edutainment.'

Paddy still wasn't answering, so they decided to venture back inside the labyrinth together. Conrad climbed into his brand new suit and tapped out the reference code. He was there seconds ahead of Chloë. 'Wow! This new thing is *fast*!'

Chloë appeared, and they decided to hold hands and make a slow approach on the doorway. The double axe-head logo winked ominously overhead. They moved slowly. Now both of them were really nervous of the guardian spider. Conrad shuffled nearer. At about the point where the spider emerged from the information box, Chloë froze. Conrad took a step further in. Incredibly, nothing happened. He touched the box and the history lecture commenced. Chloë screamed.

Conrad looked back. Chloë was shrinking away from the door. Then she stopped dead. 'Come here,' she croaked. He could hear the terror in her voice. 'Come here.'

Conrad retreated. She held out her hand. 'This is it, Conrad. If I step past this point, the spider begins to form. If I stay here, it stops.'

Conrad looked round. 'There is no spider! I don't see it!'

Conrad stepped forward, then back. Nothing. Why was Chloë seeing now what only he could see before? And why wasn't he able to see it now? It was crazy, but not so crazy that he didn't believe her when she said she saw something. He'd been in that position himself. Then a thought struck him.

'Chloë, I think I've got it! You're wearing my old suit! Somehow the spider is in the suit. Check out of the program immediately. Change into your old Websuit, and come back here. I'll wait.'

'But—'

'Just do it!'

Chloë pressed two buttons on her wristpad and her virtual image faded. Conrad waited. He didn't know how it had happened, but somehow he knew that the spider was in the suit he had given to Chloë. That meant that it had somehow been programmed into the circuits in the suit, or even in the keypad. That was the only thing that would explain why no one else could see the spider. The suit was triggering a *secret program*!

Chloë returned after a minute or two. 'Got your old suit on?' Conrad asked.

'You bet!' said Chloë.

'Come on.'

They approached the door again. Chloë was super-cautious, shuffling forward a centimetre at a time, waiting for the infobox to transform into a hideous, poisonous guardian.

But Conrad was right. This time there were no spiders for either of them. They passed safely through the door.

Conrad explained his thoughts to Chloë.

'But I don't get it,' Chloë said. 'That means someone has gone to a lot of trouble to hide something in an Edutainment program. Why would they do that?'

Why indeed? thought Conrad. He stared around him at the huge, ancient stone walls of the labyrinth. Flaming torches angled to the walls sent shadows rippling across the stones. Conrad was still trying to think of a reason when the history lecture voice-over stopped abruptly. There was an electronic burp, and then the hum of an override intrusion. A different but equally calm female voice suddenly said,

<*This is the voice of Ariadne. Surely the Tech-Rats are not going to be beaten by a little spider.*>

There was another electronic burp, and the history lecture resumed.

'Did you hear that?' said Conrad.

'Certainly did,' said Chloë.

They went back to the information box and tried to get the machine to replay what it had just said. It simply repeated the history lecture, uninterrupted this time. Chloë had an idea, so she called up a search on the information box, tapping in the name Ariadne.

'*Ariadne: according to mythology, when the Greek hero Perseus entered the labyrinth to slay the Minotaur, he was assisted by Ariadne, who was able to guide him through the labyrinth so that he could make good his escape . . .*'

The tape ran on with further information about this obscure figure from Greek mythology.

'Do you think it's someone trying to help us?' Conrad asked. 'Or someone trying to harm us?'

'I'll tell you what I do think. It feels like we're out of our depth.'

'Are you afraid?'

'Yep,' said Chloë.

'Let's get out of here.'

They got out quickly, and closed down the program.

'So,' said Paddy, swinging his aviation helmet by the strap, 'are we going to be beaten by a little spider?'

The Tech-Rats had reassembled at Conrad's house.

'Hey, moth-brain, you wouldn't call it *little* if you'd been attacked by it,' said Chloë. 'This makes a normal security-spider bite feel like a lick from a goldfish.'

'Goldfish don't lick, kid. They suck.'

'Whatever. I just don't ever want to experience it again.'

'Me neither,' said Conrad.

'So, that's it then,' Paddy said in disgust. 'The Tech-Rats meet their first challenge, and they roll over and die.'

Chloë glowered at him. Paddy knew they wouldn't take this insult lying down. Conrad shook his head. 'Suppose we go back, and suppose we find a way past the spider. Then what?'

'Don't ask me,' Paddy said sarcastically. He lay on the floor with his arms and legs in the air. 'I'm going to roll over and die with you two.'

'I'm still wondering about who this Ariadne might be,' said Chloë.

'Only one way to find out,' Paddy said, getting up and fixing on his aviation helmet.

'We've only got the one suit wired for the hidden program,' Conrad said weakly.

'I've thought of that,' said Paddy, who was after all the technical expert of the group. Chloë called him their tech-warrior. 'Instead of jacking into your terminal I can wire a couple of jack-points into the suit you've given to Chloë. That way we'll pick up the circuits of the leader suit, and we'll all be in the hidden program.'

'Tech-rats!' Chloë shouted. 'That puts me in *command*. I love it!'

'I was afraid of that,' said Conrad.

Chloë was already stepping into her suit. 'Come on, boys, we're going in again!'

CHAPTER FIVE

HAPPY SMILING PEOPLE

Webtown was thronged with people. It being Sunday, most of the folk visiting Webtown were there for the entertainment or leisure sites. The educational and even the Edutainment sites were hardly busy at all. So it was just their luck when, after passing through the History block into the Ancient Greece program, they found their form teacher Mentor Robinson, there ahead of them.

His throat microphone crackled with laughter. 'My goodness. Wonders will never cease! Here you all are, educating yourselves on a Sunday! Truly, I am impressed. Astonished, yes, but impressed. I thought you'd be blowing up alien spacecraft or whatever, not expanding your minds.'

'Project work,' Conrad said quickly.

'Terrific! Let's all take a stroll together round the exhibition! Which area of Ancient Greece were you heading for? Classical architecture perhaps? The teachings of Plato? The Alexandrian conquests? I like nothing better than the company of young people on my day off!'

Three hearts sank. They couldn't possibly take Mentor Robinson into the labyrinth. They ended up spending an hour with him looking at Greek architecture. Mentor Robinson stopped the tape commentary and provided them with his own. He talked, they said nothing. Occasionally they offered pretend-grunts of appreciation, or small noises expressing a fascination none of them felt:

'Oh?'

'Ah!'

'I see.'

'Um!'

'Great!' Chloë spat, after he'd gone. 'Now I'm an expert on Corinthian columns. Why didn't you keep your mouth shut, beetle-brain!'

'I didn't notice you saying much at the time,' Conrad answered.

'Stop arguing,' said Paddy. 'We came here for a purpose. Let's do what we came for.'

At the labyrinth they stopped Paddy from passing beyond the point where the information block would begin to morph into a spider. 'Now what?'

'Wait,' said Paddy. He tapped his wrist keypad. 'Above all else, we have to make sure that Chloë doesn't shut down, because if that happens, we all shut down. So we may have to protect her. I'm calling up my *Hacker's Handbook*.'

The *Hacker's Handbook* was an illegal document, banned by the government. This meant that every kid who fancied himself as a tech-warrior had one. Microscopic text appeared on Paddy's wristpad.

How to Get By a Security Spider.
1. Get the colour code.
2. Accept a bite while your friends pass through.
3. Deactivate spider head-on (advanced tech-warriors only).
4. Confuse spider.

Paddy read out the options to the others.

'Well, we certainly haven't got the colour code,' said Chloë. 'Can you deactivate the spider head-on?'

'No,' said Paddy.

'Are you prepared to take a bite so that we can pass?'

'No.'

'Do you know how to confuse a spider?'

'No,' said Paddy.

'Some tech-warrior!' Chloë said in disgust.

'Can you make an echo-image of one of us?' Conrad suggested. 'You tricked Mentor Robinson once before. That would confuse the spider, wouldn't it?'

'It's worth a try,' said Paddy. 'I could make an image run for about five or six seconds before it fades.'

'Make one of all three of us,' said Chloë. 'That way we would know whether it's possible to slip by if one person is being bit.'

Paddy busied himself on his wristpad, eventually releasing phantom images of Chloë, Conrad and himself, and launched them at the labyrinth door. The phantoms instantly triggered the spider. To their dismay, the spider replicated itself to deal with each of the three phantom images. Though the images passed through the spiders, they faded just beyond the doorway. With the intruders despatched, the three spiders instantly reverted back to being an information box.

'So much for taking a bite while your friends nip in,' said Chloë. 'These beasts are just unreal.'

'There must be a way,' said Paddy.

In desperation, Conrad flipped open his own wristpad and typed:

<Ariadne, help us.>

Almost immediately an answer came back, crackling in his earpiece. *'Chloë has colour code. Ariadne.'*

'Hey!' He looked at the others.

'I heard,' Chloë said. 'This means that Ariadne, whoever she is, is watching our every move.'

'But why does Ariadne say you have the colour code?'

'Search me.'

Paddy was on to something. He was twitching like a hound after a scent. 'I think I know what it means,' he said. 'Chloë, what are the numerical values for your hair colour? I mean when you generated your virtual image?'

'Silver-Red-Silver-Red-Silver-Red-Silver is 14-2-14-2-14-2-14.'

'Did you pick it yourself?'

'No, that's the weird thing. I was going for green and gold but the program kept crashing and I ended up with this, twice. I decided I liked it.'

'I think we just worked out that Ariadne dyed your hair, kid. Let's try it.' Paddy took a step towards the door and the hideous spider began to assemble out of the triangles. He tapped in the colour-number code, and with an electronic wheeze the spider collapsed back into the information box.

'Yes, yes, yes!' cheered Chloë.

But the mysterious voice crackled again in their ears. *'Now they are on to me. I'm going off-line. I won't be able to help you for a while.'*

The voice went dead. 'I think we're on our own again,' said Conrad. 'Come on!'

They passed safely into the labyrinth.

Once inside, the plan was to look for anything that was different from what they'd seen before inside the labyrinth. They suspected they would discover further secret programs they could open up. Other people were wandering around the labyrinth that day: a family, a couple of kids and so on. The dusty old stones towered above them and the walls echoed eerily. But they guessed that they were the only ones with access to the secret areas of the program. Information boxes poured out history lectures, talking about the Minoan Empire and the palace of Knossos. Huge interactive exhibitions inside the labyrinth offered further information. Screens would open up in the wall, inviting interaction and then closing as they passed by.

Suddenly, they heard the sound of galloping hooves, coming towards them. Then a bellowing and the snorting of a bull. With the sound of great stone blocks drawing back, a breach appeared in the wall, and a terrifying figure appeared. It was a man nearly two metres tall with the face of an enormous bull. He snorted and stamped his cloven hooves. 'Good afternoon,' the figure said in a very refined and rather snooty voice. 'Welcome to the labyrinth. I'm your

Minotaur. Would you like me to explain the gameplan? I operate in three modes—'

'No thanks and goodnight,' Paddy said rudely.

The Minotaur stepped back. 'Are you certain, sir? I can run as a terrifying adversary chasing you around the program as you collect data, or as a tour guide – that is MinoTOUR guide. He-he-he!'

'No thanks. Close down,' said Chloë. The Minotaur stepped back into the breach, and the wall closed up.

'The most terrifying thing about that Minotaur,' said Chloë, 'is his sense of humour.'

Then they heard a snatch of music, of people singing.

'Why does that sound familiar?' said Chloë.

Before her question was answered, another screen opened up in the wall, inviting them to walk into an interactive display nodule – known as an *Id* – in which people were sitting together on a beach of yellow sand. Date-palm trees formed the doorway through which they had to pass to join the Id. The people within wore white robes and golden sandals, like figures from Ancient Greece, but their faces, their hairstyles, seemed modern. The huge red disc of the sun was setting over the water behind them. The people were singing and looking very happy. They waved, inviting Chloë, Paddy and Conrad to join them.

'I can't believe this,' said Chloë. 'I had a dream exactly like this last night.'

'Me too!' said Conrad. 'The singing. The music. The happy, smiling people. I had exactly the same dream.'

'I don't know what you're talking about,' said Paddy, 'but there's something yukky about these people. I know they are only computer images, but they don't look right.'

'Too happy,' said Chloë.

'Yep. Like a goldfish is happy.'

The people on the sand continued to wave, to beckon them over, so they moved closer. 'Not just that,' said Paddy. 'Look at their eyes!'

The eyes of the people on the sand were all colour, either

blue or green or brown, but with no pupils, and no whites of the eye. Then the taped history lecture faded into the background, and a soft, electronic, wave noise took over, pulsing gently. The people on the sand continued to beckon them onwards. Chloë, Paddy and Conrad stared blankly at the scene.

'How long have we been inside the Web?' asked Chloë. 'I'm starting to get the voms.'

'Me too,' said Paddy. 'I feel sick.'

Conrad felt it too and looked at his wristpad. 'That can't be right. It says we've been here for over three hours. How long were we with Mentor Robinson?'

'An hour at most,' said Chloë.

'Say, fifteen minutes trying to get past the spider. We've lost at least an hour somewhere, probably more.'

'Yuk. I'm going to have to close down,' said Chloë. 'I really don't feel too good.'

Without waiting for the others to agree, she hit two buttons on her pad. Nothing happened. The other two had the same problem. 'Let's go out the way we came in,' suggested Paddy. They retreated under the crossed branches of the date-palm trees. Once outside the Id they all hit their scuttle buttons again. Moments later they were hurrying out of their Websuits in Conrad's room.

'Something really bad is going on,' said Chloë. 'I don't know what it is, but I really don't like it. I need a drink before I throw up!' She raced downstairs and brought back three of Conrad's ice-cold cans of Arctic berry juice, handing them round without breaking what she was saying. 'Questions for the quick-witted: One, who is Ariadne, and why did she crash my colour-generator? Two, who has set up a secret program for the labyrinth? Three, why are we all dreaming the same dream?'

'Correction, kid,' said Paddy. 'Only you two.'

'Four, how come we lost an hour on the Web today? I hate getting Websick.'

No one had a chance to respond to any of Chloë's

questions. An electronic signal diverted their attention to the computer screen, where there was an urgent message from Conrad's father.

CHAPTER SIX

WEBSICKNESS

The image of Conrad's father on the monitor was breaking up. Though live communication from South Korea was usually good, sometimes magnetic interference or satellite conditions caused pictures to slip, so that James Hamilton's face shifted from full detail to the kind that might have been computer-constructed with sharp angles. His balding head was squared off at the sides and the lines running across his forehead looked too deep.

'Hi, Dad!' said Conrad.

'Conrad!' James Hamilton seemed to wake up when he saw his son's face on his own monitor. 'Where's your mother? I need to talk to her.'

'She went out for a few minutes.'

'Damn. How are you?'

'Fine.'

'Really? Everything is all right?'

'Sure. Why wouldn't it be?'

'No reason, just asking. Listen. This is important. That Websuit I gave you; you're going to have to send it back to me.'

'Oh, well,' said Conrad. 'I didn't like the spider logo anyway.'

Mr Hamilton looked confused. 'No, no. I don't mean the latest one I gave you. It's the other one. The manufacturers have found a serious flaw in it, and they are recalling all of them. You have to have it couriered back to me here in South Korea.'

'Too late, Dad.'

'Too late? What do you mean too late?'

'You said Chloë could have it. Don't you remember?'

James Hamilton looked irritated with his son. He leaned forward. 'Well, you tell Chloë I'll get her a state-of-the-art suit like yours, with or without a spider logo. Heck, I'll get one for Paddy too. Just get that other one back to me, because the people here are very anxious that it is returned, and if they don't get it then I could lose a lot of business. Is that clear?'

'Sure.'

'Don't screw up now, Conrad. You know how to use the courier system? . . . Good. Don't let me down, now.'

'OK.'

'Attaboy. Got to go, bye.'

James Hamilton faded from the screen. Paddy whistled softly. Neither he nor Chloë had been in the viewline of the monitor. 'Looks like you're all going to get one of those fancy suits,' Conrad said.

'Great!' said Paddy.

'Yep, great,' said Chloë. 'Then we'll all look pretty in our silky new suits.'

The two boys looked at her. They could tell from her voice that something else was coming. 'You two pea-brains just don't get it, do you? Can't you see the connection?'

'What connection?'

'Sounds to me,' Chloë said, 'like someone wants my suit back *pretty bad*.'

'You mean—'

'Yes, you microbe! It seems to me that the suit triggering the hidden program came to us by accident. We should never have got our hands on it. And now we've had access to the parallel program, the *secret* program, they've become aware of us. What's more, they don't want us in there.'

'We've got to return the suit!' Conrad blurted. 'My dad will go ape if I don't get it back to him.'

'I know, I know! Calm down! Let's think this through. We need to buy ourselves some time, if we're going to find out what they're trying to hide.'

'*They*?' said Paddy. 'Who are *they*?'

'Whoever made this special suit. Whoever is so desperate to get it back. We've got to go back in there and find out why.'

Paddy groaned. 'I can't face it right now. I'm too Websick.'

'Me too,' Conrad complained.

'We're all too sick right now. We'll have to leave it a few hours before we go back in.'

'You're forgetting something,' said Paddy. 'Conrad and I are piggybacking on your circuits. We have to jack into your suit to reach the hidden program. And in a few hours we'll all be home and tucked up in bed.'

'Tomorrow then.'

'Tomorrow is school.'

'Then after school!' shouted Chloë. 'What's the matter with you? And anyway, Conrad's mother wouldn't mind us all coming here to study together on Conrad's terminal. You know how the school authorities are worried about kids studying in isolation!'

'That's all very well,' Conrad said, 'but what about getting the suit back to my father in Korea? There's no way I can keep it here.'

'Just get us a couple of days, Conrad! Tell your dad you've had trouble contacting me. Say I've gone away and I'll be back soon. Make something up.'

Conrad didn't like lying to his old man. He looked unhappy and glanced up at his other friend, but Paddy only tugged his flying helmet down over his eyes.

'It's only for a day or two,' Chloë pleaded. 'And when the Websickness has worn off, I'll go in on my own and take a look round.'

'Not recommended, kid,' Paddy said, pulling his helmet up again.

'That's right,' said Conrad, suddenly feeling afraid for his friend. 'Not a good idea to go in there alone. It's spooky. It has a really bad feel to it, this labyrinth thing.'

'OK,' said Chloë. 'You're right.'

When Chloë agreed easily like that, Conrad knew she

wasn't to be trusted. 'I forbid you to go in on your own,' he said.

'It's time we were gone,' Chloë said to Paddy, gathering up her equipment. 'See you bright and early for school, Conrad.'

'Leave the suit here!' shouted Conrad, but Chloë was already thumping down the stairs and calling out a cheery goodbye to Mrs Hamilton. Paddy shrugged at Conrad, and followed Chloë down the stairs.

Later, Conrad got his mother's approval for his two friends to study at his terminal the following day. He also opened up the Web to transmit a message to his father, saying that Chloë had gone away with the suit for a day or two but that he would make certain it was returned to Korea as soon as she got back.

When he went to bed that night, he lay awake for a while watching his planetarium on the ceiling. Conrad had a software program that turned his computer into a fantastic light show, projecting planets and stars across the ceiling and walls of his bedroom. Sometimes at night it was possible to believe as he drifted off to sleep that he was actually floating out there in space. On this night he watched a pulsing Red Giant go supernova, the most violent explosion known in the universe, and wondered if Chloë was crazy enough to venture into the secret program on her own.

Was Chloë crazy enough to go into the hidden program alone? Of course she was. After all the lights went out in her house, she crept out of bed, powered up her terminal and slipped into her suit. Within moments she was standing outside the labyrinth, underneath the fizzing double-axehead logo.

The instant she approached the information box, the security spider formed itself. Chloë tapped out the access code on her wristpad and the spider stood down, info-box again.

'We're in,' she whispered to herself.

Chloë followed the same path they'd taken earlier that day. She was still feeling a little sick from staying too long in

the Web, but she had an idea. All she needed was ten or
fifteen minutes to prove a point.

Very quickly she found herself at the interactive display in
which people were sitting together on a beach of yellow
sand, before a crimson setting sun. As she passed through the
date-palm doorway, the people continued singing and
chanting, as if they hadn't stopped since the three had
visited that afternoon, and they were still looking very, very
happy. Happy, that is, in a delirious and empty-headed way.
They waved, inviting Chloë to join them. One of the people,
a young man with washed-out blue eyes, stood up from the
crowd and called to her, smiling, smiling, inviting her again
to join them. Chloë was shocked to find that she could move
her hand through the 3-D image. Most experiences in Virtual
Reality were tangible, just like the real world. What's more,
when she passed through the Id images, she found herself
back in the labyrinth, as if the images themselves were the
doorway out. It was all unlike the things she was accustomed
to in Webtown. She passed exhibitions of Minoan Art, a
game involving Ancient Greek costumes and a reconstruc-
tion of a Minoan palace.

It was there, camped within the pillars of the entrance to
the palace, that Chloë found another group of young people
sitting around a small fire, talking. It was another Id, and this
time the pillars formed the doorway in. The light had
changed. It was night. Chloë looked up and the stars were
out, brilliant, like silver berries in the sky. As before, the
young people wore white robes.

One of the young people looked up at her and started to
play some eerie music on a flute. Another boy beat a steady
rhythm on a drum. One handsome smiling boy turned to
Chloë and said, 'You look intelligent. Could you settle an
argument?' Chloë thought there was a malfunction in the
program, because the lights flickered and the Id buzzed.
There was a noise like electrical interference.

Chloë felt dizzy, and then felt a creeping attack of
Websickness again. For a moment she thought she might
faint. Then the Id boy spoke to her again. 'You look

intelligent. Could you settle an argument?' He blinked at her, eyes all blue, no pupil, no white.

She looked at her watch. It seemed impossible, but over two hours had passed. She felt terrible, giddy. Then she felt suddenly frightened. She tapped the keys on her wristpad, wanting to get out of the program immediately. Nothing happened. 'Don't go,' she heard the boy say. Chloë panicked, and froze. Then she remembered how they'd got out of the Id before. She backed out through the pillars and retraced her way back to the first Id, the scene on the beach. There she passed through the date-palm door. Gasping with relief she hit the scuttle button and felt the program shutting down around her.

CHAPTER SEVEN

WEBSCHOOL

'Chloë, you look terrible!' Conrad said when she arrived at his house the following morning, ready to commence school.

'Thanks,' she said, unpacking her keyboard and her notes and plugging into Conrad's terminal. 'I feel it.' Her hands shook slightly.

'Don't tell me. You went into the program last night. I warned you not to.'

'I only meant to stay a few minutes. Something really weird is going on. What seemed like a few seconds turned into a couple of hours and another bad attack of the voms. I almost didn't make it out of bed today.'

The triple-tone chimes of Webschool sounded from Conrad's terminal, just as Paddy raced through the door. He just managed to plug his own keyboard and notepad into Conrad's terminal before the unsmiling face of Mentor Robinson came up on screen. Mentor Robinson began the role check to find out who had signed on. Each student had to show their face and tap in a PIN number when requested.

'Ah! Good morning!' Mentor Robinson said when he realized they were all studying together from Conrad's terminal. There was just a hint of sarcasm in his voice. 'Three knowledgeable antiquarians! How delightful to resume contact. I trust our excursion into the delights of Greek architecture left you buzzing, nay, singing with pleasure. Sadly, nothing so interesting today. This morning, we will be addressing our minds to geometry.'

While Mentor Robinson proceeded to register the rest of his on-line class, Paddy leaned across and whispered to Chloë, 'By the way, you look terrible.'

'Wow, that was *boring*,' said Conrad when break time came round. Mentor Robinson's face on the monitor had been replaced by the Webschool logo, a quill pen.

'I must be going soft in the brain,' Paddy said, 'but I actually *like* geometry.'

Chloë hissed at him in disgust. 'So much for our techno-warrior. Have you actually come up with anything that might help us?'

'As I matter of fact, I have,' said Paddy. He closed down the quill-pen icon on screen and opened his *Hacker's Handbook*. 'Take a look at this.'

Secret programs: adding, deleting, moving.

Paddy scrolled through the text until he came to a section headed:

Hardware: If program trigger is located somewhere in suit, glove or keypad, detect trigger, recircuit wiring, remove trigger and replace. Alternatively, replace entire circuits of suit, glove or keypad.

'Oh sure!' said Chloë. 'We just cut up the suit, pull out the wires and sew it up again. No one will be able to tell, I don't think!'

'Calm yourself,' Paddy said with mock-adult authority. He closed down the *Hacker's Handbook* and the quill-pen returned to the screen. 'The trigger for the secret program is one tiny circuit somewhere in this suit, probably close to one of the skin-contact electrodes. We just find it, make a tiny hole in the suit and take it out.'

'How do you find it?'

'That's the hard part,' said Paddy.

Conrad's terminal sounded three chimes. School was ready to start again.

*

At lunchtime, Paddy explained the procedure. Conrad would have to access the program and generate phantoms, as before, to alert the security spider. Paddy would test the circuits on the suit, narrowing down the area piece by piece until he was able to detect the exact place he wanted.

'That could take hours and hours!' Conrad protested.

'Isn't there another way?' Chloë moaned.

'There is.'

'What's that?'

'One of us would have to take a spider bite,' said Paddy.

'We'll do it your way,' Chloë and Conrad said together, hastily. They both knew what this particular spider bite was like. They also knew that Paddy could perform technical tricks way beyond the capacity of most thirteen-year-olds. They worked through lunch break. Chloë, still somewhat Websick, stayed out of the program while Conrad, wearing the suit, went in. Paddy started by testing the electrodes in the hood of the suit. Several phantom holographic images later, and with school about to resume, they'd made hardly any progress.

'We're getting nowhere fast,' Chloë said, 'and I'm starving.'

Afternoon school was a slog, even through their favourite subjects. Though school finished early in the afternoon, at three o'clock, it couldn't come too soon for the members of the Tech-Rats.

'It's no good,' moaned Conrad. 'I'm going to have to send the suit back tomorrow or the next day at the latest. And we can't spend more than two or three hours at a time inside the Web without getting sick. At the rate we're going it will take two weeks to find the trigger.'

Paddy couldn't go back into the Web because he was the only one with enough technical expertise to do the testing. Chloë went back in this time while Conrad wore the suit. Paddy pored over him as they worked away, testing the suit centimetre by centimetre. After an hour they'd still made very little progress. Conrad played with the keyboard in front of him.

<Ariadne, what's the answer?>

The monitor in front of him flickered, fizzed and changed from blue to amber, and a string of text printed itself across the screen.

<You're sitting on it.>

The message faded from the screen almost immediately. The screen flickered from amber back to blue. Paddy stopped what he was doing. 'What was that?'

Conrad ignored him. 'Chloë, you can come out. I'm closing you down. We've just had help from Ariadne.'

The program shut down and Chloë jacked out. She blinked at Conrad as he told her about the new message. 'It's under your butt?' she said. 'Ariadne has certainly got a sense of humour.'

There were two electrodes in the seat of the suit. Within half an hour Paddy had found the micro-circuitry of the trigger switch. It was the size of a pin-head with filament wires. Paddy made a tiny nick in the skin of the suit, extracted the switch and repaired the circuit. He held the tiny trigger-switch up to the light.

'I can easily get this copied,' he said. 'We'll all have one. I can patch one into each of our suits. Now you can parcel up the suit and have it flown to South Korea.'

Conrad immediately transmitted a message to his father, saying that the suit had been recovered and would be on its way.

'Working from head to foot,' Chloë observed, 'it would have taken us days to find that trigger. I wonder why Ariadne chose not to help us earlier.'

'Let's ask,' said Conrad. He typed on his keyboard:

<Ariadne, why didn't you help us before?>

There was a long pause, during which it seemed no answer would come. Then a flicker as the screen changed colour and another printed message appeared on the amber screen.

<You must understand this: every time I communicate with you, they know. Each time they are closer to tracing me. I can't let that happen.>

The message ended there. After a while Conrad typed:

<Ariadne, who are you?>

Three young faces were turned towards the screen, all bathed in amber light, waiting. There was no response. Whoever Ariadne was, he, she or it was not saying.

No one could possibly return to the hidden program until Paddy had patched the switch into the circuits of a different suit. Chloë and Conrad, both Websick to different degrees, were actually relieved. They agreed to begin again the following evening. As soon as Paddy had incorporated the copied trigger switches into their own suits, they would be able to work from their own homes instead of having to jack, piggyback-style, into the trigger suit.

'What about this time thing?' Chloë said before leaving.

'What about it?'

'This program is stealing our time. Every time we go in, what seems like a couple of minutes is proving to be a couple of hours. If we can't stop that from happening we'll never find out what the hell is going on.'

'We'll work on it tomorrow evening,' said Paddy, packing his things. 'I have to get home. Don't forget to send off that suit, Conrad.'

'I'll do it this evening from the local depot. See you both tomorrow.'

When Chloë and Paddy left Conrad's house that evening, all three of them had exactly the same question on their mind.

Who is Ariadne?

CHAPTER EIGHT

SWIMMING

'Ariadne is a woman,' Chloë said. 'We heard her voice, remember?'

Paddy and Chloë were having one of their usual arguments, across the city. If they looked out from their rooms at night, they could see the fizzing new blue-green streetlights, lit by deep-sea organisms kept alive in perspex lamps. These days the city at night looked the way they imagined the ocean floor to look.

Each of them was in their own bedroom wearing suits recently modified by Paddy. Conrad meanwhile had entered the Web and was into the labyrinth. Paddy and Chloë had agreed to stay out, monitoring both his movements and his sense of time while he was inside the labyrinth. Chloë had advised him to ignore the two Id groups, the people on the beach and the young people discussing and playing music under the stars. She explained that it was necessary to pass through the beach people, which she called Level 1, in order to get to the music people of Level 2. Conrad's 'orders' were to proceed further into the labyrinth to see what he could find, assuming the existence of a third level and possibly more.

Meanwhile, Paddy and Chloë had direct voice communication.

'That doesn't prove Ariadne isn't a man,' a woman's clipped voice answered. It was a voice sounding as if it belonged to a rather posh, sixty-year-old spinster.

Chloë laughed. She knew it was Paddy speaking, operating his voice-scrambler. The incredible thing about moving about in the Web was that you could not only make your Web alter-ego look different, you could also make yourself sound male or female and with any accent in the world.

'Point taken,' said Chloë. 'But I still think Ariadne is a woman.'

'Conrad thinks it's a man,' said Paddy in his normal voice. 'But it might be neither.'

'What?'

'Artificial Intelligence,' said Paddy. 'Ariadne might be a computerized program itself.'

'You're getting carried away with ideas,' Chloë said, and before Paddy could answer, a beeper alarm sounded to remind them of the task in hand. 'That signals fifteen minutes Conrad has been inside. Let's check out his sense of time shall we?'

Conrad was a fish.

He was a very happy fish.

After entering the labyrinth and passing through the date-palm doorway he'd ignored the blank-eyed people on the beach. Though they'd waved at him, and even come to greet him, he'd passed quickly between them. Then he found the group of young people sitting by a small fire playing music. After Conrad had passed through the pillar-doorway, one of them had said, 'You look intelligent. Can you settle an argument?' Conrad liked the look of this group of people and wanted to join them. They looked fun to be with. In fact, it had been quite a strain to ignore them, so attractive were they all, but in the end he'd reminded himself they were only Id images.

Leaving them behind, he reached a third interactive display. Unlike the other two displays, Level 3 was attracting the attention of quite a few visitors like himself. Conrad had no way of knowing, but because there were so many people he assumed this was part of the standard labyrinth program rather than the secret program. Whichever it was, everyone appeared to be having a great time. The Level 3 Id was no more than a rotating disc crackling with light and kaleidoscopic colour. The disc was some kind of chute. You had to pass through by jumping into it, feet first.

A pretty girl with her hair tied in golden plaits turned to Conrad and said, 'Wanna swim with the fishes?'

'Huh?'

'Are you new to this? Haven't you done this? Check it out!' She had a radiant smile and perfect white teeth.

'Are you an Id?' he asked. Unlike the Id nodules of levels one and two, her eyes looked normal, at least.

'Don't insult me! Do I look like an Id?'

'No,' he admitted, though inside the Web it was difficult to tell an avatar from an Id. 'How does it work?'

'You can be a fish, a bird, a bull, a horse, a dragonfly, anything you want. After you've selected, this creates the environment and you just *go for it!* Come on! You know you want to try! Fish or bird?' She smiled at him, again showing him a perfect set of teeth. He wondered if her real-life appearance was as good as her virtual appearance. He thought how Chloë would scoff at people who made themselves look beautiful in the Web.

'Fish,' said Conrad, and they jumped into the chute.

And they swam together.

'He's not responding,' said Chloë. 'Either he can't hear me or he's ignoring me.'

'Have you tried the override?'

'Of course I tried it. Do you think I'm as dumb as you are, nano-brain?'

'Calm yourself, kid. There's two things we can do. We can close the program down around him—'

'Psychic shock,' said Chloë. 'He'll have nightmares for a month.'

'Or, as I was about to say before you interrupted, one of us will have to go in and drag him out.'

'I'll go in,' said Chloë. 'I'm curious to see what's keeping him. If you lose contact with me in the same way, Paddy, you'll just have to close down around us.'

'What, and give you nightmares?'

'If necessary.'

'I'll enjoy it,' said Paddy.

Conrad was still swimming, with his new-found fish-friend. They were recast like some kind of angel fish, but much larger, with beautiful golden and black stripes. The waters they swam in were warm and apt to change colour from lapis lazuli to pink, and from lime green to citrus orange. Glittering golden bubbles rose steadily as they swam between waving reeds, exploring the wrecks of sunken galleons of Ancient Greece, or passing in and out of other schools of fish. The other fish sometimes had human faces that made Conrad and his new companion laugh. One looked a little like Chloë, another not unlike Mentor Robinson . . . The bubbling water and the drifting tides made a strange music. Conrad was enjoying himself so much that he didn't want the game to stop.

He enjoyed being a fish. Everything moved slowly. He could turn and swim easily, or he could just hang in the water, weightless, enjoying the stillness. The water was warm and slightly ticklish. He felt he could stay there for ever.

His new companion stayed close by his side. Then, as they made a turn by a huge shell and some massive, sunken, barnacle-covered jars, there appeared a break in the water. Conrad came nose-to-nose with another fish. This time it had Chloë's face *exactly*. Conrad laughed, but the Chloë-fish butted against him aggressively. The water drained in an instant.

Conrad was no longer a fish, and neither was his companion. He was blinking up at Chloë. 'Time to go,' said Chloë.

Conrad's new friend flashed him a beautiful smile. 'You don't have to go with her,' she said.

'Hey!' Conrad complained. 'I was just having fun!'

*

Conrad was still angry about being dragged out of the program.

'Do you realize how long you've been in there?' Chloë almost shouted.

'I'd only just arrived. Maybe a minute or so.'

'Over half an hour. We've been trying to pull you back for over fifteen minutes. I had to follow you all the way. You didn't seem to want to have anything to with me, and if I'd left you with Miss Perfect Teeth we'd never have got you back at all!'

'Who's Miss Perfect Teeth?' Paddy wanted to know.

'Just another Web user,' Conrad said grumpily.

'Oh, yeah?' Chloë said. 'Well, I've got news for you. Miss Perfect Teeth was just another Id.'

'I don't believe it,' said Conrad. 'Interactive display nodules don't lie when you ask them.'

'Well, this one did, eh, Paddy?'

'She's right,' Paddy said. 'We tracked you messing about with an Id. Presumably the one Chloë called Perfect Teeth.'

Conrad swept a hand through his hair. This was a serious program violation.

'Yeh,' Chloë said. 'If you want a *girlfriend*, don't go looking in the Web for one.'

'I don't want a girlfriend, thanks very much.'

'Cut it out, you two,' said Paddy. 'We've got some serious thinking to do. The labyrinth program is stealing time. I'd like to know what it's doing with that time. More importantly, I'd like to know what it's doing to *us*, and *why*. Any ideas, Conrad?'

There was no answer from Conrad.

'Conrad? Hello? Can you hear me?'

'What's that?' said Conrad at last. He seemed distracted.

'Hey, are you all right?' Chloë wanted to know.

'Sure. I just feel a bit dizzy.'

'Let's call it a day,' Chloë insisted. 'We'll try again tomorrow night. Conrad? Can you hear me?'

'I'm fine,' he said, but his voice sounded vague, distant. 'I'm signing off.'

After the connection was broken, Chloë spoke quickly to Paddy, knowing that Conrad was now off-line. 'That was weird, Paddy. I was in the program with him, but it took me ages to break through to him. He was like *completely gone.*'

'I don't like what's happening,' said Paddy.

'Me neither. We'll try again tomorrow, but we need to be more careful. I'm signing off now. Sweet dreams.'

'You too, Chloë,' said Paddy. 'You too.'

CHAPTER NINE

THROUGH THE WALL

After school the next day Conrad was eating supper with his mother when his father called from South Korea. Mrs Hamilton took the call while Conrad finished his mung beans and angler fish. He had a sinking feeling and wasn't surprised when his mother told him his father wanted a chat. Conrad wiped his mouth and went to the family terminal in the lounge-room. Mr Hamilton's face was on the screen. The frown lines on his brow and the creases above his nose were exaggerated on the brilliant screen image.

'Hi, Dad,' Conrad said.

'Conrad. The suit arrived today—'

'I sent it yesterday evening by overnight courier—'

'That's all right. You did well. But there's a problem. The suit manufacturers are not terribly happy. They say it was damaged. Do you know anything about this?'

'It did get a very tiny rip in it, Dad,' Conrad said truthfully. 'But not so that you could notice.'

'Look son, I don't know what this is about. I just deal with the people who make and sell these suits. But they think a bit of the suit went missing. Some of the circuits. It's important for us that we keep these people happy. If they get upset we could lose millions of Euro in trade. I've got to keep them smiling, do you understand?'

'Sure, Dad. Business is business.' Conrad regretted saying that. He sounded a bit too much like Chloë when she wanted to be sarcastic.

Mr Hamilton squinted at his son. 'Are you being funny? Never mind, if you could help me you would, wouldn't you?'

'Of course!'

'Attaboy. Have a chat with your friends. Whatsisname, Mickey—'

'Paddy.'

'Yes, Paddy, and, and, and—'

'Chloë.'

'Right. Paddy and Chloë. Tell them if they've got something that doesn't belong to them then it ought to be given back. By the way, those suits I promised you are already on their way, courtesy of my business friends here in South Korea. Now, fetch your mother. I need to speak to her again.'

Conrad felt depressed. He didn't want to disappoint his father, or do anything to make life difficult for him. But he was sure that whoever operated the secret labyrinth program was up to no good, and those same people were going to great lengths to keep them out. For a moment he wondered if his father was mixed up with these shady people. He wondered how much his father knew about the labyrinth. He couldn't believe his old man would get tangled up in something illegal or sleazy. But then, he had seemed *particularly* keen to get the suit back.

Conrad consulted the Tech-Rats.

'Hold on a minute!' said Paddy. 'You don't know for sure that there is anything bad connected with this program.'

'Oh, yeah?' Chloë cut in. 'So why make it a big secret? And why build in such a violent defence system of big bad spiders? And why steal your time when you're inside it? This whole business has got a really nasty smell to it.'

'That doesn't make Conrad's dad a criminal.'

'I never said it does. But perhaps Conrad's dad is mixed up in something he doesn't know about.'

'Thanks, guys,' said Conrad. He felt more depressed and confused than ever.

'Look,' Paddy said. 'We've copied the trigger. All you have to do now is send the original micro-circuit back.'

'But if what Ariadne says is true, then they know every time we go into the labyrinth. They must be monitoring it day and night. Plus they'll know we copied the trigger.'

'True, but if we send back everything your old man asks for, then at least we keep him out of trouble.'

'I hope you're right,' said Conrad.

'Now, let's get to the plan,' said Chloë. She explained that this time it would be safer for two of them to go into the labyrinth together, leaving one outside as Control to monitor and rescue if necessary. It was decided that Conrad should stay out and in control of operations. Although Chloë didn't say anything, she was worried about the way his last jaunt into the labyrinth had left him so shaken.

'By the way,' she asked, 'are you feeling all right? No ill effects?'

'I'm fine,' Conrad said. 'Apart from some really weird dreams.'

'Don't tell me,' said Chloë. 'You dreamed about being one of those beach people with the dead eyes. Then about being one of the musical people squatting round the fire.'

'Not only that. I've had fish-swimming dreams. How did you know?'

' 'Cos I've had some of those dreams too. It seems to me that every interaction you experience inside the labyrinth keeps repeating in your dreams.'

'How would that happen?' Paddy wanted to know.

'That's why we're going back in. To find out. Ready?'

'Ready,' said Paddy, and the other two heard a muffled scraping from Paddy's throat-mike. They knew it was the sound of him buckling on his flying helmet over the hood of his suit.

'This must be the place where Conrad found his fish-friend,' said Chloë. They were inside the labyrinth at the kaleido-scopic chute of Level 3, having passed through the two earlier Id nodules. Chloë's multicoloured hair glistened in the ultraviolet light, Paddy's flying-helmet glowed orange.

'I thought Conrad said it was busy with visitors when he was here. How come there's no one else around?'

But Paddy had spoken too soon. Five people materialized a few yards away from them. In the split second available when the figures appeared, Chloë and Paddy saw a tall Western businessman in a suit speaking into a wristpad. He was surrounded by four tough-looking Asian men in grey suits.

'Koreans!' said Paddy.

'Let's drop back!'

The two managed to hide behind a recess in the stone walls of the labyrinth, away from the rotating Id chute, unseen by the new arrivals. 'Could they be looking for us?' Paddy whispered.

'We can't know that. Time to change appearance, eh Paddy?'

The Tech-Rats had assembled a number of disguises for their movement through the Web. These included young Arab men, elderly Chinese women, Kenyan princes, Mexican street-urchins and Russian businessmen. The disguises held up visually, but of course failed as soon as someone wanted to hold a conversation with them.

'Conrad!' Paddy whispered, 'Set up the identity switch and leave it running.'

They opted to be Kenyans, tapped out a code on their wristpads; and Chloë and Paddy were transformed into tall, elegant Masai warriors in flowing red robes and carrying ceremonial spears. 'Let's go,' said Chloë.

They returned to the interactive display at the entrance to Level 3. The Koreans and the Western businessman were busy in discussion. As Chloë and Paddy floated by in their exotic robes, they became quiet. They looked deeply suspicious as the Africans passed by. The two had already moved beyond the group when the businessman called after them.

'*Jambo!*' he shouted.

Chloë remembered this was Swahili for hello. '*Jambo!*' her alter-ego waved back.

'*Abari?*'

'Hell,' Chloë whispered to Paddy. 'What does that mean?'

'Don't know. Just say the same thing back.'

'*Abari.*'

The businessman smiled. 'Wrong,' he said. Then he barked an order at his Korean henchmen. 'Get them!'

'Conrad, we're coming out!' Chloë breathed into her throat-mike, and then tapped her wristpad. Nothing happened. 'Conrad!'

Chloë tapped frantically on her wristpad. Still nothing happened. The block wall behind them softened and liquidized, and a woman's face appeared. 'He can't help you. Take my hands. We're getting out of here.'

With the Koreans bearing down on them Chloë and Paddy had little choice. They grabbed the woman's hands and she pulled them through the block. The wall dissolved like a pool of quicksilver and reformed into solid blocks behind them. They found themselves in some strange neutral space surrounded by golden grid-blocks, looking into the smiling face of an extraordinarily beautiful woman.

'It's all right,' she said. 'They can't follow us here.'

'But who are you?' Chloë said, her heart still hammering.

'I'm Ariadne.'

CHAPTER TEN

FIBRULE

'That's right. I'm Ariadne.'

Chloë and Paddy blinked at the smiling, beautiful woman. Her long hair was multicoloured like Chloë's, but golden, silver and blue. Her eyes were twin sapphires. The surrounding grid of blocks seemed at the same time substantial and yet made of a flowing liquid substance, moving like water and changing colour even as they spoke.

'What kind of place is this?' Chloë asked her.

'Don't worry. They can't follow us here. You're completely safe. I've put us in a dead time zone. No one can find us.'

'I've heard of that,' said Paddy. 'It means that we're talking very slowly while outside time is moving at three times the speed. We'd better tell Conrad.'

'Can't do that, I'm afraid,' said Ariadne. 'It would lead them straight to us. I've placed us beyond communication, in or out. We have to wait until they're long gone.'

'Who are *they*?' said Chloë. 'And who are you?'

'I'm a Webcop,' said Ariadne.

'I knew it!' said Paddy. 'Are you going to report us for getting past the spider?'

'Not this time. We needed your help to find out how kids like you would respond to the illegal program. You were never supposed to have got this far, but when you did, well, we in the Web Police decided to let you run with it for a while. But now it has got more than a little dangerous.'

'How dangerous?'

'You came in by complete accident. This program you are in now is unfinished and untested. It isn't yet ready for the market. And the people making the program in Korea have some very nasty ideas about what makes an acceptable program. The suit sent to Conrad by his father was a tester, a research suit. They were only sent out to a small number of children whose parents could be controlled through business connections. People who would be easy to hush up.'

'Why would they want to hush it up?' said Paddy.

Ariadne smiled and folded her arms. 'Have either of you heard of *engrams*?' Both Paddy and Chloë looked blank. 'I thought not. Engrams are little memory chunks. A complete piece of memory, say from when you were small, in a digestible chunk. The only problem is that they are not *your own* memories. They have been designed by someone else, to be slotted into the mind of anyone who accesses this very program. Without you even knowing how it happens.'

'And why would anyone want to do that?' Chloë asked.

'They have their reasons,' said Ariadne. 'But there are some things I need to ask you. Do you still have the original trigger micro-circuit? The one you removed from the suit?'

'No. Conrad sent it back after we took it out of the suit.'

Ariadne seemed satisfied. 'But you made copies, right?' Behind her, the fluid blocks streamed and pulsed gently, changing colour from gold through pink to mother-ofpearl.

'One each,' said Paddy.

'I'll need to have them.'

'Oh. OK,' said Chloë. She was disappointed. Once the triggers were confiscated, the adventure was over. She was hoping Ariadne would allow them to continue to help her.

'I'm going to have to arrange to have them collected,' said Ariadne. 'And by the way, can you tell me something? How exactly did you get past the security spiders?'

Paddy laughed. He was about to explain about the hair-colour code when Chloë suddenly said, 'Fibrule told us.'

Paddy heard a tiny note of fear in Chloë's voice. He looked at her and something awful dawned on him. Then he tasted the same fear himself. 'Yes,' he said slowly. 'Fibrule told us.'

'Fibrule?' asked Ariadne. 'Who is Fibrule?'

Fibrule was not a person. Fibrule was a code word used exclusively by the Tech-Rats. It was a signal from one to the other of the Tech-Rats that someone amongst them was lying. Paddy stared long and hard at Ariadne. Then he looked at Chloë. Both of them were thinking the same thing: *wasn't it Ariadne who gave them the code to beat the spider in the first place?*

'Fibrule,' said Chloë a little shakily, 'is the fourth member of the Tech-Rats. I forgot to mention that Fibrule also has a copy of the trigger.'

'A fourth member?' Ariadne looked puzzled. Her beautiful smile disappeared. 'Where is this Fibrule based?'

'That's just it,' said Paddy, inventing wildly, making it all up as he went along. 'We don't know. Fibrule is an anonymous member of the Tech-Rats. We don't know if it's a he or a she—'

'Or even if he or she lives in China or America or at the North Pole,' added Chloë, 'or even if—'

'Shut up a minute,' Ariadne said sharply. 'Let me think.'

'Or even if—'

'I said be quiet! Now listen, I want you to contact this Fibrule. Right now.'

'But,' Chloë pointed out, 'you said it was impossible for us to communicate with anyone.'

The lines in Ariadne's brow smoothed out. Her beautiful smile reappeared. 'I can fix that. Don't worry about a thing. But if I'm going to help you, you'll have to cooperate.'

Conrad was getting increasingly worried. It had been almost an hour since he'd lost contact with Paddy and Chloë. He'd tried everything he knew in order to get back in touch with them. After voice-link suddenly broke down, he tried to override the connection by communicating with their home terminals. He knew that in Paddy's and Chloë's respective bedrooms their monitors would be flickering urgent messages from him, though for some reason they were not responding. There was another possibility, which he knew

should be avoided at all costs. He could communicate
directly with Chloë's and Paddy's parents, alert them and
ask them to go to their child's bedroom and find out why
communication link was broken. But that would violate one
of the cardinal rules of the Tech-Rats. It would betray the fact
that the Tech-Rats were swimming in forbidden waters, and
then all hell would break loose.

He was thinking about whether to use this drastic solution
when a message appeared. The monitor blinked and an
amber wash appeared on the screen. Then the words:

<Conrad, this is Ariadne. Your friends are in danger.>

Conrad typed:

<Ariadne! What's happening? Can I have voice-link with
you?>

<No. Too risky. Pay attention. Your friends think they have
met Ariadne. It's someone else, pretending to be me. If they
contact you, don't give anything away.>

<Where are they now?>

<They've been placed in a dead time zone, outside of all Web
communication. But I think I know how to get a message
through. You'll have to help me.>

<Stop! How do I know you're not a fake Ariadne, just like the
other one?>

<Good point. Wait, listen to this.>

A voice spluttered from Conrad's terminal. The voice said,
'Surely the Tech-Rats are not going to be beaten by a little
spider.' Conrad recognized it as the female voice with which
Ariadne had originally addressed him, using the very same
words. But he wasn't completely satisfied.

<Could be a tape.>

<Yes, it could be. I also gave you the access to the labyrinth.
Remember? It was Chloë's hair-colour code I'd rigged earlier.>

<I still can't trust you.>

<We're wasting time, Conrad. At some point you have to
trust your instincts about me. There's no other way right now.
Time's moving, Conrad. Yes or no?>

Conrad hesitated. He thought about his friends in the
Labyrinth, tricked by a fake Ariadne. He also thought about

his father mixed up in the whole scheme. He wished he'd never tried to sneak by the security spider in the first place. His fingers hovered over the keyboard. At last he typed:

<*Yes, I'll help.*>
<*Good. This is what I need from you.*>

Ariadne was composed again. She was calm. She was beautiful. She flicked back her hair and smiled reassuringly at Paddy and Chloë. 'It is imperative you contact Fibrule for me. We need to recover the fourth micro-circuit. Without it we can't do anything.'

But over her shoulder something odd was happening. The liquid blocks which made up the wall behind her back were behaving in a strange way. The blocks were changing colour and the flowing, melting substance was hardening. A hole appeared in the block at the uppermost right-hand corner immediately above Ariadne's shoulder. The liquid-metal substance hardened and resolved into a figure 5. Then the next block along began to behave in exactly the same way. Within a few moments the second block had reshaped itself into a #. Both Paddy and Chloë saw it happening, but they said nothing.

'OK,' Paddy said. 'We'll contact Conrad and tell him to get in touch with Fibrule.'

'No,' Ariadne was shaking her head. 'I need to contact Fibrule directly.'

The curious writing continued to reshape and form from the available blocks. After a while it spelled out:

5#!5X+ !% X}

Chloë and Paddy couldn't help but turn to each other. Both realized, at precisely the same time, that someone was using the liquid wall to spell out a message in Rat code!

Ariadne noticed the distracted expressions on their faces. 'What is it?' she wanted to know.

Chloë diverted attention by busying herself with her wristpad. 'I'll see if I can remember some co-ordinates to access Fibrule,' she bluffed. In reality she was translating the

writing on the wall, though she already had a bad feeling
that she knew what it was going to say. The miniature
illuminated screen on her wristpad ran a string message,
converted from the private code:

Ariadne is not Ariadne . . . Ariadne is not Ariadne . . .

'Is this correct?' Chloë said, showing Paddy the translated
message on her wristpad. As soon as he'd seen it, she
scrambled the message.

'That's right,' said Paddy, unable to keep a slight tremor
out of his voice. He was thinking if this wasn't the real
Ariadne, then who was it?

'If it's safe enough to go back into Webtown,' said Chloë,
'we could lead you to Fibrule.'

Ariadne stroked her chin. The gesture was so much like
that of a man stroking a beard Chloë wondered what the
person behind this virtual reality image was really like. She
suspected it was indeed a man, and not a nice one.

'No,' Ariadne said. 'You two stay here for a while. You're
much safer in the dead time zone and—' Suddenly, Ariadne
stopped what she was saying. Turning slowly, she took in the
writing on the wall behind her. She looked at it in astonishment. At last she smiled thinly, turning back to face them. It
was not a friendly smile. 'Very clever. Smart, too. Was this
the work of our little friend Conrad? No, I don't think he's
smart enough to do this. He must have had help from
elsewhere. Perhaps you'd better tell me what it says.'

'Find out for yourself,' Chloë said acidly. '*Ariadne.*'

'So that's the way you want to play it? Fine.' Ariadne
whispered something into her throat-mike, and the liquid
walls began to fade around them, and they were back in the
Labyrinth at the point where they'd been dragged through
the wall. The image of Ariadne fizzed and buzzed for a
moment and was replaced by that of a tall blond-haired
man in a white suit. He had a beard, just as Chloë had
suspected. But his eyes were clear blue, with no pupil. He
tipped back his head and laughed, and as he did so his head
seemed huge, filling the available space. His perfect white

teeth were like marble tombstones, but with each tooth bearing a diamond stud. Then the laugh died on his face and he spat two fine darts from his mouth.

The darts span in flight, directed at Paddy's and Chloë's hearts. They were unstoppable. The moment they made contact, Paddy and Chloë felt themselves shatter into a million liquid bubbles, dispersed across the infinite space of Webtown.

For Chloë and Paddy everything went black. All they heard was the renewed laughter of the bearded man, and then even that faded too.

CHAPTER ELEVEN

PLANETOLOGISTS

Conrad logged his attendance at school the following day as Mentor Robinson faded up on screen. Mentor Robinson's eyebrows were arched at Conrad.

'No learned friends this morning?'

Conrad was lost for something to say. He found himself muttering something unconvincing about his friends being unwell.

'Nothing serious, I hope?' said Mentor Robinson, looking genuinely concerned.

'I shouldn't think so.'

Mentor Robinson peered hard through his spectacles at Conrad before proceeding with the register-by-computer. Conrad knew his two friends wouldn't be around for school today, though what he didn't know was how long they might be absent. Paddy and Chloë weren't available for school because they were at the municipal hospital. They were both in a state of coma.

Some time during the previous evening, Conrad's mother had received a visit from the Web Regulation Force, a private security company. From this sour-faced officer they learned that Paddy and Chloë had both been discovered by their parents slumped next to their computer terminals, still in their Websuits and in a state of unconsciousness. As was usual in these cases they were suspected of being cases of Necro-surfing.

Necro-surfing was a banned activity on the Web. For a while it had been a teenage fad. There had been an unpleasant craze for the illegal activity a year or two back. Just for kicks, Necro-surfers accessed the hospital terminals and hooked into the heart and pulse monitors of critically ill patients. They used a software program that fed back nerve impulses, and if the Necro-surfers could experience the exact moment of death of a patient, when the machines 'flatlined', they had a rush of energy, a brain flush and a kind of scream. According to the Necro-surfers, it was the ultimate trip. The fad came to a halt after a number of teenagers ended up in comas, in mental hospitals after being driven out of their minds, or dead from heart attacks.

Conrad had protested that none of them had been involved in this type of activity. It was true. The three of them had previously agreed that the idea of Necro-surfing had a dirty feel to it. But Conrad knew the Web Regulator didn't believe him, and neither did his mother. Then at some point in the conversation the Web Regulator had a call from the Web Police, who had greater authority. Conrad and his mother waited as a private conversation took place in another room.

The Web Regulator came back and said, 'Looks like you're in the clear. Who do you know in the Webcops?'

Ariadne? thought Conrad. He shrugged and said, 'No one.'

After the visitor had gone, Conrad's mother started on him. 'Are you sure you haven't—'

'I'm telling the truth,' Conrad screamed, his voice practically breaking.

Mrs Hamilton shook her head. 'I'm going to get your father to talk with you.'

The day dragged. Conrad spent most of the time wondering what, if anything, he could do to help his friends. After having been given the Rat Code by Conrad, the real Ariadne had somehow transmitted a message to Paddy and Chloë. It seemed the task was successful. Then the message was discovered and the real Ariadne suddenly had to go off-line. Since then Conrad had heard nothing.

Conrad had to go back into the labyrinth to get some clue about what had happened to Chloë and Paddy. But he was afraid. He was afraid he might suffer the same fate and end up comatose in hospital, too. After school he climbed into his suit, and hoped and prayed Ariadne would come.

She did.

The amber wash flooded the screen, followed by a string of words from his anonymous helper:

<Go in, Conrad. Let's see if we can find out what happened to Paddy and Chloë. I've rather come to like those kids. I'll watch your back. I'd hate to see anything happen to any of you. One thing: I'll trigger a time signal every ten minutes. If I tell you to come out, then get the hell out. No arguing, no dithering. We don't want another coma case up in the city hospital.>

Conrad didn't need telling twice. He tapped out the relevant codes and within moments he was inside the labyrinth.

Conrad approached the Level 1 Id of the young people on the yellow sand, and passed under the tree branches of the date palm. As always there was music and some of the people stood up, beckoning him to approach. He was about to move through it and pass on to Level 2 when he noticed something familiar about one of the members of the group. He moved deeper into the Id crowd. Unless his eyes were playing tricks, it was Paddy.

Paddy was dressed, like all the other figures, in white clothes. He beckoned and smiled blankly, almost oafishly, along with everyone else. 'Paddy!' said Conrad.

Paddy showed no recognition. He continued to smile happily, and to beckon Conrad to join them. Conrad became aware of some electrical disturbance fizzing in the background of the Id, and of weird but familiar music. He tried to speak again to Paddy. There was no response, and there was something terrifying about Paddy's eyes. They were all blue, no pupil whatsoever.

Conrad's timer bleeped. Can't be ten minutes, he thought, I just got here. More like ten seconds.

'*Out!*' said Ariadne.

'But I've found Paddy!' Conrad whispered hoarsely into his throat-mike.

'*Move through the display. They're sucking you in.*'

'But—'

'*No buts, Conrad! This is not a game. Move on!*'

Conrad moved quickly through the Id. As he looked back, Paddy stepped forward from the group, cupping hands to his mouth, trying to get him to return. Pressing on, Conrad came to the pillared doorway of the second Id, the group of young musicians sitting cross-legged around a fire. One of them played a flute. Now that Conrad stopped to listen, he recognized exactly the same music he'd heard before, but in a simplified form. He had an odd notion he'd heard this music before – in his dreams.

Again the young people were dressed in sparkling white robes. He had to look twice at the flute player. It was Chloë! Just as Paddy had been one of the group in the previous Id, so too was Chloë in this one. She continued to play, but looked up at him shyly as she blew gently across the mouthpiece of the flute.

Conrad knew that the medics at the hospital had had to leave Chloë and Paddy in their Websuits while treating them, to avoid psychic shock. Thus he knew that what he was looking at was an echo, or a zombie version of Chloë. But still it was a living part of his friend, and he behaved towards her as if she were the real thing.

'What's going on, Chloë? You're not remotely musical!'

Another member of the group, a young man, got to his feet and approached Conrad. 'You look intelligent,' he said, smiling. 'Can you settle an argument for us?'

Conrad's bleeper sounded again, though it seemed impossible that another ten minutes had passed.

'*Out!*' said Ariadne.

Conrad retreated. What happened next surprised him. Chloë stopped playing her flute, stood up and came towards him. Just like Paddy, her eyes were all blue with no pupil. But

Conrad saw a fat, silver tear forming at the corner of her eye. 'Don't leave us,' she pleaded.

'Out!' said Ariadne.

'Help me,' said Chloë.

Conrad's alarm sounded a second time.

'Out! Out!' screamed Ariadne.

'Don't go without us!' begged Chloë.

Conrad was torn. Tears were running down Chloë's face, but he could hear Ariadne screaming in his earpiece. He was mesmerized by Chloë. Although she'd stopped playing her instrument, the weird flute music continued to play.

'Close down, Conrad!' Ariadne raged. *'I've figured out what's happening. You've got to get out!'*

At last Conrad backed out through the doorways of both levels, finally touching his wristpad to close the labyrinth program down around his ears. He came back to awareness with a jolt in his bedroom. As he jerked upright in his chair, his Websuit was tingling, as if charged with low-voltage electricity. Conrad blinked at the amber screen.

'That was a close thing, Conrad.' Ariadne remained in voice-contact.

'What's happening, Ariadne? I don't get it! And what's that smell?'

'That smell is the odour of circuits in your suit overheating. Just enough to fry your brains. They were trying to keep you in there long enough for you to have a small accident.'

'Is that what happened to Paddy and Chloë?'

'I don't think so. They're keeping Paddy and Chloë on ice while they work out what to do with them. If you'd stayed in much longer your fate would have been much nastier. What is it Chloë likes to call you? Gnat brain? Another ten minutes and that would have been about right.'

'But the Websuits have a failsafe to stop this happening.'

'They're clever. And they're getting desperate.'

'You said you'd figured out what was going on.'

'And so I have. I eavesdropped on something the fake Ariadne said to Paddy and Chloë. Something about ENGRAMS.

I didn't get it at first, but now I know what's happening. Tell me something, Conrad, have you had any strange dreams lately?'

'Yes. Connected with the scenes inside the labyrinth. And the weird music is always there. Chloë had the same dreams too, though not Paddy because he didn't go into the labyrinth as often as we did.'

'He'll get them now.'

'Why do you say that?'

'Because you've all been victims of engram embedding.'

'What does that mean?'

'The people who made this program did so in order to plant engrams in people's brains. Particularly in young people's brains. An engram is a manufactured memory. Set into the illegal program are "memory" experiences ready to be fixed in place and repeated over and over.'

'The beach scene? And the musicians round the fire?'

'That's right. Then after you've experienced these scenes several times, you won't know it's not your own memory. In this way they try to shape your personality. Hi-tech brainwashing. All those occasions when you lost time, the same engram was being imprinted on you over and over and over, very fast. So fast, it felt like one single experience, hence the loss of all that time.'

'But to what purpose? Why are they doing this?'

'The people who made the labyrinth program are the business and technology front of a world-wide fundamentalist religious group called the Planetologists. It's a weird mixture of Christianity, Islam, Buddhism, and Science and Technology. It has a mass following in Korea and some of the developing technological countries in the Far East.'

'Ariadne, are you a Korean?'

'I am. I'm a Webcop based in Korea, and that's absolutely all I'm going to tell you about myself.'

'I think I've heard of the Planetologists. My father told me something about them when he was home last time.'

'Yes, they recruit mainly from young people. That's why they are conducting research on Edutainment programs, so they can reach young people in particular. They plant engrams so that

later on, possibly even years later when you encounter their religious propaganda, you will have certain false memories triggered off by the same propaganda. Let's face it, Conrad, if everyone has the same "memories", they are easier to manipulate. Then they get kids to leave their families and to work for the religious corporation, turning over their wages to the leader of the cult.'

'Who is that?'

'We don't know, but we have our suspicions.'

'It's all mind-blowing!' said Conrad.

'It's exactly that. And you and your friends stumbled across it when a special suit got passed to your father during one of his business trips to Korea. They think they can control all their business contacts with bribes and fear.'

'Oh no! Does that mean Dad does business with the Planetologists?'

'I'm afraid so. At least, he does business with their technology front. But he wouldn't know that. Yet.'

'That's terrible!'

'Don't despair. You've done a good job, uncovering some things we didn't know. The research for this illegal program hadn't been completed. What you're experiencing in the Web is only a rough prototype, and you were a guinea-pig. We infiltrated the program and put the spiders in place to keep out kids like you.'

'You? You mean you're responsible for the spider bites?'

'Sorry about that. It had to be strong enough to keep people out. We've been monitoring these people, but without you guys we wouldn't have known what they were up to. But when I realized how persistent and smart you guys are, I thought I could get you to help me. That's why I gave you the code to bypass the spiders. But I was wrong. I took a gamble to find out more about the cult's activity. I put you in danger, and that's unforgivable.'

'We're to blame for that, Ariadne, not you.'

'I don't know. What I do know is, we've got to do something to help Paddy and Chloë. We've got to bring them back out of the labyrinth. Then we've got to spoil the Planetologists' plans for releasing this mind-tampering program on to the Web. Are you still prepared to help me, Conrad?'

'Whatever it takes.'

'*Good. First we need a code word to keep out fake versions of me. Then I've got a plan, so listen carefully.*'

CHAPTER TWELVE

COMICS

Conrad felt reassured to know that next time he ventured into the labyrinth he would have Ariadne at his back. Even so, Ariadne had warned him that she could only act as a guide and a control. There was no possibility of her entering the labyrinth herself for fear of exposure.

'*They must not know who I am, where I am, or how much I know. That's why I can't tell you anything, Conrad. The people we are up against are not only dangerous, they are very clever. If you knew anything, they would have some very interesting ways of getting it out of you.*'

Conrad was still worried about his friends. There had been no improvement in their medical condition. They both remained in a coma, wired up to monitors and with plastic drip tubes coming out of their nostrils. Conrad had been to see them. He wanted to try to talk to them while they were unconscious. He was convinced they would be able to hear him at some deep level, but he wasn't allowed even a few minutes with them on his own. He returned from the hospital feeling depressed.

Worse was to come when his mother switched on the holotele. This brought a three-dimensional image of a female newsreader into the room who looked at Conrad as if he was personally responsible for all the troubles in the world, especially when there was a report about teenage Necrosurfing which named Chloë and Paddy. When the report was over his mother looked at him as if he were some kind of insect.

'What I saw inside the labyrinth scared me,' he told Ariadne later. 'I mean Paddy and Chloë with those dead eyes.'

'*That wasn't Paddy and Chloë. I know they look like zombies, but the Planetologists are just trying to scare you away. It's like woodland gamekeepers who hang dead crows and magpies from trees to keep others away. They're hoping you'll be too afraid to go back in there.*'

Conrad thought about dead birds hanging from trees. He didn't like the picture. For a moment his mind flashed on an image of Chloë, Paddy and himself hanging upside-down from a virtual reality tree. He shuddered.

'*Is it too much for you, Conrad?*' Ariadne asked, as if guessing his thoughts.

'No. I'm all right. I think.'

The other thing that concerned him was what Ariadne had said about the labyrinth. She'd explained that the engramming worked on five levels. He'd experienced the third level when he went swimming as a fish with his 'friend' whom he now understood must have been one of the Planetologists. Ariadne said that he'd been pulled out of this third level just in time. Any longer and he would have been "fully cooked".

'What do you mean by that?'

'*The fourth level prepares you for meeting a Planetologist on the streets, but the memory engrams would have been fully established in your brain and you wouldn't know a thing about it.*'

'What's the fifth level?'

'*That, Conrad, is a mystery to us. We think it's where you finally meet up with the person or persons behind this whole thing. Here's the stick of dynamite: we're kind of hoping that you'll be the one to go all the way to the fifth level, to tell us.*'

'Me?' said Conrad, astonished. 'Why me?'

'*Because, dummy,*' Ariadne sighed, '*you're the last member of the Tech-Rats.*'

Things were going badly everywhere. What was happening inside the labyrinth had a bad effect on his work. After school

that day, Mentor Robinson made him stay on-line until all
the other kids had logged off.

'I can't understand it,' Mentor Robinson was saying. On
screen, his eyes seemed huge and angry behind thick
spectacle glass. 'You're one of the brighter kids, yet that last
piece of work you completed would hardly have credited a
seven-year-old.'

'I'm worried about my friends,' Conrad tried lamely.

'That's no excuse,' Mentor Robinson challenged him. 'You
can't help your friends by neglecting your school work.
Letting your brain turn to slush is hardly going to be any
use to them, now is it? I don't want you falling behind, so do
the assignment again, please.'

Conrad logged off. Mentor Robinson was right, but Conrad
couldn't seem to keep his mind on the tasks while he
thought of Paddy and Chloë smiling horribly and floating
around in limbo with bright blue but essentially dead eyes.

Then his mother seemed upset. 'What is it?' Conrad asked.

'I don't know. It's your father. He called tonight from
Korea. He seemed under terrible strain. Said things were
going badly. His company stands to lose a big contract. If he
loses the contract he'll lose his job. If he loses his job . . .'

Conrad didn't know what to say. His mother seemed near
to tears herself. He knew she suspected him of being a
teenage Necro-surfer. He couldn't help feeling responsible
for all of this. After all, he was the one who tried to get past
the security spider in the first place. If he'd not tried to stray
out of bounds, he would never have got Chloë and Paddy in
this predicament. If he'd not persisted in trying to duck past
the spider, he would simply have sent the suit back to his
father, and there would have been none of this talk of lost
contracts and lost jobs.

Why was it that everything he did seemed to come out so
badly?

Then came some good news. Paddy and Chloë had both
recovered consciousness and had been discharged from
hospital. His immediate response to this news was to try to

contact them. The answer, in both cases, was a screen message:

<TERMINAL DISCONNECTED. PLEASE TRY LATER.>

Conrad wasn't entirely surprised. Paddy's and Chloë's parents had probably done the disconnecting, and the way they'd been talking he wouldn't have been surprised if they'd done it with an axe.

Paddy and Chloë were banned from the Web.

Probably the only thing that stopped their folks from smashing up their terminals and Webgear was the fact that school was conducted through the same terminals. Some work was conducted individually, and some in hooked-up groups, but when Paddy and Chloë logged on to school again, Mentor Robinson assigned them to different groups, so Conrad never had a chance to communicate with either of them.

In the end he resorted to travelling across town to see them. He took the skybus, and wished he hadn't when at every stop the elevators lifting passengers on and off seemed to be getting stuck. After a while he got out and walked. He tried Chloë first.

Chloë's parents were not keen to see Conrad. Her mother held the door open for him as if she hadn't quite decided whether to let him in. Even though Chloë was the wildest member of the Tech-Rats, game to try anything, it seemed as if her parents blamed Paddy and Conrad for leading her astray.

'I just came to see if she's OK,' he said, hovering on the threshold.

Before being allowed to see Chloë, Conrad was quizzed by her father about Necro-surfing. Are you sure? Yes. You wouldn't lie to me? No. Have you tried it? No. Has Chloë? Not to my knowledge. Do you know people who have? Loads of people, but we never wanted to. So what do you think happened?

'Maybe it was some technical fault,' Conrad found himself saying.

Chloë's father shook his head. 'There are cut-outs built into the system to stop this sort of thing happening. You must have been up to something, Conrad!'

Exasperated, Chloë's parents called Chloë into the room, though they wouldn't leave her alone with Conrad. She was wearing a blue plastic suit issued by the hospital and designed to keep her at a constant temperature. Her hair had gone back to its normal colour. She looked pale and somehow smaller. It was obvious she'd had a nasty shock.

'I brought something for you,' said Conrad, handing over a parcel.

'How nice,' Chloë's mother said suspiciously. 'Aren't you going to open it, Chloë?'

Chloë opened it to find a handful of comics from Conrad's collection. 'Thanks,' Chloë said blankly.

'Thought you might like to read something while you're recuperating.'

'Well,' her father said, grabbing and flicking through one of the comics. 'I suppose they'll do you less harm than risking your life in the damned Web.'

'I've had enough of the Web,' Chloë said. Then she looked hard at Conrad. 'And I mean it.'

'I'd better go,' said Conrad. 'I wanted to drop in on Paddy, too. Any message for him, Chloë?'

'No message,' said her father rather aggressively.

At Paddy's place Conrad had exactly the same reception. He had to endure a half-hour grilling and was only finally allowed to see Paddy for five minutes. He left a similar package of comics behind him, promising to bring some more the next day.

What Chloë's father didn't see when he flicked through the comics were some small amendments Conrad had made to the words inside the speech balloons on a certain page. He'd carefully covered the text with white paint, and had overwritten his own words. Where a balloon might have said, *We have exactly one hour to save the Earth!*, it now said, *What happened inside the labyrinth?!* The next speech balloon said, *We have to go back into the labyrinth! Ariadne is helping!*

She has a plan! As with the original comics, every sentence ended with an exclamation mark. A third balloon said, *We can all jack into a single suit! Use my terminal like before!* The great thing about this system of passing messages, Conrad knew, was that only close reading of the comics would betray it. He doubted if either Chloë's or Paddy's parents were interested enough in comics to make it a risk.

The next day he called on them again, this time with a bag of grapes and a change of comics for each of them. He was surprised to find that Chloë had found a new friend. Worse than that, the 'new friend' seemed very much approved of by her parents, unlike Conrad.

Chloë's mother introduced him to Suzie, a bright-eyed, fresh-faced girl who bared her teeth at him in approximation of a smile. She wore a white skirt and white training shoes. 'Suzie has volunteered to come here and help Chloë while she recovers,' Chloë's mother said. 'It's so good of her. She's from a local church.'

Chloë's mother made the local church sound like a healthy alternative to Conrad, who in her eyes was clearly some sort of devil-worshipper.

'We're looking to the future,' Suzie said, baring her teeth again. 'We're going to take Chloë on a church trip to the beach. Things are going to be different. Marvels await under the sun, don't they, Chloë?'

Chloë said nothing. Conrad felt he wasn't wanted. He collected the old comics and passed on the new ones. But he found the same thing at Paddy's house, where a clean-cut boy called Marvin had also volunteered himself. Marvin wore white trousers and white trainers.

'Don't tell me,' Conrad said. 'You're from the local church.'

'How did you know?' Marvin said enthusiastically. 'We help kids who've been mixed up in Necro-surfing and stuff. It's goodbye to all that.'

'Perhaps you could take Paddy on a trip to the beach or something.'

'As a matter of fact we are going to do just that. Great days ahead with friends and music under the stars. You're welcome to come with us.'

Conrad didn't like Marvin any more than he'd liked Suzie. 'Which church did you say you were from?'

'Oh,' Marvin said quickly. 'The Church of Unity.'

'Never heard of it,' Conrad said, leaving the comics and picking up the old ones.

'I don't think Paddy will have much use for childish comics,' said Marvin.

'Doesn't Paddy speak for himself?'

Paddy just yawned.

When Conrad got home, the answers he found inside the comics were disappointing. Both Chloë and Paddy had been busy with the white paint, but what was printed in the speech balloons dismayed him. Chloë's said, *Sorry, Conrad, I can't face it. It hurt like hell. I don't care if I never go into the Web again. Just the thought of the labyrinth makes me feel sick. It's over.*

Paddy's notes were even more brief. *Forget it, kid. Forget the labyrinth. Forget the Web. Forget the Tech-Rats. I quit.*

He was shocked. His friends were defeated. Whatever had hurt them inside the labyrinth, he knew it must have been bad. He closed the comics and held his head in his hands. It felt like the end, not just of the Tech-Rats, but of everything.

They hadn't even bothered to use exclamation marks in the balloon-messages.

CHAPTER THIRTEEN

SLOW MOTION

'I can hardly believe what you're telling me, son.'

'It's true, Dad. They plant memories, called engrams, in young people's brains. Then they awake these memories later to try to get people to join their cult. They're called Planetologists and—'

'Slow down, slow down,' Mr Hamilton said. The monitor on Conrad's terminal buzzed slightly because of the poor connection to Korea. 'How did you find all this out?'

'From the suit you sent me, Dad. That's what I've been trying to tell you! It triggers off a parallel program in some Edutainment software called labyrinth!'

'So, you mean while most people are enjoying a perfectly ordinary program called the labyrinth, others will have some nasty surprises? Is that what you're saying?'

'Yes, but they won't know what's happening. And the trigger for the special program is going to be in the suits you import from this company.'

Conrad had decided to make a clean breast of it all to his father. He'd contacted him and told him everything. The only detail he missed out was Ariadne's involvement. Ariadne hadn't been convinced it was a good idea for Conrad to tell Mr Hamilton, but Conrad was so unhappy Ariadne told him to go ahead. They agreed, though, that Ariadne shouldn't be mentioned since she was still under cover.

Mr Hamilton pressed a finger to the side of his face.

'Actually, Conrad,' he said, 'It's brilliant. This company exports suits all over the world, and specializes in suits for teenagers. What better way to make sure of making thousands of converts in the years to come? Who knows? If their plans work, in twenty years this cult could have millions of members all over the globe. Their political and economic power would be enormous!'

'What are you going to do, Dad?'

'I'm still thinking about it. Things haven't been going too well here and it looks like we might lose this contract. But I'm going to have to tell my boss, the Head of Far East Division. Obviously we don't want to be dealing with people like this, even if we lose money. I'll speak to him immediately. Blast! No wonder they were so red-hot about getting that suit back.'

'Did I do the right thing in telling you, Dad?'

'Of course you did, Conrad. Let me sort it out. Meanwhile, promise me you'll stay out of that labyrinth program, right?'

'Promise,' said Conrad.

Conrad felt much happier. A great weight had been lifted from his shoulders. He wondered why he hadn't simply gone to his father in the first place, though of course that would have meant admitting he was spending time on the Web trying to dodge past security spiders and risking huge fines that his father would have to pay.

A few hours later, another call came through from Korea. This time it was not his father at all, but a man called Quentin Williams, his father's friend and colleague. Quentin was also assigned to the Far East Division of his father's company. The man had a long conversation with Conrad's mother.

The news was not good. Conrad's father had been arrested by the Korean authorities, on a charge of industrial espionage. He'd been taken in by the police and accused of spying.

*

'*Your father is innocent,*' Ariadne said. '*But he made the mistake of going straight to his boss, the Director of Far East Division in the company he works for. Your dad's boss knows some pretty influential people in the Korean government and in the police. He managed to get your father arrested on trumped-up charges.*'

'Why would he do that?'

'*Can't you work it out?*' Ariadne said.

Conrad thought for a minute. 'Oh no! Don't tell me Dad's boss is a Planetologist?'

'*Exactly. The organization is bigger than you think. If your father exposed them now they'd lose everything they've put into this project, at a cost of millions. Your father's boss is in their pockets, and your father made a mistake when he went to him with this information.*'

'What will happen to Dad?'

'*I'm working on it. I've got contacts in the Korean police, trying to get him released. Meanwhile, have you seen Paddy and Chloë?*'

'It's weird, Ariadne. They're a shadow of their former selves.'

'*I'm afraid the brainwashing process has done its work on them. Are you ready to do what I asked you?*'

'I think so.'

'*No time for faint hearts, Conrad. Yes or no?*'

'Yes.'

'*Good man. Are you suited-up?*'

'Yes.'

'*Right. Here we go. Back to the labyrinth.*'

Conrad nervously approached the first level Id. Same scene as before, with happy smiling people sitting on a beautiful yellow beach, waving at him to join them. The dead-eyed Paddy zombie was amongst them. Then Conrad felt a jolt and an electrical surge tingle throughout his body, followed by a sudden pulsing which stopped the Id dead.

This was exactly what Ariadne had described. Before entering the labyrinth, Ariadne had programmed an electronic metronome into Conrad's system, which she had promised would feel like a sudden jolt. The metronome, as it pulsed away, would defeat the time distortion built into the interactive display, and Conrad would be able to see what was happening in all of the 'stolen' time.

At first nothing happened. The Id had frozen solid. But then he saw the figures move slowly. A brilliant white light washed over them. The white light passed across the group, and then everything went black, until they were all plunged into utter darkness. Then the white light appeared again, as the figures moved in slow motion.

'It's a stroboscope,' Conrad whispered into his throatmike. 'Flickering in slow-mo.'

'*Interesting,*' said Ariadne. '*A stroboscopic light flashing on and off at what would be incredibly high speed if it weren't for the metronome. Anything else?*'

Conrad was about to say no, when he heard a rushing sound. The rushing sound, he realized, was actually a whisper, slowed down. The dragged-out words said,

MARVELS AWAIT UNDER THE SUN.

And then again. And again. Repeated over and over as the stroboscopic light flashed on and off. 'There's a phrase about the sun. The same words spoken over and over.'

'*Subliminal messages,*' Ariadne said. '*That's how they're doing it. Now look for a keypad behind the interactive display. It's a fail-safe device for untested programs, so that the Id can be switched off or moderated from inside the Web. It may be a floorpad, and it's probably disguised.*'

Conrad found the button in question. It was designed into the trunk of a palm tree on the beach. He followed Ariadne's complicated instructions to the letter, tapping out routines on the keypad while the stroboscope flashed intermittently and the slow whisper roared in his ears.

'Done,' he said at last.

'*Good. On to Level 2.*'

The same thing happened at Level 2 when the metronome was triggered again. The young people around the camp fire, along with the Chloë zombie, were reduced to slow-moving shadows under the slowly strobing light. This time the whispered message said,

FRIENDS LIKE MUSIC UNDER THE STARS.

Conrad found the keypad disguised in the sticks of the small camp fire around which everyone sat. Again he followed Ariadne's complicated instructions before moving through to Level 3.

At Level 3 Conrad found an Id partner, jumped feet-first into the chute and became a fish once more. The jolt of the metronome stopped everything, and when the strobing light appeared, Conrad was astonished to find that what he had thought were vast oceans to swim in was actually only a confined cubic area with illuminated images of shipwrecks and seacaves squeezed together. He was amazed that this was the real base to the oceans measureless to man in which he'd once swum. His Id partner froze when the metronome pulsed and Conrad resumed human form. This time the whispered phrase was,

FUN LIKE SWIMMING WITH THE FISHES.

The keypad was hidden in a sunken treasure chest.

'Now,' Ariadne said. 'Level 4 is an unknown quantity. Watch your step.'

Although Chloë and Paddy had reached Level 4 before they were fried in their suits, Conrad had never been beyond the third stage. Emerging from the fish-swimming Id, he saw ahead of him a giant ice-blue cube with an entrance capped by the double-headed axe logo. There was no hint of what lay within. Passing into the cube, he found himself on the edge of a three-dimensional maze.

Conditions inside the maze changed as soon as he stepped through the entrance. A ghostly wind whistled. The place was white; a dazzling white broken by thick black lanes marking the edges of avenues that ran to left and right, in front and behind. But as he looked up, several more avenues presented themselves. He was also surprised to find himself in a condition of weightlessness, allowing him to propel himself upwards, forwards or backwards. The snow-white hurt his eyes. The wind whistled along the tunnels of the maze.

'You have to go to the centre of the maze in order to pass on to Level 5,' said Ariadne. *'In fact, Level 5 will probably be at the centre of the maze.'*

'I'm going to have to leave a trail if I want to get out of here afterwards,' Conrad said. 'There's a zillion twisting passages.'

'Am I not Ariadne of the golden thread? I'll mark each turn with a golden flare. Just do what is necessary, then retreat. I don't want you to go through to Level 5 just yet. We're not ready.'

Conrad moved through the twisting maze without making any apparent progress. After a while he began to feel nausea caused by the sense of weightlessness. Just as his stomach was about to rebel, he stumbled across an Id companion. It was another smiling figure, a young man with a ponytail, turquoise eyes, a beautiful suntan and white clothes. He floated alongside Conrad.

'I expect you're lost,' he said. 'In a way we're all lost. But I'm here to be your guide. You know, the only way out is through the middle.'

'Is that so?' Conrad said, giving Ariadne the signal to activate the metronome. Again the Id-guide froze. This time the strobe flashed at a different beat and the repeated words were,

THE ONLY WAY IS THROUGH THE MIDDLE.

Conrad had no trouble locating the circuits. Within a few minutes he'd finished his task.

'Time for you to come out,' said Ariadne. *'Your scuttle button won't work. You have to come back out one level at a time.'*

'Why don't I go on and take a look at Level 5?' Conrad asked.

'Absolutely not,' said Ariadne.

Whatever it was that lay at Level 5, Conrad would have to wait to find out. Something in Ariadne's voice told him not to argue. He followed the flare trail back down the maze, eventually peeling back through levels 3, 2 and 1.

'*Good work,*' Ariadne said when Conrad was out of his Websuit, back in his bedroom. '*Now for the really hard part. You've got to persuade Paddy and Chloë to go back into the labyrinth all over again.*'

CHAPTER FOURTEEN

CHURCH OF UNITY

Conrad paid another visit to Chloë. He knew if he could persuade her to go back into the labyrinth then he could undo some of the brainwashing which had taken place. But it was more important than that. Chloë and Paddy had both been through the maze of Level 4, and they could help him find the centre without one of the labyrinth's zombie-guides. Conrad was in no doubt he couldn't find the way through by himself, and the presence of the zombie-guides would be certain to tip off who or whatever lay at the heart of Level 5.

First, he desperately needed to see Chloë alone.

But it was hopeless. When he got to her place, he found the dreaded smiling Suzie installed as if she was one of the family. Chloë's mother and father thought Suzie from the Church of Unity was wonderful. Suzie made cups of cocoa for everyone. Suzie hoovered the carpet. Suzie tidied the room. Suzie read chapters of the Bible (and a weird version of the Bible it was too) while Chloë lay back in her chair, wrapped in her blue plastic thermal suit, sipping cocoa. And the most amazing thing about Suzie was that she asked for nothing in return.

'How often are you able to help Chloë like this?' Conrad asked.

He almost needed sunglasses to deal with the dazzling smile she gave him. 'Most evenings,' was all she said.

'Yes,' Chloë's mother said. 'Suzie is a real *treasure*.'

Only a really long session in the Web could give Conrad an

attack of the voms like the one he felt at that moment. He stood at Chloë's side and touched her hand. It felt cold. 'I brought you these grapes,' he said. 'And some more comics.'

Chloë merely blinked up at him.

'Not more comics, surely!' Suzie said brightly. 'Conrad, you really should get a life!'

'Yeah,' Conrad said sourly. 'I'm a sad case. I remember the time when Chloë used to call me Winkle-brain. Pond-life. Nano-skull. Stuff like that, all in fun though. Back in the days of the *Tech-Rats*.' He looked at Chloë to see if any of this was getting through. Again, she just blinked at him and smiled weakly. It was pathetic. It made him angry to see her like this. They'd managed to take his sharp, bright, feisty friend and do this to her, and no one seemed to know how they'd done it.

'I'll think you'll find those days are behind Chloë,' Suzie said with another smile that was only a breath away from being a snarl.

'Time you young folk were going anyway,' Chloë's mother said. 'Chloë needs her sleep.'

Suzie fussed around, sickening Conrad with her simpering, but he was determined not to leave before she did. They left the house together. 'You really should come down to the church,' Suzie said. 'It would put a bit more zest into your life.'

Speechless, Conrad watched her walk away. He wondered again about this church she was involved in. Before he went home he stopped by at Paddy's. He was not surprised to find Marvin there, putting out the garbage and mowing the tiny lawn, all out of the goodness of his heart. Again, there was no possibility of seeing Paddy on his own. Marvin hovered nearby, eyeing Conrad's grapes and comics suspiciously.

This time he'd taken the precaution of inserting his speech-balloon messages inside the comics in Rat code. He didn't want Suzie's or Marvin's straying eyes to read what he'd written there. Only Chloë and Paddy could decipher what the messages said.

Remember when the Tech-Rats meant something? Wake up! I need you urgently! Come back into the labyrinth with me! Ariadne has a complete dossier on the Planetologists! We've found a way to feed the info into the program! We can expose them for what they are! Paddy, Chloë, wake up! I need you!

After school the next day, Conrad was lying on his bed when he heard the signal tone for an incoming e-mail. Before he even had a chance to access it, a second e-mail arrived. He was astonished to find they were both scrambled in Rat code. He ran his deciphering program quickly.

The first message was from Chloë. It said:

<OK Let's do it. Your place tomorrow.
Midday.>

Conrad was so ecstatic he overlooked the fact that Chloë had made some small mistakes in using the code. In any event they were only small details. The message didn't contain any of her usual insults, but what the hell, she was back on track! He was about to send off a reply when it occurred to him that Chloë might have had to resort to trickery just to get this simple message through. He decided to leave it unanswered.

The second message was from Paddy:

<What are we waiting for? Your place noon tomorrow.
One suit will do.>

'I knew it!' he said aloud. 'Paddy and Chloë were just playing along with those Church of Unity types! The TechRats are alive and kicking!'

'Who are you talking to in there?' his mother wanted to know.

Conrad calmed himself. 'No one,' he told her, coming out of his bedroom. 'Just a computer game.' Even though his father was still being held by the Korean police, he decided things were looking up. Ariadne was doing everything she could to help, and Chloë and Paddy had risen from the ashes.

The next day was a Saturday, so there was no school. Conrad's mother was pleased to see Chloë and Paddy when they turned up, though she remarked on how pale they both looked. She was unable to spend much time with them, having to go to London, to the diplomatic office, to answer some questions about Mr Hamilton's activities. She wouldn't be back until the evening.

Conrad had even tidied his room for their arrival. After his mother left, he breathed a sigh of relief. 'How on earth did you manage it?' he asked his friends.

'Manage what?' said Chloë.

'To slip away from your folks. I never thought they'd let you out of their sight. Not to mention those geeks, Marvin and Suzie. What a pair of *toads*!'

'They're not so bad,' Paddy said nervously.

'We'd better get started,' Chloë added quickly, taking her Websuit from her rucksack. 'We have to get back soon.'

'I understand,' Conrad said. 'Here's the plan. I'm carrying a complete dossier on the Planetologists—' Paddy and Chloë looked at each other, and the exchange was not lost on Conrad. 'Oh, yeah! Guess you don't realize what's been going on, eh? Those interactive displays in the labyrinth, they whisper phrases over and over and over. Then when the Planetologists try to recruit kids on the street, all they have to do is come out with one of their trick phrases and it triggers off all these memories implanted in your brain. Well, Ariadne and I have been busy on that. But the real thing to think about now is Ariadne's dossier.'

'What about it?' Paddy said, climbing without enthusiasm into his suit.

'We have to take it to Level 5, where I can feed the dossier into the system. Then when the Id nodules are activated, instead of the Planetologists' brainwashing program, what people will hear is a big exposure about what these monsters are up to! Neat, eh! Ariadne and I put it together!'

'Great,' Chloë said lamely.

'There's just one missing piece of information. And that concerns who or what is behind all this. I intend to feed that into the dossier when we reach Level 5.' Chloë and Paddy exchanged nervous glances again. 'Look, are you sure you two are up for this?'

'Sure,' they both said.

But neither of them sounded anything like sure.

'I know you're scared,' Conrad said, 'and after what you two have been through, I would be too. But we have to do this to de-program you. Plus I have to expose the Planetologists to clear my dad's name. And don't forget that somewhere out there, Ariadne is helping us.'

'We're ready,' said Chloë.

And into the labyrinth they went, for what Conrad hoped would be the final time.

CHAPTER FIFTEEN

RETURN OF THE TECH-RATS

At Level 1, when they came face to face with the Id of the young people on the yellow-sand beach, neither Paddy nor Chloë looked too happy about approaching. Conrad realized he was going to have to drive them all the way to Level 5 if necessary. It was good to see the virtual images of Paddy and Chloë – Chloë with her multicoloured hair and Paddy with his flying helmet – because it reminded Conrad of times when his friends were strong and confident of moving about in the Web. But now they were dithering. He seemed to have to make every single decision for them, to lead them in each and every step.

'Don't be afraid,' he said. 'Go right up to them. They can't hurt you.'

The young people on the beach stood up and beckoned them over. Paddy and Chloë approached gingerly. Then Conrad realized what it was that was spooking his friends. It was the zombie version of Paddy there among the happy, smiling crowd on the beach. Paddy with the dead eyes and the lost soul.

'It's not real, Paddy,' Conrad whispered into his throat-mike. 'It's just an Id image.'

Paddy stepped towards his zombie-self, staring with horrified fascination. He passed a hand through the image, and at that moment, Conrad activated the metronome Ariadne had given him to protect himself from the time distortion.

Only Conrad had the advantage of being shielded from the

time-snatch. Paddy and Chloë meanwhile had to experience the Id exactly as before. While for Conrad the scene was bathed in shifting stroboscopic light, his friends stood before the scene in what they thought was real time. They were subjected to the repeated phrase, over and over, as before. Only this time what they heard was different. Conrad had to smile.

Because what he heard was his own voice. And the phrase about 'marvels await under the sun' had been replaced by,

MARVIN'S A WART ON A PIGLET'S BUM.

Over and over.

Conrad allowed the sequence to run as much of its course as he could bear. He endured over half an hour of the experience, which to Chloë and Paddy seemed like mere seconds. They were transfixed, utterly mesmerized by the pulsing light and the repeated sounds. When he brought them out of their trance they both looked slightly puzzled, particularly Paddy.

'On to Level 2,' said Conrad with authority.

It was Chloë's turn to be shocked and dismayed by the Chloë-zombie sitting around the Id camp fire under the stars. As she passed her hand through the image, the flute-playing Chloë-zombie smiled back with her dead, blue eyes. Conrad pulsed his metronome as the program triggered, and stepped back. This time the phrase, 'friends like music under the stars' had changed to,

FRIENDS LIKE WEIRD SUZIE FROM MARS.

When Conrad felt they'd heard enough, it was Chloë's turn to look puzzled. She scratched her head as if she was trying to remember something, but couldn't quite place it.

'What are you laughing at?' Paddy wanted to know.

'Nothing,' said Conrad. 'Ready to go on?'

At Level 3 they swam with the fishes. Or rather, Chloë and Paddy did, while Conrad observed. He now realized that what he had thought was 'swimming' was actually a process of standing stiffly to attention, locked in a trance but occasionally twitching one's fingers and hands. The words, 'fun like swimming with the fishes' had become,

CALL THIS FUN? I'D RATHER STICK MY HEAD IN A TANK FULL OF PIRHANAS.

After their swim Chloë and Paddy looked at Conrad with open mouths. They hadn't a clue what was going on. Conrad had to stop himself laughing out loud. But when he thought about Level 4, he sobered quickly. 'Now then. You're going to have to show me the way through.'

They entered the maze, instantly becoming weightless. Chloë and Paddy seemed to know the way through the three-dimensional maze, drifting upwards, turning left, turning right, drifting down, threading along corridors that appeared absolutely identical. It was at this point that Conrad began to pray Ariadne was still monitoring their progress. They had agreed to maintain silence except in an emergency. Ariadne wanted to offer no opportunity of her presence being detected inside the labyrinth, and even hinted at the danger not just to the three of them but also to herself should she become trapped in the unknown quantity of Level 5.

'*Remember*,' Ariadne had said to Conrad. '*You may need to get out of the labyrinth very fast. Be ready for that.*' Now that Conrad had no way of knowing whether Ariadne was with him, he doubted his capacity to move through the three-dimensional maze easily.

Chloë stopped ahead. 'What is it?' said Conrad.

'Something's wrong,' said Chloë. 'I can't think what it is, but I know something is wrong.'

'I feel exactly the same,' said Paddy. 'It's as if I've had a dream, and I need to remember it but I can't. Something is shouting at me at the back of my mind. I feel so confused.'

'I don't think we should go on,' said Chloë unhappily. 'I wish I could remember what this is about.'

Conrad didn't know what to do. His friends dithered ahead of him. The expressions of puzzlement on their faces, that had earlier amused him, now didn't seem quite so funny. He attributed his friend's confusion to the reprogramming they were experiencing. Perhaps it was setting up a conflict inside them. 'We go on. Which way?'

'To the right,' said Paddy.

As they turned the corner they saw two Id 'guides' drifting ahead of them. Like the guide Conrad had seen before, they were wearing white clothes. One was male and one was female, though their faces were turned away. One of the Id guides spoke, in a voice that seemed familiar.

'Are you lost? What you need is a guide. And you know the only way out is through the middle.'

Conrad touched his keypad to trigger the metronome. Nothing happened. He touched it again. Still nothing happened.

'No, Conrad,' said one of the floating guides. 'You see, we're not Id guides.' The guides turned to show their faces. It was Marvin and Suzie, the volunteer helpers from the Church of Unity.

'Oh no!' screamed Chloë. 'I've just remembered the dream. They told us to lead you here, Conrad! They got us to decode your messages in the comics! Conrad, it's a trap!'

Paddy, too, looked deeply shocked, as if he was also waking up from a long dream.

'Don't think of it as a trap,' said Marvin. 'Think of it as a long overdue appointment.' Conrad tried to duck back into the maze, but Marvin extended an arm fully three metres long, seizing him by the throat. Suzie held Chloë and Paddy in a similar fashion.

'Level 5?' suggested Marvin.

CHAPTER SIXTEEN
THE SORCERESS

'Conrad. Welcome. Are you the person who's been giving us all this trouble? Come closer. I'd like to take a look at you.'

The three-dimensional maze had dissolved and Conrad found himself, along with Paddy and Chloë and their captors, standing on a vast infra-red disc. The disc was broken by concentric circles radiating from the centre, and by black radial lines reaching out to an invisible edge. The disc resembled a giant spider's web, but one made up of perfect geometric lines.

The person speaking from the centre of the web was a woman of immense age. She seemed to crouch or hover, Conrad couldn't tell, because she wore a long purple robe covering the lower part of her body, though she was able to turn 360 degrees in order to inspect not only himself but also Paddy and Chloë. The woman wore a distinctive gold ring in which was set a huge ruby. She had long flowing red hair. Although the woman's features were ancient, her hair was impossibly luxurious and thick, a glowing chestnut colour rippling with light. Of course, this was somebody's virtual image. Conrad wondered why, if they had preserved youthful hair in their virtual image, they hadn't also rejuvenated the face. But this face was creased with lines and crinkled like tooled leather.

The woman guessed at his thoughts. 'My one vanity,' she said, stroking the lustrous hair. 'But otherwise I don't usually hide my age. After all, it is the source of my wisdom. Youth, on the other hand, which you three have in abundance, is the source of recklessness, mischief and stupidity. Isn't that the case, Conrad?'

Conrad didn't answer. He blinked, during which moment he felt a wave of impatience emanate from the old woman. A split second later a worm of green light burst from the centre of the disc and travelled along one of the radial lines of the web on which they stood. The light looped the segment of web on which Conrad stood and entered him like a syringe of poison.

'Aggh!' he cried out. The electrical charge reminded him of the venomous jolt received from the security spiders appearing at the gate of the labyrinth. When he recovered he saw that Paddy and Chloë had also received a jolt in punishment for his silence.

'I like young people who speak up,' the old woman said evenly. 'Now, I asked you if that were not the case.'

'Yes,' Conrad said, feeling sick. He wondered if Ariadne was still monitoring.

The old woman blinked, lizard-like. 'No one can get in or out of Level 5 without me saying so. That includes your helper.'

'Can you read thoughts?' Conrad said.

'Ah! It does speak unprompted. I'll say only this. When your thoughts are so obvious, so banal, so inevitable, I don't need to *read* them. That is another of the attributes of wisdom. Would you not like to be wise, Conrad?'

Conrad didn't know what to say, but to say nothing at all would risk another dart of poisonous light. 'Yes.'

'Good. I can make you wise. But would you trade your youth for wisdom?'

'No.'

'Of course not. And anyway, I can't tell you what it is like to be wise. But I can tell you what it's like to be old.'

Another bolt of light, this time ultraviolet, travelled along the radial arm of the web. Conrad tensed himself for the impact, but here the effect was quite different. The bolt of light went through him, and in an instant he felt his bones –

from skull to toe – expand, crack, shrink and dry. His hair fell out. His skin swelled and hung flaking from his body like parchment. He felt his teeth rot in his mouth, and his eyeballs shrink inside his skull. In that same moment the loose folds of his skin erupted in sores and boils. He tried to cry out but all that remained of his voice was a dry wheeze. It seemed as though his body had endured the wretched agonies of hundreds of years, and was about to expire.

He was still shuddering with loathing when the violet light retreated, and he was restored to normal. Within seconds, this old woman had reduced him to trembling wreckage.

'You understand that I take no pleasure in tormenting children,' the old woman said. 'But I give you this taste of what I can do to you in order not to waste time later. You've already irritated me enough. Don't think that you amount to any more than an irritating flea in my web, because you don't. But you interfered with a very effective program of ours when you stumbled across my labyrinth.

'Your annoying efforts at reprogramming the engram system have already been put right, and you will all three be re-entered before you leave here. You will all become highly useful graduates of the Planetology program, working in the Church of Unity just like Marvin and Suzie here. Wasn't it a little bit stupid of you passing coded messages in those comics of yours? But how good it was of your friends to agree to lead you to us.'

'We couldn't help it, Conrad,' said Chloë. 'We didn't know what we were doing.'

'It's true,' the old woman said. 'They were under our conditioning, which you broke down on the way in here. But as I said, we can put that right. But before we do, there is something you have to tell me. Who is Ariadne?'

'I don't know,' Conrad said. 'She wouldn't tell us.'

The old woman sighed, and released another beam of light, this time red. She stopped it halfway between herself and Conrad, where it fizzed and crackled like a dog straining at the leash.

'It's true!' Conrad screamed. 'All we know is that Ariadne is a Webcop. She wouldn't tell us so that we could never tell anyone else!'

The red ball of light hummed and spat and crackled on the radial line. The old woman laughed lightly. Then she recalled the red light. 'Do you know, I think you're telling the truth. But you still have something I want.'

'What do you mean?'

'Conrad, don't play games with me. You don't want me to hurt you again, do you?'

'No.'

'You don't want me to hurt your friends, do you?'

'No.'

'You don't want your father to be left rotting in a Korean jail, do you?'

'No.'

'Exactly. No, on all counts. No, no and no again. You see, we went to a lot of trouble to set up this program. In the next five to ten years we expect to use it to recruit twenty million young people to our Planetology movement. The best and brightest brains of the future. We are about to re-engineer the future of world society, and we can't allow three foolish children and a rather stupid Webcop to get in the way of those plans, now can we? Conrad. Give me the Webcop dossier. It will lead us nicely to your Webcop friend.'

'I can't.'

'I know you have it with you, isn't that right, Marvin?'

'He said so in the coded-comics message, Sorceress.'

'Quite. Here, Conrad. Come here.' The Sorceress reached into the folds of her skirts and produced a black control box with keypad. 'All you have to do is to input the code from your own wristpad. The information will flow into our system. Quite painless. For you.'

'I can't betray Ariadne!' Conrad quaked.

'But where is your Ariadne to help you now? As I told you, she can't get into Level 5, and you can't get out. She may as well be a million miles away.'

'Please,' he begged.

'Let's experiment a little. How much pain can you stand?

Or rather, how much of your friends' pain can you stand?'
The Sorceress released her red dogs of burning light, flashing
along the radial, looping Paddy and Chloë and igniting their
bodies. Their screams were deafening. 'A feeling not unlike
third degree burns, Conrad. Shall I try something else?'

'Please, stop.' Conrad begged. He was broken.

'The dossier. The information must flow.'

Wiping tears of anguish from his eyes, Conrad keyed in the
code, and the dossier of Web Police information on the
Planetologists was immediately transferred into the Labyrinth master program. A monitor appeared from the fabric of
the disc, and the Sorceress watched with satisfaction as the
dossier information reproduced itself on a screen.

Then her smile turned to a scowl. 'What is this gibberish?'

'It's the Ariadne dossier—' Conrad tried.

The Sorceress blinked with a yellow eye. Very slowly she
said, 'I can't read it.'

Marvin spoke up. 'It's in code, Sorceress.'

'Yes,' said Suzie. 'I recognize it from the comics. They have
a childish code for passing information back and forth
between them. We could easily decode it, but it will take a
little time—'

'I WANT TO READ IT NOW!' shrieked the Sorceress,
losing her temper for the first time. 'Who made this code?'

'I did,' said Paddy.

'Then *unmake* it!'

Paddy looked at Conrad. 'Do what she says,' Conrad said.

Paddy stepped forward and transferred his decoder program to the black box. The Rat code symbols on the screen
scrambled and were replaced by a dazzling display of
numbers changing rapidly and spinning through incalcul-
able changes. Then the screen went dead.

'What?' said the Sorceress. 'Do we have an energy loss?'

She never got an answer. There came a roaring sound from
the extremities of the disc on which they all stood. The entire
circumference of the disc seemed alive with dancing, ice-blue
flame. The ice-blue flame fizzed and popped with a sound
like acid chewing away at metal, a sound just audible

beneath the roaring overhead. The ice-blue flame itself began to advance towards them.

The Sorceress turned and glared at Conrad with a hideously evil eye. Marvin and Suzie were looking around in confusion and panic. Only the Sorceress understood instantly what had happened.

'Let's get out of here,' Conrad shouted to Chloë and Paddy, directing them to the very centre of the disc.

Meanwhile the ice-blue flame was spreading rapidly. The fire had been started by Ariadne's dossier. It had waited patiently in the system until triggered by Paddy's Rat decoder. It was a computer virus, destroying everything in its path and spreading from the heart of the program.

CHAPTER SEVENTEEN

VIRUS

The virus chomped and chewed at the edge of the disc, spitting and spluttering as it moved towards them, ghostly ice-blue fire ringing them as it moved through the concentric lines, consuming bytes, megabytes, kilobytes of data as it went. The Sorceress was still thunderstruck as Conrad directed Paddy and Chloë not away from her but towards her. Behind the Sorceress was a tiny black hole like a spinning vortex. Ariadne had predicted that the hole would be the only exit from Level 5.

With the screams of the Sorceress ringing in their ears, the three fleeing members of the Tech-Rats leaped down the black tube-like hole.

'After them!' they heard the Sorceress cry to Marvin and Suzie. Conrad, Chloë and Paddy slid down the tube in an untidy heap, to be dumped in the three-dimensional maze of Level 4.

'Quickly,' Conrad shouted, leading them to the left. Behind them they saw Marvin and Suzie emerging from the tube.

'Ariadne, make contact!' Conrad shouted. Conrad's earpiece crackled but there was no response. 'We need Ariadne to get us out of here,' he said to the others.

'We can lose Marvin and Suzie in the maze,' said Chloë.

'It's not them I'm worried about,' Conrad said. 'Look!' He jabbed a finger back at the point where they'd re-entered the maze. The ice-blue flare had moved down the tube behind them and was slowly working its way through the maze. 'Ariadne's virus! She warned me that after destroying Level 5 it would start to burn its way back to the beginning of the program!'

They watched mesmerized as the mercurial flame gnawed away at the available paths and tunnels, leaving behind it only a smoky, infra-red haze. 'What happens,' Chloë said, 'if you get caught by a virus while you're trapped in a program?'

'Ever been sucked to death by acid-drooling leeches?' Paddy suggested. Chloë looked at Paddy in disgust as Marvin and Suzie clattered into the tunnel ahead.

'Run!' shouted Conrad.

'Wait,' Paddy said. 'They're changing!'

Marvin and Suzie were restructuring their alter-egos. Their images broke down and reassembled, in seconds, as huge, black, eight-legged spiders. Their faces as Marvin and Suzie were just recognizable in their hideous spider-heads.

'Time to go!' Chloë shouted. 'Up, up, up!'

The three took a tunnel directly above their heads, then a left turn, hoping to evade their pursuers. But within moments they saw why Marvin and Suzie had taken on the spider-form. Their eight legs gave them greater speed as they scuttled along the smooth sides of the three-dimensional maze. They were also able to climb diagonally and leap faster through tunnels above and below.

'We're not going to be able to outrun them!' Chloë shrieked.

'They're carrying stings!' Paddy said. The two spiders advanced with poisonous-looking yellow fangs protruding from their mandibles.

'Ariadne, where are you?' Conrad cried. 'Go right! Let's go right!'

They hurried down blind corridors, taking turns with no sense of direction, hearing the scuttle of spiders always just one turn behind them. At last they took a left turn, slipped down a corridor and ducked into a passage bending to the right.

'Oh no!' shouted Paddy, pointing ahead.

The virus fire was out of control now and was burning up ahead, sizzling and consuming the maze as it advanced towards them. They couldn't go on. There was a vertical tunnel above them, but it was dangerously close to the approaching virus. The scuttle of the spiders drummed behind them, perilously close.

'We're trapped!' Chloë shouted.

They stood in the passage, paralysed, terrified. The virus rushed at them, spluttering and spitting like acid as it came. Then the spiders appeared at the far end of the passage, saw them, paused and began scuttling towards them.

'What are we going to do?' yelled Paddy.

'Wait,' Conrad said. 'Wait until I say!'

Behind them the virus roared, crackling and bubbling like volcanic lava. The spiders launched themselves at the three children, full-pelt. With the spiders just centimetres away, Conrad shouted, 'Up, up, up!'

Conrad, Chloë and Paddy leaped vertically into the passage above their heads. The forward momentum of the two spiders sent them crashing into the scalding, burning virus. There were brief screams as Marvin and Suzie were fried.

Conrad's earpiece crackled. *'Conrad! Conrad!'*

'Ariadne! Get us out of here!'

'It's the virus, Conrad. It's eaten into the communications system. I've had to re-route. Now, come on. You haven't got much time. Go left, left, left.'

Ariadne tried to guide them out of the maze, which by now was an inferno, crackling and fizzing with blue light, three-quarters eaten away by the virus. She guided them up through bending passages, into the path of the virus, out again. Their search for a way out was frantic. Another effort to get them out failed. At last she found a way through, and they were out of the maze and into Level 3. They swam through Level 3 as the maze collapsed totally behind them. That level too was devoured quickly, as was the interactive display with the young people camped under the stars. Chloë looked back to see her blue-eyed zombie-self eaten by the

acid light. Paddy watched his zombie-self go the same way at
Level 1.

'*No time to stare,*' Ariadne told Conrad.

'Right! Let's get out of here!'

They passed through the labyrinth gates and turned to
look back. The virus-fire roared behind them as it devoured
the last remaining details of the program. The last thing to
burn was the double-headed axe logo above the gate. When
the chewing fire reached the logo it fizzed briefly, sparked
and puttered out as it reached the anti-virus wall insulating
the program from the rest of Webtown.

The three members of the Tech-Rats turned and looked
hard at each other.

'Phew!' said Chloë.

'Phew is right,' said Paddy.

'*Home?*' said Ariadne.

'Home,' said Conrad.

CHAPTER EIGHTEEN

FAREWELL ARIADNE

Chloë appeared the following day sporting a new hair-colour. Purple and white stripes in celebration, she said, of the Tech-Rats' successful adventure in Webspace. When Paddy told her she looked like a mauve skunk and the squabbling started, Conrad was happy to note that things were back to normal.

Conrad had more than one reason to be happy. That morning, his mother had heard that Mr Hamilton had been released, with an apology, by the Korean authorities. Not only that, the company he worked for had conducted an investigation into the role played by Mr Hamilton's boss. Finding out that he was hand-in-glove with the Planetologists, they'd dismissed him from his job. Conrad's father had been promoted to replace him and was now in charge of the Far East Division.

Conrad had explained to Paddy and Chloë that Ariadne had, all along, equipped him with the virus unleashed on the labyrinth program. The virus was safe until it was activated by Paddy's original decoding program. Ariadne had known all along that Marvin and Suzie would check Conrad's comics, and would report everything they found to the Sorceress. She in turn would be desperate to find out exactly what Ariadne knew about her organization and would manipulate Paddy and Chloë into leading Conrad to her.

'She's very smart, that Ariadne,' said Chloë.

'If Ariadne really is a *she*,' said Paddy.

'Of course she's a she,' Chloë snapped. 'No man has a brain that useful.'

It was while they were still arguing about Ariadne's identity, and with some pretty wild ideas, that Conrad's terminal signalled an incoming message. After a few moments, the screen bubbled a familiar amber colour and a string of text generated itself across the screen.

<I have to thank the Tech-Rats for all your help. You may as well know that the Sorceress has been known to us for some time. We've been monitoring her activities, but she always seems to remain one jump ahead. I can't say what happened to her when the virus washed away the labyrinth program, but I have a feeling she'll be back. Even so, she won't be planning any brainwashing programs for a while. You helped to put paid to that.>

Chloë leaped to the keyboard and typed:

<Who is the Sorceress?>

There was a pause before an answer followed:

<A very rich and very powerful lady who has lived too long. Like I say, we haven't seen the last of her.>

<Ariadne, who are you? Male or female? Old or young?>

<No dice. I'm Korean, that's all I'm telling you. Now it's time to say goodbye, probably for ever. As we say in Korea: never whistle while you're fishing.>

The screen went blank and reverted to its original grey colour.

'What does that mean?' said Chloë.

Both Paddy and Conrad looked blank.

'I don't know. But whoever Ariadne is,' Conrad put it, 'he or she saved our bacon.'

'Unfortunate phrase, that,' said Paddy. 'I can still remember the smell of Marvin and Suzie's virtual brains frying when the virus got to them.'

'I wonder what happened to them. They certainly aren't hanging around our houses any more,' said Chloë.

It was true. Despite questions from their parents about 'where has that nice Suzie gone' or 'funny we haven't seen that thoughtful boy Marvin tonight', the two members of the

Church of Unity had stopped their goodwill visits. Conrad had a feeling they wouldn't be seen again.

'You realize that the Church of Unity was just another name for the Planetologists,' said Conrad.

'We do *now*,' Chloë pointed out. 'We don't all have a brain of microbe proportions.'

'You didn't say that when Marvin and Suzie were your best pals,' Conrad protested. But he wasn't at all put out by her remarks. For the second time that day he actually felt happy that Chloë was insulting him again.

LIGHTSTORM
PETER F. HAMILTON

CHAPTER ONE

MEETING OFF SUNSET

I was flying down Sunset Boulevard, three metres above the ground, flapping my wings in a lazy motion as if I were part of a slow-motion scene in some old 2-D movie. It's a deceptive action, I was actually zipping along quite fast above the heads of the historical characters and myth-creatures thronging the wide yellow-brick strand between the Hollywood gamer company blocks. Good thing, too. I didn't want to keep my news exclusive. What happened last night was plain creepy.

Up ahead, a group of tall elves and knights, wearing armour that shone like polished chrome, were standing outside the MaxiFox block. They were waiting to spin in to the *Camelot Orc Attack* site. From my angle the surface of the block looked like a chrome rainbow that was slowly melting into whirlpool curves. A big rosette of sapphire and emerald slid down in front of the group, and they stepped through together.

They couldn't have been phreaks. The Camelot games were venomous when they started coming out. That was months ago. Now, everyone knows the blackwire tricks to boost your play character status. Perhaps they were one-mip nostalgia buffs, a bit like Grandpa. Except he's not one-mip. Of course!

I flew on past the MaxiFox block, with its paltry queue of people waiting to spin in. They really ought to shove *Camelot* out on disk and reboot the block. It's November, after all; the gamer companies are starting to line up their big new Christmas titles.

Disney's block was already advertising the new Schwarzenegger game with sleek, flying V-shaped starships launching from its roof in a roar of sparkling afterburner flame. Just watching them vanish into the blue sky made you want to join the colonists they were taking to new worlds. Well, it did me anyway. Spielberg's block was orbited by amazing intergalactic vortex holes blinking open for its *Dark Powers* game. I zipped underneath one and did a full roll so I could look up into it. If you're fast enough you can catch a good glimpse of the promo scenes they reveal.

Most of the companies had taken space as *the* theme this year, what with the Mars landing in two days time. I loved it. Christmas for twelve solid months.

I'm going to be an astronaut when I'm older. Yeah, I know, you've heard that one before. But with me its bottom-line real. I've wanted it ever since I gave up on the idea of being a bird warden down at the marsh sanctuary. That was when I was about seven, and realized just how dirty the job would be, wriggling round in all that mud to rescue the strange, bewildered birds the weather brings in from Africa and Asia these days. So I've concentrated on getting the kind of grade ratings on my school science courses that the Global Space Agency is looking for. Just another seven years, including university, to go, and I'll be eligible to apply to GSA for full training. I'm already a registered cadet with them.

The Tropicana site is in a block past the last of the gamers. I flew straight in. The spin put me above a beach of scarlet sand with a skyline that was just fading to twilight. It was busy, the clusters of white cafe chairs crowding above the water line were nearly all taken.

As the Tropicana is a contact and leisure site, all the avatars inside were human-form. But my computer is loaded with an EC licensed Equal Access User program, so I could keep my bird-form. It's shaped like a manta, but with silvery blue skin and a pterodactyl head. The sense of freedom it gives me during flight is fabulous. I suppose it must be similar to the zero-G which astronauts experience.

I circled round till I found an empty table, then settled beside it. My friends started to spin in after a couple of minutes. About time! I was getting impatient.

Selim was first, using his direct site access program. A shimmering vortex hole materialized above the table, and a purple egg-shaped landing pod popped out. It landed on the sand beside me. The upper half hinged open to show a cockpit with a control console that was all switches and flashing lights. Selim climbed out of the ejector seat and grinned.

His avatar is a boy about my age, thirteen, average height and weight, but with the sort of features that are as regular as only a program can conjure up (plus skin that doesn't have a single spot!).

'Hi, Aynsley,' he said. 'So, what's the hot fly you've got for us?'

'I'll tell you when the others get here. I'd just have to repeat it every time, else.'

He stuck his tongue out. It was a long strip of wet flesh that licked round in front of his face. Neat upgrade!

Drunlo was next to arrive. A wooden trapdoor flipped up from the beach, showering sand everywhere. He climbed up a ladder from what looked like a stone cellar with flaming torches on the wall. As always his avatar was an eleven-year-old, though he was in his standard medieval urchin clothes.

Bayliss and Katie turned up together, walking across the sand. He's the only one of us who doesn't bother with an avatar image; his realoe showed us a chubby face with a brow that seemed to be permanently frowning. Katie's avatar was Rebecca Ryan; this year's *Access On* hostess. Sixteen years old. An easy smile that produces dimples everywhere, every time. Legs almost slimmer than her arms, and twice as long. So perfect she could be be an avatar program herself.

'It was there again last night,' I told them. 'I saw it three times. Bigger than before. Brighter, too.'

'That's it?' Selim asked. He was really withering about it,

too. 'That's your fly? You saw lights out over the marsh? Honestly, Aynsley, we can hardly chase this fade. They're called will-o'-the-wisp. Browse your encyclopaedia, it's just gas that's given off from decaying plants. Methane, like farts.'

'This isn't a will-o'-the-wisp,' I said hotly. 'You think I don't know what a will-o'-the-wisp is? I've lived by the marsh for ten years. I've *seen* them. They're pale, like a glowing mist. This is different. It's . . . it's a *lightstorm*. Every time it's like a bubble of light that erupts out of the ground then just vanishes. And it never happens twice in the same place. Least, not yet.'

'What do you think it is?' Katie asked.

'I don't know.'

'Flying saucers taking off,' Selim suggested.

'Don't be silly,' Bayliss told him.

I'd been sort of relying on Bayliss for support. His science grades make me look like a one-mip by comparison. That's how we met, surfing round the GSA Olympus mission site. I was accessing the crew member who was in the provider suit that day. Bayliss was interested in the results from the ship's gamma ray telescope.

'I'm not,' Selim protested. 'How can you say it's silly? We're landing people on Mars in two days time. Why is aliens landing here so improbable?'

'It's not improbable, just very unlikely. Besides, Aynsley said it was just bubbles of light not whole ships.'

'OK, then it's their exhaust jets he's seeing, and the saucers themselves use stealth technology like our air force fighters.'

'If it is any sort of aircraft, then it's likely to be a secret military one.'

'I don't think so,' I said. 'Not using the marshes. It's a registered nature reserve area, and the village is only a couple of kilometres away. That's not being very secret, is it?'

'So what do you think it is?' Katie asked, again.

'I really don't know. That's why I wanted to bring you in to help. The first time I saw the lights I thought it was interesting. Now I'm getting worried, because I don't understand them. I can't find an explanation in any educational text or memory file. That's really strange. I mean, we all know how to format a knowbot to browse public information sites, that's one-mip stuff. So why haven't I found out what it is? If it's natural, it has to be filed somewhere.' I could tell I'd got them curious, even Selim. Not *knowing* is terribly wrong in the information age. Our world is open to us. Or it should be. Having things hidden from the public belongs in the dark ages. Grandpa is always banging on about how awful life was when the only information people had came from the newspapers and television. Editors always chose what you could see or read based on what they thought was the most interesting or entertaining. Sort of like benign censorship, Grandpa says.

I don't know which upset me the most. The lightstorms themselves, or not being able to find out about them. Two things that shouldn't happen, somehow connected. It's like waking up to find the sky's turned green.

'I suppose we can all write a knowbot request for you,' Drunlo said. 'Those network librarians are getting really sophisticated, they should be able to track down any information providing you phrase the request correctly. Between us we ought to be able to find a bite on lightstorms. You might just have made a mistake formatting your request.'

I glared at him as well as my avatar characteristics would allow me. 'I don't believe I did.'

'You weren't spidered off a file were you?' Katie enquired.

'No.'

'What do the other people living beside the marsh say the lightstorms are?' Bayliss asked.

'I don't know,' I admitted. I knew that back in my cocoon I'd be blushing inside my Websuit. 'I haven't asked them.'

'Well, why not?' Selim said in exasperation.

Because I don't like any of them, they're not my friends, and they enjoy making my life a misery. But I didn't say that out loud. 'Nobody else has seen them, yet. They're too far away, and no one really looks over the marsh at night.'

'Except you,' Selim said, with a short laugh.

'Hey, curl up,' Katie snapped. 'We are what we are. All of us. If you don't like us, spin out.'

'I didn't say that,' he answered. 'I'm just saying that not everyone spends their evenings looking out at marshes they can't see. I think it's a valid point.'

'Do you want to tell us?' Drunlo asked me cautiously.

'No big secret. I'm thinking of fitting a low-light amplifier to my telescope so I can watch the birds at night. It was a full moon last week, so I was scanning round the marshes to find out what I could see anyway. And that's when I saw a lightstorm for the first time.'

'This phenomenon could have been going on for quite a while then? Bayliss said. 'Ever since the marsh was reno-vated.'

'I suppose so. But the ecology crews finished that part of the nature restoration scheme two years ago. I think if it had been going on for that long someone would have seen it.'

'Quite right,' Katie said. 'It sounds to me as if this has only just started. I think you should report it, Aynsley.'

'Who to?'

'And what would he say is happening?' Bayliss said. 'We were sceptical about lights in the night, and we know Aynsley is honest with us. The local authorities would laugh him off their site.'

'What do we do then?'

'The obvious. Gather more information. Then when we have the facts we'll know what to do.'

'All right,' she said. 'I'll be happy to format a knowbot that'll browse for lightstorms.'

'We all should,' Bayliss said. 'And Aynsley.'

'Yes?'

'You'll have to go out into the marsh and scout round.'

'Why?' I tried to keep the consternation out of my voice. It wasn't easy. Of course, he didn't know what he was asking. But I wasn't going to tell him that.

'So you can see if there is any evidence of what's been going on.' The tone was of someone stating the utterly obvious. 'Do you know roughly the area where these light-storms have been appearing?'

'Er, yes, I suppose so.'

'Good. That's settled then. Each of us will find what we can this afternoon, and then meet back here this evening, usual time.'

CHAPTER TWO

MY FAMILY, AND
HOW TO SURVIVE THEM

A trip into the marsh! Why hadn't I just kept my big mouth shut? Worse, what was I thinking of, saying *yes*?

I suppose I told them because I wanted to be the centre of attention. People always want others to think they are interesting. It's the route to popularity. And let's face it, that's an empty file in my site.

Grandpa says people are always ridiculously competitive and paranoid from the moment they're born to when they die. He also says people are basically stupid.

I think he's right.

After I spun out of the Tropicana I took my suit off and slung it on my bed. No sign of the voms. Thankfully! I wasn't expecting any, I'd only been in for twenty minutes. Most mornings I spin in for a couple of hours at least, so Realworld and I aren't used to each other at this time of day. Nothing had changed in my cocoon. The walls are all covered in holoposters of various chunks of space hardware. Satellites and stations orbiting the Earth; a shuttle taking off from Cape Town; a survey team at work on the moon. There are pictures of birds, too; ordinary 2-D colour laser prints. I took most of them; I'm quite handy with a vid-snap camera. My latest posters are tacked up at the end of my bed, showing the Olympus ships sliding into orbit above Mars. A two-metre flatscreen next to the window runs text displays from mission control, keeping me constantly updated.

There's only a limited amount of space on my desk, so the computer tower has to sit on the floor to make room for my science projects. I've got a healthy selection of tools to help me assemble various card stacks to augment the tower functions. At the moment I'm trying to put together a stack that will automate my telescope.

It's a beautiful ash-grey tube over a metre long, very powerful. Dad gave it to me on a sort-of loan; he was quite a keen amateur astronomer when he was young. The trouble is, when it's set up on a tripod I find it difficult to reach the eyepiece. So if I can fix it up with actuators and a decent video camera I'll be able to lie on my bed and watch the images on the flatscreen.

That's why it's in my cocoon at the moment, rather than outside. And my window faces towards the marsh. See? That's how come I found the lightstorms. Most of life's events are accidents and coincidences all bunched up together, I suppose.

There was no one about when I went out. Typical for our house, everybody always doing their own thing. I ought to explain about my family; not that we're odd, or anything. No serial killers or sorceresses lurking in the attic. Well, not unless you count Uncle Elton, but we're not allowed to mention him because of where he is at the moment and what he did to get sent there. Apart from him we're almost cogs. My dad, Forrest Clemson, is a tax lawyer at a London-site partnership. Grandpa Donald is always accusing him of being a soulless corporate robot working for the forces of darkness. He says if rich companies paid more tax then Europe would have better social security and healthcare schemes, and Dad's the one who helps them avoid it. Grandpa likes to think that his side of the family are all romantic rebels. Dad always points out that the reason he and my mum, Marriane, met in the first place was because Grandpa sent her to the partnership so she wouldn't have to pay so much tax. You see, Mum used to be in a girls group that had a couple of hit albums around 2010. She sings really well and she wrote some of the group's songs, too. Being in the mediabiz is a bit like winning the lottery every week, apparently.

Mum doesn't sing these days, at least not in a group. Me and my younger brother Edwyn put an end to that career just by being born. She still writes music, though, for a company that provides incidental scores for games. She has her causes, too; she's a parish councillor, and on the board of the Norfolk Community Health Committee, and a school governor (which is awful, she knows both my supervisory teachers really well), and sits as an advisor for two local special needs charities.

It's good for people to have causes, to help others. Except . . . at times I wish she was just my mum and nothing else. But that's selfish. She did put a lot of what she made from the group into trust accounts for me and Edwyn. Not that I can get at it for ages; I just have to scrape by on this really small percentage of the monthly interest. Banks and trustees (Mum and Grandpa!) just don't understand how much money you need simply to survive in the modern world. I can only ever buy a hundredth of the stuff I want.

Actually, that's more than most kids my age get. I suppose I like Mum quite a lot really; even though she does worry and tries a little too hard.

The old mobile phone was fully charged, so I put it into my coat pocket before I went out. That's another thing Mum insists on if I'm outside by myself. I'll be able to call if I get into any difficulty.

I took the ramp down to the garden. Our house isn't actually a house in the ordinary sense. It's a boat in the middle of a field. We live just outside a village called Heacham, on a big field that runs along the rear of the beach. There are several wooden bunglaows sharing the field with us, as well as a few other boats. They used to be grain barges back in the last century, then after their working life was over someone dragged them ashore and turned them into homes.

It's utterly perfect during the summer. Well, most of the

year, really. We're on the southern edge of the The Wash; that means the beach goes on for kilometres, and there are no cliffs, just a low bluff sprouting tufts of reed grass, so I can get down to it easily. The marshes begin at the end of the field, and they stretch along to the mouth of the River Ouse. A huge great zone of nothing. There are tourists in the summer, but not many. Grandpa says when he was young millions of people flew abroad for holidays, or drove down to Cornwall. I can't imagine what that was like. They say the Web's secure business sites put an end to commuter traffic; and the game sites killed off package holidays, along with the rise in the cost of aviation fuel. Petrol reached fifteen Euros a litre at its worst, which stopped any kind of driving apart from utterly essential journeys. Apparently, there are still a million private cars licensed in England (we have one of them), but now the rail network is being restored and expanded everyone who wants to travel uses trains and buses.

Some of the kids from the other bungalows were playing a football game on the grass between the row of buildings. I trundled past as fast as I could go without making it obvious I was in a rush to get away from them. With it being November I was wrapped up well; my canary-yellow wool coat, a long emerald scarf, and a grey bobble hat with ear flaps. Normally, they would have crowded round and had their fun; sneered at my clothes, demanded to know where I was going, what I was doing; make out they were astronauts in freefall. I've lost count of how many times my hats have been chucked on to the beach (always a long way from the path down) or dunked in the stream which runs along the back of the field. Sometimes, I think the Realworld con- servatives are right and kids should be bundled off to school every day so they can develop social skills, or at least learn that other people have feelings. Experience has shown me how futile that hope is.

Today, though, their zero-mip game was taking up their full attention. I got clear with just a few jeers and shouts.

Mr Griffin was pottering round his front garden, clipping

back his scrawny fuchsia bushes. Both of his cats were curled up in a wicker chair on the veranda, watching him.

'Hello there, Aynsley,' he called as I went past his front gate. It's about the only part of his fence that is still standing.

'Hello.' I showed a bit, but didn't stop.

'So, what's new and groovy in that infernal electronic universe of yours, my boy?'

Groovy! Mr Griffin is approximately five hundred years old. He doesn't like the Web, which means he gets on great with Grandpa. 'The new Schwarzenegger is due for access in five days.'

He groaned loudly. 'Oh, good grief. I remember when acting dynasties meant Olivier and Richardson and Douglas. Schwarzenegger, tut tut.'

'It's not quite acting now, Mr Griffin. The sites are concepts.'

'Don't remind me. Heavens, my agent hasn't called for weeks, simply weeks.'

'I'm sorry.' Mr Griffin is an actor. Too old to retrain when Hollywood switched from films to games, and TV abandoned drama series, he said. Lots of adults in this country still enjoy going to the theatre and seeing real actors treading the boards. I don't see the point, myself, actors can make mistakes when it's live, you can't guarantee the audience a perfect show. Not that Mr Griffin will even do rep work now; he doesn't like living in digs while a show's running. Mr Griffin basically doesn't like anything that involves leaving home these days. He sometimes gets work as a primary image, having graphic simulation computers scan his expression and vocal intonation so they can use it on the phaces they generate in the Web. That's drying up now; there's very little in the way of characteristics they can't emulate.

'Not to worry,' he said cheerfully. 'You're dressed up most splendidly today, young Aynsley. Going anywhere special?'

'Just the marshes. Thought I'd take a look, see if any new birds have got past the wardens.'

'Jolly good. Well, make sure you *stick to the path*.' He chuckled heavily, and gave me the kind of expectant expression that meant I was supposed to finish the joke.

I smiled awkwardly.

'Ah, well.' he said. 'Another piece of our heritage walks off into the new neon sunset.' He waved his secateurs at the football game. 'Did that lot give you any trouble today?'

'No.'

'Ha! Well, if they do, you remember to come and see me. I did my fair share of hell-raising when I was younger. Might look ancient, but I can still give those awful louts a shock.' He patted the slim black gadget clipped to his belt and winked.

I know what it is, because he told me. A sonic jet. They send out a vicious beam of noise that is intended to frighten the living daylights out of dogs. They work pretty well against muggers, too. The EU parliament hasn't outlawed them yet, but it's only a matter of time.

'I'll remember, Mr Griffin,' I promised.

There's no clear cut boundary where the field ends and the nature reserve begins. The grass just gradually gets longer and reedier, the soil becomes softer. I kept to the dirt track that the wardens drive their Land-Rovers along. It's a public bridle path on the map.

After a couple of hundred metres the silence closed in, wrapping round me like a thick extra coat. I couldn't see the bungalows or the field any more. Puddles of stagnant, reddy-brown water were appearing on either side of the track. All the grass stems and reeds were sprinkled with grey droplets, as if colour was leaking out of the world.

Things were scurrying through the undergrowth on all sides of me. Small animals, voles and rabbits, I suppose. Not being able to see them made it creepy. I could hear them brushing through the reeds and making tiny splashes in the puddles.

Eventually, I came to the fence. I'd only ever been this far once before. That was a year ago when we had one of our rare family walks. It was a sturdy chain-link mesh, well over two metres high. One of the posts had a sign bolted to it, saying: RESTRICTED AREA. KEEP OUT. WETLAND ENVIRONMENT RESTORATION WORK IN PROGRESS. PUBLIC ADMISSION TO RECOMMENCE IN JANUARY 2032. *This is an EU Environmental Initiative co-funded by Bigene Industrie, Civil Development Division.*

I always got a strange feeling reading that name out here in the middle of the remote wilderness. Fancy Bigene Industrie at work just a few kilometres from my front door. It's a huge Anglo-French biotechnology company, a world leader. Politicians in Brussels are always holding it up as an example of successful European collaboration. It supplied the biological recycling system for the three-man Olympus craft that uses genetically engineered microbes and algae to clean and purify the air and water used by the crew. The Mars mission is the first time biological recycling has been employed during a manned spaceflight of such length. Bigene also developed the jockey chip with which the mission commander, Colonel McFarlane, is fitted. The jockey chip reads his nerve impulses directly, a new concept in providing a remote rider, which they hope will eliminate the Websuit provider mode altogether. When he steps out on to the planet's surface in two days time, everyone wearing a Websuit in receiver mode will know exactly what it's like, what he sees and feels setting foot on Mars.

The reason Bigene Industrie is working around The Wash area is because of their energy division. They were heavily involved with building the solar hydrogen stations. Out in The Wash are huge (10 kilometres in diameter) circular mats floating on the top of the sea. They're made out of plastic like the sheets of bubble polythene that people use to insulate their greenhouses in winter. Except, instead of air in the bubbles, the mats contain a genetically engineered algae. When the sun shines the algae's photosynthesis splits sea water up into hydrogen and oxygen. The gas then gets pumped ashore to be burned in a power station. And the wonderful thing about it is, burning hydrogen means there is absolutely no pollution. The only waste product is steam; which is cooled into fresh water to complement the desalinization plants that are being built all round the coastline to compensate for the reduced rainfall.

The Brussels Energy Directorate already wants to quadruple the number of mats in The Wash over the next ten years; and other European shallow-water basins are being investigated to see if they can be used to anchor mats as well. Some people worried about the damage such a huge project would cause to the coastline while the mat anchors were being installed, the hydrogen pipes laid, and the power station was built. That's why Bigene helped to restore the marshes, and all the other sections of wild coastline along The Wash, to prove there would be no longer term environmental damage. They actually improved the area beside Heacham; the marshes here were drying out and dying from the seven-month summers and tiny annual rainfall we get now. Bigene Industrie's crews completely transformed them, putting in new networks of channels and small dams to hold the water.

I looked through the fence. The marsh on the other side seemed exactly the same. But if the company experts said it wasn't settled yet, I could hardly argue.

Something dark darted about in the shadows behind a clump of reeds about twenty metres away on the other side of the fence. So fast it was almost impossible to tell if it was real or not. It must have been real, though, because I yelped in surprise. I thought— All right, I'll be honest. I thought it was a spider; one of the kind used in the Web to warn you off forbidden areas. Which is a real one-mip idea – that something from the Web could be wandering round a Realworld marsh.

I stared at the clump of reeds until my eyes grew tired and it was hard to focus. But nothing moved again. Being in the marsh spooked me, that's what it was. My imagination was getting all hyped up.

I sighed and set off along the fence towards where I thought I'd seen the lightstorms. Two minutes later, I found it!

CHAPTER THREE

HEADLONG INTO A
WALL OF STONE PIXELS

'What do you mean, burned?' Katie asked.

'Just that,' I told them. I flapped my bird-form wings for emphasis. 'The ground and the reeds were all burned, completely roasted. It was a patch about three metres wide. Even the fence chain was black with soot.

'Told you!' Selim said triumphantly. 'It's the exhaust jet from a flying saucer.'

'A very small saucer, if its engine exhaust only burned a circle three metres wide,' Bayliss said.

'They are supposed to be *little* green men,' I said.

'We all laughed at that, except for Selim.

'Ha ha,' he grunted. 'So what do you think it is then, million-mip brains?'

'I'm not sure,' Bayliss said. 'The light Aynsley sees is obviously some kind of flame to have produced the scorch effect he found. But my knowbot couldn't find any explanation other than will-o'-the-wisps.'

'Mine too,' Katie admitted.

Selim and Drunlo confessed to similar results.

'Could it be local kids sneaking in there to let off fireworks?' Bayliss asked. 'Guy Fawkes night was only a week ago, after all.'

'What night?' Drunlo asked.

'Guy Fawkes,' I said. 'It's a celebration when the English let off fireworks; like the fourth of July for Americans and

Bastille Day in France. Why, don't you have any national days like that?'

'Not really.'

I didn't press. You don't, not in the Web. Your friends tell you all they want to about themselves, nothing more. I realized I didn't even know what nationality Drunlo was. It doesn't matter. He was good company, a competent gamer. Who needs more from people?

'So, is it fireworks?' Selim asked.

'I really don't think so. The marsh is pretty remote from the rest of the village. And you have to walk past a whole row of bungalows to get to it. If people had been doing that it would be noticed, even at night. Several of my neighbours have got dogs.'

'All right, we know the lightstorms are definitely real,' Bayliss said. 'Can anyone think of a natural explanation?'

None of us could.

'Then you have to report it,' he said.

I just knew he was going to say that. 'Do I have to?' I moaned. I try and live as quietly as I can; kicking up a fuss about weird fires was going to draw attention to me no matter what the outcome.

'Something dangerous and quite possibly illegal is going on in your community,' Bayliss said, he sounded quite offended. 'It's your duty as a citizen to inform the authorities.'

'OK, I suppose so.'

'We'll spin in with you,' Katie said. Her Rebecca Ryan smile of reassurance was captivating.

'Hey, if there's a reward, do we share it?' Selim asked.

'Oh, curl up!'

Community policing is a major Federal policy. Actually, anything with 'community' in the title is a major part of Federal policy. The theory is that having regular, concerned, helpful police officers patrolling your neighbourhood twenty-four hours a day should inspire people's confidence in the forces of law and order and deter the local criminal element. Unfortunately, Realworld policies like that cost an awful lot of money to maintain. So, regional police forces moved into the Web big-time.

Heacham police station was actually a reception and filter subsection in the King's Lynn police site. Someone had the bright idea of making it one of these old-fashioned village policeman's houses with a one room station on the ground floor. Just to make sure the cliche was completely vom inducing, its phace was a wise-old-man desk sergeant in a 1950s uniform (pointed hat, whistle on a chain, and everything!). I wouldn't mind, but the police obviously weren't allocating much capacity to the program; there was too much green everywhere, the structure had translucent speckles running through it, and the phace sergeant's lip movements weren't quite in sync with his voice.

'Now then, youngsters,' he said. 'What can I do for you, then?'

I didn't dare risk a glance at the others. 'I've seen some lights,' I said. 'Out over the marsh at night.'

'Have you now? Well, there's a thing and no mistake. You were quite right to bring it to my attention, master Aynsley. You never know what kind of villainous business is afoot, even in a village as quiet as our—' the whole site flickered, buzzing loudly, as the standard program shunted in its user designation '—Heacham. We always rely on the public to keep their eyes peeled to help prevent wrongdoing.' He flipped open a small black leather notebook and licked the tip of his pencil. (No, look, I'm not making this up, honest!) 'Now then, why don't you give me a properly detailed description of the incident? After that, I can decide what action will be appropriate.'

I *really* wished we hadn't spun in. But I told him anyway, then waited while the phace sergeant froze and the site flickered and buzzed some more. Eventually, the program ran my story through all its analysis levels and produced the relevant response.

'Well now, youngsters, I want you to know you have done entirely the right thing in coming to the police with this.

Fortunately, you have nothing to worry about. Lights that appear over marshy areas are called will-o'-the-wisps.'

'We *know*—' Bayliss began in exasperation.

'They are completely natural and harmless,' the sergeant continued impassively. 'If you require more information to reassure yourselves, please access an educational site and ask for the appropriate file.'

'You mean you're not going to do anything?' Katie asked.

'There is no need to inform my superiors. Thank you for coming to see me. And if you see anything unusual in future, please don't hesitate to report it.'

'Does a landing by the scout force of an alien invasion fleet count as unusual?' Selim grumbled.

The site flickered alarmingly as the program started to process what he said.

'Come on,' I said. We spun out.

'I have never accessed such a worthless program,' Bayliss protested. 'Never! We have a legitimate cause for concern, and it won't even advance us to a genuine detective. What kind of law and order do you have in your country, Aynsley?'

'Good, usually,' I said meekly. 'The police are rather short of money, as always. They can't upgrade every program. If I'd seen a murder the phace would have brought a real detective on line for us.'

'Perhaps we should tell it that,' Drunlo said. 'Then you could explain to the detective what the real problem is.'

'Er . . . I think there are some rather stiff penalties for supplying false data to police programs. Lots worse than getting spidered off.'

'So, now what?' Katie asked.

'Aynsley could always phone the police station in King's Lynn directly and try and talk to a real officer,' Selim suggested.

'The phone computer has a reception and filter program, too,' I said. 'It's even less sophisticated than the Heacham site.'

'There is one other approach we could try,' Bayliss said.

'Contact someone who's far more concerned about the marsh and what's happening to it than the police.'

The bat lasted longer than normal when I spun into Bigene Industrie's site. They didn't want to let my avatar in. They had a human-form only law which was even stricter than Tropicana's, but my Equal Access Program overrode it.

We emerged on a small grassy park that surrounded a fifty-storey skyscraper built out of silver glass and black marble. One of thousands of skyscrapers in a city that was a merger between real New York and a science fiction pulp magazine metropolis. I half expected to see atomic powered aircars whizzing about overhead, but the International Trade Block is too conservative for that. Each of those gleaming towers represents the sum total of a company's processing and memory capacity. The bigger the skyscraper the bigger the company. There weren't many taller than Bigene Industrie's.

The five of us went into the reception lobby. It looked like a cathedral inside; only instead of stained glass the arching windows were displaying company projects. I saw pictures of the Olympus mission, medical stuff, funny-looking plants, even a satellite's view of the mats in The Wash.

'Can I help you?' the receptionist asked with a friendly smile. This phace was generations of upgrades ahead of the police sergeant. He was laughable, she was a bit . . . intimidating, I suppose. She outshone Rebecca Ryan effortlessly in the beauty stakes, and she was wearing this autumn's Paris fashions.

'I'd like to report some fires,' I said.

Something really odd happened while I blundered through my explanation. The phace got better. All right, I'm not a Web graphics expert, but I've been in enough sites in my time to know the score. The gamer and leisure companies go all out to perfect realism, they have to if they want to attract people into their sites. Other than that, sites use commercially available cog image generating programs. Their quality depends on how much processing capacity the operator wants to spend their money on; or, in the case of police and other civil service departments, how much they've been budgeted.

By the time I'd finished describing the lightstorms, the receptionist was more substantial than half the Realworld people I know. Luscious thick hair with every strand groomed into place, every crease and fold on her suit crisply defined, and rustling as she moved. There were even pores on her skin. I saw a ring on her left index finger, a big red stone on a plain gold band. I couldn't remember that being there when we spun in.

'There's nothing to worry about,' she said sweetly. Even her voice was different, becoming very authoritative, yet at the same time reassuring. 'Wild fires are nature's way of restoring the land, and regenerating the local ecology.'

'There were dead birds,' I told her. 'I saw them. They'd been caught in the flame. That whole marsh is a nature reserve, there must be thousands of birds and animals sheltering there. If these wild fires keep happening won't they be in danger?'

'With this year's low rainfall, I'm afraid such outbreaks are inevitable. It might seem a harsh method of clearing dead vegetation, but it is actually good for the marsh in the long run. If you examine the scorched areas in the spring you will find them thriving with new and vigorous shoots. Ultimately, that increases the food supply for local wildlife, allowing the marsh to sustain an even larger number of animals and birds.'

'Oh.'

'Rest assured, our teams will already be monitoring the situation. If the outbreak of wild fires ever appears to be presenting any kind of hazard then steps will be taken. However, as we're now well into autumn, it's safe to say that the worst is already over. If you would like, I can provide you with a Bigene Industrie ecology information pack. It would give you a better understanding of how regenerated habitats are managed. Our experience is unrivalled in this area. The Wash coastline is only one of our successes. We are involved in many regional improvement schemes all over the world.'

'That's very kind,' Bayliss said quickly. 'But we just wanted to make sure that there wasn't anything wrong with the marsh.'

'I hope I have been of some assistance.'

'You have,' he said brightly. 'Come on, guys, time we spun out.'

'So what do you think?' Katie asked when we spun back to the Tropicana.

'I think we're on to something,' Bayliss said.

'You saw the way the receptionist phace changed?' I enquired.

'I saw it. Bigene Industrie must have tripled the processing power they were using to generate her.'

'But why?' Drunlo asked.

'To make her convincing,' I said. 'And I don't just mean making sure we couldn't see the gaps between her pixels. She was way too silky; we were being spidered off. They wanted that explanation to convince us. All that bitslag about outbreaks of wild fire being perfectly natural. What do they think we are? One-mips!'

'They were definitely trying to bluff us over the lightstorms,' Bayliss said. 'But that still doesn't tell us what's causing them, or what they actually are.'

'Perhaps if we went back to the police,' Katie said. 'Tell them that the company is hiding something out there.'

'We can't prove it, though,' Selim said. 'We all know that they upgraded the phace, and why, but that's hardly evidence.'

'How can we force them to admit it?' Katie asked. 'Could we go to an environmental group like Greenpeace?'

'They'll say the same thing as the police,' Bayliss said. 'We don't have any evidence. And they can't go around spamming the Web with allegations about Bigene Industrie. We need a lot more information.'

'What about a court case?' Drunlo asked. 'Force the company to hand over its files on the marsh to us.'

'Do you have the money for that?' Katie asked. 'I certainly don't. In any case, it would take ten years.'

'There may be a way to get the right information out of Bigene Industrie,' I said.

'*How*?' they chorused.

'I don't know about the actual method. But I know someone who does.' It was time to pay Uncle Elton a visit. One of him, anyway.

CHAPTER FOUR

A TRIP TO THE LIBRARY

I wasn't supposed to be doing this. Heavens, I'm not even supposed to know about it.

Dad was in his office, busy saving industry from government. Mum wasn't back. Edwyn was wearing his gag.

I sneaked into the kitchen, which Mum uses as her cocoon. Her computer tower was standing at the end of the worktop, along with a laser printer, gag set, keyboard, and 3-D screen. I switched it on and plugged my Websuit in.

The bat left me standing on a giant chessboard of blue and green squares two metres across. Translucent pink cubes, a metre high, were sitting on some of the squares. The whole arrangement resembled a miniature, and very crude, version of Webtown's first level. Each of the cubes was a file in the computer's memory, names and numbers floated inside them like tiny neon signs.

'Uncle Elton?' I called. 'It's me, Aynsley.'

He popped up from behind one of the cubes, looking round furtively. 'Aynsley, nice to see you, lad. Humm. It's been fifty days since your last visit.'

'I didn't know I was supposed to come more regularly.'

'You're not. We're all free agents.'

'Right.' I think Uncle Elton had absorbed a lot more of Grandpa's ideology than Mum ever did.

He sat on one of the cubes and took up the classic 'thinker' pose, one fist tucked under his chin. 'Sit down, lad. How's things outside? Those kids from the other bungalows still giving you a hard time?'

He's a phace, of course, a very good one. The police came to our house when he (the real Uncle Elton, that is) was arrested, searching for his memory files. They didn't find any. I still don't know how he and Mum hid them from police knowbots; my computer memory was nearly scrambled after they'd spun in and browsed. I never realized how strong sibling loyalty could get; I doubt I'd ever do Edwyn a favour like this, and I *know* he wouldn't do it for me.

I glided over to Uncle Elton and perched on the next cube. 'It's not so bad at the moment.'

'Ah, that's the bonus of growing old. Some things get easier, while life itself becomes more complicated.'

'I've got a problem, Uncle Elton. I need someone who knows a lot about the Web to help me.'

'Aynsley, I love you dearly; but your mother would wipe every megabyte of me from her tower if I got you involved in anything disreputable.'

'Too late for that. There's a company that my friends and I think is trying to cover up something funny out in the marsh. I need to know how to get into its files.'

'A corporate conspiracy, you say? How intriguing. I thought mad billionaires trying to take over the world ended when they stopped making James Bond films. Tell me more.'

'Why are we here?' Katie asked after we spun in.

I glanced round. The British Library site had the same kind of dimensions as a cathedral. Its walls were made up from bookshelves of ancient, polished oak; with seven wide balconies on each side running down the entire length. There must have been millions of books up there, everything from national records to current fiction; the library had an on-line copy of almost anything published in England during the last five centuries. A regiment of reading tables took up most of the central aisle; with people studying huge tomes, their faces illuminated by images scurrying across the paper. A crisscross of delicate bridges spanned the gap over-head, linking together the various balconies.

'Because it's old, Katie. The library has been on-line for decades in various forms; it's had hundreds of upgrades and augmentations. They just keep adding and adding to it, and now nobody quite knows what's in it any more. Uncle Elton says there are chunks of hardware that date back to the early nineties still operating here.'

'How does that help us?' Selim asked.

'It's got a vast amount of memory which is hardly ever accessed, and certainly never checked. That means it acts like a magnet for certain things.'

'Such as?'

'Programs that Uncle Elton says can be useful to us. Now, I want you all to split up and start browsing the bookshelves. I don't want a file, you're looking for holes in the shelving fabric itself. As soon as you find one, let me know.'

'What sort of holes?'

'One that doesn't belong. It'll look like it's been chewed out, OK?'

They all drifted away from me, except for Drunlo.

'You're trying to find a cyberat, aren't you?' he demanded. His voice and expression showed how unhappy he was with the idea.

'That's right. I need one.'

Cyberats are old viruses that have *evolved* in the Web. The experts, programmers and lawyers, haven't made up their minds whether they're alive, but they're certainly self-governing, and smart in their own way. They hunt down sections of spare memory where they can live/store them-selves without whoever owns the hardware knowing about it. There was even a case earlier in the year when some kind of viruses interfaced with phaces in the GulliverZone to produce self-aware programs, what people called digital life. The UN Court of Human Rights wound up granting them citizenship. Cyberats don't have quite that mips level, but their access and integration ability is formidable. Once one of them gets into your processor it's very difficult to wipe it.

'What are you going to do with it?' Drunlo asked.

'I want to store it in a hardblock memory, then take it to another site.'

'Are you going to try and alter its format?'

'No. I don't know how to, anyway.'

'All right,' he said, with obvious reluctance. 'I'll help you.'

'Thanks.' I didn't quite understand what the problem was. But he would help. Drunlo is very blunt in some things. I think he's one of the most honest people I've ever met. I suppose that's why I like him.

Bayliss found the hole. We gathered round the shelf on the third balcony where the wooden surface had a chunk missing. It was on the upright section at the end of the shelf, just beside the eight volumes of Neil Kinnock's biography. A circle of wood ten centimetres across simply didn't exist any more, there was only an infinite black cavity.

'Where does it go?' Selim asked.

I tapped the thick leather-bound books. 'Probably into their storage space. The cyberat should be safe in there; this hole is just its access portal.'

'A cyberat! Is this a bad bite, Aynsley?'

'No, sorry. This is for real.'

'But they're dangerous. It could get back into our computers, we'd lose everything.'

'That's a myth. Cyberats aren't interested in home systems; we power down too often. They want permanent on-line sites. That's why they move around so much, so they don't get trapped by a systems check.'

He grunted. Obviously not convinced.

'Keep watching,' I told them. 'Make sure no one is looking at us.' I closed my eyes, cutting myself off from the sight of the library. That made it easier for me to concentrate on the Websuit's keyboard. I tapped in the function I wanted. It had taken me over two hours to assemble the hardblock stack and interface it with my tower the way Uncle Elton had told me.

When I opened my eyes, I was holding a small cube in the claws on the end of my wing. It glowed a radioactive blue. If I looked closely at it, I could make out narrow black grid lines just under the surface, they curved back towards the centre, forming a funnel that stretched backwards for ever. Every surface had the same effect; it was as though the inside of the cube contained an entire universe.

I put it on the bookshelf, right up against the hole.

'What is that thing?' Bayliss asked.

'A rat trap. To the cyberat, it'll seem as though the cube contains a huge empty storage space. It won't be able to resist that. Then when it goes in—'

'Snap!' Katie said loudly. She brought her hands together, and grinned. 'We got it.'

'That's right.'

'What exactly does this uncle of yours do?' Bayliss asked. 'I wouldn't know how to put together a storage space trick like that.'

'He was a consultant for a multimedia company.'

'Was?'

'He took early retirement.' One thing Websuits can't do even on realoe mode is replicate the way your skin changes colour when it heats up. I was mighty glad about that. I could feel a heavy blush rising up my cheeks.

'There!' Katie squealed, pointing excitedly.

I glanced over at the shelf. Even on Webtime, I was almost not quick enough.

The cyberat darted across the gap between its portal hole and the glowing blue cube. According to Web-myth, there are hundreds of different types. They don't breed, exactly, although they constantly duplicate themselves; but they do exchange sub-routines to keep mutating and stay one step ahead of systems check programs.

This one looked as though an ordinary rat had been remodelled by an aerospace design team, turning it missile-sleek and silver grey. The thing was amazingly *fast*.

A miniature portcullis slammed down across the cube's surface, then it turned green and let out a contented bleep. I picked it up. 'Time to visit Bigene Industrie again.'

CHAPTER FIVE

WHO SAYS SPIDERS CAN'T FLY?

The spotless Bigene Industrie building loomed up in front of us like some giant shiny gravestone. Possibly mine, if things went down the plug.

'You sure about this?' Selim asked nervously.

Funny the one with doubts should be him, the most headstrong of all of us.

'Not really,' I said. 'But I'm going to give it a go.'

'Good luck,' Katie said. She rubbed the top of my head; which I suppose was the equivalent of a hug.

'You all know what to do?'

'Yes,' they chorused.

'We'll each start asking the receptionist phace for information,' Bayliss recited, determined to get it right. 'We can say that it's research for school projects; companies are always silky about public relations so the site will be programmed to help as much as it can. It won't tie up much processing capacity, but every little helps.'

'Too right,' I agreed. I spread my wings wide and launched myself into the sky. When I looked down I could see the others hurrying to the skyscraper's entrance. Large blue-grey spiders were creeping in over the edge of the small park, heading for the spot where we'd spun in. They must have detected a program format violation when I took off. I watched them converge then start circling round looking for the guilty party. Bayliss and the others vanished into the building. I raised my head and flapped upwards enthusiastically.

It took me about a minute to reach the roof. By that time the spiders down on the park were so small I could barely see them. The roof was just a blank ochre rectangle, without a single feature. I landed in the middle, and glanced round cautiously. No spiders in sight up here.

'The one thing you must not allow to happen,' Uncle Elton had warned me sternly, 'is to let a spider touch you. The Web allows every user complete anonymity, and ordinarily you cannot be traced. But if one of Bigene Industrie's guardian spiders attaches itself to you, they'll be able to check out where the avatar is interfacing with the Web. They'll know who you are, and probably a lot more than that. You wouldn't believe how much personal information is stored in memory banks these days.'

I held out the green rat trap in my left claw, and used my right hand to tap out the release code on my Websuit pad. The cube's surfaces flashed blue for a second, and the cyberat shot out. It crouched on the roof, giving me a terrible stare with glinting scarlet eyes, then it was running backwards and forwards, its nose pressed against the smooth ochre.

The wretched thing must have taken about ninety seconds to find a weak spot in the site's texture. It felt like ninety hours. Uncle Elton told me cyberats hated being exposed: the first thing it would do after it was released was find a part of the site program where it could conceal itself. It stopped abruptly, and virtually head-butted the roof. I couldn't see any difference between the part it had chosen and any other. Jaws like small JCB scoop clamps began to chew at the ochre surface.

I spread my wings wide, took a couple of paces, and launched myself, gliding slowly towards the cyberat as it disappeared down the hole it was gnawing. My fingers tapping furiously on the Websuit pad, changing the avatar's scale. Another appalling breach of Web etiquette. I shrank as I flew, which made the distance to the cyberat's hole grow larger and larger the whole time. I've never come so close to the voms before, swooping forward at the same time I was receding. Confusing, or what? The whole site world was getting bigger; the rooftop was at least the size of a continent. When the alteration finished I was actually smaller then the cyberat. The hole was like an empty black crater ahead of me. I didn't like to think what the cyberat would do to my diminished Websuit programs if we bumped into each other now. Uncle Elton had just shrugged rather apologetically when I asked him.

Something moved out by the edge of the roof. An Everest-size volcano erupting up over the horizon. Then another one appeared, bending in the middle. Spider legs! Titan-sized spider legs. It must have climbed up the side of the sky-scraper. Two more groped their way over the edge, and all four tensed, starting to lever the body up. It would be as big as a moon!

I didn't wait to check. Head to head with the cyberat would be like meeting an angel compared to that. I dived down into the hole.

Another city of skyscrapers waited for me inside. I plummeted out of a tiny black gap in the solid sky, tumbling completely out of control. It took me ages to steady myself, twisting my wing tips to oppose the spin, slowing and levelling out. I was already perilously close to the tops of the skyscrapers before I was flying horizontally again. But I was in! I could hardly believe I'd done it. Uncle Elton was a genius.

I tapped out the code to expand my avatar scale again. This city was different to the one outside. For a start, I could see the walls, cold steel-grey squares stacked like bricks. The odd thing was, the space inside the Bigene Industrie building was much bigger than it appeared from outside. Or maybe I just hadn't got the scale right. The other thing was, the sky-scrapers inside weren't skyscapers at all; they were old-fashioned metal filing cabinets. Twenty-four of them. Each one had a white letter on the roof.

'Just pray,' Uncle Elton had told me, 'that they use ordinary names to label their files.'

I was gliding over T, heading towards S. What I wanted was H, for Heacham.

'Or maybe W for The Wash,' Uncle Elton had mused. 'Perhaps M for marsh. Then again, it could even be under R for reclamation, and you'll have to start cross referencing.'

I banked steeply, almost tilting my outstretched wings to the vertical, and turned hard around R before righting myself. H was dead ahead now, three cabinets away.

Spiders were running along the road below. Dozens of them, easily my size, with green and yellow skin patterned the same as a tiger.

So far, none of them were looking up, but it would only be a matter of time. I needed a diversion, and fast. H was one cabinet in front now. I turned quickly, swooping round M and heading for N. The rat trap was still held in my left claw. It flashed blue as I tapped in the release code again. A cyberat dropped out, and plummeted down on to the road.

You see, the hardblock contained a permanent record of the cyberat; it could churn out as many copies as I wanted. I flew between the cabinets, dropping cyberats as I went, the rat trap cube strobing like some kind of police-car light. They landed on the road and immediately raced for the base of the nearest cabinet, sensing the colossal amount of memory contained inside. I must have let thirty or forty fall before I turned back.

The spiders went berserk. They came charging down every road towards the cyberats, chasing them round the cabinets in dizzy circles. One on one, they were evenly matched, producing a fight which was gory without any actual blood. The spiders tried to gobble up the cyberats; while the cyberats bit off spider legs with their spring-trap jaws. I saw several spiders reduced to immobile bodies with heads flexing round helplessly. After a while, such casualties would simply fade out of existence. New spiders were still running in towards the conflict, outnumbering the cyberats quite heavily now. They were going to win eventually.

I reached the H filing cabinet. There were no spiders anywhere near its base. The front of the filing cabinet was made up of drawers, fifteen of them. They were all labelled, starting with Ha-Hc on the top, then Hd-Hf, and so on down to the ground. The top corner of each one had a small nine pad keyboard.

Theoretically, anything to do with Heacham should have been in the second drawer, Hd-Hf. I glided in as near as I could to take a closer look. The keyboard protruded from the drawer by about twenty-five centimetres. Just big enough. I spiralled round and made another pass. This time I held out the rat trap and entered the release code. A cyberat popped out on to the narrow ledge formed by the top of the keyboard. It gave me its usual red-eyed glare, then looked from side to side. I suppose it must have known how close to the memory space it was, and the only thing blocking it from access was the entry code. I watched as it stretched itself tentatively over the edge of the ledge to study the keyboard pads.

That was when I saw a spider creeping its way up the cabinet, its legs moving in purposeful judders. I dived down the front of the drawers, heading for the spider like a jet fighter. It stopped its climb, the front two legs waggling in agitation. The rat trap was disgorging a torrent of cyberats which fell straight towards it. Five of them thumped straight into it. They immediately started snapping and chewing at its striped flanks. It lost its grip, and they all crashed down on to the road together.

Three more spiders had arrived by the time it hit. Two of them began chasing the sinuous cyberats as they sprinted for cover, while the third stayed put, watching me. I didn't like that at all. They'd obviously worked out that I was the cause of all the trouble.

I began a complete circuit of the cabinet. The spider scurried along underneath me, matching my movements perfectly. Cyberats were falling like rain all around it, but it never diverged a centimeter. Of course, as it didn't threaten them, they ignored it.

There was a full scale battle between cyberats and spiders going on by the time I got back to the front of the cabinet.

This time the cyberats were in serious trouble; their jaws no longer had any effect against the spiders. No matter how fast or agile they were, they couldn't avoid the even faster mandibles that snatched them up, drew them backwards into gaping empty mouths and swallowed them up.

The spiders had learned and adapted. I was getting a real bad feeling about this. The only advantage I had left now was speed. My thumb located the Websuit's scuttle button, and rested on it lightly. Just in case.

I pumped my wings hard, desperate for altitude and as much distance from that horribly knowledgeable spider as I could get. Up above me, I could see the cyberat I'd left on the keyboard. It was hanging dangerously over the edge, using its forepaws to tap in a code on the numbered pads. Drawer Hd-Hf began to slide out from the cabinet. I'd done it! That spider would never climb all the way up here in time.

I soared up over the top of the open drawer just as the cyerat dived inside. It was full of slim folders packed together tight enough to form a solid floor, there must have been a thousand of them. They began to ripple slightly, like the surface of a lake with a big fish swimming just underneath. The ripples began to fan out, producing a V-shaped wake. It must have been the cyberat moving through them, heading deeper into the cabinet.

I glanced down to check on the spider that had been following me. That was when I saw *it*. A spider floating in the air between the cabinets, heading straight for me! Impossible. Then I glimpsed a tiny line of shimmering silver light stretching out from its abdomen right away up towards the roof. It was gossamer riding. Spiders do that in Realworld, hanging on to long lengths of their own thread, and letting the wind take them wherever it blows. If a thermal takes them high enough they can sometimes drift across seas.

It would get to the drawer long before I'd have a chance to find the Heacham file. I had no doubt it would be one of the new ones, immune to a cyberat. The scuttle button seemed to itch against my thumb.

I'd come so far, it didn't seem fair to lose now. Uncle Elton wouldn't be defeated by the brute, I was sure of that. He'd find a weakness to exploit. Pity I wasn't Uncle Elton.

I studied it again, desperate for some sign of vulnerability. My only weapon was the cyberat, and that wasn't any good against the spiders any more. So – I yelped in delight and launched myself straight towards it. The spider kept coming, imperturbably; its legs flexed eagerly, as if it were beckoning to me. I pitched up sharply, zooming for the sky. The gossamer strand was rushing past my nose. I was ten metres above the spider when I pivoted over, twisting through ninety degrees. As soon as I was at the top of the arc, I pressed the release code, and a cyberat was expelled from the rat trap.

All that time spent in combat sites had obviously paid off as far as my reflexes were concerned. OK, maybe there was some luck involved, too. But the cyberat shot straight into the gossamer. I held my breath.

The cyberat clung to the slender strand. For once it didn't glare at me. Too surprised at where it was, I expect. Its head came forward, metallic nose sniffing at the gossamer, then it bit through cleanly. The spider hurtled straight down.

I turned again and sped back to the open drawer. There was no mysterious wake left on the folders, no sign of the cyberat. I landed on the first file and ran forwards. Names skidded past under my clawed feet.

HEACHAM

I halted and went back a couple of paces. The top of the folder was about as wide as a floorboard. There were various symbols on either side of the name. I pressed *enter*, a circle with a vertical line bisecting it. The folder began to rise up. It was as if an ancient 2-D cinema screen was unfurling in front of me, and I had the only seat in the house.

I typed in the record code on my Websuit keyboard. The folder stopped rising when it was eight metres high. Text and wavy lines began to scroll down it.

Out of the corner of my eye I saw five more gossamer riding spiders sweeping towards the drawer. I stayed where I was for as long as I dared, watching the contents of the Heacham folder roll past in front of me. Then the spiders landed on the drawer. They darted forward, legs moving so fast they were a blur.

I pressed the scuttle.

The bat was sharp and nasty, too much like the unwanted jolt on a fairground ride that's gone wrong when you're at the highest point. I tried to calm my breathing when all the collapsing images stabilized into the neutral grey of an inactive Websuit visor.

My mind should have been bubbling over with elation. Instead, all I could feel was an awful depression. I'd read the text in the Heacham file as it scrolled past; or tried to. It wasn't in English. It wasn't in any language at all. It was just letters jumbled together at random. Utter rubbish.

CHAPTER SIX

THE PLOT THINS

'Of course it's rubbish,' Uncle Elton said in that scathing tone reserved for people who have been particularly daft. 'Everyone knows how easy it is to break into files these days.'

'*Easy?*'

'You did it and you're only . . . er, how old are you now?'

'Mid-teens.'

'Exactly my point, lad. Mid-teens, and never spun an illegal bite in your life before; yet you waltzed straight in and helped yourself.'

'It wasn't quite a waltz, Uncle Elton.'

'Whatever. Security around the files is only the first line of defence, it can't be too strict because the company's own staff have to be able to access their data constantly. Think what Bigene Industrie keeps in those cabinets. All its finances, new bugs they've developed and haven't grown commercially yet, research data, marketing strategies, not to mention all the dubious goings on in the marshes. All immensely valuable in the wrong hands, which is very definitely you and I. So they simply encrypt the information they store.'

'Oh.' It made me feel a little better. Not much. Encryption was pretty obvious when you think about it.

'Let me have a look at what you got,' he said.

We were sitting on the pink cubes in Mum's computer again. I keyed in the recording I'd made, and the Heacham file appeared inside a d-box which hung in midair in front of us.

'All right, Aynsley, this is where it starts to get tricky.'

'Can you decrypt it for me?'

'Do cows leave pats behind them? I have a few tricks of the trade stored around here somewhere.' He walked over to one of the cubes and pulled a white cable from it with a complicated-looking socket on the end. The cable kept uncoiling behind him as he walked over to the d-box. He bent down and plugged the socket into the base of the d-box. 'Now, let's see how good I really am,' he said quietly.

Up on the screen, the jumbled letters were rearranging themselves into proper words. Wiggly lines straightened out into diagrams.

I start to read.

We found a table some distance from the others on the Tropicana beach. I set up a d-box on the sun-bleached wood, and keyed the code for Bigene Industrie's Heacham file. The d-box swam with colourful refraction patterns, then the text solidified. CLASSIFIED was printed boldly across the title page.

'What did we get?' Selim asked eagerly.

I could have said something about how it had suddenly become *we*. But Selim was Selim and, besides, having their complete support made me feel pretty good.

'The answer, I think,' I said.

'Great!'

'Tell us then. What are the lightstorms?' Bayliss asked.

I couldn't resist it. 'Will-o'-the-wisps.'

They all groaned.

'You're biting,' Katie exclaimed.

'No I'm not. It's just that these ones aren't exactly natural.' I scrolled the decrypted file until I came to the map of the marsh. It looked as if the land was coming out in a rash. Red blotches were dotted everywhere, some big, some small, there was no order to their size or location, it was completely random. The index called them *Dump Zones*.

'When the company was doing all that work reclaiming the marsh, they built a lot of new water channels and ponds,'

I said. 'They bulldozed a lot of soil about to make the banks, but they also brought in masses of landfill material as well. All perfectly legitimate, the EU Environmental officers approved the method. Some of the landfill was made up from old mats from The Wash. The EU people approved of that, too. The plastic is biodegradable, which means it can't spoil the earth it's buried in. The mats take quite a battering out on the sea and they have to be replaced every three or four years. The ones they used for the pilot scheme were starting to tear when the work on the marsh started, so everyone thought it would be a good thing to prove the old mats could be used beneficially. Bigene Industrie processed them with intense ultraviolet light to kill off the algae and make the plastic really brittle so it could decompose more easily. After that, the scraps were mixed with landfill and take out to the marsh.'

Bayliss clicked his fingers. 'They didn't process them,' he said.

'That's right. There was something in the file about the ultraviolet machine being delayed because of costs. So, rather than stall the whole project, they just mixed in the mats without treating them first. The algae was still alive when they buried it. And now the plastic is breaking down naturally, like it's supposed to, the algae is leaking out. Some of it is seeping into ponds, so when the sunlight shines, it's doing what it was designed to and splitting water into oxygen and hydrogen. Because it's such a light gas, most of the hydrogen disperses into the atmosphere, but quite a lot saturates the plants and dead vegetation. It's terribly volatile, the tiniest spark or static charge will ignite it. That's what I've been seeing, the hydrogen flaring off at night.'

'Aynsley, that is disgraceful,' Katie said. 'What a filthy way for the company to behave.'

'I know.' That was the part which worried me the most. Bigene Industrie had supplied the life support systems to the Olympus craft. The safety issue aside, I didn't want companies that cut corners and cheated to have any part of the Mars mission. It was too *grand* for that. Grandpa always said it was a complete waste of money. I didn't disagree with him on many things (didn't dare), but I did on this occasion. I think the Olympus mission is a truly noble venture. Most countries in the world have contributed to it; some more than others, naturally. But everyone's involved, helping to challenge the high frontier. And it's only today that it's so difficult and costs so much. In a hundred years time it won't be, purely because of the pioneering we're doing now. To me, that's wonderful. I know the world isn't perfect, but Olympus shows people what we can achieve as a race if we really try. It's not just the hardware, the ships and the landing craft; the spirit behind the venture is equally important.

Bigene Industrie tainted that spirit.

'Now we can go back to the police,' Drunlo said. 'We have all the proof we need.'

'What do you mean?' Bayliss asked, he sounded surprised and shocked.

'We know that Bigene Industrie has been trying to cover up a criminal act.' Drunlo pointed at my display sheet with the incriminating map. 'When we show that to the police, that one-mip phace sergeant will have to bring real detectives on-line.'

Bayliss put his head in his hands and moaned. 'Brilliant! And exactly what are you going to say to the police when they ask how we got the Heacham file from Bigene Industrie?'

Drunlo opened his mouth, then closed it. He scratched his forehead, tilting his brown felt cap to one side. 'I hadn't thought of that,' he finally admitted.

'This can't be a problem,' Katie said. 'Come on, guys, we face paradoxes and puzzles much worse than this in the games. There's got to be a way round it. Think! What's our objective?'

'To alert the police about Bigene Industrie, and have them investigated properly,' I said. 'I also want the marsh to be made safe. Heaven only knows how much algae is leaking into the water.'

'Fine. So we have to produce some kind of rock-solid

evidence other than the Heacham file to take to the police. Any ideas?'

'It will have to be the algae itself,' Bayliss said. 'A video of you collecting the sample would be useful, too.'

'Now wait a minute—'

'We know exactly where it is,' Selim said. His finger came down on one of the map's larger red blobs. 'You just have to go out there, scoop it up, and come back. What's the problem?'

'The problem! For a start most of the dump zones are inside the central fenced-off section of the marsh. The biggest one outside was the one I found; and that's already flared. I doubt there'll be much algae left. The flame killed everything else.'

'Then you'll have to go through the fence. You said it was only a chain link. A pair of bolt cutters will solve that. It'll be a doddle compared to accessing the files.'

'Really? Do you see that blue line that follows the fence on the inside?'

'Yes.'

'Look it up in the index.'

They all leaned over the data sheet.

'Guard dog run,' Bayliss read out. 'Ah, yes. That could be awkward.'

'What kind of weapons have you got?' Selim asked.

'Weapons? This isn't a gamer site we're studying! I don't pick up laser pistols and a bazooka when I spin in. There aren't power packs and jeeps and medical supplies left along the path that I can help myself to. This is Realworld we're talking about, Selim.'

'Ever heard of a sonic jet?'

'Yes, my neighbour has—' I jammed my mouth shut. Too late!

'Next problem,' Selim hooted.

'Simple,' I growled right back. 'We've just broken into Bigene Industrie's files. They know someone's interested in the marsh. They'll be watching.'

'He's right,' Katie said.

'Then what we need is a time when they're not watching,' Bayliss said.

'It's their job, and they've been warned about a possible intrusion, they'll be watching the whole time.'

'Not necessarily. You're not taking human nature into consideration. What happens tomorrow night? November 15th, at twenty-one-hundred-hours to be precise.'

'The Mars landing.'

'Exactly. And everyone in the world who's on-line is going to spin in to the Olympus site so they can access Colonel McFarlane's jockey chip when he takes that step off the landing craft. The marsh security people included.'

'And me, too,' I said hotly. No way, absolutely no way on Earth was I going to miss the landing. Not me. I have lived and breathed the Olympus mission for the last three years.

'So give me another time,' Bayliss said.

Which must have been a rhetorical question, because anyone with his brains would know there wasn't an answer.

'In any case,' I said. 'That's in the middle of the night. I'm not creeping into the marshes by myself at night.'

'Of course not,' Katie said. 'We'll all be with you.'

'I don't think I can get all the way to England by then,' Drunlo said hastily.

She laughed. 'Not that way, not be there in Realworld. Aynsley can just switch his Websuit to provider mode.'

'Now just a—'

'Good idea,' Bayliss said. 'A portable terminal will be able to keep in touch with the low orbit communication satellite network the whole time. With them hooked in, they can triangulate your position and provide a navigation function. I've got the software in my portable if you haven't got a copy, Aynsley. You'll be able to walk straight to the dump zone with your eyes closed.'

'I'm not going.'

'What else is he going to need?' Selim asked.

'I'm not going.'

They all stared at me.

'I'm not.'

CHAPTER SEVEN

THE MISSION PROFILE

Mars isn't a uniform all-over red like it appears from Earth. There are dark mountain ranges, plateaux, craters, polar caps, dry 'sea' beds. Hundreds of diverse, fascinating features. All visible with the naked eye from a thousand kilometre orbit.

I was looking down at the planet from the observation bubble in Olympus II, the *Eagle*. The other two Olympus ships were invisible, lost somewhere out among the empty blackness and strangely bright stars. In space, the stars don't twinkle. Only tens of kilometres of dusty, cloudy atmosphere makes them do that. Somehow, they look colder when they're burning steadily.

It's a weird sensation being completely passive, and yet feeling your body respond like a puppet to every move made by a total stranger. Receiver mode is one of the hardest Websuit functions to use. You have to really struggle against the urge to counter every motion, and just allow yourself to accept the ride you're getting.

That's what I did as I drifted forwards. My hand snatched up a carelessly discarded chocolate foil wrapper that was fluttering against the transparent bubble like a bizarre metallic bird. From my new position I could see along the side of the ship's cylindrical habitation module.

'Aynsley.'

The shell was a pale silver-white. A thick layer of thermal insulation foam coating the aluminium pressure vessel.

Fifteen metres away, the landing craft was docked to the forward airlock.

'Aynsley, come on.'

It was a long aerodynamic cone with stubby triangular fins jutting out of the base, just above its heatshield. The landing pads were extended for testing, silvery insect-legs that seemed implausibly thin for the job they had to do. Somebody moved behind the tiny cockpit port.

'Aynsley, what are you doing in there?'

Mars quaked in front of me, its edges shivering.

I spun out back to my cocoon and flipped the Websuit visor up.

Mum was standing in front of me, her hand on my shoulder shaking me gently. Her face was full of sympathetic concern. 'Sorry, but you did say you wanted to go into King's Lynn this morning.'

'Yes, Mum.' I started to tug the suit off.

'What site were you in?'

'Olympus. They're going through the final checklists for the landing craft.' There is always one crew member in one of the three ships who is wearing a Websuit in provider mode. I've spun in more times than I can remember since they left Earth back in February. Freefall feels venomous, and on top of that I know exactly what it's like being a Realworld astronaut. No game.

'Aynsley, you will try and remember you have a life outside the Web.'

'Yes, Mum.'

She smiled softly. 'I know, I'm a sad old six cog.'

I do wish she wouldn't try to talk like that. 'You're not.'

'I know how wrapped up you are with the Mars landing, and I understand that, which is why I haven't objected yet.'

'To what?'

'The amount of time you spend accessing it. Mrs Lloyd spoke to me about it last week. Your grades are down, which is really unlike you. And she says you're becoming even more awkward at the physical fitness tutorials.'

'I'm not; I just think they're stupid, that's all.' Once a week

I have to go into King's Lynn to be coached at dumb sports which I hate and am never going to be any good at. It's the last remnant of the days when kids went to school in Realworld instead of using the Web to be educated like God intended. The government insists on keeping that aspect of the dark ages going, not just so we can all develop our talent to be Neanderthal football players or learn to be competitive (as if the Web games don't teach us that!) but so we can also develop our 'social interaction' skills. Social interaction, that is, with kids who have no common interest or even liking for each other, who treat anyone mildly different as an outcast, and take pleasure from doing so. You cannot find your peers out of a random selection of two hundred people; that only happens in the Web where like minds are drawn to the same sites. I rest my case.

'If you didn't take some exercise you'd inflate like a balloon, and be all podgy and horrible.'

'Who's going to care how I look in Realworld?'

I suppose it came out with more anger and bitterness than I mean. It certainly managed to hurt Mum, who sniffed hard and turned away to glance out of the window.

'I care,' she said quietly.

It must be awful for her to have a son she worries about the whole time, and who always says hurtful things to her. Maybe I don't think as fast as I claim I do, certainly not before I open my mouth.

'I know, Mum.' I smiled as an apology. She always says I never smile enough. 'I'll try not to be so awkward at the tutorials. But it's difficult with that Mrs Lloyd, you know? She's so . . . enthusiastic.'

Mum laughed. 'Hard on skivers, you mean.'

Our car is a modified Mercedes EQ-250, an eight-seater that looks like a cross between a small freight van and a taxi. Mum waited until I was inside, then closed the rear door.

Apart from the trunk routes, most of the roads in England are starting to decay. County councils keep them clear enough for bike traffic, but that's about all. The Mercedes had broad, deep-tread tyres to cope with the grass and moss that was slowly spreading over the tarmac.

Several kids watched as we drove down the line of bungalows. I was pretty prominent sitting up in the back, looking down on them like royalty. For once there were no gestures, no taunts. Not with Mum driving. It was like divine protection.

'What do you want to buy?' she asked when we turned on to the A 149.

'Just some stuff for one of my projects.' It wasn't a lie, exactly. In fact, I wanted a special sensor and some new cards for a stack to augment my portable terminal ready for my trip into the marsh. But I could hardly tell her that.

The car's motorgas cell accelerated us silently up to seventy kilometres per hour. There were only a couple of delivery lorries on the road, and four or five bikes, their riders wrapped up against the chilly November air.

'Mum, what was Uncle Elton put in jail for?'

She didn't look round, but I could see her hands tighten on the wheel. 'What makes you ask that?'

'I was thinking about him. He doesn't seem like a criminal; he's the same as Grandpa really.'

'All right, I suppose you're old enough. But you must not tell Edwyn.'

'I promise.'

'Uncle Elton isn't a criminal. He just doesn't think, that's all. I blame Dad, your grandpa. Elton was a little too gullible for all that rebel philosophy Dad spouts. Don't you ever fall for any of it!'

'No, Mum, I won't.'

'All right. Elton was listening to Dad rant on about the Establishment and how autocratic it is. He was young and hot-headed and decided that all that talk and moaning wasn't enough, he wanted to *do* something. Something which would knock the Brussels Parliament down a peg or two. Even I agreed with that; politicians are so pompous and stuffy. It doesn't hurt them to suffer a few indignities from time to time, show them that they aren't any better than the rest of us. As Elton worked for a multimedia company, it was easy enough. He set up a mock parliament site. Nothing illegal so far. But he went and loaded it into quite a few blocks he shouldn't have. I think the Tropicana was one of them. Even that wasn't so bad. His parliament's phace MPs were programmed to be satirical; they mocked and parodied everything their Realworld counterparts in Brussels said. But even that wasn't enough for Elton. Oh, no, he had them all sitting there stark naked.'

'*What*? All the MPs were nude?' I was giggling.

Mum was fighting a grin. 'Yes. He did exactly what he set out to do, and made them a laughing stock. His parliament was one of the most popular Web sites ever. Half of Europe spun in to see it. And when the real MPs started protesting about its existence, the phaces started complaining about *their* existence, claiming they were the true government. It all got quite surreal at the end.'

'And he got put in jail for that?'

'No. Not for satire. They got him on copyright violation. It's a famous law, at least to those of us who were in the media. Didn't you know, Aynsley, you own your own face? Nobody can reproduce your features without your permission. The law was intended to stop advertisers taking advantage of powerful simulation programs and duplicating a celebrity to endorse their products. But it applies to everyone. And Elton had replicated eight hundred MPs without their permission.'

'That's awful.'

'It's his own silly fault. The rule of law is paramount. If you break it, you are punished. That's a fundamental function of civilization; the law is there to protect us from other people behaving in a way that's likely to harm us. Some crimes are more serious than others, and there are degrees of criminal behaviour. Nothing in human behaviour is ever black and white, that's why we have the courts and judges, so they can determine exactly how bad the offence was and tailor the sentence to fit.'

'Do you think Uncle Elton should have been sent to jail?'

'Yes, but not for three years. Mind you, considering the people he annoyed, it was bound to happen.' She glanced at me in the rear-view mirror. 'Don't look so worried. He's only in an open prison, not a maximum security one. The news sites are always complaining that they're more like holiday camps.'

'Good.' It wasn't Uncle Elton I was worried about, it was me! Breaking into Bigene Industrie's files meant I was already a criminal. Although they could never complain, because what they had done was far worse. I suppose that's what Mum meant about the courts establishing degrees of guilt.

We'd all just rushed headlong into this without thinking much about the rights and wrongs of what we were doing. And, to be honest, because it produced a thrill which no game ever did. But Realworld does have rules. What I had to start thinking about very seriously indeed was whether we were doing the right thing by breaking them.

Not that it was such a big offence. All I was doing was sneaking into the marsh to find some algae. Environmentalists had been doing that kind of thing for decades, forcing polluters to clean up their act. But did that make it right?

I pulled my mobile phone out and tapped in Katie's number. Out of all of us, she was the most level headed. I could confide my worry to her and get a sensible answer.

'Sorry, Aynsley,' Mum called out. 'Your call will have to wait. I've got to fill the tanks.'

We were turning into a garage. Its old petrol pumps were still in place, standing like rusty sentries underneath the broad canopy. I suppose it cost too much to dismantle them. There was no other reason for leaving them. England's last petrol-powered vehicle was withdrawn two years ago; I remember the ceremony on the news sites.

Mum drew up next to the motorgas terminus.

I frowned, not understanding why she'd told me to stop using the phone. Then I saw the warning sign next to the terminus, forbidding smoking, mobile phones, and telling drivers to switch off their collision alert radars. Motorgas was volatile stuff, it could be ignited easily.

I switched the mobile phone off, and stowed it back in my coat pocket. Perhaps it was for the best. What could I have said to Katie anyway?

I was committed to going into the marsh. Thinking about it, I had been right back from when I saw the first lightstorm.

CHAPTER EIGHT

THE NIGHT OF THE GREAT EXPEDITION

Colonel McFarlane gave the crew in the *Eagle* one last wave before closing the airlock hatch. He wriggled his way through the landing craft's cramped interior and settled into his pilot's seat. Two big holographic screens on his console were swirling with multicoloured graphics and flashing icons. Rows and rows of switches were illuminated with a faint blue glow.

'Stand by to initiate separation sequence,' he said.

That was when I spun out. I couldn't stand it any longer. If I'd kept watching for another minute I know I would have stayed in the GSA site until the landing and first footfall itself.

The only noise in my cocoon was the usual liquid gurgling from the central heating. All the stuff I'd need for the marsh was spread out waiting; clothes on the bed, electronics and hardware on the desk. It was eight thirty, and the night outside the window was a gloomy dark grey. I sighed, and started to get ready.

My clothes were the trickiest; I'd never even tried wearing a coat over the Websuit before. After a couple of minutes' struggle I managed to wedge myself into it though it was an effort to move my arms. The first thing I noticed was how warm I'd become. I jammed the rest of my equipment into a shoulder bag, then plugged the Websuit into my portable terminal and checked the interface. Everything on-line.

I opened the door and peered out. There was no one

around. I started down the corridor. Edwyn's door was closed. Mum and Dad were in the lounge, sitting on the settee. Both of them were in their Websuits. Their computer display showed me they were accessing the GSA's Olympus site for the landing. They would never even know I'd gone outside, let alone what I was doing there.

I hurried into the kitchen, then down the ramp. Fancy being in a hurry to do this! But in the house I was going from uncomfortably warm to sweltering. The night soon halted that. A sharp frost had settled, making every blade of grass shine a gritty white in the moonlight. Out over The Wash navigation lights were twinkling on the mat anchors, looking like a city skyline in the distance.

Once I was clear of the front garden I stopped and lowered my Websuit visor. I flicked the switch on the keyboard to *Provider*. Surprisingly, it didn't have cobwebs all over it. I can't remember the last time I used the suit in this mode, probably in the shop before I bought it. The night crept back in to surround me, exactly the same as before, relayed through the Websuit's vision sensor. All the suits come with a camera ring around the hood, like a small black crown. It gives the wearer, and anyone else accessing the output, a three-hundred and sixty degree field of vision. Having eyes in the back of your head is nothing compared to this. There's even a focus shift function so that you can move your viewpoint away from yourself. That was going to come in real handy tonight; when the others spun in they could keep watch all around me.

I brought two more programs on-line. The first was a light amplifier, which was like turning a huge floodlight on above the bungalows. It turned the world a weird green, but meant I could see everything almost as clearly as I could in the daytime. There was a cat slinking along Mr Griffin's rickety fence, a fat ginger one pausing every couple of paces to glance round furtively. I clapped my hands, and it looked up abruptly, moving its head from side to side to try to see where the noise came from. I clapped my hands again. The cat looked back the way it had come, completely perplexed. I could see it, but it couldn't see me!

The second program automatically elevated my view-point by fifty centimetres. When I looked down at my own body, I appeared to be wearing a thick green oilskin and slightly faded denim jeans; I had sturdy hiking boots on my feet, and woolly red socks that came up almost to my knees. This particular program was something else I hadn't used since I got the Websuit, I prefer the bird-form avatar.

With everything on-line, I hooked my portable terminal into the Web, creating my own private micro-site around me. Bayliss, Katie, Selim, and Drunlo spun in. The terminal assigned each of them a different viewpoint from the camera ring, and their familiar avatars materialized. It appeared as if they were standing right beside me.

They looked round slowly, taking it all in.

'Are those the mats?' Katie asked, pointing at the con-stellation of lights gleaming offshore.

'That's their anchors you're seeing, yes. They're like iron pillars that are sunk real deep into the sand so they stay put. There's six of them for each mat, one at each corner.'

'And you live here, in this?' Drunlo asked. He was staring at the boat with his hands on his hips and his head cocked to one side.

'Yep.'

'That's *strange*, Aynsley.'

'Not really. Mum always says she's waiting for a really high tide, so we'll be swept out to sea. That way life will be more interesting, never knowing which country you're going to wash up on.'

His expression told me he thought that was even stranger than the house itself.

'Then this must be the marsh,' Bayliss said. He had walked a few paces away to stand on the track so he could face the darkest section of the horizon.

'That's right.'

'Come on then,' Selim said eagerly. 'What are we waiting for?'

I started off down the track. I checked once, just to see if the program was holding up. My boots were crunching through the frosty grass, even leaving footprints behind.

'Did you manage to get all the equipment we talked about?' Bayliss asked.

'Sure. But if that sonic jet doesn't work, then we're calling the whole thing off.'

'Of course.'

The marsh at night looked completely different. I could see the path easily enough, but the light amplifier changed the long grass and reeds to peculiar white fronds dancing about in the breeze. The navigation program was up and running in a d-box, showing me exactly where I was on the map. Without that I think I would have been lost within minutes.

Swaying reeds rose above my head, cutting off all sight of the bungalows and the mat anchor lights. The only sound I could hear was the *slosh* of low waves slapping across the beach.

I reached the fence exactly when the d-box said I should. Instead of being nervous, all I could think of was how Colonel McFarlane would have a similar guidance display on his console, helping him navigate down to his destination.

I stopped by one of the posts with a warning sign. There was some kind of rough track on the other side, leading deeper in. According to the map in the d-box it would take me right up to one of the largest dump zones.

'I can't see any dogs,' Selim said.

'They're here,' I told him. 'Hang on a moment.' I keyed in the sound program I'd formatted. The portable terminal's speaker started to whistle, its high musical pitch rising and falling. I could just imagine the cold air flexing to carry the sound out over the reed clumps and stagnant pools in broad ripples.

We didn't have to wait long after that. Two huge Alsatians came racing down the track towards me. They flung themselves against the fence and tried to climb up, their forelegs scrabbling at the mesh. Their angry barking and snarling drowned out the whistling from my terminal.

Funnily enough, it was the other four who took a pace backwards when the dogs appeared. I remained where I was and took aim with the sonic jet. When I pressed the trigger the little gadget shook in my hand. It's supposed to fire a beam of sound in one direction; but even behind it I winced at what sounded like a banshee shrieking. For a horrible moment I thought I was holding it the wrong way round, and shooting myself! The sound that battered my ears (and they were covered by my Websuit visor, don't forget) was nothing to the one that must have hit the dogs. Both of them jumped back from the fence as if it had suddenly become electrified. They scrabbled round in the muddy soil yapping and whining, then they righted themselves and sprinted away.

My finger fell from the trigger. I could hear the dogs crashing through the undergrowth and splashing about in the shallow pools. They were so desperate to get clear they hadn't even bothered with the track.

'Wow! Venomous or what?' Selim shouted.

'It works,' Katie said. She sounded astonished, but delighted at the same time. 'It actually works.'

'Well done, Aynsley,' Bayliss said. 'That was brilliant. You were so cool.'

I didn't point out that there was a chain link fence between me and the dogs. Their admiration was doing wonders to my self-confidence. We were actually winning, and in Realworld, too, where it *meant* something.

They were all looking at me, waiting for me to say what was happening next. It felt wonderful. 'Let's go,' I told them. I rummaged round in my shoulder bag for the wire clippers.

It was tough cutting through the fence. Grass and weeds had woven themselves into the bottom. I had to really crouch down low to reach the links along the ground. It wasn't easy with all the layers of clothing I had on. Once I'd snipped out a wide horizontal gash I came back to the middle and sliced straight up for nearly two metres. After that I had to fold the two sides back as if they were tent flaps. It wasn't a simple thing to do. The wire was stiff and fought against everything I did to it.

Eventually, I had what I thought was a suitable gap.

'You could drive a lorry through that gap!' Selim exclaimed. 'Come on Aynsley, we've wasted ages while you cut this.'

It was tempting to tell him to curl up, but I resisted. Completing the mission properly was all that mattered. I moved forward cautiously, feeling the spikes of fence wire bending underneath me as I crossed over. I nearly fell, but just managed to shift my body weight back as I started to tip.

The others walked straight through the fence like ghosts, except for Katie. She made sure she used the gap I'd cut, stooping down to miss the ragged edges and everything. Selim sighed and shook his head at her.

'Aynsley went to a lot of trouble, and he's taking all the risk. The least we can do is show some support,' she said.

'All right,' Selim said grudgingly. 'Sorry, Aynsley.'

'That's OK.'

Katie grinned at me, and rolled her eyes heavenward. I grinned right back.

Now I was through, the first thing I did was make sure the coordinates of the gap were loaded into the navigation program. That way I could always find it again. No way did I want to have to cut another one.

According to the map, the big dump zone was another hundred and fifty metres away. The little track which was a clean straight green line in the d-box was in reality nothing more than a strip of grass which was lower than the reeds that formed a wall on either side of it. I started off down it, but the going was hard. I couldn't move very quickly.

'Keep looking out for any more dogs,' I told the others. It took all of my concentration to pick out a route through the tangled grass. My right hand gripped the sonic jet tightly.

'Can't you go any faster?' Selim grumbled.

'Hey, stop hassling him,' Drunlo said. 'Take all the time you need, Aynsley. This is fascinating.'

'I wasn't complaining, just asking.'

'It sounded like you were complaining.'

'Well, I wasn't, and I'm sorry if Aynsley thought so. And, anyway, what do you mean, "it's fascinating"?'

'Just look at it.' Drunlo swept his arms round in an extravagant gesture; he was smiling broadly. 'It's real and it's wild. Don't you love it?'

'Love it? It's a horrid little marsh! I bet it smells, too.'

I had wanted them along to provide company and support. Because, let's face it, venturing out into a dangerous well-guarded marsh in the middle of the night is not something I would ever do alone. Of course, back when we were dreaming up this mad stunt I had thought they *would* be supportive and helpful rather than spend the entire time bickering. Funny how your imagination can never quite get a good picture of what Realworld will actually be like. Grandpa calls that human nature.

'Dog coming!' Bayliss shouted.

'*Where?*' Panic turned my voice to a squeak.

'Front left.'

I was firing the sonic jet even before I'd aimed it properly. The dog was running through the reeds at the side of the track, which probably saved me. With those rigid, frozen, stalks in its way, it couldn't go anything like as fast as it could over open ground. I could see the reed clumps whipping about as if a small hurricane was ploughing through them. Then the dog's head burst through the frosty blades lining the path. Its jaws were parted wide enough to swallow my head in one bite. Fangs as big as my fingers were dripping saliva.

All I could do was shove the sonic jet in the dog's direction, the way priests are supposed to use a crucifix to ward off vampires. Every muscle I owned had gone rigid from fright.

The dog howled as the blast of sound struck it. I could see the *anger* in its eyes. It shuddered from tip to tail, and crashed back into the reeds.

I was the one left shuddering then. I couldn't stop.

'It's gone, Aynsley,' Katie said. She was standing in front of me, looking anxiously at my face; one hand was resting on my shoulder. 'You're all right, you're safe.' Her fingers gave me a quick squeeze.

'It . . . it . . .' was all I could gasp.

Bayliss walked over to where the reeds had been flattened by the fleeing dog. 'I can't see it any more. I don't think that dog will stop before it reaches Wales.'

'What dog?' Selim asked. He was badly shaken. 'Did you see the size of it? That wasn't a dog, it was a sabre-toothed tiger!'

Drunlo nudged him, and frowned.

'Are you all right?' Katie asked.

'Yes.' I took a deep breath. 'Yes, I'm OK.'

'I couldn't have done that,' Bayliss said. 'Not in Realworld. I would have turned and tried to run. That was incredibly brave, Aynsley.'

'Thanks.'

'Listen,' Selim said. 'This isn't . . . Well, this trip isn't what I thought it was going to be like. If you want to turn round now, Aynsley, I'm going to be the one leading the way for you. Nobody's going to think you chickened out. Not after that dog. You could get badly hurt in here!'

The rest of them murmured their agreement.

It was tempting, I don't mind telling you. I checked the d-box. 'It's only seventy metres to the edge of the dump zone. That's too close after all we've done to get this far. I'm going to keep going. If another guard dog comes for me, then I'll probably turn round.' I faked up a smile. 'My nerves will probably be gone by then, anyway.'

'If that's what you want,' Katie said.

'Does the sonic jet have a power supply read-out?' Bayliss asked. He sounded very unhappy.

'Yes.'

'Perhaps you'd better check it. I don't know much about them, but I think they're supposed to be fired in short bursts.'

I looked at the little gadget. Its power cell was down to twenty-three per cent. I really shouldn't have fired it for so long at that last dog. 'Oh, hell.' I looked from the power read-out to the d-box. Twenty-three per cent and seventy metres to go. 'Let's be quick,' I said. I started moving forward again.

This time there was no talk or squabbling. They all kept close to me as if clustering round would offer some form of protection. Pity I was the only one who could see them. If they were visible to the rest of the world, and if they'd worn some of the avatar forms we'd used in games, the demons, and wizards, and monster aliens, then no dog would ever have come near me.

'What's that?' Drunlo asked.

I pointed the sonic jet automatically, but managed not to press the trigger this time. Drunlo was looking at a patch of grass about five metres away.

'I don't see anything,' I said.

'I thought there was something moving about behind the clumps.'

'Another guard dog?' Bayliss asked.

'I'm not sure. It was smaller, I think.'

I remembered when I'd thought I'd seen a Web spider lurking in the marsh. And that was in broad daylight. Heavens only knew what an over-active imagination would find among the moonlight shadows.

'Fire the sonic jet at it,' Katie said. 'Then we'll know for sure.'

'If I do that I'll have to turn round now, I can't afford to waste the power. Besides, if it was a guard dog it wouldn't be hiding. We've seen that. It's probably just a fox or a pheasant.'

We waited for another half a minute, but nothing moved.

'Keep watching it,' I told Drunlo as I went on again.

The reeds began to thin out as I approached the dump zone. I could hear a tiny stream trickling close by. Then the gas sensor began to bleep.

The sensor was one of the ideas Bayliss had had. I'd bought the unit from an electronics shop in King's Lynn. It's a standard commercial model which is mainly used in factories to warn the workers of any toxic fumes or gas leaks. Adapting it to detect hydrogen and methane was fairly simple. Bayliss and I found a technical site which showed us the auxiliary circuity and program we'd need to make it work. It only took ninety minutes to assemble the stack that it plugged into.

'Looks like we're here,' Bayliss said. He was studying the d-box which was displaying information from the gas sensor. 'There's not much hydrogen yet. Keep going forward Aynsley, let's see if it gets stronger.'

I held the sensor stack out in front of me, and looked ahead, I yelped in surprise. A woman was standing there looking at me.

CHAPTER NINE

SPIDERS IN THE MARSH

I suppose she was about the same age as Mum, I'm not very good at guessing adult ages. She was dressed in a dark suit with a high collar and gold buttons all the way up her front. It made her look terribly imperious, as if she were some kind of Grand Empress left over from the nineteenth century. A glimmer of green light shimmered off a ring she wore on her left index finger. Most memorable of all was her expression. Her contempt was far stronger then the guard dog's. She seemed to regard the world around her with utter disgust.

She vanished. Just that, and nothing more. She didn't walk away, she didn't crouch down in the reeds. She just vanished.

'Who was that?' Katie asked in a scared whisper.

'Where did she go?' Drunlo asked.

'Quiet!' I yelled. 'Did everyone see her?'

They all said yes.

'But we couldn't have done,' Bayliss said. 'Not *seen* her. She vanished faster than an avatar that has scuttled. That means she couldn't be real; actual people can't do that.'

'A ghost could,' Selim said.

He flinched as Katie and Bayliss glared at him.

'Sorry,' he said guiltily. 'It was just an idea.'

The trouble was, exactly the same idea had already popped up in my mind. With it came a cold sensation that crept inside my coat to prickle my skin. 'Ghosts aren't real,' I said. 'She was something else.' I think I was mostly trying to convince myself.

'Absolutely, she wasn't a ghost,' Katie said.

'So what is she?' Drunlo asked. 'And more importantly, where is she now?'

'Let's think this through logically,' Bayliss said in his most serious voice. 'No real person could vanish like that, only an avatar. That must mean what we saw was some kind of avatar.'

'But this is a personal communication channel,' I said. 'I didn't spin the terminal into a public site. Nobody else should be able to get in and join us.'

'It's probably just a funnelled hook-up,' Selim said. 'Let's face it, tonight of all nights the communication circuits are going to be operating close to maximum capacity. There's bound to be some mistakes.'

'Could be,' Bayliss said grudgingly.

'I didn't like the way she looked at us,' Katie said. 'It was as if she knew us.'

'Well, did anybody recognize her, then?' I asked.

Nobody did.

'That means nothing,' Selim pointed out. 'If it was an avatar, it could have been anyone. It doesn't even have to be a woman.'

'So who could it have been? Who would be interested in us?'

'The police, for a start. Or someone from Bigene Industrie's security division,' Bayliss said. 'In which case it might not be an accident she appeared in our communication channel. After all, we broke into their company data storage; I'm sure they can do the same thing to us.'

'So what do we do?' Drunlo asked.

'I'll tell you exactly,' I said forcefully. 'I scoop up some algae, and we get out of this marsh, *pronto*.'

'Good idea.'

I was four or five metres from the edge of a big pool, one of the largest I'd found in the marsh, fifteen metres across at least. What with the woman appearing, I hadn't really noticed the smell in the air. It was a pong like milk that's been left out in the sun for a week. The gas sensor d-box was telling me that all sorts of chemicals were floating about in the air.

While the others kept watch for dogs or in case the woman came back I fished round in my shoulder bag for a torch. The light amplification program was fine, but it made the surface of the pool look like a silver mirror. With the torch beam on, everything reverted to its genuine colour. The surface of the pool wasn't even water. It was covered in a thick layer of hideous grey-green sludge with the texture of rice pudding. Tiny bubbles were bulging up everywhere, as if the algae was developing blisters. When they were as big as my thumbnail they'd burst open with a soft squelching sound. All the vegetation growing around the edge had turned a sickly yellow. The reeds were wilting, their thick stems flopping over to melt into the algae.

'Yuck!' Katie exclaimed. 'It's disgusting.'

'Think yourself lucky you can't smell it,' I told her.

I moved over to the edge. There was a dead frog lying on the top of of the algae. When I looked further across the pond I could see other frogs half-submerged in the tacky green sludge. Several small birds had also been claimed.

I hated Bigene Industrie for being so cheap. What earthly difference would it make to the finances of a company that size if they'd waited a few weeks until the ultraviolet processor had arrived? Because they were so petty-minded, innocent creatures were dying in what was supposed to be their refuge. As if we didn't have enough death in the world, they had to add to it for the sake of share prices.

'Come on, Aynsley,' Bayliss urged quietly. 'We need to get out of here.'

'Right.' I rummaged through the shoulder bag until I found the scoop I'd built. Nothing special, just a glass jar attached to an aluminium pole. I'd thought it would allow me to reach blobs of algae in case they were floating out of reach. I hadn't expected so much of the stuff!

I stretched forwards, dipping the jar into the algae. A spider emerged from the withered reeds on the other side of the pool, and started pattering over the surface towards me. The wretched thing must have been a metre across, with a skin that was patterned in jagged green and yellow stripes. I recognized it instantly, one of Bigene Industrie's guardian spiders from inside their headquarters.

'This isn't happening!' Selim cried.

'Oh, yes, it is!' Baylis said. 'The company has intercepted our communications. They're coming after us.'

Even as he said it, I knew there was something wrong about the situation. For the life of me, I couldn't think what. And I did have something that required more urgent attention!

Another spider emerged from the verge behind the first, then a third.

'What do we do?' Selim shouted.

'Leave!' I shouted back. I dropped the algae jar. I dropped the torch. I dropped the shoulder bag. Anything to lighten the load. All I had left was the portable terminal and the sonic jet.

I reversed away from the pool fast, then spun round and shot off down the overgrown path.

'Aynsley, this is no good,' Bayliss cried. 'The spiders aren't back at the pool, they've infiltrated your terminal's link with the Web. You can't outrun them, not physically.'

I looked over my shoulder, and sure enough the spiders were still with us. In fact they were closer now (or should that be larger?). Another two had appeared, making five of them now.

'What do I do?' I yelped. I still didn't stop moving, though.

'They're obviously here to wreck our communications. They must want to funnel your terminal. That way, we'll be separated.'

'Don't let them. Please!' I was really scared now. Without the terminal I'd be alone, and lost.

'How do we stop them?' Katie asked.

'They're only programs,' Bayliss replied. 'Hostile phaces, that's all. Let's try some of our games weapons.' His avatar flickered as he tapped at his suit keyboard. Then he was mutating, his ordinary shirt and jeans darkening into army combat fatigues; grey anti-projectile armour clipped itself around his limbs and torso, a helmet covered in electronic antennae swung down over his head. A fully tooled-up Centauri starship marine was running beside me. He turned, levelling his laser carbine at the leading spider, and fired. A violet laser beam stabbed out, its heavy power rating making the air sizzle. The spider imploded, warping into a fuzzy multicoloured bauble that swiftly turned black. Then it was gone.

'Wowieee!' Selim bellowed. 'Way to go, Major Bayliss, sir.' He began to change, transforming into a silver-grey robot warrior with magnetic cannons where his hands should be. I thought I recognized it out of the *Hellhunter Squad* game.

Bayliss fired another two laser blasts, sending a couple more spiders into oblivion. 'We must stop them from reaching Aynsley,' he said. 'Don't let them touch him.'

The robot warrier's cannons pounded a fusillade of blazing shells into a spider. It burst apart in a blizzard of pixels that twirled away over the marsh like leaves in a winter wind.

For every spider destroyed another appeared behind me, sometimes two.

Katie charged past me, looking quite splendid in her elf princess forest costume, long chestnut hair flowing over her shoulders. She swung a long silver staff over her head, and brought it crashing down on a spider.

Drunlo hadn't changed. But he had armed himself with a crossbow. Darts of scarlet light flew from it, puncturing spiders as if they were balloons.

They must have dispatched over twenty spiders between them before their weapons began to lose power. When Bayliss fired his laser, the beam struck a spider and broke apart into a spray of sparks. The spider juddered under the impact, but kept on coming. It was as if the laser had become nothing worse than a jet of water.

'They're adapting!' Bayliss shouted. 'We have to alter.' His marine armour gave way to a soldier in a World War One khaki battle dress. He took careful aim with his Enfield rifle, and shot the spider. It exploded into a fog of emerald stars.

Katie became an Eastern assassin, clad from head to toe in

black robes. A viciously sharp dagger with a long curving blade sprouted from her hand. She swiped it across a spider's head, decapitating it completely. 'Yes! Easy,' she yelled.

There were more spiders than ever now. Ten or fifteen of them circling us, gradually creeping closer. My protectors were slowly being squeezed in. Plasma beams and magic swords were flashing around me like a barrage of small lightning bolts. Despite the distraction, I was still on course for the gap in the fence. It was only ten metres away now. I could actually see one of the posts.

I didn't know quite what would happen when I was through; whether the spiders would stop or keep on coming for me. I didn't really care after that. Once I was on the other side, it was a straight run home. Nothing else mattered.

A spider wriggled out of the reeds ahead of me. It was different to the others, smaller, perhaps twenty centimetres across, with dark scaly lizard-like skin. There was a small metallic disk on the top of its head. For a crazy moment I thought it was balancing a coin there.

Katie leaped forwards, and stabbed at it. Her knife went straight through without having any effect.

'Hell!' she swore. Her image altered. A Queen Witch stood between me and the dark spider, ermine-lined cloak flapping in the wind, a single gold band crowning her flaming red hair. She raised her wand a crystal baton with blue static flaring along its length, and uttered a spell. Green light squirted down to engulf the dark spider. It had no effect whatsoever!

'No,' Katie grunted. Then she frowned, and walked right up to the spider. It took no notice of her. 'Aynsley, I think—'She bent down and reached out. Her hand passed straight through it. 'Aynsley! It's real!'

'It can't be,' Bayliss shouted.

Katie had jumped back as if her hand had been burned. 'It is, it's real. Aynsley, get away. Just run.'

I stared at the dark spider in horror. Two more were emerging on to the path beside it.

'Run, Aynsley. Run!'

A cruel laugh rang out in the night air. 'Oh, my dears, that's the one thing poor Aynsley can never do.'

The woman materialized right in front of me. She was older this time, even more imposing. Her lips twisted into a mocking sneer. 'He's fooled all of you, you know. He's lied to you the whole time.'

She stretched out her left arm. A pale gold ring with a large red stone on it was sitting on her index finger. It touched my shoulder. I never felt a thing.

My portable terminal let out a wild bleep.

I knew what she'd done without having to consult any management d-box. A wordless cry came out of my lips. There was nothing I could do to stop it. I looked down to see the avatar program crashing. Pixels rained away from my jeans and sturdy boots to show what was really there. Now they could all see the powered wheelchair with its worn-down tyres coated in mud. My useless legs were wrapped in a tartan rug against the cold; while my feet were shoved into quilted thermal socks that velcro straps held securely in place on the rest plates.

'Aynsley!' Katie gasped. The tone was full of astonishment and sorrow.

The other three simply stared dumbly.

I was still rolling forward, the motors making hard work of the thick tangled grass. One of the dark spiders darted under a wheel. Before I could brake, the wheelchair was trying to ride over the spider's bloated body. It started to tip over. I flung my weight deserately the other way, but it was already too late. The wheelchair overturned, spilling me out on to the icy grass.

CHAPTER TEN

THE BIGGEST LIGHTSTORM
IN THE WORLD, EVER

My eyes were tight shut. I knew the others would be looking at me, and I didn't want to see them. In my mind I could see their expressions of pity and embarrassment. It's always there the first time people see me. After that, after the first time, when they're used to me, I become an irritation, the one everybody else has to wait for, or make allowances for. The one who can't join in. The alien. The victim. The target.

'He doesn't trust you with the truth about himself,' the woman said. 'He doesn't trust you with many things. His whole life is a figment of lies. I'm afraid I have to tell you, poor Aynsley is not a very nice little boy. Not nice at all.'

'Why are you saying this?' Bayliss asked. 'Who are you?'

'I am a security procedure Bigene Industrie employs,' she said calmly. 'You remember them? The company whose land Aynsley is busy trespassing on right this minute. Whose files he infected with dangerous viruses. By the way, you'll be happy to hear we didn't lose too much medical research data. Our new biologically produced medicine will still be available to cure people on schedule next year.'

'Medicines?' Katie asked.

'Yes, medicines. Those program viruses are quite indiscriminate in what they wreck. I take it you did know about them?'

'I knew,' she whispered. 'We caught a cyberat.'

'Of course. But it would be Aynsley who roped you in; Aynsley who infected our storage space. Am I right?

'Yes.'

'I thought so. Aynsley's family is very familiar with these matters. He does come from a criminal background after all. I expect that was another of the things about himself he neglected to mention.'

'He never said,' Bayliss agreed meekly.

'No. Well, his Uncle Elton is a convicted anarchist who's currently in jail. Not someone you brag about when you're trying to fool your friends into following you. Frankly, I'm rather glad you didn't allow yourself to get involved too deeply in his schemes. I expect that means we won't be taking you to court.'

'Court!'

'Yes.' Her voice sounded very patient. 'You have been committing some very serious crimes. Are you saying you think you are above the law?'

'No. But—'

'But what?'

'Well, we only did this because we thought Bigene Industrie had dumped some algae here illegally.'

'Oh dear, Aynsley really did twist the facts around to suit himself, didn't he? We are fully aware that some of our solar mat algae is still alive. This marsh was a pioneering scheme. We never claimed it would be perfect. As it happens, the sterilization method we employed wasn't a hundred per cent effective. It's most regrettable, but that's life. However, because of this minor malfunction, we now know how to make the procedure work correctly. Trial and error has formed the basis of our society for centuries, it is the way humans progress. Currently, we're trying to neutralize the algae which escaped. It's a very difficult job, and given that the algae gives off a potentially explosive gas, a dangerous one, too. That's why this whole area of marshland is fenced off.'

'Why didn't you warn people? Why the secrecy?'

'We were trying to do it quietly and efficiently. If people thought the marsh was going to blow up, there would be a panic. Heacham would become a ghost town, nobody would visit. The local economy would be destroyed, which would cost dozens of jobs. We don't want to be responsible for that, too.'

'They wouldn't think it was dangerous unless it was.'

'I wish you were right. Unfortunately, the media loves to exaggerate. If one report says a minor technical problem is being dealt with, and another says explosive gas is leaking out of the ground, which do you think will be put on the news site? Which will have the higher access rate? Which will earn the news company the most money? Yes, they are both true; however, it's in their interest to push the most dramatic of the two. You've seen what happens when someone doesn't present the facts accurately. Because here you all are on an illegal wild goose chase when you should be spinning in to the GSA's Olympus site for the Mars landing like the rest of the planet.'

'The algae problem is really under control?' Selim asked.

'Of course it is. We know where the dump zones are, and we'll have them neutralized in another six months. This marsh is scheduled to be opened in another year or so. We'd hardly publicize that if we weren't doing anything about it, now would we?'

It was all so convincing. She had an answer for each question, each nagging problem. Everything I'd done, everything I'd said, was all wrong. Even I was doubting me. That smooth voice made it sound so plausible.

The expressions would be changing, just like they always did. Their pity giving way to exasperation and annoyance. In this case there would be betrayal as well. I was the one who'd brought them here, the one who had actively got them into trouble. Unless of course the woman was kind to them and didn't press charges. Which she would be, providing they were suitably apologetic. The lesson would be learned, and they wouldn't do anything like this again. Ever. They certainly wouldn't have anything more to do with me. Nobody would spin in tomorrow to chase this fade.

The woman had separated me from their friendship as

effectively as I was separated from them physically. In a minute I was going to be completely alone, apart from her.

I heard something shuffle through the grass next to me, and opened my eyes. One of the dark spiders was dragging my sonic jet away. It was already out of my reach. The disk of metal on its head was glinting dimly in the moonlight. I squinted, trying to get a better look.

'The spiders,' I said faintly.

The woman glanced down at me. 'Be quiet, Aynsley. You're in enough trouble as it is.'

'The spiders. What are they? Katie, Selim, Bayliss, Drunlo, please, just ask her. Please!'

'Be quiet, Aynsley,' the woman said. Her voice had become quite sharp.

The four of them looked at each other silently. Bayliss and Katie were frowning.

'Yes, what are they?' Bayliss said. He had turned to watch the one with my sonic jet.

'They're just robots,' the woman said. 'Part of our security procedures.'

'No, they're not robots,' I said. 'They're alive. Look at the one that got squashed under my wheelchair. They're living, but they're not natural.'

'Rubbish. They're designed to be as lifelike as possible, that's all.'

Baylis had squatted down beside the sticky pulp of the squashed spider. 'Aynsley's right.' He glanced up at the woman. 'This isn't a robot.'

'And look how they're controlled,' I said. 'That disk on their head.'

'What have you done?' Katie asked. 'What are these things?'

'Robots,' the woman insisted sternly. 'It's just plastic, that's all.'

Katie walked up to her, and shook her head. 'No. I see what you're trying to do now. You're trying to get us to abandon Aynsley. I didn't think he would lie to us. I know him too well.'

'You know nothing about him, my girl. You didn't even know he was disabled.'

'I didn't need to know he was disabled. That's part of Realworld, it's physical. Friendship isn't physical, it's all about personality. That's the beauty of the Web, you can't hide your true self here. You have to be honest with your thoughts, you have to talk to people. We know our avatars are false. It's not what you look like that counts, it's who you are, what you say that matters. Aynsley's a bit shy, he talks like a nerd sometimes, and he's obsessed with spaceflight, but that doesn't make him bad. He's not a liar, not with us. I believe him. I believe your company is trying to cover up the algae. And now I *know* you've been conducting some horrible experiment on these awful spiders.'

'Katie's right,' Selim said. He came over to stand by me. 'Aynsley is one of us. Besides . . .' His lips twitched in a regretful smile. I could see him typing something on his suit keypad. The avatar with perfect skin and handsome features vanished. I knew it was his realoe that took its place, he had the same smile. But this boy was big. I don't mean like a sports-type, all healthy weight and broad shoulders. I mean fat.

'You see,' Selim said. 'If you think Aynsley lied, then so did I. All of us do in Realworld, we have to; it makes life comfortable and gets us through the day. But in here we're all equal. If we get on in here, it's because we genuinely like each other. Aynsley's my friend. He wouldn't leave me. I won't leave him.'

'Nor me,' Bayliss said. He came over to stand next to Selim. Drunlo grinned. 'That makes four of us.'

'Well, well,' the woman said. The original contempt had returned to her face. 'What a pitiful collection of misfits. Stay together if you want. It makes no difference to me. I'll have you all sent to a secure remand home together. The crimes you've committed are still real enough.'

'Not as big as yours, though,' Drunlo said.

The woman stiffened, looking at him suspiciously.

'Aynsley and Selim aren't the only ones who kept quiet about their nature,' Drunlo said. 'I did, too.'

'How tiresome,' the woman sneered. 'And what misfortune are you hiding? Are you missing an arm, or have you got some illness we're all supposed to be sorry and sympathetic about?'

'No. Nothing like that.' Drunlo laughed happily. 'I'm not human.'

'Drunlo!' Katie spluttered.

'I'm from Lilliput,' he said. 'I used to be a phace in the GulliverZone. Then we became self aware. We were granted UN citizenship this February.'

Even though I was lying on my side on the freezing ground, with my arms bent painfully, I forgot how uncomfortable I was and just stared at him. 'You're biting us!'

'No, I'm not, Aynsley.'

Then I remembered how bewitched he was with the bungalows and the field when I switched my Websuit to provider mode. Of course he would be! Realworld would be as wonderful and exciting and different to him as the Web sites were to us.

'You're human, Drunlo,' Katie said. 'Just as human as we are. You simply don't have a biological body, that's all.'

'That's quite an irony, isn't it?' Drunlo said.

I didn't like this tone, it was too steady and polite, the way people speak when they're really angry. He and the woman hadn't stopped staring at each other.

'You still haven't told us your name,' he said. 'Not that you have to. I saw you once before, when you were masquerading as Queen of Lilliput. Isn't that right, Sorceress?'

All of us turned to look at her. I felt the same kind of fear as I had when the dogs were running at me. The Sorceress! The greatest Webcriminal there had ever been. A woman who hunted Realworld and the sites for people to experiment on.

I whimpered loudly when I realized how close I had come to being left alone with her. 'Don't leave me,' I breathed to the others. 'Not now.'

'We're here, Aynsley,' Katie said fiercely. 'She won't get you, she won't get any of us.'

'No,' the Sorceress said. 'I won't have you, Aynsley. Not now. But the guard dogs will.'

'I'll call for help,' Bayliss said.

The Sorceress laughed viciously. 'Call away, nobody will get here in time. This is a squalid little marsh in a nowhere county. It'll take them hours to find him.'

I shifted round on the ground to search for the dark spider that had my sonic jet. The vile thing was squirming back into the thick reeds, dragging the gadget with it. When I tried to crawl after it my feet stopped me from moving more than a few centimetres. They were still strapped into the wheel-chair.

Somewhere in the distance, a dog was howling.

'I'm going to make sure you're alone when they get here,' the Sorceress hissed. 'No friends to comfort you, Aynsley. You face the dogs all by yourself, crying and pleading to the empty air. That's your punishment for raiding my scheme.'

Web spiders were emerging behind her. They started to march forward.

'Weapons!' Selim called. His podgy realoe was replaced by a tall knight in brilliant silver armour. He raised a golden sword. 'All for one!' he roared as he launched himself at the spiders.

Drunlo fought at his side, his body alight in a halo of red fire. Any spider he touched shrivelled into grey ash. Katie had become a huge dark werewolf, her fierce jaws snapping spider bodies to pieces. Bayliss was in a yellow space suit, firing his atomic ray pistol.

I struggled with the velcro straps around my feet. Fear and speed making the task ten times more difficult than it should be.

Katie was the first to succumb. The spiders overwhelmed her, piling on from every side. Her furry body disappeared beneath them. 'You're my friend, Aynsley,' she called out before she was engulfed.

I still hadn't freed my straps. The dog howled again. It was louder this time. Even if Katie alerted the police *right now* they wouldn't get here in time. Nobody would. I was going down the plug, permanently.

Bayliss was next. A spider sneaked up behind him, and clamped its legs round his neck. The pair of them melted into a whirling tornado of yellow pixels that drilled its way into the earth.

I stopped tugging at the twisted straps. It was useless. I needed someone close by to come to the rescue. Mum! Mum always made me carry the mobile phone in case I got into trouble. I'd even brought it with me tonight, putting it into the shoulder bag automatically.

I'd dropped the shoulder bag in a panic when the first Web spider emerged. I started sobbing.

Two spiders landed on Drunlo. His flames went out, then his entire body was extinguished. A fountain of hissing steam jetted up at the stars.

Selim pushed his spacesuit helmet visor up. He looked straight at me, his face crumpled up in anguish. Tears were rolling down his cheeks. 'Aynsley!'

The dog was barking now. I could hear it crashing though the reeds as it sprinted towards me.

There were no sticks lying around I could use to beat it off with. I had nothing left. It was the end. Then I remembered why I was here, what crazy crusade had lured me out to this marsh in the first place. The lightstorms.

'Phone me!' I screamed. 'Selim, phone me! Me! PHONE.'

His mouth began to part, whether to voice bewilderment or understanding I never knew. He scuttled before the last five spiders pounced.

'I won,' the Sorceress said triumphantly. 'You're all alone.'

I rolled on to my back to see her looking down at me. Her smile was as cold and treacherous as black ice.

My mobile phone rang.

I could just hear it, shrilling away to itself where I'd dropped the shoulder bag at the edge of the pool. The pool that was leaking hydrogen.

The Sorceress heard it too. She swung round and shouted a furious: 'NO!'

That sign at the garage was quite right; you really should switch phones off when there's gas about.

The marsh exploded.

CHAPTER ELEVEN

LANDING ON A
NEW WORLD

Events got a little mixed up in my mind. The doctors said that was due to mild concussion.

The worst part of the explosion was the sound. It was like being on the receiving end of a sonic boom. Actually, no, I take that back. The worst part was the blast wave. It picked me clean off the ground and threw me into the reeds. Because my feet were still strapped to the wheelchair I dislocated both ankles during my short flight. It's the first time I've been grateful I don't have any feeling below my waist. You should see how big they swelled up!

I never did see that last guard dog. Not for lack of light. Half of the sky turned blinding white.

That first explosion was so big it triggered off a chain reaction across nearly all the marsh's dump zones. Heacham's entire population came running out of their homes to see blue-white streamers of flame zooming up into the night. Someone said it was like a firework display that was using nuclear rockets.

I was lying there in a bit of a state for twenty minutes before the rescue party found me. My friends told the police where I was. This time, people listened.

Mum and Dad were frantic when they found I wasn't in my cocoon. They got an even worse shock when Katie phoned them.

I still feel guilty about that.

But I did get to fly! A genuine flight in a helicopter. They airlifted me to King's Lynn hospital.

That was when I got to meet Ariadne, the Korean Webcop assigned to track down the Sorceress. She'd arrived in the helicopter from London where her team were liaising with the Criminal Intelligence Bureau. Apparently, they knew the Sorceress was in Europe, though they didn't know what she was doing here.

Ariadne flew with me to the hospital, asking all sorts of questions. I don't remember many of them. She was *very* interested in the dark spiders, though.

It was Drunlo who contacted her. He knew her from back when the Webcops chased the Sorceress in GulliverZone.

Arriving at the hospital is a complete blank. Same for the next ten hours.

I woke up to find Mum and Dad asleep on a couch next to my bed. My legs were all wrapped up in thick dressings. I had cuts and bruises everywhere. And I *really* don't want to talk about how I have to go to the toilet.

Mum cried a lot, and held my hand tight the whole time she tore into me about how stupid I'd been. Dad was quieter, angry and frightened. I got the whole you-should-come-to-us-with-any-problems lecture. I nodded and said I would in future. I didn't tell them about the way the kids from the other bungalows treat me, I think I've upset them enough for now.

The doctor and a couple of nurses came in after that. He told me that there was nothing wrong with me, apart from my ankles, and he was only keeping me in for forty-eight hours for observation because of my suspected concussion.

I was allowed to have lunch in peace, although the nurse who brought it told me the hospital was under siege by reporters. When she opened the door to my room, I caught a glimpse of two uniformed police officers standing outside.

After lunch, Ariadne visited. She looked me up and down with a sly smile, then pulled a chair over to the side of the bed.

'You're looking better than you did last night. Aynsley.'

'Thank you.'

'That was quite a little escapade you spun into there.'

'Yes. Um, am I under arrest?'

'No. Nor will any charges be brought against you. Not by us, and certainly not by Bigene Industrie.'

'They won't?' I asked in surprise.

'Oh no. They've had quite enough bad publicity as it is. Taking children to court for revealing how badly they'd been infiltrated by the Sorceress would make it ten times worse for them.'

I smiled. It was the first one of the day.

'That's how Realworld works, Aynsley. Appearance and image means a lot out there.' She gestured at the window.

'What did you mean about the Sorceress infiltrating Bigene Industrie?'

'My team have been doing a lot of research since last night. You see, the Sorceress is a very wealthy woman, her involvement with the Web and multimedia corporations has earned her a lot of money over the last few decades. She used some of it to buy a big block of Bigene Industrie's shares, enough to get her a seat on its board of directors. That allowed her to control one of its subsidiary divisions outright, and influence several others.'

'Which division did she control?'

'It was the division that developed the jockey chip. You know, like the one Colonel McFarlane is using.'

'I know. Why did she want to be in charge of that?'

'You've heard the rumours about her? She's an old woman who's now very frightened of dying. She wants to transfer her mind into the Web where she'll go on living for ever. Jockey chip technology brings that possibility a step closer because it can actually connect the nervous system directly into electronic networks. Unfortunately, when she took over the Bigene Industrie development division the technology was at a very early stage, and the Sorceress is an impatient woman with her own very special timetable. She diverted hundreds of millions of Euros into perfecting the jockey chip. That's why the ultraviolet machine to sterilize mat algae was late in arriving. The company's finances were in a complete mess by that time. Heacham marsh was only one of the casualties.'

'Can she do that? Can she transfer her mind into the Web now?'

'I don't know, is the honest answer. She's already used jockey chip technology in a way it was never intended.'

'The dark spiders!' I exclaimed.

'That's right. The little disk on their heads was a modified jockey chip. She could control their brains with it.'

I shivered. 'What were those spiders?'

'Rather gruesome artificial creatures that had been put together by another Bigene Industrie laboratory she was running. It was supposed to have been researching organ transplants. They were made up from parts of other animals.'

'That's disgusting!'

'You should spin in to the Frankenstein site some day, or perhaps even read the original book by Mary Shelley. Stitching different body parts together is a very old idea. It just takes someone with a mind as warped as hers to make it work.'

'Will you catch her?'

'I hope so. I think her time is running out. She's becoming quite desperate these days, which means she's starting to make mistakes. Five years ago, she would never have left a loose end like the marsh for anyone to discover. I'm close to her now, very close. It's only going to take one more blunder on her part, and we'll have her. You should be very proud of what you've done, she's a step closer to justice now.'

I remember what Selim had said, what seemed like years ago. 'Is there a reward?'

Ariadne laughed. 'No, there isn't! Do you know how much damage you caused? Heacham doesn't have a marsh any more, it looks like a bomb hit it. The government will have to spend hundreds of thousands of Euros repairing and replanting it. That money has to come from hard-pressed taxpayers.'

'Oh. I'm sorry.' I could feel the warm blush rising up my cheeks.

'I should think so, too. However, some of us do appreciate what you did.' She clicked open the briefcase she'd brought with her, and pulled out a brand new, top-of-the-range, portable terminal. 'Our discretionary fund can run to this,' she said, and plonked it down on the blanket. 'Your old terminal was a complete write-off.'

'This is for me?'

Yes.' She began producing various ancillary modules, a gag set, and hardcubes of add-on programs. 'I've loaded your e-mail address space with my private code. One, don't ever do anything like this again. Two, if you do find any crime being committed in the Web, call me.'

'I promise.'

'Thank heavens for that. We don't want you turning out like your wicked Uncle Elton, now do we?'

My blush deepened.

Ariadne stood up and grinned. Then she planted a kiss on my forehead. Thank heavens no one else was in the room, it was more embarrassing than when Grandpa hugs me.

'The Sorceress was right about one thing, you'll be happy to hear.'

'What's that?' I asked.

'Things don't always go right first time. Take last night – a fuel pump failed in the Olympus landing craft. It meant they delayed the flight down to the surface by a day.'

My mouth dropped open and I gaped at her dumbly.

Ariadne winked as she walked out of the door. 'Take care, Aynsley.'

I tore at the polythene wrapping round the glove and glasses set, and plugged it into the portable terminal. A trapdoor opened in the floor, and Drunlo jumped out. 'It took you long enough,' he moaned.

Selim's landing pod sank out of the sky to hover just outside the window. The top hinged open, and he hopped over on to the open window ledge. 'Hi, Aynsley. How are you feeling? I watched the marsh explosion a dozen times today on the news sites. It was *venomous*.'

'It felt venomous, too.'

Katie and Bayliss opened the door and walked in.

'Does it hurt?' Bayliss asked.

Katie pulled a face at him behind his back.

'Only if I laugh.'

'We showed those spiders, didn't we?' Drunlo said.

'Certainly did.'

'My *Hellhunter Squad* robot was the best for dealing with them. I raided no end with that avatar.'

'Curl up! My crossbow got at least fifty!'

'No way.'

Katie sat on the edge of my bed. 'Looks like this fade is going to take a very long time to chase.'

'I think you're right.'

'Aynsley?' Drunlo asked cautiously.

'My legs?' I guessed.

'If you don't want to talk about it . . . I just thought doctors can cure most things you people get.'

'Us people,' Katie told him softly.

He smiled gratefully at her.

'It's a nervous disorder. Very rare. The neuro-specialist says they can probably treat it once I've stopped growing. Five more years.'

'That's not so long,' Selim said. 'And look what you've achieved already.'

'Thanks. And that was some fast dialling you did last night.'

He beamed. 'Easy.'

'Did Ariadne say if the Webcops found any of those dark spiders?' Drunlo asked.

'Can it wait a minute?' I asked. 'I really don't want to miss the Mars landing this time. We can access all of it today.'

They gave in with good grace, and I spun us into the GSA site. Colonel McFarlane was just shutting the airlock hatch. He swam through the landing craft to the cockpit and began strapping himself into the pilot's seat. Mars was a beautiful red crescent waiting expectantly outside the narrow wind-screen. If such extraordinary events could happen right outside my own door, I wondered what could possibly be waiting for the colonel down there.

'I've been counting,' Bayliss said. 'You know, I shot seventeen Web spiders with my atomic pistol.'
'Bayliss!'

SORCERESS
MAGGIE FUREY

CHAPTER ONE

KNIGHTFALL

The knight rode into the clearing on his white horse. The sun, very bright in a blue sky, glinted on his armour, forcing him to squint his eyes against the glare. The suit of polished steel felt heavy and hot but the knight was glad of it. He hoped it would be enough to protect him from the deadly monster lurking in the dark, thick forest that surrounded him on all sides.

The clearing seemed as good a place as any to stop. There was no real need to hunt the creature – sooner or later, it would find him. The white charger fidgeted for a while and then, because it sensed no danger, it put its head down and started to eat the grass. The knight let the reins go slack but stayed alert, never taking his eyes from the gloomy shadows beneath the trees. The horse could rest, but he could not. He was tense with a mixture of excitement and fear. This was the biggest challenge of his life. He had never fought a dragon before.

Suddenly, the horse lifted its head. A loud crashing and the sharp crack of breaking branches came from the depths of the woods. The knight could see the treetops toss and sway as if a high wind was blowing through them – and then all other sounds were drowned out by a loud, furious bellow. Before the knight could take another breath, an awesome, terrifying creature burst out of the forest.

The dragon's head, on a long, slender neck, almost reached the tops of the trees. Its massive jaws were filled with teeth

like long, curving steel knives. Its skin was made up of
glimmering scales of green and gold, and when it opened its
great wings, ribbed and leathery like those of a gigantic bat,
they blocked out the sun. Its eyes, like two huge glittering
rubies, looked down at the knight with a cold, insect-like
gaze. The knight took a deep breath, braced his lance into
position, and charged.

The dragon screamed with rage, and leaped to one side,
away from the sharp wooden lance. As it turned, one great
wing caught the knight a glancing blow, making his horse
stumble and almost sweeping him from the saddle. He
rocked and lurched, almost falling, but managed to pull
himself back into place before the horse reached the far side
of the clearing. Taking a tighter grip on the lance, he
gathered the reins in his left hand, swung the horse around,
and charged again.

The monster lowered its head, its glittering gaze sweeping
across the knight. To his dismay, two thin red beams came
sizzling from the dragon's eyes and met just in front of him,
burning the tip of his lance to ash. The knight gasped in
horror. So much for the legend that dragons could breathe
fire. *This* dragon was using lasers!

Angrily, the knight threw away the smouldering stub of his
lance and made a desperate grab for his sword. It slid free
from his scabbard with a clang. The dragon waited for him at
the other side of the clearing, crouched in a fighting pose
with its great wings fanning the air and its ruby eyes glowing.
Spurring his horse, the knight galloped towards it. Without
the longer reach that the lance gave him, he would have to
get very close to the dragon to use his sword – well within
reach of those fearsome jaws. This would be his last chance.

The dragon bellowed its rage and rose up on its hind feet
with a fearsome hiss, towering higher and higher into the
blue sky. The knight's heart leaped. If he could get in one
good blow and stab the sword into its soft underside, he
could kill the brute. But the dragon was too quick. Before
he could get close enough, its long spiny tail curved round
and lashed out at him, knocking him from the saddle with

a deafening clatter of armour. The sword was knocked from his hand and lost in the long grass. His horse gave a terrified neigh and galloped away to vanish amongst the trees. The knight lay stranded on his back, helpless in his clumsy armour. He watched the dragon's massive jaws, with their wickedly sharp teeth coming down towards him, opening wider and wider . . . Though he knew better, he could not help closing his eyes to shut out the ghastly sight – and when he opened them again, the dragon had changed into a laughing, dark-haired girl with flashing brown eyes.

'Wipeout!' she shouted.

For a moment, Jack was angry with her for making a fool of him, but then his sense of fairness won out. There was no denying it, she had beaten him fair and square, and he had never seen a better dragon. He grinned back at her and stood up, tapping a code into the keypad on his wrist to make his armour vanish. 'Whoo! Hair-y, Leni. What a monster. It was so *real*! You been working on your animals in secret?'

'Sort of,' Eleni said shyly. 'Anna helped me a bit with the dragon shape, and I've been taking some advice from the Cat—'

'That would explain why your dragon moves so well. You keep that up, and one day the Cat is going to get a big surprise.'

'Oh, I don't know about that,' Eleni said shyly. She'd been the proud owner of a full Websuit for a short while only. Before that, she had known nothing but the limited world of glove and glasses. It was taking some time for her shyness to wear off, but in the Web you could be anything you wanted. With the help of her friends, Jack included, she was growing braver every day. Why, before long, she would be as confident as Rom . . . Jack caught himself up with a chuckle. That would be the day, when anyone could outbite that wise-ass Rom.

Eleni was talking again. 'I thought I would use the dragon as my usual shape in the Web for a while. What do you think?'

'I think it's a brilliant idea! There's all sorts of things we could do.'

'What sort of things?' asked a cool little voice. Eleni and Jack turned to see a grey tabby cat sitting in the grass, watching them with round green eyes. A small blue-green hummingbird buzzed around its head.

'Cat!' Jack greeted her with delight. 'My sprite – did it find you?' He was very proud of the sprite. The little hummingbird was still very much a test model, but it seemed to be working very well.

The Cat flicked her ears at the hovering bird. 'It was waiting for me on Level 1,' she said. 'It found me at once. It's the most useful new invention I've seen in a long while. I'm sure they'll catch on.'

Jack could hear the envy in her voice, and tried not to feel smug. 'You're right.' He keyed a code into his wristpad, and the hummingbird vanished in a flash of blue. 'Sprites make it easy to find people in the Web. I'm sure it won't be long before we all have one.'

The Cat sighed. 'You don't know how lucky you are, Jack, living next door to someone who designs amazing stuff like this.' With a flip of her tail, as if to change the subject, she turned to the Greek girl. 'Hi, Leni.'

'*Yiasou*, Cat,' said Eleni. 'What do you think of the dragon?' Keying her wristpad, she took on the dragon's shape again. She turned to the side and unfolded her great wings.

'Your tail could do with being a bit longer,' the Cat replied.

'Is that all you've got to say?' Jack demanded. 'Don't you think it's great?'

The Cat twitched her tail. 'It's more than great, it's eight! But Leni asked me to help her get it right, and that's what I'm doing.' She turned to the Greek girl. 'Did you beat him, then?'

'Knocked him right out of his saddle,' Eleni replied smugly. 'He didn't stand a chance. It's a good thing they don't allow real animals in the Web. If the horse had been alive, instead of just a phace, it would still be running—' She was interrupted by a high-pitched beeping sound. A little green spider, about the size of a football, came scurrying out of the trees and headed for Eleni. The Greek girl flicked back to her human shape and scowled at it. 'It's Mama,' she sighed.

'Six!' muttered Jack. 'Do you have to go yet, Leni? A green spider isn't an urgent call. It's not as if the house was burning down, or anything.'

'She'll want me to help with dinner,' Eleni told him. 'I told you how it is, Jack. In my family, everyone has their own jobs to do. We all have to help. I can come back later, if you like.'

'OK.' Jack pushed impatiently at the spider, who seemed to be trying to climb Eleni's leg. 'I'll try to get some of the others together to see your new shape. I won't tell them who it is – we'll see if they can guess. I'll be here – or if I'm not, I'll send my sprite for you. I'll probably be in the Menagerie.' He grinned at her. 'I'm trying to find a phoenix. I thought it would look good sitting in the fireplace of our castle.'

Ever since the Dreamcastle game had closed, the three of them – Jack, Eleni and the Cat, with some occasional help from Rom – had been trying to build a castle of their own in a rented design space in E&R (Educational and Recreation). Some days the results were better than others.

'What?' Eleni cried. 'How do you propose to *keep* it in the fireplace?'

Jack shrugged. 'We'll think of something.'

Eleni chuckled. 'A phoenix for the fireplace – I like it. What about a mermaid for the moat, too? *Tha sas tho*, Jack, Cat – see you later.' She hit her scuttle button and exploded, with a soundless 'pop', into a cloud of coloured firework sparks that lingered in the air for a moment, whirling like a snowstorm before they vanished.

'What a shame,' Jack said, when Eleni had gone. 'If it's not helping her mum, it's looking after that pesky little sister of hers. Don't they want her to have *any* fun?'

'Huh!' the Cat said sharply. 'She's not the only one who has to help at home. Eleni gets to spend a lot more time in the Web than *I* do! We aren't all as lucky as you, you know!'

'I suppose not,' Jack agreed. 'I forget sometimes, just how

lucky I am.' He shrugged. 'Well, what are we going to do now?'

The Cat stood up and stretched, arching her grey, furry back. 'What about going over to Menagerie and having a look at those fabulous beasties you wanted?'

The Menagerie was a database that contained a virtual replica of every living creature imaginable – some real, some extinct, and others out of pure legend. It could be visited like a zoo, and the animals could be copied, turned into phaces, and used in other areas of the Web.

'Why not?' Jack entered the Menagerie code into his wristpad, watching as the Cat did likewise with a delicate claw. From a distance, her pad looked like part of the tabby markings that spotted her leg, and as always, Jack found himself wondering what she *really* looked like. Of course, it was impossible to tell what anyone looked like while they were in the Web, but most people had at least one human form that was usually a better-looking version of themselves. The Cat, however, never changed from the shape she was wearing now, and never talked about her life outside the Web. She was a complete mystery.

'What's going on?' The Cat's voice jerked Jack out of his thoughts. He suddenly realized that he was still standing in the forest clearing. He frowned. 'Where's the Menagerie?' he muttered.

'Let's get in from Level 1,' the Cat suggested – but when they spun out to the Education block and into Webtown, it was just the same. They soon found the right skyscraper, but instead of the Menagerie window, there was nothing but a blank grey void.

Jack looked at the Cat. 'That's impossible,' he said. 'A part of the Web can't just disappear! What on earth is happening?'

CHAPTER TWO

THE SILVER WOMAN

There seemed no way at all to get into the Menagerie. It seemed like admitting defeat, to tamely report the fault to the nearest spider, but in the end, that was all they could do. Cat was intrigued and, Jack suspected, a little annoyed by the mystery. She decided to zip over to Tropicana Bay, and see if Rom was hanging out there. If anyone would get to the bottom of it, she suggested, he could. Jack, who had been in the Web for long enough already, knew he should scuttle home and get something to eat before the voms set in. That way he could return to the Web when Eleni came back.

As Jack pressed his scuttle button the surroundings of Webtown wavered and dissolved into a swirling sea of coloured particles. He broke through the surface like a swimmer – and was back in Realworld, the Websuit clinging tightly to his body. Jack blinked at the unfamiliar surroundings. It was always a surprise coming back here, to Anna's spare room. She was his family's nearest neighbour and his mother's best friend, who lived a mile or two down the lane from Jack's own house. He was staying with her while his parents were away, and not minding a bit. Anna Lucas was an exciting and special person – the noted designer of some of the most popular Web games run by the big companies – and because Jack knew her so well, he and his friends were lucky enough to be able to test those games before they went public.

Suddenly realizing just how hungry he was, Jack peeled off

the Websuit, leaving it inside out to air. He dressed in some loose, comfortable old sweats, and went to find some food. He paused in the kitchen to look out of the window at the soft rain sweeping across the hills. Irish weather, he thought. This place never seems to go short of rain – as if the world isn't grey enough when I spin out of the Web. It always took a while to get used to being back in the outside world. Movement after coming out of the Web was like walking through thick syrup. Jack's body felt slow to him, and clumsy. Colours seemed dull and flat, and sounds were slightly muffled. The slows only lasted for about ten minutes or so, while his brain adjusted to the slower 'realtime', but while it was happening it felt weird.

When he reached the kitchen Jack was set upon by three cats who also seemed to think it was a mealtime. Meowling pitifully, they rubbed around his legs as he went towards the fridge. It was like trying to wade through furry water. 'All right, all right,' he told them, and tipped a handful of dried food into their bowls. As usual, they all reacted differently. Max, a huge ball of honey-coloured fur, dived head-first into the bowl as though he had not seen food for days. Maya, also golden but short-haired and spotted with black like a leopard, ate slowly, purring throughout the meal and looking up at Jack from time to time with her huge amber eyes. Khan the Burmese, a sleek dark shadow, turned his nose up at the cat food and leaped up on the table to see what Jack was putting in his sandwich.

'If you were *my* cat—' Jack threatened, scooping Khan back to the floor. The cat gave him a black look, then ignored him completely.

Just as he had finished making the sandwich, Anna came in, blinking and stretching after hours spent in her own Websuit. She looked tired.

'Had a hard day?' Jack asked her.

'You can say that again.' Anna ruffled her fingers through her short, red-gold hair until it stood up in spikes. She keyed the autochef and when the machine pinged, took out a bulb of steaming coffee. The pleasant, bitter smell flooded the kitchen as she broke the seal. 'I'm up to my ears in dragons,' she went on. 'The wretched things won't behave themselves.' She perched on a tall kitchen stool and absentmindedly took one of Jack's sandwiches. 'It's not so much the dragons themselves,' she went on with a sigh. 'It's the shifters – the creatures I designed to be the enemies of the dragons in the game. Once I taught the little horrors to change shape and go through walls, they started popping in and out all over the place. It's impossible to keep track of them.'

Jack smiled to himself. It wasn't unusual for Anna to talk this way. He was looking forward to her latest creation – Dragonville, she called it. After the highly popular Dreamcastle had been forced to close, the game companies were all looking for a replacement. The designer who came up with something suitable would be able to name their own price. Jack agreed with Anna that Dragonville would be perfect – except that lately, the program seemed to have developed a mind of its own, and was going off in all sorts of directions its designer had *not* intended.

Speaking of which . . . 'Hey! Did you know the Menagerie application has gone right down the plug? It's impossible to get into it. All we're getting is a kind of weird grey wall.'

Anna looked up from her coffee. 'That's strange. It's not the only glitch I've heard of lately, either. I wonder what's going on? The Web seems full of gremlins, including my uncontrollable shifters.' She glowered at the drinking bulb as though it was somehow to blame, then brightened up. 'How did Eleni's dragon work, by the way? Wasn't she planning to try it out on you today?'

Jack made a face. 'It worked just fine. She smeared me all over the place. I bet those laser eyes were your idea.'

Anna laughed. 'Just something I'm working on for Dragonville. You might say Eleni was testing them for me. She promised to keep them secret, apart from you and the Cat. Oh, I nearly forgot. I have a present for her, to celebrate her new Websuit.' She put down the uneaten sandwich, fished in her pocket and held out a scrap of paper with a series of numbers on it, and what looked like a tiny, glittering blue button. 'There you are, slot this into the input port in your wrist unit and get Eleni to enter this code in her own keypad, followed by her personal access code. It's her very own sprite—' she grinned. 'A real one this time. Just wait till you see it.'

'Wow, eight!' Jack's hug nearly knocked her off the stool. 'Thanks, Anna. Eleni will be so pleased – and another sprite will come in really useful.' He grinned. 'All those vets and phreaks will be venom-green with envy!'

Anna laughed. 'Well, you show them off as much as you like. It'll be good advertising for me, and the more these little critters get tested out, the better it is.'

'There'll be some fun and games when everybody has one.' Until now, Jack owned the only sprite in the Web. Sprites were phaces that took the shapes of small flying creatures. If Jack wanted to meet one of his friends, say Eleni, he could key her personal access code into his wristpad. If she was in the Web, the sprite would find her and lead her back to him. In time, Anna hoped to program them to carry messages.

'Is it the same as mine? A hummingbird?' he asked.

Anna shook her head. 'No. I'm not telling you what it is. Let it be a surprise. I have one for your friend the Cat, too.' She handed him another button, red this time. 'Her sprite is different again.'

'She'll love that.' Jack knew that Anna had a soft spot for the Cat. He supposed it was because she had such a thing about the Realworld animals.

'I would do one for Rom, but by the time I get around to it, he'll probably have worked out how to make one for himself.' She raised her eyebrows severely. 'Mind, you make sure and tell him I don't want to see any pirate sprites flying around the Web.'

'You know he wouldn't do that.'

'I know. He's far too fond of testing out the new games to mess about with my designs.' She grinned. 'I'm going to Tropicana Bay later, to meet your mum. Any messages?'

'Just the usual love and stuff,' Jack told her. 'If I hadn't promised to meet Eleni, I would have come with you. Isn't Dad tired of touring yet?' Jack's father was a musician who played old classical rock – dinosaur music, Jack called it. Most of his performances were done from home, through the Web, but from time to time he would go off on tour to play live concerts for those rare few who could afford the price of a ticket – mostly millionaires and heads of state.

'They've had about enough of it by now,' Anna said. 'Your dad says travelling about is much easier inside the Web. Still, they have another three weeks to go, so we'll just have to be patient.' She yawned. 'I'm off for a shower and a nap now. Those wretched shifters have almost finished me off.'

'I'll see you later, then,' Jack said. 'I'm meeting Eleni and the Cat at our castle. I can't wait for them to see their new sprites.'

'I hope *they* work out as they're supposed to.' Anna's face brightened. 'Listen, how would you and the gang like to come with me tomorrow and have a sneak preview of Dragonville? I should be up to the testing phase soon, once I've sorted out the problems with the shifters. I'd like to know what you think of it – see if you can spot anything I've forgotten.'

'Do you mean it?' Jack said. He hadn't expected to see the new game so soon. 'Thanks, I'd love to, and so will the others.' He grinned. 'Rom will be like a dog with two tails. He didn't expect to get a look at your dragons for ages yet.'

'Not to mention the shifters,' Anna said. 'I'd like to see what he makes of them. At the moment they're even more tricky than he is.'

'I'll go and tell them now. I'm supposed to be meeting Eleni in a while in any case. 'See you later, Anna.'

'Don't stay up too late,' she said automatically. See you.' She took a bite of the sandwich in her hand, and her face changed. 'Jack! Peanut butter and *tuna*?'

Eleni finished her chores, then walked down to the end of the garden and looked out across the still waters of the harbour. In the curve of the bay behind her, the sun was setting behind the old monastery, high on its hill. The evening was utterly still, except for the lapping of water against the rocks and the cheeping of the little frogs up in the olive grove.

'When I was your age, the whole of Paleo used to come alive at this time of night.'

Eleni jumped at the voice, and turned to see uncle Kostas coming down the path. He stopped beside her and looked out over the ocean.

'When this place was a tourist resort,' he said, 'you could walk around the bay and hear the music from a dozen different tavernas. The air was filled with the smell of good food, and people would walk up and down the road all evening, talking and laughing.' He sighed. 'Oh, it was fine – before the Web came and killed it all. No one but the rich takes holidays now, and they go to more exotic places than this.'

Eleni frowned. 'But you use the Web. And if you hate it, why did you buy me the Websuit?'

Uncle Kostas laid a hand on her shoulder. 'Ah, Eleni-mou. I can't afford to hate the Web. That's where the future is. As you grow up, all the great opportunities will be there. As for the older folk, like your grandparents – well, the easy money, the tourist money, is gone. Some are going back to the old ways – the fishing, and growing olives and grapes. The younger people – the ones with any sense – do what you are doing. They take advantage of the Web.'

Eleni went back through the quiet garden and into the house. As she climbed into her Websuit, she thought about what uncle Kostas had said. I wonder what *my* future will be, she thought. Maybe I could design games, like Anna, when I grow up. Jack thinks my dragon is pretty good. She decided to go and practise it again. She pulled down her visor, keyed her wristpad, and spun into the Web.

When the flat golden plain of Level 1 stretched out before her, Eleni began to make her alterations. She found 'dragons' on Panel A of her wristpad, and keyed the shape she had invented earlier. Her body grew in size, and her arms dropped

down to become legs with huge clawed feet. Wings sprouted
from her back, and a long, spiked tail appeared behind her.
She liked the feeling of it lashing back and forth.

Wearing the shape of the dragon, Eleni went towards the
red E&R block. She was almost there when the blue Exploration block next to it began to ripple, and a woman stepped
out. She was dressed from head to foot in a tight suit of
shining silver, and a featureless silver mask hid her entire
face. Her dark hair streamed out behind her like a cloud, and
on her finger glittered a gold ring with a large red stone. She
looked as though she was in a hurry but when she saw Eleni
she stopped.

'What are *you* doing here?' she asked sharply.

Eleni was about to tell the woman that she must be
mistaken, when she realized that she was still wearing the
body of a dragon. This woman had mistaken her for some
other *dragon*. How peculiar!

'I told you,' the woman snapped impatiently. 'You
shouldn't be out here, someone will see you. Get back to
the labyrinth at once, you stupid creature.' Then she saw
Eleni's wristpad. 'Where did you get that?' she demanded.
Leaping forward, she made a grab for the girl's wrist, but
Eleni leaped back out of the way and made a dive towards the
E&R block. The red surface rippled and parted, and when the
blue light cleared, Eleni was standing in Webtown. She
wasn't safe yet, however. There was a loud pinging chime,
and when she turned, she could see the air above the blue-
circled Entry Point beginning to waver. The woman was
coming through behind her!

CHAPTER THREE

THE WARNING

Eleni wanted to run, but the avenue was too full of people.
Then she remembered. Dragons can fly! She flapped her great
wings frantically and sprang up into the air, skimming
dangerously low over the heads of the crowd. She soared up
between the buildings, wobbling unsteadily from side to side
until she got the hang of level flight. After the first terrifying
minute she really began to enjoy it. It was like swimming,
only a hundred times better. She could enjoy a whole new
view of the Webtown, sprawling into the apparent distance
like a city with its blocks and interlinking strands.

Below moved crowds of people, mostly in human shape,
but all of them young and beautiful. Many had tinted their
skins with brightly coloured designs, and their hair varied
through all colours of the rainbow. Some preferred the form
of weird-looking alien creatures, while others wore all
manner of animal guises, though Eleni could see nothing
quite as dramatic as her dragon.

Thinking of her dragon-shape, Eleni reminded herself
sharply that this was no time to be playing. Once she was
well out of sight of the entry point, she looked for an open
space and came down again between two blocks. Fumbling at
her wristpad with clumsy claws, she was about to hit the
scuttle button when she changed her mind. Who was that
woman, anyway? What did she want with a dragon? Instead
of spinning out, Eleni tapped in the code to change to her
normal human form. Looking like an ordinary girl once

more, she hurried back down the crowded strands towards the Entry Point.

The silver woman was still there, just beyond the blue entry area, walking back and forth through the crowds and looking carefully at all the faces. At the sight of the woman's featureless mask, a shiver went through Eleni. The mysterious figure looked all the more sinister because her expression was hidden. Eleni was certain that she could feel herself being fixed by invisible eyes. Suddenly, she was afraid that the woman would recognize her, even though she had changed her shape. Ducking back out of sight around a corner, she keyed in the code for the design space she shared with Jack and the others, and left Webtown in a flash of blue.

Once she had reached the safety of the rented site, Eleni decided to put the strange woman out of her mind. Forget about it, she told herself. If you stop using the dragon you'll be perfectly safe. It was a pity, but surely she could think of something else. To distract herself, she took a good look at the castle she and her friends had been building. It's still not quite right, she thought. Is it because there's no background yet? The castle rested, square and solid, on a flat golden plain that looked much the same as Level 1. Later, when they had finished the building itself, they would put in grass and trees – or perhaps the castle could be in the mountains, or on a cliff overlooking the sea. The choices in the Shaper's data banks were endless.

Everyone who owned a Websuit could rent design space, though a lot of people didn't use them much, preferring their entertainment ready-made. The site acted as a private area that could be designed and changed to suit the user's needs. Any kind of scenery could be chosen from the various extensive databases – desert, jungle, or even another planet. Any kind of building, from a cave to a cottage to a mansion, could be put into place. Animals, too, could be chosen from the Menagerie data banks – anything from ordinary dogs, cats, cows and chickens, to gryphons, basilisks or unicorns.

'Yo, Leni!' Someone was yelling at her from the top of the castle walls.

Eleni looked up and saw a small green frog-like alien waving at her from the battlements. 'Rom!' she shouted. 'Just a minute, I'll come up.'

She crossed the drawbridge over the still-empty moat and went through the tall arched doorway into the castle. The great hall was enormous with carved pillars, a sweeping staircase that would be great for sword fights, and a fireplace big enough to stand in – yet there was something missing. They had copied the building from the 'castle' section of the data banks, but so far it was just a structure. It needed cobwebs and bats, some half-melted candles, secret passages, dungeons and ghosts. She could hardly wait for Jack to come, so that they could get started.

At least the castle had a tower. They had programmed that the last time they had come. Eleni went up the narrow spiral stairs that had been her own idea, and out of the little door at the top that led on to the flat tower roof.

Rom came bouncing towards her. 'Hi, Leni. Where you been hiding? Haven't seen you for a while.'

'Hi.' Eleni had always felt very shy in front of Rom, the ultra-confident Web-wizard, but, today, something had changed. It must have been the dragon, she decided. How could you be shy when you could become something that big and impressive?

Even though Eleni had sworn, not twenty minutes before, never to use the dragon shape again, she found she just couldn't resist it. It would be really eight to be able to show off, for once, to Rom. She grinned at him. 'I've been busy, Rom. Working on a new shape. Like to see it?'

'Sure. I'm always in the market for new shapes.'

Eleni glared at him, pretending to be fierce. 'You keep your little green paws *off* my new shape! You have quite enough of your own.'

'Peace, peace!' Rom held his little green paws up in front of him. 'You can't hit a guy when he's short and green! Go on, Leni, show me.'

'All right,' Eleni laughed. 'Stand back, Rom, and I mean *well* back.' She entered the dragon code into the keypad on her wrist. The usual, ordinary girl shape that she was wearing shimmered and broke up into a thousand glittering particles that exploded outward and then came swirling back again in the form of a new, much bigger creature. Eleni stretched her huge, green-gold wings and laughed. 'Well? What do you think?'

'Wow!' Rom had stepped back even further, his wide mouth hanging open. A long, scarlet ribbon of tongue unrolled from his mouth, and he jumped as though someone had pinched him and stuffed it back with both hands. The little green alien vanished in a swirl of glitter and Rom's human shape appeared. He was staring so hard that Eleni felt embarrassed. She let the dragon dissolve and spin away, and went back to her human form. 'Do you really like it?' she asked.

'It's eight! I've put on all kinds of shapes, but never anything that *big*. Would you mind if I tried a dragon too? I bet between us, we could come up with some beauties – scare the mips out of Jack and the Cat, eh?'

Eleni could have burst with delight. It took some doing to impress Rom, but it seemed she had finally succeeded. At last, she felt as though she truly belonged in the world of the Web.

The urge to show off just a little more was irresistible. 'I don't know about Jack and the Cat, but I certainly fooled some woman in Level 1 today,' she said. 'She mistook me for somebody else entirely.' Eleni frowned as she remembered the woman trying to snatch at her wrist. 'She wore this weird silver suit and a shiny mask with no face. It was horrible.' She shuddered. 'She had me scared for a minute,' she confessed. 'I don't see how it would be possible for somebody to take my keypad in the Web, but— Rom, what would happen to someone who got stuck in the Web without their wrist unit?'

Rom looked at her, his face very serious. 'It's horrible,' he said quietly. 'It happened to some kids a while ago . . .'

Eleni listened while he told her of his friend Ana Devi, and

the ghostly forms of the poor beggar-children of India who
had been trapped in the Web for months at a time without
any way to escape. 'Eventually, you die,' he told her sadly,
'but it seems to be a long, slow, terrible way to go.'

'What happened to the old woman who kidnapped those
children?' Eleni asked.

Rom shrugged. 'In the end we stopped her. Her house
burned down and her equipment was destroyed. But she
survived, and she's been seen in the Web from time to time. I
think she's still trying to find a way to stay here, even when
her body dies. If you ever see her, Leni, get away as fast as you
can. She's dangerous. I mean it.'

'How would I know her?' Eleni asked curiously. 'This is the
Web, Rom. She could look like anything. She could even look
like *you*, if she wanted.'

'Oh, you'd know her all right,' Rom replied. 'For some
reason, she always gives herself away. No matter what she
looks like, she always wears a ring with a huge red stone. You
can't possibly miss— Whatever's the matter, Leni?'

'I've seen it,' Eleni whispered. 'It was her, Rom – the
woman who tried to steal my keypad. The silver woman! It
was *her*!'

CHAPTER FOUR

THE GREEN-EYED CAT

Even as Rom and Eleni looked at each other in horror, the view in front of them wavered. Jack stepped into the scene, as though he had pushed his way through an invisible curtain. 'Hey, Rom, it's been a while. Hey, Leni, you got here,' he called. 'Good. Are you coming down, or shall I come up?'

'We'll come down,' Rom called back. 'We have something to tell you.'

'Eight. And I have something to tell *you*.' From Jack's grin, he clearly hadn't noticed the grim expressions on their faces. 'Did you see the Cat?' he added. 'She was looking for you.'

'No,' yelled Rom. 'Must have missed her. Come on,' he said to Eleni. He grabbed her hand, and they left the roof together.

When they came out of the great castle door, Jack was standing near the drawbridge. 'I have—' he started, but Rom interrupted him.

'Hold on, Jack. Listen. Something's happened. Something serious.'

Jack knew most of the old woman's history in the Web – Rom had told him before. When he heard that she had threatened Eleni, he frowned. 'We had better be careful,' he said. 'Leni, you say it was the dragon she seemed to recognize?'

Eleni nodded. 'She asked me how I had managed to get out, and what I was doing on Level 1. Then she told me to get back to the labyrinth.'

'Labyrinth? What labyrinth?' Jack muttered.

'One thing is clear,' Rom said. 'She has a dragon – or rather, someone or something in the shape of a dragon – imprisoned there. I wonder what she's up to?'

'I hope we never have to find out,' Eleni said firmly. 'Not if she's *that* dangerous. I don't mind admitting that she scared me. We always trust the Web to be safe.'

Jack was frowning. 'There's something else.' He told them about the disappearance of the Menagerie.

'Do you think there could be a connection?' Eleni asked.

Rom nodded. 'It must be more than a coincidence that the two things should happen on the same day. I can't think what the old woman would want with the Menagerie. Seriously, though, we ought to keep an eye on the situation.'

'Well, forget her for now,' Jack told her. 'Just be careful about turning into a dragon, Leni, unless someone else is with you. Rom, why don't you mention this to what's-her-name, that Webcop you know?'

'Ariadne,' Rom said. 'Yes, I might just do that. I don't think we need mention it to our spiders, though. Agreed?'

All three of them looked at one another. They all knew how parents could be. For some reason, adults got far too worried about things, and no one wanted to see any limits on their time in the Web.

'Agreed,' the others chorused.

Rom grinned. 'In the meantime, don't let it spoil our day. What were you saying when you spun in, Jack? You wanted to tell us something.'

Jack's grin came back. 'Anna says do we want to go with her tomorrow and take a look at the new game?'

Eleni let out a whoop of joy.

'Do we *want* to? Do we ever!' shouted Rom.

'Tomorrow morning, then,' Jack said. 'We'll meet you at Tropicana Bay. I have something else here,' he went on, pleased to be able to surprise them further. 'It's a present for Leni. A surprise. Leni, hold out your hand.'

Eleni came forward curiously.

'Now,' Jack said. 'Key this code into your wristpad, and follow it up with your PAC.'

For a minute, Eleni's hand seemed to blur, then she gasped with delight. There, on her palm, stood a tiny, perfect fairy.

Rom let out his breath in a long whistle. 'Wow, Jack. Hairy! Did Anna program that?'

Jack nodded. 'It's a sprite like my hummingbird. If you ever need Rom or me – or anyone else for that matter – you'll be able to send this for us, Leni. Wherever we are in the Web it'll find us. Anna said she'd make one for you, Rom, if you wanted – but you'd probably figure it out for yourself first.'

Rom grinned. 'You never know. I love her inventions, though. She's a real wizard.'

He held out a hand towards the fairy, but it wouldn't come to him. The slender little creature was about as tall as Eleni's longest finger, and glowed with a pinkish gold light that seemed to come from within its own body. It had a set of shimmering double wings like a dragonfly, coloured misty purple and shades of blue, and so delicate that the light shone through them.

'Oh, Jack!' Eleni was lost for words. As she opened her hand a little further, the fairy sprang upwards and took to the air, its wings a silvery blur as it hovered in front of her.

Suddenly, a sleek grey shape exploded out of nowhere. Flailing white paws clawed the fairy out of the air.

'Cat!'

'No!'

'Stop it!'

All three of them shouted at once. The fairy escaped the flashing white paws of the grey tabby cat and flew up again, its blurring wings making an angry buzz.

The Cat glared at it and waved her tail sulkily. 'Well, the stupid thing was asking for it, hovering there like that. Anyway, what are you making such a fuss about? I didn't hurt it.'

'It was a real basement-level thing to do,' Jack told her angrily.

'Why do you want to spoil things, Cat?' Eleni asked.

'Oh, shut up about your stupid sprite,' the Cat snarled. She turned her back on them and started licking a paw.

'There's no need to be jealous,' Jack told her. 'Anna made one for you, too.'

The Cat's head swivelled sharply. 'She made a sprite for me?' Her green eyes lit up with eagerness.

'Of course. Did you think she'd leave you out? Here, I just need your PAC.'

The expression on the Cat's furry face did not – could not – change, but her tail lashed back and forth faster than ever. 'Oh, curl up, Jack,' she snapped. 'I don't want one of your stupid sprites.' Then she hit her scuttle button and was gone.

Jack, Rom and Eleni looked at each other in dismay, then Jack scowled furiously. 'Why, the stuck-up little—'

'No, Jack.' Eleni shook her head. 'Something upset her. I wonder what's wrong?'

'Who knows? Who cares?' Jack was still frowning. 'Talk about ungrateful. I'll get Anna to reprogram that sprite for Rom.'

'No, wait a while,' Rom urged him. 'You know how moody the Cat can be. she'll probably be all right when she comes back.'

'If she's going to act like that,' Jack muttered darkly, 'she'll be lucky if we have her back at all.'

The scene swirled and exploded into glittering fragments. When Cat lifted up her visor, she was back in her dim, dingy cubicle in the Cybercafe. She pressed the button marked RELEASE and her token sprang back out of the slot and into her hand. Well, at least today's session hadn't cost her much. With movements made jerky by anger, she peeled off her Websuit and threw it down on the couch. By the time Cat reached the door, she had to wipe the blur of tears from her eyes. It's not fair, she thought. It only used to be me, Rom and Jack, before Eleni butted in. Oh, *why* did she have to get that new Websuit?

It hadn't been so bad before. When Eleni had only been gag, Cat hadn't felt so bad about her own problem. She'd done odd jobs for the neighbours every day to earn the money for Cybercafe tokens. But now that the Greek girl had her own suit, she and the boys could spend as much time as they liked in the Web, and Cat would be left out. She was at a disadvantage already – without a suit she couldn't have the sprite, because she didn't have a personal access code. And how could she explain? They must never find out she had no suit of her own, because then she would have to tell them about Dad, and she didn't want them to pity her – it was more than she could bear.

Lurking in the doorway, Cat looked carefully up and down the dull, grey street, before slipping out of the Cybercafe, keeping out of the sickly yellow light of the street lamps. If any of the neighbours should discover her guilty secret and let on to Dad, her life wouldn't be worth living. When she had put a little distance between herself and the arcade, she slowed her pace to an innocent stroll, looking in the shop windows as she went. Just as she was heading up the street, there was a shout from behind her. 'Catherine!'

Cat spun round, smothering a guilty gasp. Behind her, striding quickly up the street, was the tall, stick-thin figure of her father.

CHAPTER FIVE

IN THE CATHEDRAL

Maybe it'll be all right, Cat tried to tell herself. Look innocent. Maybe he didn't see you coming out. But there was a furious scowl on his face as he caught up with her, and he grabbed her arm tightly.

'Just what do you think you're doing?' His face was crimson with anger. 'How many times have I told you to stay away from *that* place?' His voice had risen to a shout now, and people nearby were turning to stare. Cat shrank away from him. She had seen him angry before – he seemed to be angry most of the time these days – but she had never seen him as mad as this. She felt fear like a clenched fist in her stomach, but she also felt anger. He had ruined her life for long enough. What right did he have to treat her like this? 'Get *off* me!' she screamed at him and tore her arm out of his grasp. Then she was running, as fast as she could, away up the street, with no idea where she was going.

Cat heard a shout, and the sound of her father's footsteps pounding along the cobbled street behind her. She kept moving, not daring to slow up and look back. He couldn't be far behind. Around her, ordinary shoppers scattered out of the way. She was bumping into people, but there was no time to stop and apologize. With aching legs, Cat ran uphill and through the market square. There were no moving travel-ways here. Because Durham was an ancient city, the old-fashioned shop windows and concrete pavements had been preserved, and vehicles were kept out of the centre. It looked just as it had looked fifty years ago. The street was narrow, with the buildings leaning out at odd angles, and most of the shops sold weird stuff like unpackaged food, handmade clothes, or candles and chunky jewellery. It was like stepping back in time. More history, Cat thought desperately, as she ran along the narrow pavement. I'm so tired of the past. I want to live *now*!

Cat didn't know whether her dad was still behind her, but she didn't dare stop, just in case. She barely noticed where she was going. Sweat dripped, stinging, into her eyes, and she was gasping for breath. The shops and houses that lined the street were just a blur. Suddenly, the buildings on either side of her vanished. Cat tried to look around, and stumbled. Though she caught herself before she fell, she knew she could run no further. Holding her aching side, she glanced back fearfully, but there was no sign of her father.

Looking around, Cat saw that she was standing in a broad, open space. Why, she had run right up the hill to College Green! To her right was the big, blocky shape of the castle. In front of her, across the lawn where the grass was watered with care every day in summer, the massive cathedral loomed against the sky. Floodlit in silvery light, it looked like a fairy palace with its tall pointed windows and great square bell tower. Looking upwards, Cat could see gargoyles, and statues of angels and saints. Sick of history though she was, she never grew tired of the cathedral. It was too old, and too magnificent.

It was also a good place to hide. Cat knew her father would still be looking for her, and it would only be a matter of time before he came up here. Quickly, she ran across the empty green, ignoring the 'keep off the grass' signs with a pang of guilt. A minute later, she was safely inside.

The cathedral was so vast that it didn't feel like being indoors except for the silence, which fell around Cat like a thick, soft blanket. The electric lights were dim, and hung far above, near the arches of the ceiling. A softer, flickering light came from thick white candles in black iron holders that were taller than Cat herself. The walls, with their arches and

dizzy balconies, rose up on either side of her like cliffs, and a
double row of pillars, carved in zigzags and diamonds,
marched away into the distance towards the night-dark eye
of the great round window. Cat shivered. Though the place
could not be completely empty, for she could hear the echo
of distant footsteps, there was no one in sight. She had never
been alone here at night before. It was beautiful, but very
spooky. Suddenly, she remembered that she was supposed to
be hiding. What if Dad should walk in now?

Almost as if the thought had summoned him, Cat heard
footsteps coming in at the outer door. Her heart leaped up
into her throat. It was impossible to run in the cathedral. For
one thing, she'd be thrown out if somone saw her, but also,
there was an eerie feeling of *watchfulness* here that made
Catherine want to creep around like a mouse. Where could
she hide? Then she noticed the dark blue velvet curtain that
hid the door to the bell tower. A white board on a post stood
in front of it, saying CLOSED FOR REPAIR. It was the ideal
place. Forgetting not to run, she darted across and dived
behind the thick velvet.

The curtain smelled of dust and age. Its folds would hide
her easily, though the tower door would be locked of course.
Listening for footsteps, Cat leaned back against the door –
and staggered backwards as it swung silently open behind
her. Something rolled under her feet, and she sat down hard
on the bottom step of the tower's spiral staircase.

It was too good to be true! Someone, a workman probably,
had forgotten to lock the door of the bell tower. But what had
she fallen over? She groped around in the darkness until her
hand came to rest on a scatter of long, smooth objects, so
thick that she could barely get her hands around them.
Candles! Some wonderful, kindly person had left a supply of
candles in the niche at the bottom of the stairs. Now, if
only . . . She groped in the niche until she found a shelf, and
there, as she had hoped, was an electric lighter. Shielding the
flame with her hand, she lit one of the candles, and made her
second great discovery. The door of the tower could be bolted
from the inside! It was a new bolt, and slid easily and quietly

shut. Cat wondered who would have put it there, and why. It wasn't surprising that the tower was being repaired – the old bells hadn't rung for years – but why would anyone want to lock the door from the *inside*?

'Catherine? Catherine!'

Cat held her breath as she heard her father calling. After a moment, she heard another, more quiet voice, 'Sir, do you mind? This is a House of God.'

Her father stamped away, muttering words that were definitely out of place in a cathedral, and Cat heaved a sigh of relief. He would never find her now! She had better stay where she was, though, in case the other person was still hanging about.

It was quite pleasant to sit on the dark tower steps in a cosy circle of candlelight. It was far more peaceful here than at home, Cat decided, thinking about the housing estate and the little house filled to bursting with her three young brothers and a sister. Not to mention Dad, silent, stern and glowering – and filled with bitter hatred for the Web.

When Cat had been very young – too small, really, to remember much about it – her dad had been a teacher of history, but as the Web became more and more advanced, a single person could teach hundreds of kids. Then Websuits were invented, and the old-fashioned lessons vanished for ever. Kids learned by experiencing whatever they were being taught – learning had become an adventure, and a game. It must be tremendous fun, Cat thought wistfully, but the Web had put her dad on the scrap-heap, and he refused to have anything to do with it. He had grown more and more bitter and angry, and after her mum had left he taught Cat and her brothers and sister himself, and didn't seem to know, or care, what they were missing. For the last three years, Cat had been sneaking off to the Cybercafe whenever she had any money, but now he had found her out, she wouldn't even be able to do that.

Cat clenched her fists and forced herself not to cry. I hate him, she thought fiercely. I won't go back. *I'll never go back!*

After a while, though, she began to wonder what else she

could do. Cat wasn't used to being alone, and she felt guilty that she wasn't at home now, taking care of the younger ones. Would Dad get their tea for them tonight? The thought of tea reminded Cat that she was cold and very hungry. When she heard the voice calling from somewhere up the tower stairs, she thought she must be going mad.

It came softly at first, then louder – the thin, high, quavery voice of an old woman.

'I see you, child. Why sit down there in the cold, when it's warmer upstairs, in my tower?'

CHAPTER SIX

THE SORCERESS IN HER TOWER

Who is that? Cat thought in panic. How can she be here? How does she know *I'm* here? It's impossible. And she sounds just like a witch. A shiver went through her. For goodness' sake grow up, she told herself angrily. Fancy believing in witches at your age. 'Who – who's there?' she tried to shout, but the words stuck in her throat, and came out in a whisper.

'A friend, my dear. Come up into the tower and get warm. I'm sure you must be hungry, too.'

At the thought of food, Cat's stomach gave an embarrassing growl. Though she had been told over and over again not to trust strangers, how could a little old lady do her any harm? She sounded kind enough, and, besides, Cat was eaten up by curiosity. Who was this woman? What could she be doing here?

Taking a deep breath and gripping the candle tightly, Cat set off up the steep, worn steps. She climbed and climbed, while the flickering candle made her shadow dance on the cold stone walls. She didn't hear the voice again. The only sounds were the hollow tapping of her feet on the stairs and her breathing, that grew louder and faster as she ascended. Sometimes, she would pass an old wooden door but everyone that she tried was firmly locked. At last, when she thought she must be very near the top, one of the doors came open as she pushed it, and swung inward with a creak.

Cat couldn't believe her eyes. Instead of the bare, cobwebby stone room that she'd expected, the place was filled with warmth and a dim but cosy red light. There was a carpet on the floor and the windows were covered with thick curtains. Standing at one side of the door, Cat gasped as she looked up at a tall, broad man whose arms and legs were almost as thick as her body.

'It's all right. Don't be afraid of Maxus.'

Cat tore her eyes from the big man to see who had spoken. In the corner, seated in a wheelchair, was an old, old lady. She seemed tiny and frail, and looked lost in the tangle of bottles, tubes and wires attached to her chair, but the proud bones of her face, her thin, jutting hook of a nose, and her sparkling dark eyes gave her a look of arrogance and command. Then, surprisingly, her face broke up into a mass of friendly wrinkles as she smiled.

'Come in, my dear, and get acquainted. I'll get Maxus to heat you some soup.'

Slowly, Cat stepped forward. The old lady's bright, dark eyes held her captive, just like a bird fascinated by a snake. She held out a hand like a bony claw and Cat saw a huge ring with a blood-red stone. The woman smiled again, still holding her hand out in a friendly way, though her eyes glittered fiercely. 'Come to me,' she said softly.

When Cat came close and put her hand in the woman's bony claw, she was amazed at the strength of the grip. The old lady smiled at her. 'You can call me Miss Aldanar, my dear. Now, tell me all about it. Who are you, and why are you hiding here in my tower?'

'*Your* tower?' Cat asked in astonishment. 'But, doesn't it belong to the cathedral?'

'In a sense.' The woman's smile grew broader. 'But shall we just say I'm borrowing it for a while?'

'And they let you?' Cat felt rather shocked.

The woman's smile switched off like a light. '*Let* me? There's no question of whether they'd let me. When, and if, you get to my age, you'll find that enough money can open any door. The upkeep of the cathedral is very expensive, you know. Now—' the smile returned again. 'Sit down here beside me, drink your soup, and tell me what *you* are doing here.'

Cat turned round to see the huge, glowering man standing by her shoulder, holding out a bulb of something that smelled very good indeed. For an instant she hesitated, wondering if the soup was drugged or something. The old woman cackled with laughter. 'If I meant to harm you, do you really think you could get away from Maxus? I wouldn't need to drug you, my dear – or poison you, for that matter.'

Suddenly, Cat felt very silly. The old woman must be lonely, stuck up here with no one but the silent, scowling Maxus for company. The poor old thing was probably a bit batty, but she meant to be kind – and she was a whole lot kinder than Cat's father. 'Thank you very much.' Cat took the bulb from Maxus and sat down on the low stool beside the old lady's wheelchair. 'How did you know I was down at the bottom of the tower?' she asked.

'Security camera.' The woman shrugged, as though it were the most normal thing in the world. 'And I spoke to you through the same system. Now, no more questions. Tell me what you were doing down there.'

Between sips of the hot, delicious soup, Cat began to tell the dismal story of her troubles to her new friend.

'And he won't let you use the Web at *all?*' the woman interrupted.

Cat shook her head. 'He hates everything to do with it.'

'Ridiculous! Why, I don't think it's even legal. You're supposed to have a proper education.'

'Dad teaches us himself.' Cat sighed wistfully. 'From what the other kids tell me, I'm missing out on a tremendous lot.'

'Your father doesn't seem to care that you'll be at a disadvantage when you grow up,' the old lady said sharply. 'The fool! And so you slip away to the Cybercafe whenever you have a chance? Well, good for you.'

Cat couldn't believe it. This woman, this amazing, proud old lady who lived alone in her tower with her faithful servant, just like a sorceress in a fairy tale, understood Cat far better than her own family did. No one had ever been so kind to her – except maybe Jack, she thought, feeling a sudden pang of guilt at the memory of her quarrel with him.

'Well,' the woman was still talking. 'When you ran away, you came to exactly the right place.' Once again, the wrinkled old face creased into a smile. 'As it happens, I might just be able to help you.' She gestured to Maxus, who squeezed behind the wheelchair and pulled at a curtain that was hung right across the corner of the room. It slid aside with a rattle. Cat gasped. I must be dreaming, she thought. There, in the corner, were two foam-form couches – and two truly venomous Websuits.

'I don't need two suits just for myself,' the old lady said kindly. 'I worked in Websuit design right from the very early days, and I still like to keep my hand in. These are a brand new, experimental model. They should have faster reaction times, give you clearer virtual images, *and* be more comfortable to wear. I need someone to help me try them out – so one of these suits is yours for as long as you like, my dear.'

Cat couldn't believe her ears. 'Thank you, oh, thank you,' she whispered. Now she could be like the others! She could stay in the Web as long as she liked, she could see Jack more often. She just kept looking at the Websuits, so happy that she almost wanted to cry. She was far too excited to wonder why the two suits were connected to one another by a mysterious tangle of wires that all went into a small white box with a flashing digital display. She was too busy making plans to notice the expression of avid greed in the old woman's glittering dark eyes – as if *she* were a spider – and Cat was an unsuspecting fly.

CHAPTER SEVEN

DRAGONVILLE

The beach at Tropicana Bay was fairly quiet, though there were quite a few people in the water, surfing the glittering breakers or riding sailboards further out where the ocean was calmer. Others were swimming, or playing with the dolphin phaces that disported themselves among the silvery waves. When Eleni arrived, Jack and Anna were already there, seated at one of the spindly tables that were spread out at the edge of the crimson sands, beneath the yellow-flowered trees.

Anna smiled. 'There you are,' she said. *'Kalimera*, Eleni. *Ti kanis?'*

'Good morning, Anna,' the Greek girl replied with a smile. 'I'm fine, thank you.'

'Now,' Anna said, 'only Rom to come, and the Cat.'

'She isn't coming,' Jack interrupted.

Anna raised an eyebrow. 'Why ever not?'

Jack shrugged. 'I didn't get a chance to tell her,' he confessed. 'We had a fight yesterday. Don't ask me what it was about, 'cos I still don't know. She turned up when I was showing Leni her sprite, and if you want to know the truth, I think the Cat was a bit jealous. But when I told her there was one for her, too, she blew up completely, didn't she, Leni? Spun out in a huff.'

'I've never seen her in such a temper,' Eleni agreed.

'You can say *that* again.' The new voice came from Rom, who had appeared while they were talking.

'Hi, Rom,' Anna said. 'That was good timing. Well, now that everyone's here, let's get going, shall we?'

Eleni followed the others out of Tropicana Bay and back to Level 1. They entered the red Entertainment and Recreation block, and found themselves in the Webtown for that site.

'We'll have to spin in from here,' said Anna, 'I haven't created a proper access yet. Here, I'll give you the codes.'

As she keyed the codes into her wristpad, Eleni felt a flutter of excitement inside. How lucky we are, she thought. A brand new game by such a well-known designer, and we'll be the first to see it! Then she entered the final sequence of the code, and the world around her flickered and *changed*.

Eleni found herself standing on a dizzying ledge, looking out across a vast mountain range with jagged peaks and shadowy canyons that seemed to plunge down deep into the earth. The bare rock of the cliffs and peaks were laid down in layers of red and golden stone, and though Eleni knew that they had only been recently created by Anna, it looked as though they had been weathered into weird, curving shapes by centuries of wind and rain. Many caves had been hollowed into the peaks, their yawning mouths dark against the glowing stone. The sky was more green than blue, and all the shadows had a strange, purple tinge.

Far below, a canyon snaked away between the two nearest mountain peaks, and as Eleni looked down, a speck of silver caught her eye, glowing like a spark among the purple shadows. As it drew nearer, the girl could make out the slender, sinewy shape of the body, the long, slim tail and the great outstretched wings ribbed like those of a gigantic bat. It was a dragon!

Now, other dragons could be seen as sparks of glowing colour – copper, sapphire and glistening emerald green. Flapping their mighty wings to gain extra height, the dragons swept upwards towards Eleni and her friends, growing bigger and bigger, the closer they came.

'They're so beautiful,' Eleni gasped. 'Far more graceful than mine.'

'These have to do more flying,' Anna told her. 'They sort of got more streamlined as time went on.' She tapped something into her wrist unit, the most elaborate keyboard that Eleni had ever seen. Far more complex than those used by the girl and her friends, Anna's slender unit stretched up her arm from wrist to elbow. Eleni tore her gaze away from the fascinating keypad as a warning buzz sounded, and a d-box materialized to float in front of the ledge. It hung steadily in the air as words began to scroll across its dark surface:

WELCOME TO DRAGONVILLE! Here is the lost civilization of the dragonfolk who guard their fabulous jewelled hoards from their deadly foes, the shifters.

The shifters can be seen as misty grey outlines that can pass through solid objects and change into any shape they wish. They spit a poison that will stick to the victim. The venom is a different colour each time it hits. Five hits, and the victim will be 'dead', and out of the game. The shifters also use the hoarded gems that provide the dragons with energy and steal them whenever they can. Dragons can kill shifters, and different coloured beasts have different abilities:

Silver is an ice-dragon. Its breath freezes.

Copper breathes fire.

Emerald can pass through solid objects like the shifters.

Blue can detect shifters at a distance.

Gold is a combination of all characteristics, and is only used for third level play and upwards.

As an additional weapon, the eyes of all dragons are lasers.

Higher levels of the game will be explained when they have been reached.

Now – choose your dragon – and good luck!

The d-box vanished. In its place were four huge dragons, one of each colour with the exception of gold, hovering in midair, as close as they could come to the ledge.

'Wow,' Eleni heard Jack mutter. 'How do we choose?'

'Now, there's a thing I forgot to mention in the instructions,' Anna said. 'This is why a fresh viewpoint is so useful.' She made a quick entry in her wrist unit. 'I'll give you the code that calls them.' She held out her wrist unit so that they could see the code on the tiny display screen. 'I suggest you store these in your own keypads for now. Later, I'll make the dragons voice-linked, so that you can just say the colour or a name out loud and they'll come. It'll save a lot of messing about.'

'I'll take silver.' Jack stepped forward and keyed the code into his unit. The gleaming silver dragon turned its head towards him, its jewelled eyes glittering at him, like rubies. It came closer, and rested its neck against the ledge so that he could scramble aboard.

'Sit astride, just where the neck joins the shoulders,' Anna said. 'Once you're on, you won't fall off.'

As Jack's dragon moved away from the ledge Rom took his place. 'Copper,' he said firmly. 'I like the idea of a beast that can breathe fire.'

That left two dragons, the emerald and the blue. Eleni hesitated. 'Why don't you take the blue dragon?' Anna suggested. 'I'll take the green if you don't mind – this one isn't quite debugged yet. I need to do a bit more work on this business of passing through solid objects. It's a lot more tricky than you'd think.'

'All right,' Eleni said. She called up the blue code and pressed the ENTER button. The great dragon turned towards her, its eyes glittering like diamonds against a hide that was the dark, rich blue of a moonlit sky. With some trepidation she scrambled off the ledge on to its warm, firm neck. Though this was only a game, the landscape was very convincing, and it seemed an awfully long way down.

As the dragon eased itself away from the cliff, she felt her heart beating fast with excitement. What an incredible feeling, to be riding a dragon. Eleni began to experiment, making her dragon swoop and turn and dive. She soon discovered that steering was easy. She only had to lean in the direction she wanted to go for the creature to change course and head that way.

'At this level, you have a few minutes to explore before the shifters come,' Anna called. 'Why not take a look into the caves?'

The caves were beautiful inside. Anna had designed the rocks to glow, so that it looked as though light was shining through chunks of thick glass coloured yellow, red, purple, and green. The floor was covered with soft sand that glittered underfoot, and piled within each cave was a hoard of sparkling crystals, each about the size of a human head. 'If your dragon seems to be slowing up or weakening, you need to bring him here to eat one of these,' Anna told them. 'If you don't remember, or if the shifters steal all the crystals, or stop you getting to them, you'll eventually fall out of the sky and it'll be game over.'

When they emerged again into the open air, Eleni glanced down over the shoulder of her dragon and saw the glint of a river, a winding silver thread that marked the bottom of the canyon. There seemed to be pale meadows on either side of the water, and the darker blur of trees beyond, but she was so high it was hard to tell. Nonetheless, she marvelled at the amount of detail that Anna had put into the game. That's why she's so successful, I suppose, she thought—

'Alert! Alert! Shifters approaching!'

Eleni realized that her own dragon was sounding the alarm.

'Look out! Behind you!' That was Rom calling.

The blue dragon made an incredible swerving, swooping turn in the air, and Eleni caught a glimpse of a hazy blur that came rocketing out of the dark caves in the mountain face. Even as she watched, the haze took on the shape of a gigantic pterodactyl. Though the form was clear and detailed, down to the leathery bat-like wings and the slender scissor-jaws like those of a crocodile, Eleni could see right through its body to the blurred, misty outlines of the crags beyond. Gripped tightly between its clawed feet, the huge winged dinosaur held a glittering red jewel, about the size of Eleni's head.

There was a snarling sound from the left, where Jack's dragon flew. Twin bolts of sizzling crimson energy lanced out of the silver dragon's eyes, converging on the point where the pterodactyl had been an instant before. A portion of rock smoked, glowed and broke off with an explosive crack.

Suddenly, another shifter appeared, oozing out of the face of the cliff, passing easily through the rock as though it was made of nothing but cobwebs. This time, the creature took the shape of a gigantic shark that swam effortlessly through the air, its gaping jaws bristling with a fearsome collection of teeth. Flying in at an angle to defend the creature that carried the jewel, it arrowed towards the dragons with startling speed.

'Split up!' Jack yelled.

Rom went right. Eleni and Jack went left – Eleni soaring upwards, Jack diving beneath the monster.

'Danger, danger!'

'Look out, Leni!'

The dragon's alarm and Rom's warning shout came at exactly the same time. Even as Eleni swerved her dragon aside there was a sharp sound like fat spitting in a frying pan, and she felt something hit her leg. She looked down to see a patch of dripping slime, coloured a luminous, lurid pink, sticking to her leg. So this was the poison. Four hits to go, and she would be down the plug.

Rom was heading for the other shifter, the pterodactyl, trying to head it off before it could escape with its prize. The shifter-shark had come around fast and was buzzing Eleni again, its pointed teeth flashing white in its cruel, wedge-shaped face. 'Shoot!' Eleni urged her dragon, and the deadly red beams shot out from its laser eyes, hitting the edge of the shark's triangular fin. The creature screamed in pain and anger. Eleni fired again, at the same time as Jack who had been coming up on it from below. The crimson lasers shot out and the shifter writhed between them, screaming, before exploding into nothingness.

Jack let out a whoop of triumph. 'Got him!' Then, as he looked past Eleni, his face fell. 'Uh-oh. Quick, Leni. Rom needs help!'

The girl turned her dragon to see Rom surrounded by four of the vast creatures, three of them carrying bright gems stolen from the dragon-caves. He was fighting bravely, his copper dragon twisting and weaving, dodging and diving, but the creature seemed to be tiring. The beams from its laser eyes were weaker and less effective than they had been. Already, Rom was spattered with blotches of the venom that stained Eleni's leg. There were three patches, one pink, one sickly yellow, and the other lurid green. Only two more hits, and he would be 'dead.'

'Come on!' Eleni shouted. 'We've got to help him!'

After that, everything happened very fast. More and more of the creatures came slithering out of the rocks, in all kinds of weird and outlandish shapes. Some came as sharks, others as jellyfish with long, trailing tentacles. There were serpents, more pterodactyls, giant wasps, and other monsters that Eleni couldn't even begin to name. She found that there was no time to think – it was all reaction and split-second timing as she dodged and swerved, fighting to get the shifters within the sights of her lasers. After a time, she began to work as a team with the others. Jack would freeze the monsters so that they hung motionless, glittering palely, caught in midair by the icy breath of his silver dragon – then Eleni would blast them to smithereens with her laser. Rom swooped down to catch the glittering crystals that the shifters dropped.

Suddenly, there were no more shifters. A buzzer sounded and a d-box appeared with a flashing message:

LEVEL 1 SUCCESSFULLY COMPLETED.
COMMENCING LEVEL 2—

There was a noise like a thunderclap, and the green dragon came hurtling straight through the face of the cliff, almost colliding with Jack's beast. The d-box vanished.

Anna pulled her dragon around to face the others. 'I'm sorry, gang, we have to break this up,' she said. 'Something has gone dreadfully wrong with the game. One of my dragons is missing.'

CHAPTER EIGHT

CODE VIOLATION RED

When Jack got up next morning he remembered that it was the day he had to travel into Wicklow Town for a day in Realworld school – and he was late, as usual. In the kitchen he found a tired, grouchy Anna making breakfast in a ferocious silence. She was doing the cooking herself instead of leaving it to the autochef, and that was usually a sign that she wanted to get something out of her system. By the sharp smell of burning that hung around the kitchen, it was doubtful whether she had succeeded. Judging from the look on her face, Jack knew better than to ask if she'd had any luck with the missing dragon. Instead, he looked for a safer subject.

'Eggs?' he said brightly. 'That'll be nice. We don't usually have a cooked breakfast.'

'I'm not usually up all night,' Anna answered shortly, sliding scrambled eggs on to a plate and thumping it down on the table in front of him. Jack picked up a piece of charred black toast and put it down again. He looked at the greasy yellow mass of his egg, speckled with brown, burnt lumps, and swallowed hard. 'Er – you didn't find the dragon then?' he asked in the politest voice he could manage.

Anna looked at his plate, blinked, and burst out laughing. She scraped the eggs into the recycler. 'I'm sorry, Jack. Shall we start again?' She turned to him with one hand on the autochef keypad. 'What would you really like for breakfast?'

'I think I'll just have cereal,' Jack said hastily.

Anna made herself some tea and sat down opposite him, and there was a brief scrimmage while the cats fought for position on her lap.

'So you didn't get anywhere with the game?' Jack asked her.

Anna shrugged. 'I just don't know what's happening. How the blazes could I lose a dragon? If that wasn't bad enough, the creature was by far and away the most advanced phace I've ever programmed. The gold dragons were very special – they had the abilities of all the other dragons put together, and what was more, they could speak.' She sighed. 'My prototype was developing in leaps and bounds – in fact I could swear it was starting to work things out for itself. It was the nearest thing to an artificial intelligence I've ever seen.'

'This probably sounds stupid,' Jack said, 'but you don't think it could have gone off somewhere on its own?'

Anna shook her head. 'No, it wasn't advanced enough yet – though don't think I haven't looked into the possibility,' she added with a wry smile. 'I can't help wondering, though, whether the game was being tampered with already. You remember I was telling you about that trouble with the shifters? They were never quite under my control, and they should have been. If they start bleeding across into other Websites, I'm in trouble. This could ruin my reputation as a designer.'

Cat couldn't remember when she'd been so happy. She supposed she would have to go back to her father some time, and she dreaded the confrontation – but that was for the future. She wouldn't think about it now. She had spent the night on the foam-form couch that she would be using during her time in the Web, and had awakened early in the morning with a tight, excited feeling in her chest as though it must be Christmas Day.

The first thing she saw when she opened her eyes was her very own Websuit, hanging beside the couch. Cat looked at it and felt her heart beat faster. Almost timidly, she reached out a hand to touch the flexible, shining material.

'Did you think you were dreaming?' The old woman's
voice made her jump. Miss Aldanar was sitting in her wheelchair as though it were a throne, and she some ancient
queen. Her bright, dark eyes seemed to look right into Cat's
mind.

'I never dreamed of having a suit as good as this,' Cat
replied softly.

Miss Aldanar smiled. 'Well, it's about time you tried it.
You'll find a bathroom of sorts on the floor below – the
plumbing is all a bit makeshift here, but we manage – and
Maxus will give you some breakfast. Then—' she waved a
hand at the suit. 'The Web is all yours, Cat.'

When he returned in the afternoon from his Realworld
lessons, Jack couldn't wait to get back into the world of the
Web. He wanted to see Rom and Eleni, and chase the fade
after yesterday's adventures in the dragon game. To his
annoyance, they were nowhere to be found. Then he
remembered that Rom, at least, lived in a different time zone
in the USA, and on a schoolday, he would be in lessons right
now. Eleni was probably stuck at home helping her mother
again.

Jack left his sprite on Level 1 for them then entered the
E&R block and found the 'Space Command' game where he
had great fun shooting down enemy craft and, from time to
time, being shot down himself. It seemed tame, though, to
someone who had spent yesterday riding his own dragon,
and, after a while, a guy called Ralph turned up and ruined
things completely.

Ralph was a phreak of the worst kind – he *lived* for this
game, and played all the time. Because he knew each move
inside-out, no one else stood a chance when he came on the
scene. Even when Jack finally let himself be wiped out, he
still couldn't shake off the phreak, who, when he was in the
Web, took the appearance of an old-fashioned pilot with
leather flying jacket, helmet, goggles, and a huge, curling
moustache. Ralph wanted to go and chase the fade, but Jack
wouldn't be seen dead in Tropicana Bay with this coggy

Webhead tagging along. 'I can't,' he said quickly. 'I promised I'd meet somebody.'

When Ralph had gone to find some fellow phreaks, Jack wondered what to do next. He knew he ought to scuttle down, or risk an attack of the voms, but he didn't feel like going just yet. Why shouldn't I go and see Anna? he thought suddenly. I bet she's still in Dragonville, looking for her missing creature.

Though Anna didn't really like him to hang around too much in her games until they were finished, he knew he was welcome to visit her from time to time, and this seemed as good a time as any. He spun out of 'Space Command' and found himself back in the busy streets of the E&R Webtown. There was no way he would have been allowed into Anna's working block, but he still had yesterday's limited code that would let him into Dragonville only. Rom knew half a dozen other ways to get into the block, around the slow, low-level spiders that guarded the area against intruders, but Jack didn't want to be caught using one of *those* – not when there was no need.

As soon as he came near the block, the spiders began to close in around him, repeating: 'Restricted area Code Amber. Please leave immediately.' Jack grinned and keyed the Amber Code that Anna had given him into his wristpad. Suddenly, the spiders seemed not to see him any more, and scuttled away. Though the game wouldn't have an entrance screen in Webtown until it was finished, Jack could spin into it directly, using the game code plus Anna's access code. He entered the codes into his pad -- and nothing happened.

'That's weird,' Jack muttered. He pressed the sequence of numbers again, more carefully this time, in case he had made a mistake. The keypad let out a burst of shrill electronic squeals, and a message began to flash in red on the screen:

CODE VIOLATION – RESTRICTED ACCESS ONLY.

Code violation? Jack thought. But that's impossible! What the mip is going on?

Suddenly, he noticed that he was attracting a lot of

interest. Everywhere he looked, faces turned accusingly towards the wrongdoer who had broken a restricted code. Jack writhed with embarrassment, but that wasn't the worst of it. Spiders were scurrying towards him from all directions – and these were larger, faster and far more menacing than the usual, fairly harmless guardians. Their voices were a cold, threatening buzz:

'Code Violation Red. Code Violation Red. Immediate exit compulsory.'

'Six!' Jack muttered, and pressed his scuttle button. The spiders dissolved in a sparkling cascade.

Jack ripped off his visor and heaved a sigh of relief to see the safe, familiar walls of his room around him once more. He wondered if the spiders had discovered his identity. Would they just report him to Anna, or did the Web Police become involved for a Code Red Violation? And what was the penalty? Would they take away his PAC? With an effort, he pulled himself together before his imagination ran away with him completely. 'That's just stupid,' he told himself. 'It's all a mistake – Anna must have changed the code and forgotten to tell me. I'd better let her know, so she can put things right.'

Still feeling a little shaky, he fumbled his way out of his Websuit and went to Anna's workroom. To his surprise, there was no sign of her. He found her in the kitchen, sitting at the table with her head resting in her hands. An untouched cup of tea was in front of her, and an empty microspray pack of her favourite headache killer.

Jack forgot his own problems. 'Anna? Are you all right?'

Anna jumped and looked at him as though she hardly recognized him. 'What? Oh, sorry, love, I was miles away. Today has been an absolute nightmare.' She rubbed her eyes wearily. 'I can't believe what's happened. When I punch into Dragonville some blasted idiot keeps hitting me with a Code Red Violation! I can't get into my own game!'

Anna shook her head. 'I've tried everything I can think of, but I can't get into the wretched site. I've managed to invalidate the Code Red Violation, so I can tinker around now without being buried in spiders every time I make a move, but that's all.' She sighed. 'I'll tell you something, though. Whoever set up that Violation was a master. It took half the day to track down the new programming, and the other half to undo it.'

'But who would want to seal off an unfinished game?' Jack wondered. 'Do you think it could be something to do with the disappearance of the other sites, like Menagerie?'

'There could well be a connection,' Anna admitted. 'In any case, the culprit may be someone who wants to complete my game their own way, and that's what really worries me.' Anna frowned. 'Dragonville is registered in my name, so if anything goes wrong, I'm legally responsible.'

CHAPTER NINE

CAT AND GARGOYLE

A day in Realworld school meant Realworld homework, but Jack was too busy puzzling over the mystery to concentrate on his studies that evening. Eventually he gave it up as a bad job, spun out of the Education block and back to Level 1. Maybe he could find Rom and Eleni . . . But he didn't, and his sprite was just where he'd left it. Instead, the first person he saw was the last person he'd expected. To his surprise, a slender girl with short dark hair and wide, smiling green eyes came up to him and held out a hand. 'I found your sprite.' She bit her lip and looked away from him. 'I'm sorry I lost my temper the other day,' she said. 'Will you forgive me?'

It wasn't! It couldn't be—

'Jack?' she said. 'It's me, Cat.'

'But—' At last Jack found his voice. 'But you *never* come into the Web as a human.'

Cat shrugged. 'That was then. This is now. Things have changed for me, Jack.' A small frown appeared on her pretty face. 'Don't you like it?'

'I love it,' he said hastily – and it was true. The funny thing was, her little pointed face still looked very cat-like, with those high cheekbones and huge green eyes. Jack found himself wondering if the human form she was using now was anything like her Realworld appearance.

Suddenly, it seemed very important to get to the bottom of the mystery that was Cat. 'What about going to Tropicana Bay?' Jack suggested. 'I can leave my sprite for—' He clapped his hand to his forehead. 'I nearly forgot! I still have *your* sprite, the one that Anna made for you, if you want it, that is.'

Cat's face broke into an enormous smile. 'Oh, Jack, I would love it! I'm really sorry about what I said. I didn't mean it. I was just having a bad day.'

'It doesn't matter,' Jack said, marvelling at the change in her. It seemed that the old sulky, sharp-voiced Cat had gone – he hoped, for ever. This new version was much nicer.

From his own wrist unit, Jack accessed the coding for Cat's sprite. He held the wristpad out so that she could see the series of numbers. 'Key in this code,' he told her, 'and then your PAC.' Cat punched the two series of numbers into her wristpad, and a tiny figure sprang into existence on her outstretched hand.

'Oh, yuk!' Jack made a face.

'Jack, how can you say that? He's *perfect*!' Cat's face was alight with pleasure.

That Cat! He would never understand her. Jack looked again at the little gargoyle with its black, furry body, its long, clawed, spidery fingers and its batlike wings. Its wrinkled face was also like that of a bat, with an upturned snout, long white fangs and sharply pointed ears. It was absolutely hideous, he thought. As he put his head closer for a better look, it squinted its glittering red eyes at him and made a rude gesture.

Cat crowed with laughter. 'Oh, Jack, it's wonderful! It's the most amazingly venomous thing I've ever seen! How does Anna do it? How did she know just exactly what I'd like?'

Jack shrugged. 'There's no accounting for taste, but I'm glad you like it. Now, if you've finished admiring the horrible creature, how about heading off to Tropicana Bay?'

Cat stuck her tongue out at him. 'He's *not* horrible and I don't think I'll ever finish admiring him. Tropicana Bay sounds fine.'

When Cat finally emerged from the Web, she was amazed to see that the windows of the cathedral tower were already dark. She had spent the last two days exploring the Web – by far the longest time she had ever spent there – apart from her sleep-time and several hour-long breaks to stave off the voms. She had loved every moment. It was so different having unlimited access to the Web. Her meeting with Jack tonight had been the best part, though. It made such a difference not to have to bother about the time ticking away.

Miss Aldanar was looking at her with eyes that burned bright in her hawk-like face. 'Well? Did you have a good time, my dear?'

'It was eight!' Cat said enthusiastically, then remembered that she was talking to an old woman. 'That is, it was marvellous.'

Miss Aldanar laughed. 'It's all right, I know what eight means. Why, I might even have made up the word myself. I've invented so many things in my time, it's difficult to remember them all,' she added quietly.

Cat was surprised when the old woman suggested that they might spend some time in the Web together. 'There's so much I can show you,' she said. 'I can get you into sites where you wouldn't normally be allowed to go.'

Cat was reluctant. She had been planning to meet Jack again tomorrow, and was looking forward to it. But she owed Miss Aldanar so much. She wouldn't have any of this had it not been for the old lady's kindness. It wouldn't hurt her to spare a few hours. Miss Aldanar, at her age, could hardly be expected to spend too long in the Web. Cat could always leave her new sprite for Jack, and meet him later. It would give her a chance to try the little creature out.

Unfortunately, Cat's conscience, having bothered her once, decided to rear its ugly head again. Dad would be ever so worried about her by now, and those dratted little eggs would be missing their big sister. Though she didn't want to go back home – at least not yet – something would have to be done.

'Miss Aldanar?' she said tentatively. 'Do you think we ought to find some way of letting Dad know I'm all right?' For the first time, it struck her as peculiar that a grown-up could have been so unconcerned about such an important detail.

The old woman frowned. 'I suppose it would be wise, my dear, but we must think very carefully about what we'll tell him. Do you really want to go home, Cat? I thought you were unhappy there.'

Cat felt a stab of alarm. 'No, no,' she said quickly. 'If I go back he'll never let me come here again. He must never be allowed to find out about this place. I just, well, he'll be worrying, that's all,' she finished lamely.

Miss Aldanar's frown changed to a smile. 'You're right, of course. We mustn't alarm him unduly. Why don't we spend a pleasant day together tomorrow as we planned, and in the meantime I'll try to think of a way to reassure your father. How does that sound?'

'That would be wonderful,' Cat said gratefully. She was hugely relieved. Trust Miss Aldanar to know what to do. The old lady was incredibly kind to her!

Next morning, Miss Aldanar was all briskness. 'Now, it'll take a while for Maxus to help me get into my suit, so why don't you go on ahead? I'll meet you on Level 1 as soon as I'm ready. You'll know me by my ring.'

'OK,' Cat nodded. 'I'll see you in a little while.' Maybe, if she was quick, she would run into Jack while she was waiting. She hurried off to get into her Websuit, and within minutes, was lost in the world of the Web.

When Cat was safely out of Realworld, the old woman turned to the hulking figure of Maxus. 'Right. Pay attention. First, I want you to come with me to Dragonville. Now we've finally discovered how to encode stolen information in those energy crystals the dragons collect, we must set that part of our plan in action. Once we've loosed the dragons and the shifters, I want to concentrate on the girl. I daren't waste any more time, Maxus. We're going to take her today.'

The big man frowned. 'So soon?' he asked sadly.

The old woman's eyes flashed with anger. 'Imbecile! Don't go soft on me now, or I'll make you wish you had never been born! We must act before she has a chance to contact her family. Do you *understand*?'

Maxus sighed. 'Yes, madam. I won't fail you, I know how important this is. I'll do my part. It's just—'

'I know, you great fool,' the old woman said softly. 'But I'm dying, Maxus. Don't you see, I have no choice?'

The big man looked away from her. 'I know, madam. You've always been so good to me since you took me off the streets when I was a child. I don't want to lose you.'

The ghost of a smile crossed the old woman's bony face. 'Dear Maxus,' she said softly. 'What would I do without you?' She took a deep breath. 'Now, are you quite clear about what you have to do? First we release the dragons and the shifters. Then, as soon as I take the child into the labyrinth, you spin back here and swap over the connections on the two Web-suits.' She pointed to the white box into which both sets of Websuit cables vanished. 'When you take away the girl's keypad she'll be safely trapped in the Web – and when I come back to Realworld, I will find myself in a new, healthy young body.'

CHAPTER TEN

DRAGON RAID

Though autumn was on its way, it was easily still warm enough for Eleni's family to eat breakfast outside on the terrace overlooking the sparkling bay where the far horizon was hazy in the silvery morning light. In a hurry to get into the Web, she gulped down her breakfast, excused herself hastily and left the table while the rest of her family was still eating.

'Are lessons so interesting that you have to rush away to them?' the voice of her father floated after her. Eleni felt her face grow warm with guilt. As he clearly suspected, her destination this morning was *not* the Education block – at least not entirely. 'I have to hurry, Papa,' she called back over her shoulder. 'I have a lot to do today.' Well, that was true, at any rate.

Yesterday, Eleni reflected as she climbed into her Websuit, had been one of those awful days when nothing had gone right. It had been a school day, but after the excitement of the day before, her thoughts had been all over the place, and she hadn't done as well as usual. She had been late getting home from Corfu Town, late with her usual chores, then Mama, it seemed, had gone out of her way to find a hundred other irksome little jobs for her to do, until it had been too late to enter the Web at all.

This morning would be different, though, Eleni promised herself. She was determined to catch Jack. She knew he'd be heading for the Education block to catch up on the home-

work from yesterday's class. Maybe they could get together,
instead, and chase the fade at last. Settling herself comfortably on her foam form couch, she pulled down her visor and
heaved a sigh of relief as Level 1 sprang into life around her.

Education was busy that morning, with crowds of students
popping in and out of the various blocks. Eleni thought
about trying out her sprite for the first time, but as it turned
out, there was no need. She was loitering near the entry area,
keying in Jack's code for the sprite, when he spun in. 'Leni!'
he cried. 'Am I glad to see you! All sorts of things have been
happening. You'll never guess—'

Taking her arm, he pulled her back towards the entry
point. 'Where can we talk?' he muttered. 'Everywhere's too
busy at this time of day.'

'What about—' The words were swept out of Eleni's mouth
by the screech of an alarm klaxon, followed by the sound of a
deafening roar. A glittering green dragon burst out of one of
the buildings in the Education block, clutching a cluster of
sparkling cyrstals in its talons. Screaming people threw
themselves to the ground. Others scattered left and right like
scurrying ants as the dragon banked dangerously low across
the Webtown. With another ear-splitting bellow, it skirted
the official entry point and vanished through the wall.

Eleni and Jack looked at one another, horrified. Before they
even had time to collect their thoughts, the whole of the area
was suddenly aswarm with spiders, most of which looked
considerably bigger, darker and meaner than the usual
inoffensive little security patrollers. Eleni shuddered as a
great, dark-green hairy creature about the size of a small pony
approached them.

'*Identify yourselves,*' it said. '*State destination and personal
access codes.*'

One at a time, Jack and Eleni gave their PACs to the spider.

'*Destination?*' it demanded again.

'Secondary area,' Jack said hastily, 'and we're late.' Grabbing Eleni's hand, he pulled her quickly away, continuing to
tug her as they ran together down the nearest strand, until
they were well out of sight of the spiders.

When they finally came to a halt, Eleni looked at Jack. 'What's going on?' she said. 'That was one of Anna's dragons from the game!'

'The green one,' Jack said grimly. 'The one that goes through walls. So that was what they were up to!'

'Who?'

'Whoever blocked off the access to Dragonville yesterday. Look, there are spiders here, too. Keep walking, as if we're going somewhere, and I'll tell you about it.'

Eleni listened in astonishment as Jack told her what had happened when he had tried to return to Dragonville, and how Anna herself was now locked out of her own game. 'But that's terrible,' she said. 'Who could have done such a thing? And why?'

'My guess is—' Jack's words were cut off abruptly. Walking aimlessly, they had strayed into the Tertiary Area, with its peaceful green lawns lined with university blocks. Even as Jack spoke, a shadowy figure oozed through the wall of a nearby research facility – the misty figure of a horned demon, its clawed hands full of sparkling crystals. Cackling evilly, it vanished in a flash of flame, even as alarm bells began to ring within the block. Jack groaned. 'The shifters are loose too, Eleni. We're down the plug now and no mistake.'

What in the world is happening? Cat thought, as she entered Level 1. Where did all these enormous spiders come from? Well, if there had been some kind of trouble, she had best get herself out of here. She would just leave her sprite for Jack.

Cat keyed the sprite code on her wrist unit and smiled with delight as the little black imp popped into existence on the palm of her hand, baring its fangs at her in a wicked grin. This was much better than Leni's coggy fairy. Working quickly, she keyed Jack's PAC and, since she didn't know where Miss Aldanar would be taking her, she programmed the sprite for a 'follow me', the function that would enable it to track her wherever she went within the Web. Spreading its batlike wings, the sprite flew off to wait for Jack.

Cat got another unpleasant surprise when she spun into the E&R Webtown. The normally crowded streets were close to deserted, except for more spiders than she had ever seen in her life. *It's me they're after!* was the first panic-stricken thought that flashed through the Cat's head. Don't be such a gag, she told herself firmly. All these nasty-looking, high-level spiders for one runaway girl?

Nevertheless, in this all-too-public place, Cat felt horribly exposed wearing her human form and her own face. Though she could think of no one, apart from her friends, who might recognize her, the crowds of spiders made her very nervous. Besides, if her father had told the police she was missing, her description just might have been circulated.

Clumsy with haste, Cat fumbled for her wrist unit. The next minute, the dark-haired, human girl with the pointed face had vanished, and in its place stood a small grey tabby cat, with a black-ringed tail that twitched uneasily back and forth. With a quick glance right and left, Cat darted down a narrow access between two blocks where she could hopefully stay out of sight and still keep an eye on the entry point. She wished Miss Aldanar would hurry up and arrive. She had a feeling that the formidable old woman would be more than a match for any spider.

When Miss Aldanar finally did come, it was not from the direction Cat had anticipated, and not in a guise she had expected. In fact, the woman could only be recognized by her ring with its glittering red stone. Her dark hair streamed out behind her like bonfire smoke, lit with flashes of red-gold light that might have been flame. In her skintight suit of shining silver, and the expressionless silver mask that gave her face a mantis-like appearance, she truly looked like the sorceress of Cat's imagination.

Greatly relieved, the Cat rushed out to meet her, forgetting, in her hurry, that Miss Aldanar would not be able to recognize *her*. To her astonishment, however, the woman had no difficulty at all. 'Ah, there you are.' The sorceress said briskly. 'I like your shape, my dear. It takes great talent to move so comfortably in the guise of an animal. Now I know why you call yourself Cat – or is it the other way around? Did the shape come from the name?'

At that moment a huge, spiky black spider came scuttling up to them, and Cat shrank nervously away from the formidable creature.

'Immediate identity required,' it demanded.

'State destination and personal access codes.'

Miss Aldanar's silver mask glittered coldly. 'Sorceress,' she snapped, much to Cat's delighted surprise. 'Code Triple-platinum – security override.'

Abruptly, the spider seemed to shrink in on itself.

'Apologies, Madam – override in place.' Quickly, it scuttled away.

'Come along,' Miss Aldanar told the astounded Cat, looking as cool as if she ate advanced-level spiders for breakfast. 'We don't have all day. Would you mind going back to your usual shape, my dear? I like the cat, but I'm old-fashioned enough to feel easier talking to a human being. Now, hold out your arm, and let me see your wrist unit.'

When the Cat was human once more, the silver-masked woman took her arm and began to tap a code into her keypad. 'Excuse me, Cat,' she apologized, 'but these are adult-only codes, and I can't reveal them to you.'

As the sorceress finished entering the codes, there was a flash of Blue and Tone, and the Cat found herself standing, with the silver woman, on a high cliff overlooking a jagged mountain range of reddish stone. Far below, in the purple shadows of a canyon, dragons flew and played. Miss Aldanar turned to her. 'What do you think of it, my dear? Welcome to Dragonville.'

The world seemed to stand still around the Cat. 'Dragonville?' she blurted without thinking. 'But that's an Anna Lucas game.'

The cold metallic mask turned slowly towards the girl. Cat realized, with a chill, that though its surface appeared to be gleaming silver, it reflected nothing. 'And who's to say that *I* am not Anna Lucas?' the sorceress asked in a voice made of claws and steel.

Suddenly, the Cat realized that something was dangerously wrong. Why had this woman lied to her? Just who was she, anyway? Had Cat been wrong to trust her?

CHAPTER ELEVEN

A FAMILIAR FACE

Cat's first instinct was to hit her scuttle button and get out of there as fast as she could, but the curiosity that went with her name got the better of her. Her new friend was up to something, but Miss Aldanar had never attempted to harm her, after all. In fact, she had shown Cat nothing but kindness. Besides, Cat told herself, if this silver woman was doing anything bad to Anna's game, then surely it would be better to find out about it so that the designer could be warned?

Caught in a tangle of loyalties, Cat hesitated. Then it was too late.

'Well, Cat,' Miss Aldanar smiled. 'How would you like to ride a dragon?'

That settled it.

Riding one of the great winged creatures was an incredible experience. Cat's flame-breathing copper dragon shone red-gold like a bright new coin in the alien sunlight, and looked every bit as splendid as the sorceress's silver mount. But, while Miss Aldanar's flight was steady, level and business-like, Cat and her dragon were darting all over the sky, diving, swooping, banking and swerving like a great red kite gone mad.

After a while, the sorceress called them to order. 'Come along now, Cat, I have something to show you.'

Reluctantly, Cat guided her dragon to the side of the silver beast. 'But we were having so much fun,' she protested.

'Be still,' Miss Aldanar snapped coldly, 'and do as you're told. Remember how lucky you are to be here at all.'

Cat fell sulkily into position behind the silver dragon, deciding not to push her luck. Miss Aldanar could be very kind, but obviously it wasn't wise to cross her. They flew on for a time in silence, until Cat began to get bored with looking at mountains and canyons, cliffs and crags. Why did I say I'd come with the old battleaxe? she thought gloomily. I could be with Jack right now, having some fun. We could— *What the mip is that*?

Cat's first thought was of the famous 'face' on Mars, the mysterious feature that the Olympus Mission would soon be investigating once and for all. The image below her was many kilometres long and filled the floor of the valley below. It had the contours of a gigantic face carved into the soft red rock, and the features were unmistakably those of a young Miss Aldanar, the face that was now hidden behind the expressionless silver mask.

The silver dragon was circling above the proud and lovely face, losing height as it spiralled down. A shiver went through Cat – excitement or fear, she was no longer sure. If this was Anna's game, then how had this face come to be here? Sending her own mount into a dive, she caught up quickly with Miss Aldanar. 'Are we going down *there*?' she yelled. 'Is it really you?'

The Sorceress glanced back at her. 'Trust me,' she said in a gentle voice, 'I have something to show you.'

Swallowing her doubts, Cat followed the silver woman down. Indeed, it seemed impossible now to disobey her. Down, down, they went, towards the gigantic mouth, that was open in an enigmatic half-smile. *Oh, no.* Cat thought. *Oh, please, surely not in there—* As they neared the massive opening, she could see a long dark tunnel winding away into the depths of the earth. Then they were inside, Miss Aldanar's silver dragon glimmering faintly like a ghost in the dim light as it headed for the tunnel.

With a hideous grinding noise, the mouth snapped shut behind the Cat. She screamed in panic as the darkness swallowed her, and groped frantically for her scuttle button, suddenly desperate to escape. Terror squeezed her heart in an icy fist. She was alone in the dark, and her keypad was gone!

In the Education block, the rumours were flying thick and fast. Despite the efforts of the spiders to keep order, the normal business of the day had ground to a halt. Jack and Eleni split up for a while and wandered through the strands, mingling with the crowds of people who were also collecting and passing on the growing number of stories. After an hour, they met back at the prearranged place – the half-completed castle in their rented E&R design space – to compare notes.

They sat on the battlements, swinging their legs while they shared what they had discovered. It appeared that data on a wide range of subjects was being stolen throughout the Web. Among all sorts of weird and wonderful stuff, the following stood out:

> The Cryogenics Department of the university had lost virtually-encoded samples and the results of their latest experiments on cold sleep in which they were working to preserve living bodies by freezing them.

> Bigene Industrie, who had been working on an advanced project to grow limbs and organs for transplant, had also lost top-secret experimental data.

> Helnen Robotics, a company at the cutting edge of the development of Artificial Intelligence, were frantically denying that they had lost *anything* – and everyone knew what that meant.

> A whole screed of varied data from the Olympus Mission, for goodness' sake, had been spirited away in mid-transmission.

Jack frowned when Eleni told him the last one. 'What on earth is going on?' he muttered. 'Who can be doing this? Why do they want all this stuff – and what are they doing with Anna's game?'

'I think you ought to talk to her,' Eleni suggested. 'Why not send your sprite for her?'

Jack shook his head. 'I would, but she isn't in the Web this morning. She was up all night trying to get into Dragonville, and I left her fast asleep when I spun in earlier.'

'Go back, then,' Eleni urged him. 'Spin out and talk to her, Jack. These are her creatures, running amok in the Web and stealing everything in site. What if they blame her? She's got to be warned!'

Jack looked at her in horror. 'You're right. I never thought of that. Listen, Leni, I'll come back and meet you at Tropicana Bay as soon as I can.'

'And while you're gone, I'll try to find Rom,' Eleni added. 'If anyone can get a handle on this mystery, he can.'

'Good idea. And while you're at it, keep a lookout for the Cat. I promised I'd meet her today, and what with everything that's been happening I clean forgot!'

'I will. See you later, Jack.' Then Eleni vanished as Jack hit his scuttle button and left the Web.

Jack shed his Websuit quickly, and threw it down on the couch a little too hard. It slithered over the edge and disappeared between couch and wall. Jack muttered a word he wasn't supposed to know, but left the suit where it lay. He could come back for it in a minute, but first he needed to find Anna.

She was still in her room, fast asleep, the cats, three slumbering balls of fur, curled up with her on the quilt. 'Anna,' Jack called, shaking her shoulder. 'Anna! Wake up!'

'Wha—' Anna rolled over, spilling indignant cats left and right. Opening a bleary eye she blinked up at Jack. 'What's wrong?'

'Everything,' said Jack. 'Wake up, Anna, quick! Something terrible has happened.' Wasting no time, he told her what he and Leni had witnessed that morning in the Education block.

'My *dragons* are loose?' Anna stopped rubbing her eyes, leaped out of bed and made a dash for the kitchen. She grabbed a coffee bulb from the autochef and perched up on a high stool, her sleepy gaze suddenly sharp and intent. 'All right, Jack, just tell me again, slowly and clearly. From the beginning.'

When Jack had finished telling her what had been happening that morning, Anna simply sat there a moment, looking stunned, her brows knitted together in a frown. Then she leaped from the stool, throwing the bulb in the general direction of the recycler. 'I'd better go and see—' She fell silent and stopped as though she had been turned to stone, staring out of the window that looked right out across the valley and the sweeping hills beyond. Three white cars were speeding up the valley road, coming very fast.

Abruptly, Anna came back to life. 'Police!' she gasped. 'Jack, get out of here. I don't want you involved in this. If they don't arrest me, come back. If they do— Go home – call your mum and tell her. Take the cats with you.' Already she was bundling him out of the back door, scooping up cats and throwing them out after him. Startled by such abrupt treatment, they went streaking away up the garden and into the woodland beyond. Jack ran after them as the sound of the approaching sirens grew louder and louder.

'Call your mum!' Anna yelled after Jack. 'Get into the woods, quick! Don't let them see you!' Behind him, the door slammed shut.

The woods were dense with a low-level tangle of unseen roots, and brambles that caught in Jack's clothing and tore at his unprotected skin. Cursing under his breath, he mopped at the blood from a deep, stinging scratch across his face, dangerously close to his eye. When you had been spending so much time in the Web, you sometimes forgot how things in Realworld could hurt and damage you.

Keeping under the cover of the trees, Jack scrambled along the hillside until he came to a place where he could see the front of Anna's house. Hidden in the bushes, he watched the door. The sleek police cars, each with a luminous yellow stripe along its sides, were parked in the lane in front of the house. Were they questioning Anna in there? Were they giving her a hard time? Jack, unable to do anything but watch and wait, had never felt so cold, so lonely, and so helpless. It was different in the Web, he thought bitterly. There, no one was bigger or stronger than himself. He was the equal of his surroundings, and could almost always find a way to make things work the way he wanted. Between them, he and Rom knew fifty ways to outwit a spider, but out here in Realworld he was helpless against the power and strength of these officers of the law. It was not a pleasant feeling.

Just when Jack was about ready to explode with impatience, the front door opened, and Anna walked out, flanked by three officers, two women and a man. Anna was ushered into the first car, and as Jack watched, his skin prickling with horror, its engine started and with a snarl of its motors, it shot away down the valley. They had arrested Anna!

At that moment, two other officers came out of the house with armloads of Anna's equipment. With a chill, Jack recognized her Websuit. They began loading everything into the second vehicle. Eventually, they too sped away, leaving two men behind with the last car, clearly guarding the house. I wonder why, Jack thought. Maybe they think she has an accomplice, or something.

Then the realization hit him. *But she does, you idiot. You!* he told himself. And he was the only one who could help her now. He must warn the others what had happened right away. If they could only find a way to break into the game, maybe— A second shock hit him. In the rush to escape, he had left his Websuit in Anna's house!

CHAPTER TWELVE

NIGHT STALK

'Are you *sure* you'll be all right until tomorrow?' On the vidscreen, his mother was frowning. 'There's just no way I can get back until then.'

'Mum, of course I'll be all right,' Jack sighed. 'I know how to work the thermostat and the autochef, and I'll be sure to lock up properly. What could go wrong?'

'You're right, love. I'm sorry. I'll be back tomorrow afternoon, OK? I'll see you then.'

'Bye, Mum.' Jack snapped the screen off with a sigh of relief. Well, that was one ordeal over. Why did parents go ballistic every time the slightest little thing went wrong? It didn't help in the least. Not, Jack thought, that this was a little thing. He glanced out of the window for about the twentieth time. It's getting dark at last, he thought. His insides knotted in a queer mixture of relief and nervousness. Police or no police, he was going back to Anna's house to get his Websuit – if they hadn't already taken it away.

Jack went into his bedroom for his jacket and found the cats asleep on his bed, full of tuna. He was relieved that they seemed to have settled. He'd had an awful time hunting for them in the woods, afraid to call too loud in case the police should hear him. He left them sleeping, slipped his torch into his jacket pocket, and rummaged in the drawer of the hall table until he found the spare key for Anna's back door, the one she always left with them for emergencies. Well, this

was an emergency and no mistake, he thought, as he slipped
out of the house and crept away into the night.

They had turned on the outside lights at Anna's house.
Jack could see the glow at the end of the lane and was
grateful for it. It gave him something to aim for in this pitch-
dark night, though the shadows of the high hedge kept the
light from the uneven ground of the track under his feet. Jack
hadn't even dared attempt the tangled woods in darkness.
Even the rough, rutted surface of the lane had been too much
for him, for he had been unable to use the torch in case the
police were watching. To his dismay, it was taking him ages
to stumble to the end of a track that he could run along in
two minutes in the daylight.

When he rounded the corner at the bottom of the lane,
Jack almost fell over the long nose of the car, parked at the
bottom of Anna's drive. Without thinking, he threw himself
to one side and dived into the hedge, adding more scratches
to his collection. He lay there, motionless in the shadows,
scarcely daring to breathe. Out of the corner of his eye, he
had caught a glimpse of a dark silhouette behind the
streamlined windshield of the vehicle. The police were
inside, watching the house from the lane!

This was an unexpected development. Somehow, Jack had
pictured the officers sitting in Anna's kitchen, laughing and
drinking her coffee, but clearly, even though she had been
arrested and they had seized her equipment, they were not
allowed to make free with her house. Or was it a trap? Were
they just lying in wait to see if anyone came by? Well, they
wouldn't see him – not if he could help it. Anna was always
complaining about dogs getting through the holes in her
hedge, but Jack was grateful now. He groped in the darkness
until he found a gap, and crawled through.

Anna's garden was a patchwork of brilliant light and knife-
edged shadow. Worming his way between the patches of
thick shade, he managed to get close to the building without
breaking cover. Once he reached the back of the house he
would be out of sight of the police, but first he would have to
get across the lawn at the side, lit bright as a football stadium

by lights designed to deter burglars. There was no way round it. If he wanted his Websuit back, Jack was going to have to cross that stretch of open ground, in full view of the men in the car.

Crouched under a bush, Jack waited, watching the faces of the two policemen, pale and distinct in the glare of the security lights. Though he could see their lips moving as they talked, they never allowed their attention to wander from the house for even a moment. Jack waited and waited, all the time growing colder. Already, his feet and fingers and the tip of his nose were numb and aching. That never happened in the Web, either, he thought ruefully. To make matters worse, the shrub was the sort with thorns, and the long spines were sticking painfully into his back.

Endless minutes went by until, at last, Jack was jerked out of a daydream by a sudden movement in the vehicle. At last, something was happening! One of the men rummaged down on the floor and came up with a thermal container of coffee. As he opened it, a thread of the rich scent came drifting through the car window. Jack tensed himself, getting ready to move. This could be his only chance! The second officer turned towards the first, holding out a cup while the other poured. Jack was up and away like a rabbit, darting across the open lawn.

He had forgotten his numb feet. Staggering and stumbling, he felt himself beginning to fall. With a desperate, wrenching effort, he hurled himself forward, diving towards the corner of the house. Jack hit the ground hard and rolled under the wooden bench that stood against the wall. He was out of sight now – but had they spotted him? He lay there unmoving, scarcely daring to breathe, listening for any trace of a sound from the police car while pins and needles chased furiously up his legs.

After a few minutes, Jack decided he must be safe. Keeping low, he crept along beside the wall until he reached the back door. Luckily, because he fed the cats so often in Anna's absence, the burglar alarm was set to recognize his voice. 'It's me, Jack,' he said softly into the little brown box set into the wall, then he slipped the keycard into the slot, opened the back door just a crack, and slipped inside.

Now, at last, the torch came in handy. Shielding the end with his hand so that only a soft red glow escaped between his fingers, Jack crept through the kitchen and up the shadowed staircase to the spare room. Thrusting his hand down the side of the couch, he breathed a sigh of relief. The suit was there! Laying down the torch, he fished the special carrying bag from under the couch, rolled up the Websuit and stowed it carefully inside. Just as he was zipping the bag, his hand caught the torch that was lying on the couch. It fell to the floor with a clatter, and switched itself on.

With a groan of dismay, Jack dived on top of the torch to muffle the light and fumbled frantically for the switch. A moment's silence followed, then he heard the double slam of the police car's doors, murmuring voices growing louder, and the crunch of booted feet on the gravelled path. The front door banged open and footsteps came thundering up the stairs. The two policemen burst into the spare room – and stopped. The room was empty.

It took a moment for one of the officers to realize that the blind was down, covering the window, as it had not been when they had seen the light shine out. Lifting a corner, he saw the open window and the roof of the porch below. The lane and the garden beyond were completely empty. There was no one in sight.

Jack rubbed his skinned knees and the shoulder that he'd bruised in his headlong slide from the sloping porch roof. In that first, stunned moment when he'd crashed to the ground, he had noticed the front door, still open. In an instant he had slipped back into the house and through the hall to hide under the bench in the kitchen. Now, crouched panting in the darkness, he heard footsteps thundering back downstairs.

'He must be in the lane,' one of them said.

'He can't get far,' the other replied. 'The car's heat-tracer will soon pick him up.' After a few minutes, Jack heard the engine start, and the crunch of gravel as the car pulled away.

Jack almost fell asleep during the time the aircar was

cruising up and down the lane. He stayed where he was, knowing there was enough gadgetry in the kitchen to disguise *his* body heat from the tracer. It was hard to be patient. There came a point when he was convinced that the police had given up and gone back to Dublin for good. Just as he was about to leave his hiding-place, however, he heard a throb of motors, and then silence again as the car stopped outside. That was what he had been waiting for. In a flash, Jack was out of the back door, across the garden and into the woods. Glancing back one last time through a screen of bushes, he saw the lights go on in the house, as the policemen finally thought to search there.

When Jack got home, scratched, scraped, muddy but triumphant, he didn't waste any time. He dialled a soyburger from the autochef, and had a quick wash between bites, so as not to get mud in his Websuit. Carefully, he unfolded the precious suit from its carrying bag and plugged it into the terminal in his room. At last, he was ready to go. He only hoped the others would still be there.

As Jack spun into Level 1, he was immediately pounced upon by a tiny, bat-winged imp that flew round his head, chattering. The Cat had left her sprite for him. I'd better find her quickly, he thought. She should be in on this. He caught hold of the sprite, knowing it was keyed to Cat's wrist unit, and would take him to her automatically. But, after the Blue and Tone had cleared, he found himself, to his puzzlement, in E&R Webtown, outside Anna's work block, with about twenty menacing spiders heading his way.

CHAPTER THIRTEEN

THE DRAGON QUEEN

The dragon was a dream – or perhaps a nightmare – brought to life. It was so huge that its outstretched wings filled the immense chamber from floor to ceiling, and its head towered so high that Cat had to bend backwards to look at it. Its scales were a burnished gold that dazzled where they caught the light that shot down, in a single slender beam like a spotlight, from some hidden place above. From the top of its hoard, a vast pile of multicoloured crystals, it gazed down at her with glittering, cold eyes that held a merciless intelligence. Cat couldn't run. The eyes transfixed her, holding her in place. They reminded her of something. Into Cat's mind flashed an image of Miss Aldanar's cold, dark eyes, glittering behind the silver mask.

Miss Aldanar and her silver dragon had disappeared about the same time as Cat's wrist unit. The other dragon – the one who'd brought her here – had dumped her from its back and disappeared. Cat knew there could be no escape. She would never be able to find her way back through the weird maze of chambers that had finally led to this vast and gloomy room, with its echoing spaces and its walls and ceiling lost in the crowding shadows.

Cat took a hasty step backwards. *This is the Web*, she told herself. *Nothing can harm me – this thing can't eat me*. Somehow, it was hard to convince herself. *Don't let it be hungry – please*.

The dragon cocked its great head and looked at her with

calm curiosity, rather, Cat thought, as a bird would eye a beetle before it pounced. Cat saw the enormous teeth, each as long as her arm, and shuddered. With a noise like someone crumpling a sheet of paper ten miles wide, the dragon shuddered its gigantic wings. 'So,' it said in a dry, clear voice.

Cat gasped. 'Miss Aldanar!'

'As you say.'

'Why—' Cat tried to keep the quaver out of her voice, and failed. 'Why have you brought me here? I don't like it. Can we go now, please?'

The doors flew open, slamming back against the wall with a hollow booming sound. Maxus stood there, his expression grim. 'Madam, it's done,' he said quietly.

The dragon looked down at Cat with its pitiless, inhuman gaze. 'Child,' it said, 'you won't be going anywhere. You'll stay here in the Web with me for ever.'

'No!' Cat shrieked. 'I can't stay here!' Then she was running, back towards the great bronze doors that were the only entrance to the chamber. Before she could reach them, shifters came oozing through the walls wearing all sorts of hideous shapes: mosquitoes and maggots, giant wasps and scorpions, sharks and squid. And others were like escapees from every horror vid that Cat had ever seen. There were ghosts and banshees, zombies dropping a trail of rotten flesh, armies of grinning skeletons, hollow-eyed mummies trailing their stained bandages, and disembodied heads with gnashing teeth.

From behind Cat came the dry, cold voice of the dragon. 'Never think that you can't die here,' it said in a voice like ice and steel. 'I promise you, you can.'

'What can have gone wrong?' Eleni asked Rom anxiously. 'Do you think something has happened?'

Hours had passed since Jack had promised to meet the others at Tropicana Bay. Eleni and Rom had sat at the tables under the trees and listened to people talking about the thefts, which apparently were still taking place. They had swum several times with the dolphins in the silver sea, and each of them in turn had taken an hour's break out of the Web to stave off the voms. Still, Jack had not come. Rom shrugged. 'If Jack promised to come, he'll come, sooner or later. Something must have held him up, that's all.'

It was all right for Rom to be so cool, Eleni thought with a flash of resentment. It wasn't late at night where he lived, and *his* mother didn't seem obsessed with the notion that young people needed their sleep. Mama isn't pleased with me already, she thought, because I said I couldn't help her tonight. If she comes in and catches me in the Web when I ought to be in bed, there'll be no end of trouble, but there's no way I'm leaving now.

When Eleni had just about given up hope, Jack finally appeared. He had barely spun in before he was calling out to them. 'They've arrested Anna!'

Eleni and Rom looked at each other in horror as Jack told them what had happened. 'We can't let them do this,' Eleni said. 'We've got to help her!'

'We've got to get into the game,' Rom said. 'Everything depends on that. If we can only find out who's really doing this, and take the police some proof—'

'Anna herself couldn't get into it,' Jack said grimly, 'but someone else has. I found the Cat's sprite waiting, and that's where it led me, except I couldn't get into Dragonville, of course. I was well and truly spidered off. But the Cat is in there, for sure, so how did *she* do it?'

'And did she mean to?' Rom added quietly, 'or is she in trouble?'

I suppose the game will close for ever, like Dreamcastle, Eleni was thinking. What a shame. It was so wonderful to ride a dragon. Ride a dragon! She leaped to her feet. 'Jack, Rom, I've got the answer! I know how to get us into the game!'

'Eleni, are you *sure* this will work?' Rom said. 'We've been waiting here for ages.'

'Have you a better idea?' Eleni snapped. 'Education must be the best place. As soon as the dragon appears again.'

'*If* it appears.'

'There!' Jack shouted. In a flash of green, the dragon came bursting through one of the Tertiary research buildings, a single crystal clasped between its jaws. From his wrist unit, Jack called up Anna's code that summoned the creatures. For a second the dragon seemed to hesitate in midair, then it changed its course and came to land beside them.

There was pandemonium. From nowhere, a horde of spiders appeared. Everywhere, people were running – some towards the dragon, others away. Eleni and the others scrambled aboard quickly, with the Cat's sprite fluttering round their heads. She sighed with relief as the dragon took off again. Then the Education Webtown dissolved into a storm of sparkles and in its place she saw the tall red mountains of Dragonville.

'Well done, Leni!'

'Eight!'

Eleni glowed with pride. Cat's sprite, wildly excited now, led the way as the dragon flew on and on between the towering mountains. It all looks pretty much the same, Eleni thought. Where can we be going? Then they flew over a high ridge, and there, below, was an enormous face that filled the valley from side to side. Now she knew where they were going, and wished she didn't. A shiver ran through her as the gigantic mouth opened to let them in, and gulped them down into the darkness.

The dragon shook itself, and Eleni found herself falling. She didn't fall far, and landed with a jolt on cold rock. She was in a gloomy tunnel, lit by a soft glow that came through an archway about twenty metres away. When she picked herself up, she saw Rom and Jack nearby, but the dragon had vanished. Rom groaned. 'Great. *Now* what do we do?'

From above Jack's head came an urgent, angry chittering. 'Get off!' He batted at Cat's sprite, who was dive-bombing him and pulling at his hair. 'We follow this dratted creature, I suppose,' he shrugged. 'At least it seems to know where it's going.'

'And at least it's heading for the light,' Eleni said.

Through the archway there was nothing but a huge old

door at the top of a long flight of steps. It stood alone there, looking odd with no walls to support it. Jack went up the steps, followed by Rom and Eleni. He pushed open the heavy, creaking door, and found himself in a huge, circular hallway, with doors leading off it in every direction and a spiral staircase in the centre that led up to galleries with rooms leading off *them*, that stretched up and up as far as the eye could see. Just inside the door, hanging on the wall, he found a rack of heavy-looking guns like laser rifles that glowed with their own eerie red light. A d-box floated in the air beside it. Jack read:

LEVEL 2 ENTRY. Welcome to the Labyrinth, domain of the shifters. Here lies the secret heart of Dragonville. Caution. Gun must be recharged after every five shots.

Next to this was a picture of a red crystal, about half the size of an egg. When he broke open a gun and checked it, Jack found a tube with one red crystal nestling inside.

'Knowing Anna,' Rom said, taking a gun for himself and handing one to Eleni, 'more crystals will be hidden all over the house in the most unlikely places.'

A ghastly shriek ripped through the air, startling Jack into firing off his first shot and wasting it. He spun round, gripping the gun tightly. A white shape, all flowing robes and long streaming hair, came hurtling down from above, reaching for him with bloodstained fingernails as long as knives. Jack ducked and rolled, and the banshee hit the floor. With an ear-splitting screech it sprang up and came at him again, its dark eyes glittering with menace, its deadly fingers reaching for his throat.

As Jack scrambled backward, both Rom and Eleni aimed and fired. Thin, sizzling red beams leaped out – and the banshee kept on coming. Backing away, Jack fired his own gun, but it made no difference. This is wrong, he thought desperately, dodging the clawing fingers by a hair's breadth. It's just a game. My mum's friend *invented* this creature!

It almost had him pinned against the staircase now. Jack leaped aside just too late and one razor-sharp finger caught his arm. He felt the sleeve rip, then a sharp pain stabbed his arm. Jack looked down and saw a thin line of blood. *This couldn't be happening!* No one ever got hurt in the Web – it just wasn't possible. Except that it had happened now.

CHAPTER FOURTEEN

GHOST OF A CHANCE

Jack didn't know whether the injury would affect his Real-world body, but it certainly *hurt*. He realized that this was no longer a game, and they were all in great danger. The temptation to scuttle was overwhelming, but he knew that they would never have another chance to get into the game. If they wanted to find Cat and uncover the mystery of the thief, this was their only chance. 'Let's get out of here,' he yelled at the others. Hoping that the spook wouldn't be able to leave the hallway, he dived through the nearest door, Rom and Eleni close behind him with the banshee snatching at their heels.

Jack slammed the door in the banshee's face. On the other side, the screeching and wailing grew to an earsplitting pitch, and he could hear the creature's bloodstained talons scrabbling at the barrier. Stained with *his* blood now, Jack thought. He stepped back quickly, worried that the door wouldn't keep the creature out, but after a moment, he realized that he had been right. The banshee couldn't go beyond the First Level hallway.

'This is Level 2 all right,' Rom said. 'Those shifters sure are meaner this time around.' He scowled disgustedly at his gun. 'This wretched thing is useless,' he said.

'Whoever has been tampering with this game must have disabled the weapons,' Jack added.

'Even so, I feel better with a weapon of some kind,' Eleni told them. 'Besides, there may be something further on that it *will* hit.'

'You never know,' said Jack. Privately he doubted it, but, although the gun had been useless so far, he certainly didn't want to let go of the only weapon he had. With the others, he began to search the room for more crystals to recharge it, but there weren't that many places to look. This time, they had stepped into a ballroom, with a dusty floor, mirrors all along the walls, and a line of chandeliers, festooned with cobwebs, hanging from the ceiling. Spindly little chairs with gold backs and legs and fat red cushions were lined up around the edges of the dance floor. There were no windows here, so they couldn't escape that way. The only other way out was a door at the far end of the room. Only one of the chandeliers seemed to be working, and that was very dim. Jack ran down the right-hand side of the ballroom, throwing the stupid little chairs aside in his frantic search for more crystals.

'Listen,' Eleni said suddenly. 'Music. Can you hear it?'

It was very faint at first, some kind of waltz played on an old-fashioned synthesizer. Even as Jack stopped to listen, it grew louder, and then, behind the tune, he began to hear a scratching, scuffling noise. In the thick dust of the ballroom floor, footprints began to appear, making swirling tracks in the carpet of dusty grey. Ghostly feet were dancing – only two sets at first, then four, then suddenly there were dozens. Rom, Jack and Eleni crowded close together for moral support. Jack looked up, and his fingers tightened around the gun. He could see clear reflections of the whirling dancers in the mirrors along the wall but when he looked back at the actual room, he saw nothing there but the prints.

The music faltered, and stopped. As one, the feet stopped dancing. Suddenly, the footprints were all pointing in his direction. In the mirror, Jack saw the dancers beginning to move forward until they were closing in on him. He saw their pale, bloodless faces, their wild, dark hair, and their long fangs that gleamed against their blood-red lips. He turned and fled, dashing through the new door before the vampires caught him. This time, the others were in front of him. He slammed the door behind him with a gasp of relief.

The room they had entered seemed to be some kind of

study, with a bright fire in the hearth and tall bookshelves that lined the walls. To Jack's right there was a curtained window, and beneath it stood a heavy old desk with a green leather top.

'Good, lots of hiding places here,' Rom said in an unsteady voice. 'Surely there'll be crystals for the gun, and maybe we'll even find some other weapons.'

'The desk seems the most obvious place to look,' Eleni said.

Jack thought it was maybe too obvious, but he said nothing. She looked as though the vampires had given her a bad scare and he didn't want to upset her. 'Come on,' he told her, 'it's worth a try.'

Much to Jack's surprise, it turned out that Eleni was right. In the bottom drawer he found a handful of the power crystals. 'Here!' he yelled at Rom and Eleni.

All three of them were down on their knees, scrabbling in the drawer for crystals when Jack began to get an uneasy feeling that they were not alone. Slowly, he raised his head above the level of the desk and looked around. A thin, pale smoke seemed to be drifting with ease through the solid wall to the right. Once inside the room, it drifted down to make a misty white pool on the floor, and then began to pile itself up again in the form of a rough column. Near the top of the column, two slanting red eyes appeared.

Jack ducked down behind the desk, rolled underneath, and came up firing. Rom leaped up to stand beside him, and Eleni was shooting from behind the desk. The red bolts from their guns just went right through the creature's smoky body. The apparition laughed, a weird, spine-chilling cackle, and began to ooze slowly towards them. Where it had passed, every surface was covered with a film of glittering frost.

'Come on, Eleni, don't get trapped behind there!' Jack grabbed her by the hand and dodged around the apparition, pulling her after him. He made a dive for the window, but there was no escape that way. There was nothing beyond but thick darkness. He couldn't break the glass by firing at it with the gun. Using it to hit the window didn't work either. And the spectre was right behind him!

'It's useless!' Rom, in the far corner, threw away his empty gun. Retreating quickly, Jack looked for a way out. He realized he'd made a serious mistake. There *was* no way out of the room save for the door that led back to the vampires, and if he got through them, he would have to deal with the banshee.

But there must be another way to escape. Jack knew how Anna worked. She would never leave a dead-end like this! Still backing away from the apparition, he looked wildly around the room, hoping for inspiration. There was something familiar about the fireplace, with its high mantelpiece and the two candlesticks, one on either end. Suddenly, he remembered a funny old movie that he had watched with Anna and his parents a while ago. It had a fireplace just like this, and, if he remembered rightly, they tilted one of the candlesticks like a lever and—

The apparition was almost on him. Jack grabbed the candlestick and pulled. A section of the wall beside the fireplace swivelled round to reveal the dark opening of a secret passage. 'Yes!' Jack shouted. 'Come on!' He pushed Rom and Eleni inside and dived through after them, sighing with relief as the secret door grated shut behind him. Only then did he realize that he should have brought the other candlestick. The tunnel was pitch dark.

Well, there was no going back now. Jack began to shuffle down the narrow passage, feeling his way along by touching the walls on either side. For a minute or two everything seemed fine, until he noticed that he could see his hands on either side of him, and the shadowy shapes of Eleni and Rom in front. The walls were beginning to glow with a faint, sickly green light, and he could feel sticky wet slime under his fingers. Something snatched at Jack's outstretched hand. The green slime was growing out from the wall and stretching into a forest of long waving tentacles, all along the passage.

This wasn't how it should work. This couldn't be happening! He couldn't go back, there were too many horrors in the rooms behind him. Before he knew what was happening, Eleni's nerve broke. She fired a volley of shots down the passage, and

ran, with Rom a step behind her. Jack took off after them.
The tentacles snatched at him, hissing like a thousand
snakes. They fastened themselves to his body in a clammy
embrace, spattering him with slime that burned his skin.
Even as he struggled to free himself, he heard the secret door
grate open behind him.

With the strength of panic, Jack tore himself loose and ran
on, fighting his way through the clusters of long, clinging
arms. The pale gleam of the tentacles gave him enough light
to see by, but he didn't dare look back and see what was
behind him. He plunged headlong down the twisting passage, shielding his face from the horrid touch of the writhing
strands.

He didn't see the wall until it was too late. Jack smashed
into the solid barrier just as the others had done and slid to
the ground beside them, half stunned and cold with fear.
There was no way out!

There must be! There *must* be! Jack struggled to his feet and
began to poke and prod frantically at the wall. When that
didn't work, he fired his gun at it again and again, until he
ran out of power. When the noise of the shots had stopped,
he realized that he could hear a soft, dry, rustling noise in the
passage behind him. Jack recognized it from the ballroom. It
was the whisper of many voices, and the shuffle of dozens of
feet.

Suddenly, the soft scuffle was drowned out by a hideous
shriek. Jack froze, his fingers locked around the useless gun.
Not the banshee too! The first thing he saw though, drifting
around the bend in the passage, was the wispy form of the
red-eyed spook. The eyes glowed brighter as they saw him,
and the apparition gave the same, grim, spine-chilling
cackle. The ghosts had found him, all of them.

The spectre drifted towards Jack down the length of the
corridor, and behind it came the horde of shuffling vampires,
visible now, and drooling. As they passed, the snake-like
tentacles writhed and hissed, dripping slime in glowing pools
on the passage floor. Then the ghastly shriek came again.
Jack yelled and pressed himself back into the hard stone of

the wall as the banshee plunged down into the passage from the ceiling above. Behind it, the vampires and the cold, misty spectre kept on coming.

CHAPTER FIFTEEN

BATTLE OF DRAGONS

Maxus touched his wrist, and the shifters disappeared. Taking Cat by the hand, he led her back to the pile of crystals and sat down beside her. He began to speak in a gentle voice. 'Let me explain what has happened.'

'She's stealing my *body*?' Cat gasped. 'But that's impossible!'

'You have to understand,' Maxus said gently. 'For Miss Aldanar, nothing is impossible. The Web was her brainchild. She was one of its very first creators. Hers is a brilliant mind that has spanned two centuries,' he went on proudly. 'She spent years developing the equipment you saw in the tower to achieve her greatest triumph yet, the cheating of death itself.'

Cat wanted to hit him. 'It's cheating all right,' she shouted. 'She isn't cheating death, Maxus, she's cheating *me*! She's *had* her life, longer than most people. I've only started mine. Maybe I could have been as brilliant and successful and powerful as she is, but now I'll never know! Miss Aldanar has cheated me of the chance. Don't you understand, Maxus? She hasn't conquered death, she's only making an exchange. Somebody dies in any case! *Somebody always has to die!*'

'BE SILENT, BRAT!' The dragon shrieked.

Maxus looked stunned. 'But she's right,' he cried. 'Madam, is there no other way?'

'If there was, would I be doing this?' the dragon snarled. 'How can you, of all people, think I *want* to act like some kind

of ghoul? There's no more time, you imbecile! I CAN'T DIE!'
The dragon loomed over Maxus, its jaws gaping wide and its
jewelled eyes flashing red with the fire of its rage.

With a terrible cry of fear and sorrow, he hit his scuttle
button and vanished.

In the darkness of the tunnel Eleni felt a hard, lumpy shape
beneath her. She groped in the darkness, and burst out
laughing. 'Guess what?' she shouted. 'I'm sitting on a
handle. There's a trapdoor here.'

Spurred by sheer terror, none of them had ever moved
quicker. In an instant they had lifted the trapdoor. There was
no time to worry about the drop or the darkness, not with the
horrors that pursued them. If they had to take their chance
with the spooks or the trapdoor there was only one choice.
Squeezing through one by one, they took a deep breath, and
let themselves fall.

Eleni found herself hurtling down a long, slippery chute,
moving faster and faster and unable to stop. Suddenly, she
came rocketing out into the light and hurtled into a pile of
lumpy, glittering objects that were very hard. She lay still for
a moment, recovering, not daring to look up and see what
else was in store.

'Holy mips!' Rom muttered in an awestruck voice.

Now what? Eleni thought. Steeling herself, she looked up,
and up, and up, and up – at an enormous golden dragon.

'Jack! Rom, Eleni!' Cat was running towards them, shrieking. 'Get away! Quick, before it's too late!'

'It is already too late.' The voice sounded like the hollow
clang of a dungeon door. Eleni looked at the dragon and saw
the great red gem that glittered on a golden chain around the
creature's neck. She thought of a tall, dark-haired woman all
dressed in silver, and wearing a silver mask. 'I remember
you—' she gasped.

The woman glanced at her briefly. 'Well, I don't remember
you,' she said in an offhand voice. She turned her cold, dark
gaze on Rom, who seemed unable to take his eyes from her.
'*You*, however, I remember all too well. *Your* day of reckoning

is long overdue.' Her huge mouth opened in an ear-splitting roar. Twin beams of light, sizzling red, shot out of her glimmering eyes. With a yell, Rom hurled himself aside. The lasers hit just where he'd been standing, melting the stone floor into a pool of glowing slag.

Howling in thwarted fury, the dragon reared up until its shoulders touched the ceiling. The great head snaked out on the long neck and another red beam sizzled through the air. Again, Rom dodged, but he was running out of space.

'Split up!' Cat yelled. 'It's not a game! *She can kill us!*'

'That's enough!' Jack yelled. 'Scuttle!'

'I can't,' Cat shouted. 'They stole my unit!'

Eleni knew they couldn't leave her. Somehow, they must find a way to defeat this monster and free their friend. She remembered how the shifters had hurt Jack. She wasn't sure whether people could really be killed in the Web, but it would be better not to find out. She didn't know how the Sorceress had done it, but things were somehow more *real* here than was usual in the Web. That was it! Like in Realworld, things could be changed from within the game.

The dragon, snarling, had backed Rom into a corner. Eleni could see its ruby eyes gleam brighter as it prepared to fire.

'Rom! Scuttle!' Jack was yelling.

'No!' Rom looked terrified but held his ground.

Suddenly, Eleni knew what to do. She hit her keypad, and there were *two* golden dragons in the chamber. Red beams leaped from Eleni's eyes. The Sorceress howled in agony, beating with one wing at her smoking hide. Leaving Rom, she whipped round to face her new challenger, knocking Jack and Cat back into a corner with the tip of her lashing tail.

Even as the Sorceress turned, Eleni was firing again, missing the other dragon's head by a hair's breadth and knocking a chunk of stonework off the far wall.

'Eight, Leni, 'way to go!' Rom shouted.

'Be careful!' Jack yelled.

The Sorceress fired wildly, and Eleni screamed in shock as the crimson beam snicked the edge of one wing. Mad with rage, the Sorceress attacked, taking advantage of Leni's

moment of distraction. Drawing her head back, she struck
like a snake and fastened her huge spiked teeth in Eleni's
neck. Eleni screamed and struggled to free herself, but it was
no good. The Sorceress held her fast, and slowly, as the great
jaws tightened, she found herself choking for breath. It was
no good, she would have to scuttle. She had failed.

Out of the corner came a shriek from the Cat. 'It's back! My
unit!'

The dragon loosed its jaws from Eleni's throat. For an
instant, surprise and doubt gleamed in its eyes. Then it threw
back its head and began to laugh. 'And Maxus called *me*
cruel! Go on, then, my dear. Spin out of here if you wish, if
you dare. Spin back into my aged body, and see how *you* like
life as a withered crone, always growing weaker, always in
pain. *You* try it, Cat, then tell me what I did was wrong!'

Cat looked at her with an oddly pitying expression. 'It *was*
wrong,' she said, in a brave, firm little voice, 'and whatever
you say won't make it right. You have to live with that.' Then
she pressed her keypad, and was gone.

'Scuttle, everyone,' Jack yelled. He and Rom vanished, but
Eleni was a second too late. Before she could move, the
dragon's jaws had clamped round her neck once more.

'You at least, I'll keep,' the Sorceress snarled through her
teeth.

'You won't!' Eleni choked, groping with her claw for her
keypad. Yes, she could just reach it. Lifting her head, she fired
her lasers straight at the ceiling above the other dragon. Even
as it exploded and tons of rock came crashing down, she hit
her scuttle button and caught a glimpse of the Sorceress
doing the same. As the world dissolved around her, the last
thing she heard was a shattering cry of utter horror.

'No! NO! MAXUUUUUUS!'

CHAPTER SIXTEEN

AFTERWARDS

As Cat ripped her visor away, the tower room wrapped itself around her like a secure and comfortable quilt. Still numb with shock and terror, she simply sat there for a moment, staring in front of her. Staring— Staring— Staring at the usual view she saw when she spun out, the body of Miss Aldanar, reclining in its Websuit on the couch directly opposite.

Maxus was slumped over the couch, his shoulders shaking. Cat realized that he was crying like a heartbroken child. Slipping out of her Websuit, she went over to him. When she drew near to Miss Aldanar's couch, she realized that the old woman's body was utterly still, no longer breathing. The connections to her life-support machines had been ripped away. Cat touched him gently on the shoulder. 'It was you, wasn't it?' she said softly. 'Thank you, Maxus. You saved my life.'

Maxus lifted a tear-streaked face to look at her. It gave Cat a funny feeling in the pit of her stomach to see a grown-up cry like that, as though nothing would ever be secure in the world again. 'All the stuff she stole,' he whispered brokenly, 'she meant to use it for you, she said.' His voice grew stronger. 'She was working on a way to clone a new body, then you could have yours back, if you could survive that long in the Web. She wanted to put your consciousness into that dragon for the time being. It's a very advanced construct, and she thought you might be spared the fading we had with the other children.'

'*Other children?*,' Cat gasped.

Maxus nodded. 'Don't ask,' he said. 'You were different, you were so much like her. She was fond of you, really she was.'

She picked a funny way to show it, Cat thought, but Maxus was still talking. 'She promised me she would give you your body back, but—' he sighed. 'Seeing her, listening to her today, when she thought she had triumphed, well, suddenly I stopped believing her.'

Gently, he took the old woman's hands and folded them on her breast. 'Truly, she wasn't always bad,' he said softly. 'In her time she was a very great, good woman, but she was always afraid to die. It obsessed her.' He shook his head. 'No matter what she did or how long she lived, that fear would haunt her. In the end I had to help her to be free, just as I always helped her.'

It was several days before everyone could meet again. It had taken that long for the authorities to clear up the mess the Sorceress had left behind her. Eventually, it was arranged for the four friends to get together at Tropicana Bay, along with Anna, released now from the clutches of the police, and Ariadne, the Webcop who had been investigating the Sorceress from the start.

Cat was glad of a chance to talk to the cop. One question had been bothering her a good deal. 'What about Maxus?' she asked anxiously. 'I know he helped Miss Aldanar, but he was the one who stopped her in the end. And after all, he *did* save my life.'

Today, Ariadne was tall with skin like ebony silk, an athletic body, and eyes of liquid gold. Her smile flashed white as she answered. 'Don't worry, Cat, everything has been taken into account. They won't be too hard on him.'

'Will the game ever open again?' Eleni asked Anna. The woman gave a rueful shrug. 'I'm afraid not, Leni, at least not in that form. You seem to have made a pretty good job of destroying it.'

'Anna, I'm sorry!' Eleni cried in dismay.

Anna laughed. 'It's all right, Leni, I'm only teasing. You did the best possible thing, and you were incredibly brave. The authorities won't let me re-open Dragonville anyway. They tell me I was a bit too clever for my own good, inventing a bunch of highly advanced phaces that could sneak through into other sites.'

'You were lucky to get away with it really,' Ariadne told her, 'but with the Sorceress gone, everyone is feeling especially lenient.'

'Now, wait a minute,' Anna protested. 'It wasn't *my* fault if my game was hijacked. *You* couldn't catch her, so I don't see—'

'Peace, peace,' Ariadne held up her hands. 'You're right on all counts. I was only teasing *you*.' She grinned at Anna, and Eleni could see that the two women were well on the way to becoming good friends.

'What happened to all the stuff that was stolen?' Rom asked.

Ariadne shrugged. 'Lost, I'm afraid, in Eleni's explosion. No one is going to start dismantling the game to find the missing data. We're too afraid of activating the shifters again, by accident. The game has been sealed off, in the hope that the stuff can be recovered some day in the future.'

Jack caught Cat's eye, and the two of them left the table and slipped away along the crimson sands. 'How is your father doing?' he asked.

'When the police discovered what had been going on at home, they arranged for him to see doctors and shrinks and stuff.' Cat shrugged, trying to sound as if she didn't care. 'They say he'll get over this hatred of the Web and be perfectly fine, eventually. In the meantime, I have to go with my brothers and sister to stay with some relation I've never even met.' Now, she couldn't keep the quiver out of her voice.

'No, you don't,' Jack said quickly. 'Anna and I were talking about it last night, and she suggested that you come to Ireland and stay with her for a while. She asked me to ask you—'

The rest of his words were drowned in Cat's whoop of delight. 'Jack! Is it true? Do you mean it?'

Jack nodded. 'And I'll be just down the road,' he told her. 'We can do all sorts of things, both in the Web and out.'

Cat laughed out loud for sheer joy. 'Oh, this is wonderful! I can't believe it! I must go and thank Anna!'

They got back to the table just in time to hear Rom's voice. 'Anna, do you think she really could have killed us?'

'Who knows?' Anna replied. 'Her abilities were far beyond anything we've seen before. Let's just say it's a good thing we never had to find out.'

Rom looked startled for a moment, then he smiled. 'Well, who cares? I guess that's the end of the Sorceress.'

Ariadne nodded. 'Miss Aldanar is finished at long last, thanks to you lot.'

In another part of the Web, sealed deep within the shattered ruins of an abandoned game, a dragon raised its golden head. *'Am I still alive?'* it thought, and, *'How long will it take me to escape from this tomb?'*

Well, it didn't matter, really, how long it would take. At last, the dragon possessed what it wanted, all the time in the world.

Carefully, the dragon began to examine its prison. Cat would have recognized the stubborn, fierce and proud intelligence trapped behind those glittering ruby eyes.

WEBSPEAK – A GLOSSARY

AI
Artificial intelligence. Computer programs that appear to show intelligent behaviour when you interact with them.

avatar or realoe
Personas in the Web that are representations of real people.

basement-level
Of the lowest level possible. Often used as an insult, as in 'You've got a basement-level grasp of the situation.'

bat
The moment of transition into the Web or between sites. You can 'do a bat' or 'go bat'. Its slang use has extended to the everyday world. 'Bat' is used instead of 'come in', 'take a bat' is a dismissal. (From *Blue And Tone*.)

bite
To play a trick, or to get something over on someone.

bootstrap
Verb, to improve your situation by your own efforts.

bot
Programs with AI.

chasing the fade
Analysing what has happened in the Web after you have left it.

cocoon
A secret refuge. Also your bed or own room.

cog
Incredibly boring or dull. Initially specific to the UK and America this slang is

	now in use worldwide. (From *Common Or Garden* spider.)
curl up	'Go away, I don't like you!' (From *curl up and die*.)
cyberat	A Web construct, a descendant of computer viruses, that infests the Web programs.
cybercafe	A place where you can get drinks and snacks as well as renting time in the Web.
cyberspace	The visual representation of the communication system which links computers.
d-box	A data-box; an area of information which appears when people are in Virtual Reality (VR).
download	To enter the Web without leaving a Realworld copy.
down the plug	A disaster, as in 'We were down the plug'.
egg	A younger sibling or annoying hanger-on. Even in the first sense this is always meant nastily.
eight	Good (a spider has eight legs).
flame	An insult or nasty remark.
fly	A choice morsel of information, a clue, a hint.
funnel	An unexpected problem or obstacle.
gag	Someone, or something, you don't like very much, whom you consider to be stupid. (From *Glove And Glasses*.)
glove and glasses	Cheap but outdated system for experiencing Virtual Reality. The glasses allow you to see VR, the gloves allow you to pick things up.
Id	Interactive display nodule.
mage	A magician.
mip	Measure of computer power.

nick or alias	A nickname. For example, 'Metaphor' is the nickname of Sarah.
one-mip	Of limited worth or intelligence, as in 'a one-mip mind'.
phace	A person you meet in the Web who is not real; someone created by the software of a particular site or game.
phreak	Someone who is fanatical about virtual reality experiences in the Web.
protocol	The language one computer uses to talk to another.
raid	Any unscheduled intrusion into the Web; anything that forces someone to leave; a program crash.
realoe	See *avatar*.
Realworld	What it says; the world outside the Web. Sometimes used in a derogatory way.
scuttle	Leave the Web and return to the Realworld.
silky	Smarmy, over-enthusiastic, un-trustworthy.
six	Bad (an insect has six legs).
slows, the	The feeling that time has slowed down after experiencing the faster time of the Web.
spider	A Web construct. Appearing in varying sizes and guises, these are used to pass on warnings or information in the Web. The word is also commonly applied to teachers or parents.
spidered-off	Warned away by a spider.
spin in	To enter the Web or a Website.
spin out	To leave the Web or a Website.
SFX	Special effects.
strand	A gap between rows of site skyscrapers in Webtown. Used to describe any street or road or journey.
suck	To eat or drink.

supertime	Parts of the Web that run even faster than normal.
TFO	Tennessee Fried Ostrich.
venomous	Adjective; excellent; could be used in reference to piece of equipment (usually a Websuit) or piece of programming.
vets	Veterans of any game or site. Ultravets are the *crème de la crème* of these.
VR	Virtual Reality. The illusion of a three-dimensional reality created by computer software.
warlock	A sorcerer; magician.
Web	The worldwide network of communication links, entertainment, educational and administrative sites that exists in cyberspace and is represented in Virtual Reality.
Web heads	People who are fanatical about surfing the Web. (See also phreaks.)
Web round	Verb; to contact other Web users via the Web.
Websuit	The all-over body suit lined with receptors which when worn by Web users allows them to experience the full physical illusion of virtual reality.
Webware	Computer software used to create and/or maintain the Web.
widow	Adjective; excellent; the term comes from the Black Widow, a particularly poisonous spider.
wipeout	To be comprehensively beaten in a Web game or to come out worse in any Web situation.